Nathaniel Neal Solly

Memoir of the life of David Cox

Nathaniel Neal Solly

Memoir of the life of David Cox

ISBN/EAN: 9783337142865

Printed in Europe, USA, Canada, Australia, Japan

Cover: Foto ©Raphael Reischuk / pixelio.de

More available books at **www.hansebooks.com**

MEMOIR

OF THE

LIFE OF DAVID COX

MEMBER OF THE SOCIETY OF PAINTERS IN WATER COLOURS

WITH SELECTIONS FROM HIS CORRESPONDENCE,
AND SOME ACCOUNT OF HIS WORKS

BY

N. NEAL SOLLY

Illustrated with numerous Photographs from Drawings by the Artist's own hand

Bettws-y-Coed Old Church.

"Observe that thy best director, thy perfect guide, is Nature. Copy from her. In her path is thy triumphal arch. She is above all other teachers; and ever confide in her with a bold heart."
CENNINO CENNINI. Rome, 1437.

LONDON:
CHAPMAN AND HALL, 193, PICCADILLY
1873

PREFACE.

UPWARDS of fourteen years have passed away since the great landscape-painter, David Cox, was carried to his last resting-place in the quiet churchyard of Harborne, followed by many warmly attached friends and relatives.

I have long felt that a memoir of this good man and true artist, and a record of his principal works, was a want in the literature of our day, and one which ought to be supplied, as a labour of love.

I have waited in the expectation that some writer would undertake this biography, equally willing, and more entirely qualified by reputation, for so honourable a task; but finding that there was no immediate prospect of this, and being encouraged to go forward in this work by several old friends and admirers of David Cox, and assured also of generous help from various quarters, I now appear before the public, soliciting an indulgent construction of my endeavours to do justice to the simplicity and truthfulness of his character and to the originality of his genius.

The name of David Cox, although familiar to most lovers of art throughout Europe and America, will probably not convey to the majority of my readers the deep and varied meaning which it suggests to those who have made a long and careful study of his drawings and paintings. I shall endeavour, therefore, to show as I proceed some of the grounds on which his fame rests as the representative painter of English and Welsh scenery, and also to indicate many of those rare and peculiar merits which are now acknowledged to exist in his works, merits which recommend them especially to all true lovers of natural scenery.

My aim will also be to introduce my readers to the *man* just as he was in every-day life, genial, gentle, simple-minded, and modest, yet full of penetration and ardour in all matters pertaining to his profession. With this object I shall give some quotations from familiar letters and relate various anecdotes, which, although trifling in themselves and occasionally without any very special reference to art, will, I believe, assist in my object of showing David Cox as he was known to his friends, and as he still lives in the memory of those who have survived him.

Although it may be considered a truism, I cannot but remark how completely Cox's life has been expressed and written in his works.

The study and enumeration of what his hand and his *mind* produced, year after year, shows with what patient industry and lifelong practice he wrought out the ideal of his life and fulfilled his mission.

Continually changing the scene, but ever keeping in mind one and the same object, he gradually rose to the consummate knowledge and power which culminated in the deep, grand feeling of his latest works.

I trust that very few who follow the career of David Cox from his boyhood to his grave will feel disappointed at the absence from this narrative of all exciting events. In a life of such constant work, following but one pursuit, the chief incidents must necessarily consist in his onward progress, step by step, up the steep and rugged hill of fame.

The history of this onward progress, beset as it was in early years with many difficulties, and an account of the events which befell him during his long life, will, I hope, be thought not only interesting but eminently encouraging by many, who, like Cox, have only their own exertions to rely on for their advancement. I shall endeavour to lay before my readers a truthful picture of David Cox the artist, to indicate how ardent was his love for nature, and how unwearied his industry. As to his genius, I need hardly insist on that; it is so plainly declared in his works.

David Cox left no auto-biography, and not very many letters of general interest.

Those which have been preserved, and which are interwoven with this memoir, will, I believe, be read with interest, not on account of their possessing any particular literary merit, but because they help to illustrate his character and disposition, and also contain some of his views and reflections on matters connected with art; they also give some account of his sketching excursions.

It was only in the year 1866 that the first short biographical notice of David Cox appeared in that well-known work, by Messrs. Richard and Samuel Redgrave, entitled "A Century of Painters." But from the compass and scheme of those volumes only a few pages could be devoted to the life of each artist, and, although interesting and instructive, much is necessarily left unrecorded.

The same may be said of the short memoir of this artist contained in a newspaper article in the *Illustrated Midland News*, in May, 1870, written by Mr. William Hall, of Birmingham, to whom I am indebted for much assistance.

Some of the old friends and companions with whom Cox was on very intimate terms have already passed away, and with each succeeding year the difficulty of obtaining full and accurate information has increased. One or two chapters will be found at the end of this book, giving an account of many of his principal works in water colours and oils; and in the Appendix there is a complete list of all the drawings exhibited by him in the gallery of the old Society of Painters in Water Colours, of which he was a member for forty-six years; there is also a chapter on the genius and character of Cox at the end of the book.

It now remains for me to tender my sincere thanks for the kind assistance which has been rendered to me in the progress of this work, not only in the way of information and original letters, but also by the loan of drawings and paintings, the works of David Cox, to be copied by photography, and which appear in this volume. These illustrations, by the artist's own hand, of works painted by him at various dates, will, I trust, be regarded with especial interest by many who have no very ready means of access to the originals. To Mr. David Cox, junior, and to Mrs. William Roberts my grateful acknowledgments are peculiarly due; likewise to Mr. F. Craven, to Mr. H. T. Broadhurst, to Mr. Peter Allen, to Mr. S. Mayou, Mr. S. Quilter, and to Mr. Blacker, for the loan of valuable works. To Messrs. E. Everitt, W. S. Ellis, George Fripp, Alfred Fripp, G. P. Popkin, William Holmes, William Hall, J. Hollingsworth, B. A. Hallam, J. Banner, and Dr. Gibbs Blake, I am also indebted for various communications and assistance.

As "Bettws-y-Coed" is so peculiarly identified with the name of David Cox, I have added a chapter with that title, which I have devoted exclusively to a description of the place and its immediate neighbourhood, and to an account of the excursions he made there. Bettws was the scene of the "Welsh Funeral," perhaps his most famous work. A photographic copy of this will be found at the beginning of this preface.

In conclusion, I venture to express a hope that this record of an honourable and successful life—successful in the truest sense of the word—will be the means of enabling some of my readers to appreciate better the artist and his works, and also be welcomed by a few old friends, who sincerely loved the man, and who still cherish his memory.

N. N. S.

EDGBASTON, *December*, 1872.

CONTENTS.

CHAP.		PAGE
I.	EARLY LIFE, 1783 TO 1804	1
II.	FIRST RESIDENCE IN LONDON, 1804 TO 1814 .	15
III.	HEREFORD, 1814 TO 1827 . . .	34
IV.	WORKS ILLUSTRATED BY DAVID COX . .	51
V.	SECOND RESIDENCE IN LONDON, 1827 TO 1835 . .	61
VI.	SECOND RESIDENCE IN LONDON *(continued)*, 1835 TO 1840 .	78
VII.	PROGRESS IN ART AND REMOVAL FROM LONDON, 1840—1841	93
VIII.	FIRST YEARS AT HARBORNE, 1841 TO 1844	107
IX.	LIFE AT HARBORNE TILL DEATH OF HIS WIFE, 1844 TO 1846 . .	129
X.	LIFE AT HARBORNE, AND SUCCESS IN OIL-PAINTING, 1846 TO 1849 .	141
XI.	BETTWS-Y-COED . .	158
XII.	PAINTING IN OIL-COLOURS	181
XIII.	OIL-PICTURES	189
XIV.	LIFE AT HARBORNE *(continued)*, 1849 TO 1855 . .	216
XV.	TESTIMONIAL PORTRAIT BY SIR J. W. GORDON, 1855	235
XVI.	WATER-COLOUR DRAWINGS .	246
XVII.	LAST YEARS AT HARBORNE, 1855 TO 1859 .	284
XVIII.	CONCLUSION	302
XIX.	SUPPLEMENTARY—ON THE GENIUS AND CHARACTER OF DAVID COX .	308

APPENDICES.

I.	DRAWINGS EXHIBITED IN THE WATER-COLOUR SOCIETY, 1813 TO 1859	318
II.	NOTICE OF SALES OF DRAWINGS AND SEPIAS, 1856 TO 1872 . .	327
III.	CRITIQUE ON THE EXHIBITION IN THE GERMAN GALLERY, 1859 . .	333

LIST OF ILLUSTRATIONS.

To face page

I. FRONTISPIECE.—PORTRAIT OF DAVID COX, a photograph from Life, taken in 1855.

II. VIGNETTE ON TITLE-PAGE. View of Bettws-y-Coed Old Church.

III. THE WELSH FUNERAL at Bettws, photographed by A. Brothers, Manchester, from the celebrated water-colour drawing by David Cox, exhibited in 1850, now in Mr. F. Craven's collection. Date of original 1850. Size of ditto, 2 feet 6 inches by 3 feet 3 inches v

IV. MINIATURE HEAD ON A LOCKET, photographed by A. Brothers, from the original painted by D. Cox in early life. This Locket is in the possession of Mr. David Cox, junior 1

V. KENILWORTH CASTLE, WITH A FLOCK OF SHEEP, a Composition. An Autotype from the original very early drawing by David Cox, in the possession of Mr. Blacker. Date about 1808. Size, 16⅛ inches by 21¼ inches 15

VI. THE LUGG MEADOWS NEAR HEREFORD, photographed by A. Brothers, from an early water-colour drawing by David Cox, now in Mr. Peter Allen's collection. Date about 1817. Size of original, 17 inches by 26½ inches . 34

VII. PARRY'S COTTAGE, NEAR AILSTONE HILL, HEREFORD, partly built by David Cox, and inhabited by him from 1817 to 1824. Print by the Heliotype Company 50

VIII. OLD WINDMILL ON MOSLEY COMMON, BIRMINGHAM. Copy by Heliotype Company from soft ground etching. Etched on copper by David Cox. Date 1819 51

IX. THE HORSE FAIR, BIRMINGHAM. Autotype from the original water-colour sketch by David Cox, now in the collection of Mr. S. Quilter, date uncertain. Size of original, 7¼ inches by 10⅜ inches. Being from a rough sketch, it requires to be viewed from a distance 61

X. RAPID STUDY FOR THE SUBJECT OF AN OIL-PICTURE, being Scene on the Coast near Hastings, low water. Photographed by R. W. Thrupp, from water-colour sketch by David Cox, in the possession of Mrs. W. Roberts. Date 1843. Size of original, 6¾ inches by 8¾ inches . . 78

XI. BOLSOVER CASTLE, DERBYSHIRE, photographed by A. Brothers, from water-colour drawing by D. Cox. Exhibited 1843, now in Mr. F. Craven's collection. Date 1843. Size of original, 1 foot 11 inches by 3 feet 1 inch . 93

XII. FLINT CASTLE AND COAST OF NORTH WALES. Heliotype of large sepia drawing by David Cox, from the original in the possession of Mr. David Cox, junior. Date 1844 107

XIII. GREENFIELD HOUSE, HARBORNE, David Cox's residence. Heliotype from a sketch made about 1848, when Cox was living there. It shows the garden front of the house, and the bow window of the parlour on the side . . 128

To face page

XIV. BOLTON ABBEY, YORKSHIRE, photographed by A. Brothers, from celebrated drawing by D. Cox. Exhibited in Water Colour Society in 1847, and now in Mr. H. T. Broadhurst's collection. Date of drawing 1847. Size of original, 2 feet by 2 feet 10 inches 129

XV. BEESTON CASTLE, CHESHIRE, photographed by A. Brothers, from water-colour drawing by David Cox. Exhibited in the Old Water Colour Society, and now in Mr. F. Craven's collection, dated 1849. Size of the original, 2 feet by 2 feet 10 inches. This is one of the most successful drawings, and of the best period 141

XVI. PEAT GATHERERS returning from the Moors near Bettws-y-Coed. Autotype from the water-colour drawing by David Cox, now in Mr. David Cox, junior's, collection. Date 1856. Size of original, 19 inches by 29½ inches 158

XVII. BATHERS FRIGHTENED BY A BULL. Photograph by A. Brothers, from a water-colour drawing by David Cox, now in Mr. H. T. Broadhurst's collection. Date 1853. Size of original, 10½ inches by 14½ inches . . . 181

XVIII. GOING TO THE HAYFIELD, photographed by R. W. Thrupp, Birmingham, from the fine oil-painting by David Cox, in Mr. S. Mayou's collection, Edgbaston. Date 1849. Size of original, 2 feet 4 inches by 2 feet 10 inches 189

XIX. BROOM GATHERERS ON CHAT MOSS. Photograph by A. Brothers, from the well known water-colour drawing by David Cox, exhibited in the Water Colour Society; formerly in Mr. Mayou's collection, now in that of Mr. F. Craven. Date 1854. Size of original, 2 feet by 3 feet 10 inches . . 216

XX. PORTRAIT OF DAVID COX, painted by Sir J. W. Gordon. Heliotype from proof engraving by Bellin. This is the Testimonial Portrait, now in the Public Gallery, Birmingham. Date 1855. Size of original, 3 feet by 4 feet . 235

XXI. STOKE-SAY, NEAR LUDLOW—STORMY WEATHER. Photograph by A. Brothers, from water-colour drawing by David Cox on rough paper, now in Mr. Peter Allen's collection. Date 1853. Size of the original, 11 inches by 15 inches 246

XXII. THE SKIRTS OF THE FOREST—Part of Old Sherwood Forest—High Wind. Autotype from water-colour drawing by David Cox, being his favourite one of this subject, from the original in Mr. David Cox, junior's, collection. Date 1855. Size of original, 18½ inches by 21½ inches 284

Eight pages of letters, of which three contain sketches, printed as fac-similes by the Heliotype Company, from the originals written by David Cox:—

The Letters dated 1st January, and 12th January, 1841 106

The Letter dated July, 1844, from Tynllan 128

THE LIFE OF DAVID COX.

I.

EARLY LIFE.

1783 TO 1804.

IN a small house near the bridge, in Heath-mill Lane, Deritend (anciently Der-yat-end), a poor suburb on the south-east side of Birmingham, surrounded by workshops and small forges, David Cox—the subject of this memoir—was born on the 29th of April, 1783. His father, Joseph Cox, followed the calling of a blacksmith and whitesmith, forging gun-barrels, bayonets, horseshoes, and other similar articles during the war, and putting his own trade-mark upon them.

CHAP. I.
—
1783—1804.

His son has related, that in after years, he used to take any opportunity that offered to examine the soldiers' bayonets in the London parks, in search for his father's mark; and also that on one occasion he derived much pleasure, when out on a journey, by discovering a horseshoe with his father's initials stamped upon it. The forging of iron and steel had been, from a very early date, one of the representative trades of Birmingham, and Joseph Cox appears to have been an industrious and thriving artificer in iron, but without much mental cultivation. His wife, whose maiden name was Frances Walford, was the daughter of a farmer

CHAP. I. 1783—1804. and miller, having a windmill on a high gravelly hill, which existed formerly on the left-hand side of Holloway Head, as you go up from St. Martin's Church, and in the vicinity of St. Thomas's Church. She was, in some respects, a superior woman, with highly religious feelings, better educated than her husband, and with a good deal of force of character and natural good sense. Her son David has often attributed a good deal of his success in after life to the watchful care and good judgment of his mother, and to the right principles which she instilled into his mind in early years. David Cox's excellent mother died about the year 1810; but his father, who had removed to Hill Street some years before, married a second wife, and afterwards went to live in a cottage at Saltley, not far from Aston. He lived to a good old age, and died in 1829 or 1830, having been in receipt of an annuity from his son for many years, and which was continued as long as he lived. David was an only son, but he had one sister named Mary Ann, older than himself. She had helped to take care of him when a child, and he was always much attached to her throughout his life. She married an organist and teacher of music at Manchester, named Ward. For some years he kept a musical academy there; but they had no family, and after Mr. Ward's death he was succeeded in business by his nephew. Mrs. Ward was a brunette, with a good natural expression, but without any claim to be considered pretty. Although possessed of a fair share of common sense, she was fond of "having her own way," and she was also described by some of her acquaintances as a *strong-minded* woman. After she lost her husband she used frequently to visit her brother at Harborne, and he rarely allowed a year to pass without going to see her at Sale, near Manchester.

It would be difficult for any one who now visits Birmingham —the metropolis of the trade of the Midland Counties, numbering a population of 350,000, with its interminable streets, busy warehouses, vast railway system, stately halls, and large works and factories driven by steam-engines—to realise the wonderful changes that have taken place since 1783. Wide indeed is the difference between the aspect which the town presented at that date and its present one. Heath-mill Lane, the scene of Cox's birth, was a narrow thoroughfare. Passing by an old pool, it joined the main approach to Birmingham near the bridge over the Rea, and its south corner was formed by that ancient and renowned inn the Old Crown, built of black oak, with curious gables, still standing, and mentioned as long ago as 1531, in Leland's Itinerary. The greater part of the lane, including Joseph Cox's house, has been swept away of late years, to make room for the railway approaches, and the quaint old timbered buildings in that part of the town are rapidly giving place to modern red-brick houses.

At the date I am speaking of, or, rather, two years earlier —viz., in 1781, when the last census was taken—the entire population of Deritend and Bordesley together only numbered 2,125, and there were but five streets, mostly very narrow. At this time the community of Birmingham altogether boasted of but thirty-six private carriages; the highest rent of any house, except the inns, was ninety pounds per annum, and some houses, with shops and gardens in good situations, were let at ten pounds. The old covered market crosses—"The Old Cross," on the site of Nelson's monument in the Bull Ring, and the Welch Cross, at the junction of Bull Street and High Street—still existed, and were then used for the sale of butter, poultry, and other country produce. The large room over the Old Cross having been used in olden times as the Court of Request, and as most of the town meetings used to be held there, we must infer they were not very large ones.

When about six or seven years old, Cox was sent to one of the day schools which existed in Birmingham in those days, and where the teaching was altogether of a very elementary character. At this time he fell over a door-scraper and broke his leg. During the confinement caused by this accident, and whilst his leg was in splints, a cousin of the name of Allport (probably son of John Allport, a painter in general, at 54, Bull Street, Birmingham, at the end of the last century) gave little David a box of colours, and he amused himself in painting paper kites which his school companions brought him. The box of colours proved a source of delight and unfailing amusement to the boy; when better, he procured some paper and copied a number of small pictures from engravings, which he coloured, and disposed of for the merest trifle.

As soon as he had entirely recovered, he was sent to the free school in Birmingham: but he did not long enjoy the advantages of instruction there, as his father withdrew him as soon as he thought he could make the lad useful in his own workshop.

He was by no means a strong boy, being thin and lanky, and on one occasion—when at the free school—a big boy annoyed him by calling him by some derisive epithet, expressive of his legs being thin and lanky. David told his tormentor that if he said that again he would give him a hiding. The offence having been repeated, the lads had a good set-to; and, although our hero does not appear to have claimed the victory, still, his pluck had the desired effect—that of silencing his opponent.

After a short trial, it was found that the work in his father's shop was too much for David, and his fondness for colouring pictures increasing, it was proposed that he should be apprenticed to some one of the toy trades then carried on in Birmingham, in which his natural bias might be turned to advantage. That he might be better prepared, he was sent to attend an evening school for drawing, kept by Joseph Barber the elder, at the corner of Edmund Street, where it joined Newhall Street. Mr. Barber was the father of the artists, Charles Barber and Joseph Vincent Barber, who were learning drawing there at the same time, and David Cox formed a warm and lasting friendship with Charles, a man of the most estimable character. Samuel Lines was also a pupil. Mr. Barber is reported to have been very strict, and very particular in enforcing *correct* drawing: he made his pupils repeat the same subject in outline many times, until accuracy was attained. There is no doubt that David made great progress in drawing at this school, and laid the foundation for much of his after success.

The so-called toy trades which first gave employment to young David had originated about the year 1775, through the enterprise of a Birmingham worthy, Mr. John Taylor. They consisted in the manufacture of buttons, gilt and lacquered buckles, snuff-boxes, lockets, &c., mounted in metal work and painted. The painting varied much in quality; but that it was, in those days, sometimes not very good may be inferred from the fact that one man in Mr. Taylor's service is recorded to have once earned three pounds ten shillings a week by painting the tops of snuff-boxes at one farthing each.

After attending Mr. Barber's school for some time, David at the age of fifteen was apprenticed to a locket and miniature painter in Birmingham, of the name of Fieldler. He soon overcame the difficulties of the work, and eventually learned to paint lockets in miniature very well indeed under his master's instruction, as is proved by a locket painted by him in early life, representing the head of a young man, in the possession of Mr. David Cox, junior; it is really a beautiful work, especially for a young man, as my readers will, I think, allow, after examining the photographic copy which appears at the beginning of this chapter. After he had been thus employed for rather more than eighteen months, his apprenticeship was brought to a sudden close by

CHAP. I. 1783—1804.

the death of Mr. Fieldler, who committed suicide. On going upstairs, David was the first to discover the body of his master hanging on the landing. This caused a great shock to his sensitive nature, and one which he certainly never forgot as long as he lived. Before finally dismissing the subject of the Birmingham toy trades, I must relate an anecdote of this date in connection with them :—Mr. Fieldler, the miniature painter, had another apprentice at the same time as David Cox, named Haseler, whose son has informed me, he saw, when a boy, lockets that had been painted at Fieldler's, with Cupids and subjects of Heathen Mythology, besides heads. They were first traced on the ivory by means of coloured paper, and then outlined with lake. The elder Haseler related that he had a companion, a painter of snuff-boxes, who excelled in a subject much in request seventy years ago, in the early days of the French war; a group of artillery or men-of-war's men, loading and firing off cannon with plenty of smoke. . . . . Six figures besides accessories were painted on each box at six shillings each, and by dint of great assiduity the painter realised four or five pounds a week. . . . . His success rather exalted his head, and one pay-Saturday he drove to his employer's house in a hackney coach to receive his earnings. The master, surprised to see a carriage at his door, inquired the cause, and on learning it, quietly observed he should "take a wheel off it" next week. So the following Saturday, without making any remark, he paid five shillings and sixpence instead of six shillings for each box, and so on each week, till he had taken off three sixpences. The limner said nothing, but painted a figure less each time; at last the master observed that there were only three figures on each box, but a great deal more smoke, and asked "the reason why," in a tone of complaint. "Oh!" said the painter, "you must understand that the three gunners are gone to look after the three missing sixpences." The master was convinced by this argument, and they soon came to a fresh and satisfactory arrangement.

After the unfortunate termination of David Cox's engagement as a locket painter, his cousin Allport, who was fond of frequenting the theatre at Birmingham, which had lately been rebuilt, and who was acquainted with the manager and actors, took him there sometimes to see the scenery. The broad and effective style of scene-painting took a great hold on his imagination, and he was much pleased when Allport got an engagement for him to grind colours and wait on the scene-painters, and he was also enabled for a time to resume his evening attendance at Mr. Barber's drawing class.

The elder Macready, father of the tragedian, was then lessee and manager of the theatre. He spared no pains to have his dramas well got up, and he had recently engaged an Italian scene-painter from the Opera House in London, De Maria, for whom young David worked as a humble assistant.

He found his occupation a very congenial one, and he soon made many new friends. His taste and love for art were beginning to be clearly developed, and he had abundant opportunities of watching the progress of De Maria's work, which he admired very much. De Maria had been a friend and associate of J. M. W. Turner, and Cox used to compare some of the scenery painted by De Maria to Wilson in colour, and to Claude in composition. Even to a late period of his life, Cox was never tired of speaking of De Maria's works, and often regretted that they had probably been long since destroyed. On one occasion (at least forty years after his employment at the Birmingham Theatre), Cox was staying at a friend's house at Sevenoaks, the terrace of which overlooked the beautiful Knowle Woods: there he used to enjoy walking up and down smoking a cigar, and he would then describe with enthusiasm the scenes painted by De Maria, especially a wooded landscape, and after

CHAP. I. 1783—1804. a detailed account of its effect and breadth, he added earnestly, how very much he should like to see it again.

Cox was too modest to offer to assist in the painting of scenery, but he made friends with the chief carpenter, who had charge of all the mechanical arrangement of the theatre, and this led to his confiding to him his previous training in art, and his desire to be allowed to try his hand in that department. The carpenter was not slow in communicating to De Maria what young Cox had said about his practice in painting, and that he thought he could assist him with the side-scenes. He was allowed before long to make a trial; the subject to be represented being some groups of village folk, congregated together at a country fair, with a rustic having his pocket picked.

Cox's success in this first essay led to his further employment in the same line.

The facility and ease of handling, as well as the mastery of effect, which are learnt by scene-painting, and which Cox had the opportunity of studying under a good master, greatly assisted him in his subsequent career. It gave him a large manner and taught him breadth, as has been the case with Stanfield, Roberts, and many other good artists.

As I may not have occasion to revert to De Maria again, I will now mention an anecdote in connection with him, although somewhat anticipating dates. Cox lost sight of his friend and master, De Maria, for some years after he left Birmingham, and it was not until Cox had joined the Society of Painters in Water Colours, in 1813, that they met in this wise:—Cox one day, according to his habit, was standing *incognito* near some of his own works in the Exhibition, listening to the remarks and criticisms of the visitors, when an elderly gentleman, who was looking at one, happened to turn round, and Cox recognised in him his old friend the scene-painter. Cox said he was very glad to meet him after so many years, and that he had always considered himself very much indebted to him in matters of art. "What!" said De Maria, "are you the David Cox, the painter of this picture, the same young lad who used to grind my colours at Birmingham? Then, indeed, I assure you that, if I taught you something formerly, I have now learnt a great deal more from you."

Some time after Cox commenced to paint the side-scenes, a play was to be brought out which had never before been acted in Birmingham, in which the denouement of the plot depended on the production of a lady's portrait, the likeness of the heroine. Search was made, but nothing could be found that would at all answer the purpose; time pressed, the chief scene-painter happened to be absent, and the performance of the evening seemed likely to be nonplussed. Cox, feeling confidence in his own ability, having painted so many heads on lockets, and hearing of the difficulty, was overheard to say that he could do it. This was at once communicated to Macready. Cox had been too modest to apply himself to the manager, but when sent for said, "I think, sir, I can produce what is wanted if you will allow me to try." Macready looked at the young man with surprise, as he doubted his ability; but he said, "Well, you *shall* try." The actress, a Miss Decamps, was coming to the rehearsal. Cox was told to look well at her. He at once commenced the picture, she sat to him afterwards for its completion, and it turned out a complete success. Thus Cox's promptness and ability enabled the piece to be performed, and this led to his engagement by Macready as his scene-painter. This was of the more importance, as, besides the Birmingham Theatre, he had several other provincial theatres under his management, where scenery required to be painted. Cox was about eighteen or nineteen years of age at this time, and he retained this engagement for about four years. Macready's son, W. C. Macready, who became so celebrated as an actor

CHAP. I. 1783—1804.

in after life, was then a child; and Cox, with his usual kindness, painted a complete set of miniature scenery for various dramas, to be used in a toy or puppet theatre, which had been made for the little boy probably by one of the carpenters. These scenes were so much prized and so well taken care of, that they were still in existence only a very few years ago. The esteem so early formed for the youthful scene-painter in young Macready's mind, lasted until the end of his career, as is proved by a most friendly letter written half a century afterwards by the great actor, when the testimonial portrait of David Cox was projected, and to which he sent a subscription of two guineas.

It was the custom in those days for a company of provincial actors, or players as they were then generally called, to move from town to town, giving representations sometimes in extemporised theatres, and accompanied by the scene-painter.

In this way Cox travelled about with the "players" to Bristol, Leicester, Sheffield, Manchester, Liverpool, &c., and occasionally he would take a minor part on the stage; and once, when Macready was at fault, he used to relate that he enacted the rôle of clown in a small country town.

Although Cox seems to have caught a relish for the humour and intellectual stimulus of such society, he was not at all pleased with the freedom of manners, nor with the scanty and dirty accommodation which they had often to put up with on their travels. On one occasion he was particularly disgusted at being requested, after breakfast at an inn, to keep a sharp look-out to see that nobody was coming whilst one of his companions cut off as much cold beef as made a meal, and pocketed it. After working hard at painting for some hours, by way of change and exercise he used sometimes to summon the carpenters to hold the blanket for him, that he might take a harlequin leap. In those seasons of the year when his services were not required at the theatre, young Cox turned his time to account by drawing and sketching from nature with the Barbers. After he had led this life for some years, during which he gained much experience in producing scenic effects, the hasty temper of the elder Macready was the cause of a quarrel. I have heard the following account of the misunderstanding, although, probably, there were other causes of dissatisfaction. Cox had failed to please Macready at all times, and the latter pointing to a scene that he was under the impression had been painted by some other artist, told Cox it was far superior to anything he could produce. The remark was resented by Cox, as the scene in question had really been painted by himself some time before (as his signature at the foot afterwards shown to Macready proved), and he determined to embrace the first opportunity that offered of terminating his engagement at the theatre.

His practice in scene-painting was regarded by him as merely a stepping-stone to something higher, he had set his heart on becoming a landscape-painter, and in giving up his appointment at Birmingham, he thought he should be clearing the way in that direction. He was the more fortified in this resolve by his mother's wish, as she feared that the continued companionship with actors might contaminate his morals, and she particularly objected to his travelling about the country with them. She is reported to have used her influence with Mrs. Macready to get her son David liberated by Mr. Macready, and the matter, after some difficulty, was arranged to their mutual satisfaction. Cox appears, before going to London, to have made use of his temporary leisure in making some sketching excursions, amongst other places to Kenilworth. There still exists in his son's possession a view of Kenilworth Castle, date 1804, very correctly and boldly drawn; and he cut his name with this date on one of the old staircases, leading, I believe, to Cæsar's Tower. About this time Astley, the proprietor of Astley's circus, visited Birmingham, and, seeing what Cox could do as a

CHAP. I. 1783—1804.

scene-painter, offered to employ him at his circus or theatre, in Lambeth, if he would come to London. Cox was then twenty-one years of age, and his great desire to go to London induced him to accept Mr. Astley's proposal; and as soon as arrangements could be made, he started by coach on his first journey to the metropolis, accompanied by his mother, who rather dreaded the gaiety of London for her son. This was in 1804. Travelling in England was a very different thing then from what it now is, and sleeping on the road was a necessity. On arriving in the metropolis they proceeded to Lambeth, and there, in a quiet road, not far from the Elephant and Castle, near the back of Astley's Circus, Mrs. Cox secured board and lodgings for her son, at the house of a widow lady, Mrs. Ragg, who was residing there with her two unmarried daughters. The eldest of these, Mary, was destined in the course of a few years to become David Cox's wife. Mrs. Ragg had also another daughter, married to Mr. Hills, and her youngest daughter afterwards married Mr. Gardener, who held a situation under Government, in connection with the sale of the ordnance and other maps. To the widow and her two daughters Mrs. Cox confided her son, begging them to look to his comfort and welfare, and so she left him and returned to Birmingham. Cox soon went to Astley's Theatre, in the hope of entering on his promised engagement in the scene-loft, but he found that there were already several painters employed, and, it being the end of the season, he felt a delicacy as to forcing himself in their way. He therefore never painted at Astley's, but he had some commissions for scenery for the Surrey, and also for the Swansea theatre. Determined to seek other employment in London, he succeeded in this before long, as we shall see in the next chapter. At the time Cox went to London, in 1804, he was on friendly terms with Mr. Allen Everitt (grandfather of the present Mr. Allen E. Everitt), who at that time kept a shop for the sale of drawings, drawing materials, and paper, in

Union Street, Birmingham. He always kept up a friendship with Mr. Everitt's family, and often stayed at their home in after years. Mr. Everitt's son Edward was one of his earliest pupils, and he introduced Cox to many of his early friends. Cox had at that time two young companions who intended to become artists, and who were his special friends, Charles Barber, already mentioned, and Richard Evans. They followed Cox to London, taking lodgings near him, and all three used to go out sketching together. Richard Evans was poor in those days, and Cox, who was much more proficient in landscape art than his friend, kindly lent Evans many of his own sketches in indian ink, which Evans copied and sold to help himself along. I have seen several of these drawings by Evans in indian ink, copies after Cox, of that very early date. The subjects are chiefly buildings, such as castles, cottages, or old houses, rather square and simple in form with decided shadows. Richard Evans became a portrait-painter of some distinction, and used to work under Sir Thomas Lawrence, making duplicate portraits of members of the Royal Family, which were much in request. Charles Barber, after exhibiting landscapes without much success for a few years in London, removed to Liverpool, where he soon took a good position, and where he continued to reside as a landscape-painter for a period of forty years. He filled for many years the office of President of the Liverpool Academy of Painting, exhibiting occasionally at the Royal Academy in London.

He was also one of the earliest members of the Liverpool Literary and Philosophical Society. Cox made many sketching excursions with Barber in early years, and till within a few years of his death he used frequently to meet him at Bettws; indeed, their friendship endured throughout life.

Among the deceased landscape artists who also commenced their career in Birmingham, and who have afterwards attained to a high position and wide-spread re-

CHAP. I. 1783—1804. nown, the names of Thomas Creswick, R.A., and George Mason, A.R.A., must not be overlooked. With Creswick Cox was for several years on very friendly terms. The death of George Mason has happened whilst these pages are being prepared for the press. Like Cox, Mason was endowed with a very poetical mind, and one that was in harmony with all that was graceful and impressive in nature; he possessed great power added to a thorough knowledge of art, acquired during a long residence in Italy; he had risen rapidly to the foremost rank of landscape-painters, and his loss will be severely felt and lamented by all true lovers of art in England.

II.

FIRST RESIDENCE IN LONDON.

1804 TO 1814.

DIRECTLY after David Cox was located in Lambeth in 1804, he commenced sketching from nature and making drawings, which he offered at very low prices to the London dealers; among others to one of the name of Simpson, who kept a shop in Greek Street, Soho, for the sale of works of art. These drawings were often bought up by country drawing-masters, who wanted them as copies for their pupils. CHAP. II. 1804—1814.

Cox has related that he sold some of these at this time at the almost nominal price of two guineas a dozen.

Mr. Simpson was pleased with what the young artist brought, but he told him that he thought his art knowledge would be much improved by copying the works of some of the old masters. Cox having replied that he should like nothing better if the opportunity of doing so offered, Mr. Simpson, who possessed a fine landscape by Gaspar Poussin, gave him permission to make a copy of it, provided he liked to do it in his shop. The offer was accepted, and, in spite of the difficulties of the locality, Cox made a very good copy of the oil picture in water-colours, which is now at Brixton Hill. It represents classical figures, and a flock of sheep passing by a pool, with old buildings and trees in the distance. The composition is good, and the colour rich but rather dark. The influence of this picture may be traced in some of Cox's works painted shortly afterwards, especially a mill at Penmachno, of the date of 1807. In order to improve himself in composition, Cox purchased, soon after he came to London, a collection of etchings from paintings by Gaspar Poussin, Salvator Rosa, and Claude, published by Pond in the years 1741, 1744, and 1746, and well known as "Pond's Etchings." These he found very useful with regard to composition and light and shade, and he used to refer to them frequently in after life. He greatly admired the works of the artists above named, as well as those of Hobbema and Velasquez.

Soon after Cox had completed his copy of the Gaspar Poussin in Simpson's shop, he made a large drawing, about 16 by 20, in rivalry of that work, the subject being a composition, with a flock of sheep and a man and dog, also some trees and Kenilworth Castle. The arrangement and effect are good, but the touch is somewhat constrained.

It is interesting as being one of the earliest drawings of large size which he made. The date cannot be later than 1806 or 1807, and, I believe, before he had lessons from Varley. It is now in the possession of a gentleman in London, Mr. Blacker, and through his kindness I am enabled to give a photographic copy of it at the commencement of this chapter.

In order to provide subjects for his drawings, Cox used at this time to frequent Battersea fields, Old Bonner Hall, in Lambeth, and the wharves on the banks of the Thames; indeed, for many years the Thames, with the grand and picturesque buildings adjoining it, such as Westminster Abbey, Greenwich Hospital, Somerset House, and the London Bridges, afforded the materials required for many of his drawings.

Cox used frequently to offer his drawings at the shop of Palser, then living near Astley's Theatre, in the Westminster Road. There he saw drawings by other London artists, which he admired and tried to emulate, especially those of John Varley. Cox thought he might get on better if he had some regular instruction in water-colours, and he considered for some time whether he should apply to John Varley, John Glover, or William Havell. Finally he determined to apply to Varley, and he often said, in after life, how much he rejoiced that he came to that decision.

At this time John Varley lived at No. 16, Broad Street, Golden Square, and there Cox made the acquaintance of several other artists. He took several lessons in water-colours, for which he was to pay at the rate of ten shillings each; but, after he had had a few lessons, Varley, addressing his pupil, said, "I hear you are an artist, Mr. Cox." "No, sir," he replied, "I am only trying to become one." "Well," said Varley, "however that may be, I shall be happy to give you any advice or assistance in my power, and I hope you will come here and see me draw as often as you please; but I cannot take any more of your money."

In 1805 Cox made his first journey into North Wales. He appears to have been joined by his friend Charles Barber, and the two young men made an interesting tour through the wildest parts of Merioneth and Carnarvonshire. The love for North Welsh scenery which sprung up in Cox's heart on this occasion was never extinguished as long as he lived. Some of the sketches made at this time, dated 1805, represent the following subjects:—"Bridge leading to Cain and Mowddach Waterfalls," "Near Llanilltyd," "Bwlch-y-Garnedd," "Llansilian Vale," "River Dee," "Owen Glyndwr's House," "Pistyl-y-Cayne, on the road to Trawsfynydd," "Moel Shabod," "Vale of Gynnarit," &c. They are rather slight; some only in outline, and others tinted with indian ink, good in composition, but without much effect. I have also seen sketches made in Wales in 1806, when he carried with him a few colours—indigo, gamboge, purple lake, and sepia, dissolved in bottles, with which he painted on the

CHAP. II. 1804—1814. spot; likewise a broad and effective water-colour of Kenilworth Castle, dated 1806.

The colour is low in tone in these sketches, but truthful, and somewhat in the manner of Barrett and Varley. At this time he used also to sketch rather boldly in chalk on blue paper. On returning to town he occupied himself in making drawings from his sketches, visiting exhibitions, and occasionally painting scenery for provincial theatres. A commission was offered him for some large scenery for the West of England, I believe by "Little Cherry." Cox demurred at first because he had no room large enough for the work; but Mr. Hills, a connection of Mrs. Ragg, happening to possess a builder's yard, and being himself a carpenter, kindly offered to set up a hoarding of boards and frame in the yard where Cox might paint. This was done, and Cox has often described his anxiety to get his work done before rain fell. The time of year was midsummer, and he fortunately completed a set of scenes in distemper, the weather being fine.

An interesting proof still exists, however, that Cox occasionally turned his knowledge of scene-painting to account after he went to live in London, in the shape of a bill in Cox's own handwriting, which I have seen, and of which the following is an exact copy:—

1808. Mr. STRETTON to DAVID COX, Dr.
Feby. 15th. To painting 310 yards of scenery at 4s. pr. square yard, £62 0 0

The above document is in the possession of Mr. John Wood, of High Street, Wolverhampton, where it may be seen, and I have to acknowledge his courtesy in allowing a copy to be taken. I am informed that this Mr. Stretton was either the lessee or the manager of the Wolverhampton Theatre in 1807 and 1808, and the scenery was probably painted in the summer or autumn of 1807 in the carpenter's yard in Lambeth. The receipt came into Mr. Wood's possession from Mr. Roebuck, whose family resided at

Manchester, near to Mr. and Mrs. Ward, and were said to be friends of Mrs. Ward (Cox's sister). This account of painting done at four shillings the yard suggests the strange vicissitudes which time brings to pass. Work by the same hand has lately been competed for at prices which may be computed at some thousand pounds per yard.

In the spring of the year 1805 the Society of Painters in Water Colours opened their first exhibition at Lower Brook Street. At first it consisted of sixteen members only. Cox did not join that society until 1813; but a rival society was started in Bond Street, to which Cox belonged. I have not been able to obtain an exact list of the members. Heaphy, Henry Richter, Luke Francia, S. Owens, Dorrell, Goodwin, and some others exhibited there; I believe probably also W. Turner, C. Fielding, and Robson, as these artists did not join the regular Water Colour Society until some years after it commenced. This rival society was not very prosperous; and I may as well state here that, after a few years, it came to a disastrous close, as the expenses exceeded the income, in consequence of which the works of many of the exhibitors were seized to pay the rent of the gallery. Among the principal sufferers on this occasion was David Cox. His finances were by no means flourishing at the time, and the blow fell on him very heavily. Mr. J. Allnutt, of Clapham Common, purchased several of Cox's drawings at the forced sale which took place at the time. Fifty years later, namely, about 1861, after the death of Mr. Allnutt, his executors were preparing to sell his collection at Christie's, and amongst the drawings were the identical ones just referred to. One of these was a fine drawing, 4 feet by 3 feet, representing Windsor Castle rising up grandly beyond a reach of meadows, with trees and water in the foreground, the distance dark and powerful, and the whole highly finished. The sides of the drawing were pasted down on a stretching-board, and the edges having got stained, were

CHAP. II.
1804—1814.

slightly decayed under the frame. Mr. David Cox, junior (who had been asked by Mr. Carr, Mr. Allnutt's son-in-law, to look over the collection), removed the drawing from the board, when, to his surprise, another very nice drawing of the same size appeared underneath, representing the Vale of Llanilltyd; and, more surprising still, on removing this one, again a third drawing, of which the subject was a Pool at Sutton Coldfield, with trees and hills in the distance, was discovered. No doubt, in the early days when these drawings were produced, Cox placed but small store on his works, of which he had great difficulty in disposing. His mind was depressed, and he may have thought that, as he should paint many better ones before long, he would place these three to support his exhibition drawing of Windsor Castle, or he may have forgotten that he had placed other drawings already on the board.

In 1808 David Cox, who had continued to board and lodge in the house of Mrs. Ragg, married her eldest daughter, Mary, and shortly afterwards he rented a small cottage at the corner of Dulwich Common, just passing the College on the road to the right.

Into this cottage the young couple moved soon after their marriage, and there their only child, David, was born in the following summer. Mary Ragg was a slight, gentle, delicate woman, and had never very strong health, especially in early married life. Her son David says that his first recollection of his mother was of the "pale lady who could just walk round the garden." This refers to a period when the child, a few years old, had been staying away from home at his aunt's. Mrs. Cox had good taste in literature, and used to read a great deal out loud to her husband while he drew. Works of biography, travels, and occasionally a novel, were what he liked best to listen to. She always took much interest in art, she occasionally drew herself, and her opinion was always asked and valued by her husband on his works during their progress. She was some years his senior, naturally of a cheerful disposition, and, without doubt, she exercised great influence for good on his character. When Cox first went to live on Dulwich Common it was a lonely and rather wild spot, much frequented by gipsies, who hovered about the extensive woods belonging to Dulwich College, which then fringed the common in unpruned luxuriance. He made many studies on the common of gipsies, their donkeys and encampments, and these served him in good stead as "incidents" in his drawings in after life. Cox used to relate that on one occasion he was coming home from London late at night, his pockets stuffed with packets of tea, sugar, &c., and he had nearly crossed a field leading to the common, when suddenly he espied the legs of a man, crouched down close to the stile, as if lying in wait. Immediately he started off at full speed, and gained his home by a wide circuit, the sugar beating a tattoo on his sides as he ran. In 1809 Cox took his wife and son on a visit to his father and mother in Birmingham, who were then living in Hill Street, near the corner of Swallow Street. His young friend Edward Everitt took lessons from him on that occasion, and he well remembers how Cox would leave off in the middle of the lesson for a few minutes, saying he *must* go and nurse the "baby." They went out sketching frequently, and made studies of Moseley Common, Sutton, Aston, and many other places. I have seen these drawings, which still exist, and which are broad and powerful, with little finish, now somewhat faded in colour, but still pleasing and truthful.

As I have already stated, Cox used to sell his early drawings at Palser's shop in the Westminster Road, and there they were seen and admired by Colonel the Hon. H. Windsor (afterwards Earl of Plymouth), who at once determined to take lessons from him, and inquired where the artist lived. Palser at first hesitated to inform him, but on being pressed he said that he was a young man from the country, who now

CHAP. II. 1804—1814.

lived in a cottage on Dulwich Common, "*a long way out of town.*" That was, however, on the Colonel's way as he drove in every day from Beckenham, so he called at once. Cox was fortunately at home, and the first lesson was given. Cox used humorously to observe that this first lesson cost him his dinner. A joint or a fowl was down at the fire roasting, and almost ready to serve, when the Colonel arrived. Before the lesson was over the meat was, as Cox said, crying out aloud that it was burnt, and that he was astonished the Colonel did not smell it, for it was quite spoilt. Colonel Windsor proved a valuable friend, he took many lessons from Cox at various times; but what was of more importance, he introduced and recommended him to the Hon. Misses Eden, to Lady Gordon, to Lady Arden, and to other families of distinction. Cox used to walk all the way from Dulwich to the West-end and back; but he said that seeing his new style in art appreciated gave him confidence. He had obtained quite a start in teaching at the West-end during the London season, and he was soon enabled to raise his term for an hour's lesson from five shillings to half a guinea. He used generally, at this time, to leave his work with his pupils, and some of these little drawings, which cost their possessors only ten shillings, have since been sold for thirty or forty guineas each. Amongst his early pupils at the West-end, besides those already named, were Miss Tylney Long, Lady Sophia Cecil, and Lady Burrell. Whilst he was living at Dulwich, Cox had the misfortune to be drawn for the militia. Besides his instinctive repugnance to anything resembling a military life, he felt that to sacrifice the time necessary to serve would sadly interfere with his progress in art. He made the necessary representation at head quarters, but without success, as they declined to take his name off the roll, although others, who were less truthful than himself, had got off. He therefore paid for a substitute at Croydon, but for some cause he was refused, and Cox left home quietly for a time. Afterwards, when the prospects of peace caused less strictness in the enrolment, he was able to return, being no longer afraid of being arrested as a deserter. Times were hard for poor artists, and Cox struggled on, giving what lessons he could, and occasionally selling a drawing at a low price. Still he could not but feel anxious for the future, and often felt troubled in spite of the cheering sympathy of his wife, who was always ready to take a hopeful view of the situation. It was on a day of unusual despondency that Mrs. Cox suggested to her husband that, by way of trying something new, he should advertise to give lessons in perspective. This struck Cox as being a good idea, and he set to work at once to give it effect, and hastened to procure some books in London to brush up his recollection of the rules. The elements of Euclid were recommended to him, amongst other books, as containing the instruction he was desirous of imparting to others. Cox had never learned geometry, and he did not know exactly what to expect; but he sat down after tea to study his new acquisition. He soon found he had got more than he had looked for; the longer he endeavoured to master the propositions, the more the difficulties increased. At last his head began to ache, and his courage to fail, and, after one or two more useless attempts, he shut the book up with an exclamation of disgust, and flung it from him in despair. The partition of the room in which he sat was old, and being merely composed of lath and plaster, the book—flying like a shot—made a hole through it, and fell down inside the battens. Cox, in his humorous way, used to tell this story with much glee in after life, remarking that without doubt the book was still lying where he had flung it. The experiment was, however, in other respects more successful, as Cox soon got pupils, to whom he taught the elements of perspective—builders, and the more respectable class of artizans, who required to make drawings and elevations in connection with their work. It is interesting

CHAP. II.

1804—1814.

to note the prices obtained by Cox about this time—1811, 1812, and 1813—for his lessons and drawings. In an old account book of the date are the following entries in his own handwriting:—

1811.			
Nov. 15.	Sold to Mr. Everitt, Birmingham—		
	View of Lambeth and London . .	£5 5 0	
	Village of Crowhurst, in Sussex . .	4 4 0	
	Nymphs Bathing	3 3 0	
	View of Warwick Castle . . .	2 2 0	
Nov. 30.	1 dozen Sepia drawings at 8*s.* each .	4 16 0	
	Village of Castor, Wilts . . .	1 10 0	
	Old House, near Knowle . . .	1 0 0	

1812.

July 23. Coloured Drawing of Stack-yard, £1 11*s.* 6*d.* Coast Scene, £1 1*s.* 0*d.* Ditto of Perry Bridge, £1 1*s.* 0*d.* Pevensea Castle, 15*s.* Ditto of Westminster Bridge, £2 2*s.* Barley Field, £1 11*s.* 6*d.* Sion House on the Thames, 15*s.* Thames Fishermen, 18*s.* Smugglers, 18*s.* Hastings Fishermen preparing to go out, £2 2*s.* 0*d.* Hastings Fishermen landing Fish, £2 2*s.* 0*d.* Chertsey-on-Thames, £1 1*s.* 0*d.* Windsor Castle, from Datchet, £1 5*s.* 0*d.* London, from Kennington Common, £1 1*s* 0*d.* Near Hampton-on-Thames, 10*s.* 6*d.* Rocks near Hastings, £1 1*s.* 0*d.* Hay-field near Windsor. Seventeen Drawings.

Total £21 7 0

NOTE.—D. C. agrees to let Mr. Everitt have the above for £18 18*s.* 0*d.* instead of £21 7*s.* 0*d.*

LESSONS.

1812. Lady Arden, a double lesson, £1 1*s.* 0*d.* Single lesson, 10*s.* 6*d.*
1812—1813. Miss Tilney Long, lessons at 7*s.* each.
" " Miss Tongs, Croydon, lessons. Mr. Goodwin, ditto.

SALES.

1811. Mr. Goodwin (a London dealer), 2 Heath scenes, £1 10*s.* 0*d.* Small Heath scene, 15*s.* Cader Idris from Llanfair, 15*s.* Small Drawing, near Norwood, £1 1*s.* 0*d.*

In the same book the following sales of water-colour drawings are entered to Mr. Smith of Birmingham:—

1812.

Jan. 23. View near Bromley, £1 1*s.* 0*d.* Stacking Hay, £1 1*s* 0*d.* Fisherman's Cottage at Hastings, £1 1*s.* 0*d.* View on Sydenham Common, 10*s.* 6*d.* Sketch from Nature, 10*s.* 6*d.* Half a dozen Sepia Drawings, £2 8*s.* 0*d.*

Also in the same year, 1812, another small sale to Mr. Everitt as follows:—

View of Lord Auckland's Farm	
Gravesend Fishing Boats .	
Stackyard	£5 5 0
View of the Sussex Coast .	

The following entries of drawings sold to Mr. Radclyffe, the engraver at Birmingham, also occur :—

1811.

Oct. 17. One Small Drawing, 7*s*. Nov. 21, one Coloured Drawing, 10*s*. 6*d*.

1812.

Jan. 13. One Coloured Drawing, 10*s*. 6*d*. One ditto, 12*s*. One ditto, 15*s*. One ditto, 18*s*.

Dec. 9. One ditto, £1 11*s*. 6*d*. One ditto, £1 11*s*. 6*d*. One ditto, 10*s*. 6*d*.

1813.

Feb. 4. One ditto, £1 11*s*. 6*d*. July 22, £1 11*s*. 6*d*. Sept. 19, one large coloured drawing, £6 0*s*. 0*d*.

,, Mr. Macdonald, view of Chertsey, £5 0*s*. 0*d*.

1814.

Jan. 8. Sale of Drawings to Mr. Everitt, Birmingham—
Sheep-shearing, £1 11*s*. 6*d*. Lane near Dulwich, £1 11*s*. 6*d*. View near Norwood, £1 11*s*. 6*d*. Windmill and Heath, £1 11*s*. 6*d*. Edinburgh Castle, £1 1*s*. 0*d*. Wrekin, Shropshire, £1 1*s*. 0*d*. Hay-field, £1 1*s*. 0*d*. Cold Harbour Lane, 15*s*. Hastings Fishing Boats, 15*s*. Hastings Fish Market, 15*s*.

Nearly every year during his residence in London, and afterwards at Dulwich, Cox made a journey to his native town, Birmingham, to visit his old father and his other friends there. He often sold drawings there, as we have noticed by the extracts copied out of his account book, and he sketched a good deal on those occasions in Warwickshire, and sometimes also in Staffordshire. When at home his favourite excursions were on the banks of the Thames both above and below London—Battersea, Chertsey, Windsor, and Eton; also Millbank, Lambeth, Westminster, and Gravesend. Views in these places are very numerous among his early drawings.

At the latter end of the spring of 1812, Cox took his wife and child to Hastings, where he found many subjects for his pencil. I have seen several of these a good deal like the coast scenes in Turner's "Liber Studiorum;" the effects of storm and rain, with fishing boats and figures in their every-day occupation on the coast, and rough seas with the moon rising, are beautifully drawn and fine in feeling. He engaged lodgings at Hastings in a street just opposite to a house in which his friend, William Havell, the artist, was staying at

CHAP. II. — 1804–1814.

the time. They went out sketching together, and Cox brought home, in addition to the studies by the seashore, several inland views—Battle Abbey, and other places in the neighbourhood.

At that time Hastings was a picturesque old place with a great many fishing boats, and St. Leonards did not exist. David, although a very little boy, often accompanied his father to the beach. One day the child, in his rambles, discovered a silver watch on a ledge of rock under the cliffs, and brought it to his father, who was sitting near sketching. Presently they saw a fisherman wandering about in rather a distracted manner; Cox hailed him, and he had soon the pleasure of restoring to him his lost watch. During this visit to Hastings Cox painted occasionally in oil. There are many little oil sketches on millboard of this period. Havell was also beginning to turn his attention to oils. Early and late they pursued their employment, and Cox used to boast that he painted a sunrise in June, and then awoke his friend by flinging pebbles at his bedroom window to show what he had done whilst the other slept.

In the year 1813 Cox was elected a Member of the Society of Painters in Water Colours on its reconstruction. It now exhibited in the great rooms in Spring Gardens, and had hitherto confined itself exclusively to water-colours. This year, however, the society determined to give a wider scope to their exhibition by admitting oil pictures also, as was explained by the following notice which was issued :—" 1813. The Society of Painters in Water Colours, stimulated by public encouragement, and gaining confidence from success, have ventured this year on a considerable extension of their plans. Pictures in oil and in water-colours, portraits, models, and miniatures are admitted into the present exhibition ; and, should these increased efforts receive from the public that liberal support which has always accompanied the former exhibitions of this society, every year may produce fresh sources of amusement, and each succeeding exhibition become more worthy of approbation and patronage." This new plan does not appear to have been attended with the good results which were anticipated, as in the year 1821 the society reverted to the original plan of an exhibition in water-colours only. In the first year of his membership David Cox exhibited seventeen drawings. They were chiefly views near Dulwich, but the subjects also comprised Llanberris Lake, the Wrekin, and many views on the banks of the Thames. Although joining the society was a great event in Cox's life, he does not appear to have gained much advantage from it for some years in the way of the sale of drawings. They were ignored by the public, who were unable to appreciate their originality and peculiar merits, for even at that time David Cox had a distinct style of his own, but his name was almost unknown. The long war which had been waged with France had depressed trade, and made living dear, and people generally had but little to spare for objects of luxury. Cox had many difficulties to contend with; but he continued to work steadily on at his art with untiring industry and perseverance. He often drew the same subject several times over, making changes in the arrangement, or additions, until he had succeeded in realising the idea and expression he desired. The drawings of this period, and, indeed, I may say the same of most of those produced in the first years of his residence in London, partake of many of the qualities which distinguished his more mature works. There are generally much breadth, a feeling of repose, and an absence of any attempt at drawing-master dexterity, or at the still more objectionable prettiness which are the characteristics of feeble work. His handling was less free and colouring less fresh and pure than in later years, and partook unmistakably of the low tones of some of the older masters; his foliage also was somewhat heavy. Cox was one of the earliest subscribers to the "Liber Studiorum," which was being published by J. M. W. Turner. That he did so at this time, when his means were so straitened, is a proof how highly he prized this admirable work. With respect to the "Liber Studiorum," Cox related that Turner hung up a prospectus of that work in his rooms on first opening an exhibition of his works, also a frame containing the drawings in sepia for the first proposed numbers; it was reported also that Turner was induced to undertake this work from the advice of a friend at Tunbridge, a water-colour artist, in this wise:—They were turning over Claude's "Liber Veritatis" together, and when near the end, his friend exclaimed, "Turner, you could do better things if you chose." The idea appeared to be acceptable to Turner, and, after further conversation, some of the illustrations were at once determined on.

There can be no doubt that no artist appreciated Turner's genius more than Cox did, and every year during his residence in the neighbourhood of London, he used to watch with ever-increasing interest for the appearance of the noble pictures which Turner was producing at that period. The following anecdote will be welcome to my readers as tending to illustrate this feeling. On one occasion Cox had to give a lesson to Lady Arden, at the West-end, and, on arriving at the appointed time, he found she had not yet descended to breakfast. Cox, therefore, took the opportunity of going to see some of Turner's recently painted pictures, and was particularly charmed with "A Harvest Dinner, Kingston Bank, on the Thames," reapers at dinner, painted in 1809, and now exhibited in the Turner Collection in the National Gallery, No. 491. He remained for a long time in front of this picture quite entranced, and on his return to give the lesson to her ladyship, Cox said he had been so delighted with Turner's "Kingston Bank," that he could think of nothing else, and that he should like to draw a recollection of it for the lesson. No drawing paper could be found at the time, except the cover of a piece of music, but on this Cox made a small but charming and delicate drawing, very like the "Kingston Bank" in arrangement and colour. His remembrance of Turner's picture was much valued by Cox, and it still exists in his son's collection at Brixton Hill. The original painting by Turner is quiet in tone, and Cox's drawing is perhaps rather more sunny. The figures, especially that of the lad stooping down with his head close to the water to drink, are admirably given. Cox used to relate, that during the years he lived at Dulwich, many and many were the works which he tore up and put down the drains of London, without consulting his wife, as she always took the opportunity of rescuing them from destruction whenever she could. In later years, when walking with a friend on the south side of London, he stopped suddenly on one occasion opposite to a large grating, and said, "Look *there!* That was the favourite spot where I used to send the fragments of my drawings floating down into the Thames." When out sketching he frequently felt dissatisfied with his work, even in later years, and with the modesty always inherent in true genius, he would throw down his brush exclaiming, "Ah! I cannot do it! it's of no use trying. Nature beats me. She is very beautiful, in all her aspects, and I will not disgrace her."

It was in the summer of 1813 that Cox was offered an appointment as teacher of drawing at a military college—to this we shall refer more at length presently. The difficulties he had lately had to contend with, and his anxiety about the future, induced him to accept this, but probably without sufficient reflection. This engagement caused him to break up his pleasant home at Dulwich, where he had passed several years, happy on the whole, although not unchequered with care. Before leaving, he sent his first contributions to the Water Colour Society's Exhibition, in Spring Gardens, thirteen drawings in all. Among the subjects were views in North Wales, Westminster Abbey from Lambeth, Windsor

Castle from St. Leonard's Hill, &c. Besides the members of the society, other artists were at this time allowed to send works for exhibition to the gallery in Spring Gardens, and I observe that in this year Cox's early friends, Charles Barber and J. Vincent Barber, exhibited one or two pictures each: they had rooms at 49, Brewer Street, Golden Square, a favourite locality for artists in those early days.

When Cox gave up his cottage on Dulwich Common, his wife removed to her mother's house in Camberwell, and their little boy was sent to stay for six months with his grandfather at Birmingham, and from thence he went on a visit to his aunt Ward at Manchester. Cox himself, at the same time, proceeded to Farnham, and took up his abode in the military college there, as teacher of drawing to the senior officers who were studying in that establishment. I understand this college was founded by the British Government, in consequence of the want felt by many officers during the war of a more thorough training in the scientific branches of military knowledge. The French, and other foreign officers, were reputed to be more proficient in those respects, and Sir William Napier, and other officers of distinction, had joined the college, and Cox used to speak of the pleasure he derived from becoming acquainted with them. The junior officers were taught drawing by Mr. Andrew Wilson, a Scotch artist, a friend of David Cox, who persuaded him that he would be able to undertake all the duties of the appointment. Cox applied for it and obtained it. Whilst at Farnham he resided in the college, and had the complimentary title of "Captain," with a servant to wait on him. He, however, soon found that he had made a mistake. The mechanical drawing and military mapping, mapping out the configuration of ground, were very irksome, but the restraint and discipline were still more so, as he could not go to London without asking leave of absence, and he became unhappy. Sir Howard Douglas, the governor, was very kind. He and the other officers appear to have recognised the talents of the artist, but also that he was not quite suited to the position which he occupied at the college, and after the end of the first term or two he was allowed to retire, and he then rejoined his wife at her mother's house. There is little doubt Cox's residence in the military college was attended with some advantages. He himself used to acknowledge that the discipline was of use in strengthening his character, and that it helped him towards the success which he afterwards achieved. It, however, interfered a good deal with the temporary progress of his career in art, as may be judged from the fact that in the following year, 1815, he did not exhibit a *single drawing* at the Water Colour Exhibition. Soon after Cox's return from the military college, he saw in the *Times* an advertisement that a good master to teach drawing and painting was wanted in a ladies' school in the city of Hereford, and that a liberal salary would be given. He answered it, and the consequence was that the head of the establishment, a Miss Croucher, came up to London, and had an interview with Cox, who referred her to two of his artist friends. The terms proposed were £100 a year for teaching in Miss Croucher's school twice a week, with liberty to take other pupils in the town and neighbourhood.

Cox used to say that several reasons conduced to determine him to accept this engagement besides the certainty of the salary. These were that the cost of living in that part of the country was very moderate as compared with London; that there would be cheap education at the Hereford Grammar School for his son, and also that it was so near to North Wales and to the picturesque scenery of the Wye. I think it must be allowed also, that as far as Cox's advancement in his profession was concerned, no more fortunate event than a residence in the rural county of Hereford could possibly have occurred. There was full scope on every side for the development of his love for homely country subjects

CHAP. II.

1804—1814.

connected with farming; and how well he availed himself of this, and *worked the mine* almost under his feet, such grand pictures as "Changing the Pasture," "Going to the Hay-field," "Carting Vetches," &c., painted in after years, fully proves.

Cox at first went down to Hereford alone, to look round and see what accommodation he could find for his family; at the end of two months he engaged a cottage, and returned to London for his wife and child, who forthwith accompanied him to the picturesque old city.

Lady Arden advanced him £40 to defray the expenses of their removal, and in order to discharge this debt, Cox painted on commission for her ladyship "A Fish Market at Hastings," and one or two commissions for other parties which made up the amount.

A short time before leaving London, Cox received a letter from one of his old pupils, a lady of rank, which I will here insert, as it shows how much he was esteemed by those to whom he taught drawing; but, being on this subject of his teaching, I must first copy what one of his old pupils and dear friends has written: "I am sure no man was ever so lavish of his favours as David Cox; none ever communicated every atom of what a pupil wanted to know with such a winning simplicity; none scattered his treasures of knowledge so bountifully. I remember his saying to me once on a private view day that a lady had said to him, 'Oh, Mr. Cox, how do you manage that foreground?' without a moment's pause he replied, 'I take a dry brush and dip it into rather strong colour, and sweep it lightly over the paper. I find it gives the rough effect I want.' On another occasion he told me that one of his brother artists had laughed at him as having showed all the tricks of the trade; but the fact was David Cox had no tricks." I think that one of the secrets of Cox's success in life was his openness, his genial kindness, and thorough unselfishness. He always made *friends* wherever he went, and became known quite as much with the poor as with the rich: indeed, the way in which he was loved and trusted by the poorer classes was very remarkable. The pupil's letter referred to above was as follows:—

"Burgley, July 14th, 1814.

"Lady Sophia Cecil's compliments to Mr. Cox, and is much obliged to him for his good wishes for her recovery. Lady S., in her way to town last August, called at Mr. Cox's, to discharge her debt, but was told the house was let, and the people could not inform her of Mr. Cox's direction. Lady S. has enclosed three pounds, as she perceives Mr. Cox has omitted the lesson he gave her last year of etching. Lady Exeter and Lady Sophia most sincerely trust that no disappointment occasions Mr. Cox to leave Dulwich, and assure him of their very best wishes for his health and prosperity in Herefordshire.

"Lady Exeter desires Mr. Cox, if he should again come to town, to call at Privy Gardens, as both she and Lady S. will be always happy to see him, and to hear of his welfare. They both hope Mrs. Cox and his child are well. Lady S. will be very glad if Mr. Cox will send her his direction when settled in Herefordshire."

III.

HEREFORD.

1814 TO 1827.

CHAP. III.
1814—1827.

AT the close of the autumn of 1814 Mr. and Mrs. Cox and their little boy arrived at the ancient city of Hereford, famous for its venerable cathedral and churches, and in olden time for its extensive monasteries and castle. The latter, situated on the northern bank of the pleasant river Wye (deservedly renowned for its scenery), was formerly considered one of the strongest fortresses in England, and, with the massive town walls and embattled watch-towers, defended the inhabitants of the city from the attacks of their turbulent Celtic neighbours.

During the civil wars the castle and city were frequently besieged; but, with the advent of more peaceful times, the defences have been swept away, except here and there a few dilapidated and detached portions of the old walls which still remain, overgrown with moss and weeds, relics of an age now happily passed away. The Wye winds partly round the city, and is spanned by a fine old bridge, from which there is a pretty view looking up the river and over green fields towards distant wooded hills. Not far off is the river Lugg, with its rich meadows well shaded with fine trees, destined to become the favourite sketching-ground of Cox.

When they arrived at Hereford their fortunes were at an unusually low ebb, and they first rented an old cottage at Lower Lyde, in the parish of Homer, near Ailstone Hill, and

about two miles and a half off on the north side of the city. It was in a very lonely situation in a small wood, and, in olden times, had probably been a small farmer's or game-keeper's house. The floors were paved with flagstones, the accommodation was of the simplest character, and in winter the night winds whistled mournfully through the branches of the surrounding trees. Doubtless it *was* a very dreary place to pass a winter in, so in the spring following, that of 1815, Cox removed into a small but more cheerful house rather nearer the city, called George Cottage, in the adjoining parish of All Saints, and situated on the north side of Ail-stone Hill. Their son David was then only five and a half years old, but he has a distinct recollection of this cottage, in which they resided for two years.

Cox set to work making sketches of the city and neighbourhood as soon as he was settled in his new and humble home. I have seen several of his drawings of these subjects of the years 1815, 1816, and 1817. They are low in tone, but pleasing in composition and in the arrangement of light and shade. The colours have often faded, especially the blues; the prevailing tones now being various shades of browns, russets, and greys. His residence at Hereford was very useful in producing a love for rustic subjects—ploughing, haymaking, lane scenes, &c., but his drawings were seldom exact copies of what he saw. Skies appear from a very early date to have been much studied, and in many of his earliest drawings it is easy to recognise the same fondness for gloom and grandeur which characterized his latest works. He has often in late years said, on looking at some of his old sketches, "Ah! I began in the right way." Early dawn—twilight—storm on the coast, moor scenes, and heaths under cloudy or rainy effects, are certainly very often found among his early works, and are the subjects he most frequently reproduced.

Throughout the year 1812, and at the commencement of

CHAP. III. 1814—1827.

1814, Cox had been employed by S. and J. Fuller, of Vere Street, afterwards of Rathbone Place, to make soft ground etchings on copper from his own drawings, with the view to the publication of a work on landscape art, which was published in 1814.

They, however, gave him a further commission for more of these soft ground etchings after he arrived at Hereford, and at these he worked in 1815. It gave him more trouble to carry this out at a distance from all the appliances needed, but he was very successful and very original, as the works themselves (to which I shall refer more at length in my next chapter) fully prove. Some of the plates were to be worked off in colour, and in these he tried to vary the effect of daylight as much as possible.

The boarding-school kept by Miss Croucher, at which Cox had been engaged to teach, stood at the bottom of Widemarsh Street, on the right-hand side going out of the town, and is called "The Gate House," being close to the site of the old Widemarsh Gate, demolished in 1798. This house, reported to have been the residence of the governor when Hereford was a walled city, is of the Early Tudor period, with much quaint carved woodwork outside, and the rooms wainscoted inside with old oak. It has a good-sized garden or playground at the back, running down to a portion of the massive old city wall still remaining. Here Cox spent many weary hours every week, as he did not find his pupils very promising; and the young artist, whose mind was tuned in sympathy with nature in her grandest aspects, was obliged to take to flower-painting, still-life subjects, and other similar work; indeed, to meet the wishes of pupils, he often quitted his own style, and taught figures, hands, and heads. There are also in existence some excellent groups of flowers, with natural treatment, which he drew at this time in water-colours. He did not even disdain to work on white wood in Chinese fashion, including bronzing! Cox's natural good-nature setting him to accomplish, in his own original way, whatever was requested and sought for. Unfortunately he found little appreciation at Hereford for landscape, the only walk in art for which he really cared. Some time later he copied the knife, kept at Home Lacy, with which, according to tradition, Felton stabbed the Duke of Buckingham. This was a commission from Walter Fawkes, Esq., and it drew forth a gratifying letter of thanks.

I find, by a memorandum written by Cox in one of his old account books, that he began to teach at Miss Croucher's school on the 26th October, 1814, and that he taught there continuously till the end of 1819. He also commenced to teach at the Hereford Grammar School on the 2nd February, 1815, and he continued to do so for a great number of years. That he also taught at a school kept by a Miss Poole is proved by the following entry in his note-book:—

1816.	MISS POOLE Dr. to D. COX.			
Half-a-year's instruction to five young ladies, each 3 guineas		£15	15	0
Entrance money		2	2	0
Five drawings		2	12	6

The arrangement for teaching at the Grammar School was by no means an advantageous one for Cox, as he only received for this work a yearly stipend of six guineas. In those days, especially in the provincial towns, the art of design was regarded altogether as rather an inferior and unimportant accomplishment.

He soon found that there was little to be done in Hereford in the way of obtaining private pupils, and he was obliged to seek for these at the residences of the county gentry at some distance, and also to eke out his income by giving lessons at schools in Leominster and some other neighbouring towns. This took up a great deal of time. About the second year of his residence at Hereford he made the acquaintance of the Rev. Mr. Hopton, of Canon-Frome Court, by whom he was engaged to give lessons to his daughters. Mr. Hopton had an old worn-out hunter running about the park, and, as he had been used to carry weight, he thought he could certainly carry Cox (who was not a tall man) in his rides to and from the houses situated a few miles from the city, and he offered to make him a present of the horse. Cox gladly accepted this offer; but it soon became lame, and had to end its days in the park. He was next persuaded by a young man (an apprentice of the bookseller Mr. Watkin), to whom he gave early morning lessons in drawing, to try a young horse. Cox mounted him in a field, but the horse was too fresh and restive; Cox was thrown on the first trial, and unfortunately dragged, with his foot in the stirrup, round the field. He still made another essay. This time it was an old pony which had belonged to an apothecary, and had been ridden by the boy who took out the basketsful of draughts, mixtures, &c., considered so essential in those days for the cure of all human ailments. The pony, which was called "Jack," however, had a will of his own; he had been used to stop at nearly all the white gates leading to the houses and cottages around Hereford, and whenever Cox approached one of these gates, Master Jack, who thought *he* knew best what was right, came to a dead halt, in spite of all his rider could do. Cox thought this more trouble than walking, so he soon parted with Jack, and made no further experiment in horse-flesh all the remainder of his life, considering that three failures were enough for any man.

In the first or second year of his residence at Hereford he made an excursion down the Wye as far as Chepstow, visiting Ross, Monmouth, and Tintern, and making many sketches. In the year 1816 he exhibited seven drawings in the rooms of the Water Colour Society in London, some of which were near Hereford and on the Wye. I believe that they did not meet with a very ready sale; the public were beginning to feel the pinch of the hard times which followed the close of the long French war. The following year, viz., in 1817, Cox sent nothing whatever to the Water Colour Exhibition. This was caused in part by the great absorption of his time in going about the neighbourhood giving lessons, but still more by a serious illness which laid him low for some time in the spring of that year, and for which he had to be bled. He was attended by Mr. Samuel Cam, a well-known and highly respected surgeon in Hereford; and this led to his forming a warm friendship with that gentleman, which lasted for many years. Mr. Cam had several early drawings from Cox, which still exist, and which I have seen in the house of his nephew and successor, Mr. Thomas Cam, in St. Owen Street, Hereford. One of these is a river scene, probably the Lugg, somewhat in Varley's style. Another, dated 1815, is interesting as being a view in the High Street, of the Butchers' Row, and other old houses in the centre of the city which have since been pulled down. It is very carefully drawn, with a great many characteristic figures, and the effect is pleasing.

Cox made the acquaintance at Hereford of Mr. Honiatt, of St. Owen Street, who took much interest in his drawings; also of a Mr. P. B. Watkin, bookseller, stationer, and dealer in engravings, &c., at the corner of Widemarsh Street, whose shop was a very favourite lounge; Mr. W. H. Cole was another stationer and dealer in drawings, with whom Cox often disposed of his works at exceedingly modest prices. Mr. Spotsy, manager of a bank at Hereford, was also a valued and early friend. I believe these are all now deceased.

At the end of 1817 Cox left George Cottage, and moved into a thatched one in Parry's Lane (*alias* Holmer Road), Ailstone Hill, of which I give a view at the end of this chapter. When Cox first thought of renting this cottage, which was prettily situated in a country lane, there was not sufficient accommodation in it for his family, and no room that would do as a studio; so he asked the owner, Mr. Parry, if he would add what was required. To this Mr. Parry replied, that, as artists' ideas did not always agree with those of other people, instead of making the alterations himself he

CHAP. III. would give forty pounds towards any change or additions that

1814—1827. Cox might desire, which he could then make to please himself; and that he would not raise the present rent, which was only eight pounds per annum. There was a good garden opposite, belonging to the cottage, full of fruit-trees, and Cox gladly closed with this offer. He added twenty or thirty pounds of his own, and built a comfortable room on the north side, which served as studio and parlour, and a good bedroom over it. In front of the cottage Cox put up a broad verandah, covered with thatch and supported on rustic columns. In the course of years the verandah, having become decayed, has been taken down and a simple porch put up in its place, as shown in the picture. When Cox resided there the little garden in front, which is now full of bushy evergreens and other shrubs, only contained hollyhocks and roses, which must have bloomed there in profusion, as appears in a sketch of the cottage made at that time by Mrs. Cox. This is rather interesting, as it shows that the love for hollyhocks, which was manifested in Cox's garden at Harborne in 1855, existed nearly forty years earlier at Hereford.

In this cottage Cox resided for five and a half years. At that time the windows of the studio looked into a pleasant meadow, but of late a road has been made alongside the cottage where grass used to be. At the bottom of the garden there was an old-fashioned draw-well in a shady spot, and here, in summer weather, when the cottage larder was not cool enough, Mrs. Cox used to hang the joints of meat down the well that they might keep better. It was a joke against her that on one occasion, a guest being expected to partake of the Sunday's dinner, a leg of mutton had been suspended in the well, but in the night a rogue, more sly than honest, having discovered the secret, forestalled Mrs. Cox, who found nothing there in the morning, and the party in Parry's Cottage were obliged to partake of less substantial fare. This well, which had the disagreeable habit of overbalancing the winders if not very strong, was afterwards bricked over. CHAP. III. 1814—1827.

Cox took several pupils during his residence at Hereford, both in Parry's Cottage and Ash Tree House, to whom he taught drawing and painting. The first who came was the son of the agent of the Duke of Beaufort, a young man of the name of Turton, who remained two years. He was succeeded by Mr. J. M. Ince, son of a surgeon at Presteign. Frederick Birch, from Norwood, and a young man of the name of Parry, from Monmouth, were the two last. Of these pupils, Mr. Ince is the only one who appears to have attained to any success as an artist in after life. Mr. Ince got a good appointment at Cambridge as teacher of drawing and painting, and also resided some years in Presteign and London, painting landscapes, which sold fairly, by which he realised a good independent property. He was always very careful in his expenditure, and never married. It appears by his notebook that Cox received at the rate of seventy pounds per annum for some of his pupils, and seventy guineas for others, for board, lodging, and instruction.

Cox exhibited thirteen drawings this year (1818) in the Water Colour Society, one of the most important being a view on the river Lugg, near Hereford. The Lugg meadows were early selected by him as a favourite place of resort, as some very fine trees grew near the river. He used to visit London every spring to see the exhibitions, often giving lessons there to some of his old pupils, who also purchased some of his drawings. His sales, too, at the exhibitions gradually increased, and he was now enabled to lay by a little each year towards his favourite project of building a cottage for himself on his own freehold.

In his annual journeys to and from London he passed through Birmingham, where he still kept up several of his old friendships, and where he was in the habit of selling drawings. He generally stayed in Birmingham, at the house

CHAP. III. 1814—1827.

of Mr. Everitt, on his way home. I find the following sales to Mr. Everitt noted down, made on one of these visits:—

1817.
May 15. Mr. EVERITT, Birmingham, Dr.
Six Indian ink drawings, at 7*s*. each.
Six ditto ditto at 4*s*. each.
Drawing of Warwick Castle. Snowdon from Beddgelert. Morning. No price.

Also the following drawings sold to Messrs. S. and J. Fuller, London:—

1818.				
Feb 18.	One Drawing, Berry Pomeroy . . .	£1	5	0
	One ditto, View below Gravesend . . .	1	5	0
	Four ditto, 18*s*. each	3	12	0
	Twenty-one ditto, 8*s*. each	8	8	0

On one of these journeys, about this time, he revisited Hastings, and made several drawings. He also made an excursion to North Wales in 1818. In May, 1819, a young maid-servant, Ann Fowler, whose parents resided near Hereford, entered the service of Mr. and Mrs. Cox, where she remained for forty years. She became housekeeper after the death of Mrs. Cox, and never left her master as long as he lived. She proved herself a very faithful, efficient, and attached servant. This spring Cox took his son with him to London to see the exhibitions for the first time. They made a great impression on him, especially Wilkie's picture of the "Chelsea Pensioners." Cox had ten drawings in the Water Colour Society's Exhibition, chiefly views on the Wye and in North Wales, and also a view of the town of Hereford. The picturesque bits of the old city afforded many subjects for his pencil; one, which was afterwards lithographed, was of Old Cabbage Lane (near the cathedral), in which there was a quiet eating-house where Cox and his friends used occasionally to get their dinners. In this year (1819) Cox also made a journey by himself into North Devon, and he revisited Bath, where, two years previously, he had executed a commission for views, six of which, including a general view of the town, Lansdown Crescent, the Pump Room, &c., were published by

S. and J. Fuller in 1820. This journey was often referred to by him as a very dull one because he was *alone*; he always liked to have a companion whenever and wherever he could. Cox also made a tour in North Wales this year during the summer vacation, and was accompanied by some young friends from Hereford—Mr. Bulmer, and Mr. John Parker, and William Henry Parker. They went along the Upper Wye, Rhaiadr Buillt, and Hay, to Aberystwith, and thence through some of the chief points of interest in Merionethshire and Carnarvonshire. His companions appear to have been more bent on amusement than art, so his sketches on this occasion were chiefly in pencil, or memoranda in chalk, which he worked up at home. They were not very satisfactory, and, although he made a great many studies, few of them were ever worked up into drawings.

In 1820 Joseph Hume, the political reformer and economist, visited Hereford, and was warmly welcomed by the Liberal party. Cox, whose opinions were of the advanced Liberal order at that time, formed one of the committee to receive him, and, with two others, subscribed to present him with a hogshead of the best Herefordshire cider. A public dinner was given on the occasion, followed by the usual speeches. This was one of the very few public dinners at which Cox was ever present. On his return home in the evening, Cox said he would celebrate so important a day by planting a number of acorns and chestnuts in his garden. He had always an especial love for forest trees. The young trees came up and grew till they were too large for the garden, and Mr. Parry informed me that they have since been transplanted into the adjoining fields. Cox had taken great interest the preceding year in the trial of Queen Caroline, and many were the arguments which he had on the subject with his friends. His wife, whenever the discussion waxed warm, used to step in as a pacificator. At that time Cox took in Cobbett's "Register," the raciness of which he

CHAP. III. 1814—1827. appreciated. Not relishing the high taxes then in force, and disliking the policy which had led to their imposition, Cox tried to drink Hunt's roasted corn, and, not liking that, the idea occurred to him that *new hay* would make a morning beverage to the detriment of the revenue, so he purchased some and had a tea-pot full prepared. On the return of Sir R. Price for the county he went to hear him address the electors, and at the conclusion of the address, Cox exclaimed, "That's the man who *can* speak," a compliment not always echoed even by his supporters. Although Cox was a reformer in principles, and advocated Liberal measures at this period of his life with the enthusiasm that might have been expected considering his ardent temperament, his views became very much moderated with the advance of age, and in his latter years, although he used to enjoy occasionally hearing the *Examiner* and other Liberal papers read out loud, he took little interest in politics, his mind being absorbed in the pursuit of art. He also devoted a good deal of time to his garden, the produce of which was a valuable aid to the economy of his house.

In the year 1820 Cox exhibited the unusual number of seventeen drawings in the Water Colour Exhibition. Views in Herefordshire predominated; but there were also some Welsh scenes, and several other subjects, such as "Haymakers," "Ploughing," "Boy Angling," &c., of which very few appeared in his earlier exhibited drawings, but which had been suggested by his walks round Hereford, and which form the staple of his best and most characteristic works in later years. Indeed, he ever held that the matter or subject of a sketch was inferior to its treatment or sentiment.

It has already been remarked that Cox had great admiration for the works of Turner, and he never omitted an opportunity, when he paid his annual visit to London at the time of the exhibitions, of going into the Turner Gallery in Queen Ann Street. Turner was on friendly terms with him, and used always to greet him as "Daniel." "Well, Daniel, how are you?" The origin of this joke I believe Cox himself could never explain. On Cox's return home in 1821 he determined to paint a large drawing, 2 feet 5 inches by 3 feet 7 inches, in recollection of the glowing and imaginative pictures lately produced by Turner. This resulted in the large drawing now in the possession of Mr. W. Quilter, of Norwood, "Æneas approaching Carthage." This drawing was exhibited in 1825 in the Water Colour Society's Exhibition, under the title of "Carthage, Æneas, and Achates," and sold for fifty pounds. The passages from which it is taken are as follows, from the first book of the Æneid:—

> "Ipse uno graditur comitatus Achate,"

and

> "Instant ardentes Tyrii; pars ducere muros."

The drawing was a long time in hand; it is very unlike Cox's usual work; the colouring is bright, and the foreground highly finished. The buildings have some resemblance to the grand, stately architecture of Martin's works.

In the year 1821 Cox exhibited only four drawings, twelve in 1822, and eighteen in 1823. This latter year there was also a loan collection of drawings exhibited in the Water Colour Society's rooms, which comprised five works by Cox. The greater number of the drawings exhibited in the above years are views in North Wales, where Cox went almost every summer, also views on the Thames, especially near Gravesend, and at Hastings. Cox used to stay with his relations in London for a month or two, before the exhibitions opened, when he used to complete his works for exhibition, and was enabled to make sketching excursions on the Thames, &c., when the weather permitted. Some of the latter years of his residence at Hereford he gave as many as three lessons a week to some of his old pupils, who were very glad to avail themselves of his temporary abode in London. His teaching had by

CHAP. III. 1814—1827. this time a good deal increased, as appears by his old account books, fortunately preserved, and which I have seen. The prices charged were still very moderate, varying from seven-and-sixpence to half-a-guinea a lesson. In 1824 he had also several private pupils at these rates in the neighbourhood of Hereford: Miss Parkinson, the Misses Hopton, and some of the family of the Rev. J. Lelly, of New Court. He made a pretty sketch of that gentleman's seat, which he afterwards lithographed himself, and it was printed by G. Hullmandel. He also made an etching of the new Town Hall, Hereford, which is interesting from the vast concourse of people, about eighty, in the old-fashioned costumes of the period. In the summer of 1824 Cox had a commission from Monsieur Ostervald, of Paris, for seven drawings, which he charged to him at three and four guineas each. The subjects were as follows:—"View of the Town of Hay;" "Fishing Boats on the Thames;" "Fishermen at Hastings;" "Corn-field View in Herefordshire;" "View of Goodrich Castle;" "Tintern Abbey;" "Lymouth Pier." Mr. Ostervald was a publisher and dealer in works of art. And this was followed by another commission from him to paint some French subjects, views on the Mediterranean, &c., from outlines forwarded to him from Paris. He used also, at this time, often to dispatch small drawings—views on the Wye, on the Thames, and in Wales—to Mr. Clay and other dealers in London, views of Rhaiadr Bridge, Devil's Bridge, &c., for which he charged two guineas each.

Cox's great industry during the last few uneventful years at Hereford, added to the receipts from taking pupils, &c., had resulted in considerably improving his finances, and he now began to turn over in his mind his favourite project of building a house for himself, the cottage he lived in in Parry's Lane being too small for much comfort. There is, under date 5th April, 1824, in one of his account books, a calculation of how much money it would take to build a small house, with an estimate in detail amounting to £317 10*s.* 4*d.* Every brick and piece of timber are carefully detailed in this calculation. About this time he purchased a piece of land, very pleasantly situated on the brow of Ailstone Hill, and he then lost no time in commencing to build. He was his own architect and clerk of the works, rising at five o'clock to inspect the work of the day. The house was built on gravel, and stood sideways to the road; it was finished by the end of the year, was thatched with straw, and had also a thatched verandah, which ran round three sides of the building. In front was a circular drive up to the house, in the centre of which stood a large ash-tree, in consequence of which it was named "Ash Tree House;" and behind was a good-sized garden, surrounded by some elms and other large trees, which are still flourishing. This house is now known as "Berbice Villa," and is in excellent repair. The thatched roof having caught fire, has been replaced by tiles, and the verandah has disappeared. Cox removed into this house at the end of 1824, but he only lived there two years, as at the end of 1826 he had an offer to purchase his house from a Mr. Reynolds, who had lately returned from Berbice, in the West Indies. The bargain was soon struck, the price being about a thousand pounds, and early in the year 1827 Cox left it.

Mr. William Radclyffe and Mr. Edward Everitt, of Birmingham, visited Cox at Hereford more than once, and he often went to stay with them in return. On one of these occasions, in 1825, Mr. Everitt introduced Cox to Mr. Charles Birch, then residing in the Black Country, who not only admired his drawings, but entered thoroughly into their meaning and understood their originality, and with this gentleman he formed a long-enduring friendship. Mr. Birch had a true feeling for art, and Cox deferred very much to his judgment and opinion, which was generally right.

The Water Colour Society moved into their new gallery,

CHAP. III. 1814—1827. 5, Pall Mall East, in 1823, and from that time Cox increased the number of the drawings he exhibited. Indeed, he and Copley Fielding were the largest contributors for many years. In 1824 he sent the large number of twenty-three drawings, and thirty-four in 1825. The subjects were exceedingly varied, those in North Wales, Hampshire, (especially on the Wye), and on the Thames, being the most numerous. Lord Northwick appears to have been a purchaser in 1825, but the prices Cox realised were much too low, averaging chiefly from three to six guineas each, as marked on one of his own catalogues.

Mr. Edward Everitt relates that he spent a fortnight with Cox in Wales, in 1825, and also visited Tintern, Goodrich Castle, and other places on the Wye; on this occasion Cox made a very highly finished view of the castle in black-lead pencil, which he presented to his friend, and also an etching of a cottage and pigsty, equally highly finished, both of which exist. I have stated that Mr. W. Radclyffe visited him more than once, and on one of these occasions, viz., January 19th, 1825, he sold him the following drawings: one small drawing, £1 5*s.*; "View of a Windmill," £6 6*s.*; "Water Mill at Festiniog," £6 6*s.*; "Cader Idris," £12 12*s.* The following drawings were forwarded to Mr. Clay, London, in February, 1825: "Oxen at Plough," "Cows up the Medway," "Greenwich," "Passengers going on board an East Indiaman," "Greenwich from Sydenham Hill," "Vale Crucis Abbey," "Tunbridge Priory."

In 1826 Cox again sent twenty-two drawings to the exhibition, and went to London, accompanied by his son, a few weeks before it opened. His brother-in-law, Mr. Gardener, was then established at No. 163, Regent Street, as agent for the sale of the Government Ordnance Maps. Soon after their arrival in town Mr. Gardener told Cox that he held a commission from government to proceed to Brussels to see a large map of the world, which had lately been published there, and he urged him to accompany him and take David also, adding that the trip would not occupy much time. So agreeable a plan wanted but little persuasion, and they shortly started by coach for Dover, crossed to Calais, where they stayed a day or two, and then travelled on by boat and diligence, *viâ* Dunkerque and Bruges, to Brussels. After engaging lodgings, they visited the Museum, Town Hall, and other sights, including Waterloo, and Cox made several drawings in the city, and sketches of the country people and market women, in their quaint caps. He had heard that the Hoptons, of Canon-Frome, were travelling on the Continent, and on inquiring at a bookseller's, he ascertained that they were lodging in the next street. Mr. Hopton welcomed him warmly, and said he had actually written lately to ask Cox to join him and his family in a tour through Belgium and Holland, which they were making in their travelling carriage, and in which he pressed him to take a seat. Cox consented to join the Hoptons, and they left Brussels for Ghent and Antwerp in a few days, whilst his son returned with his uncle Gardener to England. After quitting Belgium, they visited Dort, Rotterdam, Delft, the Hague, Leyden, Amsterdam, and Haarlem. Cox made many sketches on this tour, chiefly in pencil, as time pressed. Those still existing include very clever street views at Ghent, a view of Haarlem, from the Amsterdam canal; the Fish Market at Amsterdam; Dort, on the canal; view on the canal from Leyden to Haarlem; sketches near Rotterdam, Barges at Dunkerque, &c. They were made as they glided along the canals, and have the colours sometimes written down, as cobalt, yellow, &c. They have low horizons, with figures and cattle cleverly introduced, reminding one of Cuyp, with the clouds in outline, slight, but graphic. Drawings from some of these sketches appeared afterwards in the Exhibition of the Water Colour Society.

It was in the autumn of this year, after his return home, that Cox negotiated the sale of his house. Several considerations appear to have weighed with Cox, and to have determined him to take this step. He rarely came to any important decision without due deliberation; but he had been long convinced that it would be desirable if a good opportunity offered to remove from Hereford; the following were some of his reasons:—He felt that London would afford a better opening for his son, then just growing up, and destined to be an artist. Also that he would himself be able to associate more with other artists. Living for so many years constantly amid rural scenes, Cox had often felt a longing (as his son relates) for the inspiration to be derived from intercourse with artists and art lovers. It is certain nevertheless that the intimate knowledge he acquired of the routine of farming and of English country life in Herefordshire, immensely assisted and led forwards to the success which he afterwards achieved. Early in 1827 Cox and his family quitted Hereford, and took up their abode at No. 9, Foxley Road, Kennington Common, on the south-east side of London. Mrs. Cox's health had been very delicate for some years, but after her return to London she soon became stronger, and was able to take longer walks; she had also the pleasure of being near her own relatives.

HELIOTYPE.

IV.

WORKS ILLUSTRATED BY DAVID COX.

THE first work containing soft ground etchings on copper, etched by Cox himself from his own drawings, was published in 1814, by S. and J. Fuller, of 34, Rathbone Place. It was entitled, "A Treatise on Landscape Painting and Effect in Water-Colours," by David Cox. It had been in progress for upwards of two years, some of the plates having been etched as far back as the beginning of 1812. The same firm published several repetitions or editions of this work at different dates, and again, in 1825, they brought out "The Young Artist's Companion, or Drawing Book," by David Cox. These series are illustrated in a very interesting manner, being all studies from nature by the artist himself. Some are in outline, with a little free-hand shading; some in aquatint, to represent sepias, and some are also coloured. They are intended as examples of composition, light and shade, effect and colour. The illustrations bear various dates between 1812 and 1823; many have much of the originality and feeling of his later works. It is interesting also to trace the same idea in these very early etchings as in the subjects of many of his latest pictures, such as "Changing the Pasture," "Going to the Mill," &c. Besides landscapes and sea-coast subjects, there are several studies from still-life. The first few sheets are for beginners, and are simple, unaffected, and well selected. In the "Treatise on Landscape Painting

CHAP. IV. and Effect," there are twenty-five pages of etchings and thirty-two ditto of aquatints. In the "Young Artist's Companion" there are forty pages of etchings and twenty-four pages of aquatints, some of the latter being coloured.

By a memorandum in Cox's account book I learn that in February, March, April, and May, 1812, he received eighteen guineas each month for etching six copper plates, at three guineas each; he was also paid five shillings for colouring four sporting prints. In September of the same year he received £39 7*s*. 6*d*. for twenty-five plates of sepia drawings; in October at the rate of three guineas per plate for four coloured drawings, and for four ditto at £1 8*s*. per plate. In January, 1814, he received for colouring six large sepia plates twelve shillings, and for colouring twelve small sepia plates also twelve shillings. In 1816 Messrs. S. and J. Fuller are debited by Cox, for etching twenty-four copper plates, at £2 12*s*. 6*d*. each, for the months of January, February, March, April, May, and July = £63. March 27th, 1818, they are also debited for four views in Bath, sixteen guineas, and afterwards, for two ditto, eight guineas. These were made for the illustrated work on Bath they were about to bring out. It is rather rare now, but I have fortunately seen a copy, of which I will give a description. It is entitled, "Six Views of the City of Bath," from drawings made by David Cox, price, in colours, £1 10*s*., dated 1820. The views are engraved by Smart and Sutherland. The drawing and perspective of these views are excellent, and prove how admirably Cox could draw street architecture. The first in order is the "Town Hall and Abbey, Bath." In the foreground is a stage-coach and horses, with passengers, market people at a stall selling poultry, and a man driving a brewer's horse, with beer barrels on a sort of trolly. The next subject represents the "Royal Crescent, Bath," with figures promenading in quaint costumes, the ladies with very short waists. The third is "Lansdown Crescent, Bath," two sedan chairs with their bearers are waiting on one side of the road, and the other is crowded with ladies and gentlemen. The fourth is "The Pump Room, Bath." The buildings in this view are all admirably finished, and it is very amusing from the number of Bath, *alias* sedan chairs, eight or nine carried by young men in livery, and young fops bending forwards to salute the ladies. The fifth view is of "Pultney Street, Bath," with a beautiful perspective effect; and the last is a general view of "Bath from the Beacon Cliffs:" its arrangement is like some of the older masters. These views must have been made by Cox in 1817, as he was paid for them all at the beginning of 1818, although the book bears date 1820. Without doubt a year or two was necessary for the engravers to complete their work, and for the colouring, which was done by hand. As regards arrangement and effect they are superior to most views of cities published in the present day.

The subjects of "Cox's Treatise on Landscape Painting," published by Messrs. Fuller, comprise views at Edgbaston, Dulwich, Hampton-in-Arden, Kenilworth Castle, Aston Hall, Hereford, Hastings, Northfleet, Bridgwater, Lambeth, Windsor, Eton, Battersea Marshes, the banks of the Wye, and many parts of North Wales. Picturesque bits of Old England abound in these books—rustic bridges, cottages, and quaint old houses, such as scarcely exist in these latter times, when so much that was endeared to the artist has been swept away by the hands of modern "improvers." It will, I think, be interesting to ascertain the ideas and views of Cox, at that early period of his career, on the scope and aim of landscape-painting, as published in the Treatise: I will therefore give an extract, containing the hints which he thought would be of use to the student of landscape art at that day, showing what, in his opinion, should be aimed at, and what avoided:—

"The principal art of Landscape Painting consists in

CHAP. IV. conveying to the mind the most forcible effect which can be produced from the various classes of scenery which possess the power of exciting an interest superior to that resulting from any other effects, and which can only be obtained by a most judicious selection of particular tints, and a skilful arrangement and application of them to difference in time, seasons, and situations.

"This is the grand principle upon which pictorial excellence hinges, as many pleasing objects, the combination of which render a piece perfect, are frequently passed over by an observer because the whole of the composition is not under the influence of a suitable effect. Thus a cottage or a village scene requires a soft and simple admixture of tones calculated to produce pleasure without astonishment. On the contrary, the structures of greatness and antiquity should be marked by a character of awful sublimity, suited to the dignity of the subjects, indenting on the mind a reverential and permanent impression, and giving at once a corresponding and unequivocal grandeur to the picture. Much depends on the classification of the objects, which should wear a magnificent uniformity, and much on the colouring, the tones of which should be deep and impressive.

"In the selection of a subject from nature the student should ever keep in view the principal object which induced him to make the sketch, whether it be mountains, a castle, group of trees, a corn-field, river scene, or any other object. The prominence of this leading feature in the piece should be duly supported throughout; the character of the picture should be derived from it; every other object introduced should be subservient to it, and the attraction of the one should be the attraction of the whole. The union of too great a variety of parts tends to destroy, or at least to weaken, the predominance of that which ought to be the principal of the composition, and which the student, when he comes to the colouring, should be careful to characterize by turning upon it the strongest light. All objects which are not in character with the scenes should be most carefully avoided, as the introduction of any unnecessary object is sure to be attended with injurious consequences. This must prove the necessity of becoming thoroughly acquainted with and obtaining a proper feeling of the subject. The picture should be complete and perfect in the mind before it is ever traced upon the canvas. Such force and expression should be displayed as would render the effect at the first glance intelligible to the observer. Merely to paint is not enough, for when no interest is felt nothing is more natural than that none should be conveyed. When the pupil has made a correct and decided outline all timidity vanishes, and he will work with spirit and freedom. The reverse is the cause of so many failures in the commencement of art. The last and surest method of obtaining instruction from the works of others is not so much by copying them as by drawing the same subjects from nature immediately after a critical examination of them, while they are fresh in the memory. Thus they are seen through the same medium, and imitated upon the same principles, without preventing the introduction of sufficient alterations to give originality of manner, or incurring the risk of being degraded into a mere imitator."

The following is an extract from "The Young Artist's Companion, by David Cox, 1825:"—

"The great merit of a picture depends on the most appropriate *effect* given to each scene. Abrupt and irregular lines are productive of a grand or stormy effect, while serenity is the result of even and horizontal lines. Morning effect, for instance, may be displayed in any composition, the form and character of which are pleasing to the eye, where the pendent forms of trees, combined with other objects, communicate to the mind a delightful impression. Owing to the great glare of light in mid-day effects, hay-fields, corn-fields, or any busy scene on rivers, are suitable. As regards evening and

CHAP. IV. twilight, such effects being calculated to convey to the mind impressions of grandeur, the composition should be studied to produce the same, and the colouring ought to be perfectly in unison with the peaceful repose or the gloomy majesty which contrasts the scene.

"A flat country on the marshy banks of a winding river should be seen beneath a grey-coloured sky. The transient effect adapted to such a landscape is provided by the fleeting lights of the sunbeams struggling between the interstices of the flowing clouds. The old pollard-willow is strictly characteristic of this scene and its situation, and its situation in the landscape might be such as to carry the eye through all the various meanderings of the stream.

"In landscapes which are low, and on the whole less prolific in interest, and less gratifying to the eye, an additional feature of interest should be thrown into the sky, to aid, by the contrast it would afford, the effect of the whole; and where the scene itself is naturally full of interest, the picture will of course admit of a less beautiful and imposing sky."

In 1840 a new edition of the "Treatise on Landscape Painting" was brought out by S. and J. Fuller, in twelve monthly folio numbers. It was preceded by rather an elaborate prospectus setting forth the advantages and objects of the work. How this came about will be best explained by the following letter addressed by Mr. Samuel Fuller to David Cox:—

"34, Rathbone Place, January 31st, 1840.

"MR. D. COX.

"DEAR SIR,—It is now six-and-twenty years since we published your work, 'A Treatise on Landscape Painting and Effect,' and during this time a new family and many aspirants to the art have appeared, and many are forthcoming, so that I think if your work was to appear again there are many who would be inclined to take to it. With this in view, we propose to republish it, in monthly numbers again, the first number to appear next March. The plates have been proved, and found to be in good condition, particularly the soft ground, which I consider as good as ever. The sepia or shadow and effect will want some little attention, and which I shall thank you to be so good as to look over; but I believe that I am in possession of some proof impressions that may assist the engraver. As I propose to advertise this to the world, it will give much publicity to your name, and I hope it will give an interest and a demand for the art again. I have no doubt but you will be surprised to find that it is twenty-six years since you commenced this work. Time has passed away, and many changes have taken place, but I do not think myself that anything has been added new by those who have brought out similar publications. I have been these last three weeks laid up with a cold, but should the day prove fine on Sunday next, I will take the advantage and come and take my tea with you. Hoping you and Mrs. Cox are quite well,

"I remain, dear sir,

"Yours truly,

"SAM. FULLER."

About the year 1835 Cox was engaged, in conjunction with Cattermole and Creswick, to illustrate the "Wanderings and Excursions in North Wales," about to appear from the pen of Mr. Thomas Roscoe. Of the fifty-one beautiful engravings in this work, twenty-nine are from subjects sketched from nature in water-colours by David Cox. They are all well-chosen and effective, but the following are especially noteworthy from their spirit and their grand representations of mountains overhung with mists and clouds, wild passes and rock-bound torrents:—"Pass of Llanberris," "Falls of the Machno," "The Trifaen Mountains," "Llyn Idwal," "Falls of the Ogwen," "Nant Frangon," "Entrance to

CHAP. IV. the Menai Straits," "Penmanmawr," "Pont Aberglaslyn," "Harlech Castle," and "Rhaiadr Cwm." The view of Chester is also a fine work, with a good deal of delicate finish in the distance, and with something of Turner's feeling. The "Vale of the Llugwy" is interesting partly on account of the introduction in the foreground of a girl blowing a cow's horn. Cox used to be summoned to dinner in this way when staying in a remote part of North Wales, and he painted a figure subject of the girl with her horn from nature. I shall never forget the pleasant evening I spent in 1836 in the company of David Cox, looking through the whole of these sketches soon after his return from North Wales, and the pleasant anecdotes and descriptions with which he illustrated them, whilst showing them to Mr. Charles Birch and myself.

David Cox also supplied the following illustrations for a second work published by Thomas Roscoe, "Wanderings in South Wales, including the Scenery of the River Wye," which came out shortly after the "North Wales:"—"Hereford," "Rhaiadr," "Brecon Church," "Coldwell Rock," "Goodrich Castle," "Vale of Towey," "Hay on the Wye," "Scene near Trecastle Road, Carmarthen," "Langharn," "Kilgarren," "Ragland Castle New Weir," "Water Mill on Tervy," "Devil's Bridge," "Cardigan," "Kidwelly Castle," and "Llangadog Bridge." These are as good artistically as the North Wales series, although the scenes themselves are generally less grand and interesting. These sketches were made in consequence of an agreement with Wrightson and Webb, the publishers, New Street, Birmingham, who agreed to pay at the rate of four guineas each for half, and five guineas for the remainder. This charge was the more moderate when it is taken into account that Cox had to travel over four hundred miles to complete the scenes.

In 1829 an account of Warwickshire was published, with illustrations by D. Cox, P. de Wint, Clarendon Smith, J. N.

Barber, J. D. Harding, Mackenzie, and W. Westall. Those by Cox were done in sepia, and the original drawings are now exhibited in the Public Art Gallery at Birmingham. They are beautifully finished, and very charming, as showing how differently subjects may be treated. They were engraved by W. Radclyffe. The following are some of the subjects of the illustrations by Cox:—"The Session House, High Street, Warwick," a beautiful, highly finished water-colour, with numerous figures; "St. Martin's Parsonage," a commonplace subject, but delicate in treatment; "Guy's Cliff, Warwick;" "Stoneleigh Abbey," a very beautiful, tender sepia, with figures and dogs introduced; "Market Place, High Street, Birmingham, and St. Martin's Church in the distance:" this is the gem of the series, as the arrangement and treatment of the foreground, composed of market folk, poultry stalls, &c., with rows of ducks and geese, are wonderfully clever, and show Cox's readiness of resource and admirable drawing.

In 1862 and 1863 the Art-Union of London published a series of twelve beautiful line engravings by Edward Radcliffe, from water-colour drawings by David Cox. The subjects are all characteristic ones, and well selected. They comprise well-known pictures, such as the "Welsh Funeral," "Lancaster Sands," "Outskirts of the Forest," "Peat Gatherers on a Windy Day," &c.

In 1866 the *Art-Journal* published "Hay-Time," from Cox's painting; and in 1868, "Carreg-Cennen Castle," from the beautiful drawing by Cox, in the collection of Mr. Tom Taylor. The first named is engraved by Edward Radcliffe, and the *Art-Journal* remarks on it at some length. The following is a short extract:—"The character of the scenery is Welsh, probably on the borders of one of the lakes, a portion of which is seen in the distance. It is one of those open landscapes we often find in the works of this artist—a wide, outspread tract of level ground, backed by a range of hills here standing out in partial sunshine against a mass of purple clouds. Cox possessed a rare faculty of representing space and distance by light and shade intermingled, and this power is abundantly evident in this picture."

Of "Carreg-Cennen," which is engraved by W. Chapman, it is remarked:—"The ruined fortress before us tells its own story far more fittingly, as we now see it, than if it were represented under a bright, sunny sky and a breathless atmosphere. The artist has surrounded it, as it were, with all the attributes of its own fortune—storm, disquietude. Clouds career wildly over its head, and the rain-torrents are driven against its massive walls. The intelligent observer will not fail to note how beautifully the light is thrown from the lifted clouds on to the centre of the picture."

When Frederick Tayler brought out his portfolio of original designs in lithotint in 1844, and G. Cattermole produced a similar work from his drawings in 1845, Cox thought he might like to follow in the same track, and with that intention he made several clever lithotints, still in existence, from his own works, which I have seen. He was probably not satisfied with the result, as he shortly afterwards abandoned the idea. His time and thoughts, too, became so much engrossed by his increasing practice in oil painting, in addition to water-colours, that henceforth he was unable to take up again any description of book illustrations.

V.

SECOND RESIDENCE IN LONDON.

1827 TO 1835.

DAVID COX'S removal from Hereford and return to London must be regarded as an important epoch in his art life. He felt the need of being more in the world of art, and of a wider scope for the development of his practice and increasing powers of execution. It is to be noted that it was after this change of residence that he sought in Derbyshire, Nottinghamshire, Yorkshire, and Lancashire new scenes for the exercise of his pencil. For many years, beginning with 1831, I find a series of visits recorded to Haddon Hall, Hardwick Hall, Bolsover Castle, Bolton Abbey, and the neighbourhood of Lancaster.

CHAP. V.

1827—1835.

He left London at the end of 1814, when difficulties appeared to be looming around him on every side. The public patronage of art at that time was at the lowest ebb: so low, indeed, as compared with the present day, that it is difficult to realise the great change that has taken place. When he returned to London, in 1827, the trade and resources of Great Britain, fostered by many years of peace, had greatly improved, and the pursuits connected with art had shared in the general return of prosperity. Cox himself was now possessed of a certain though very modest independence, and he felt that he was justified in moving into a better and more commodious house, which he engaged at No. 9, Foxley Road, Kennington. He continued his London teaching, and during

CHAP. V.

1827—1835.

the season he had as many pupils as he desired. It was the fashion in those days for ladies to have albums containing highly finished drawings by various artists, and Cox used to relate that when teaching in London he often occupied many consecutive lessons in making a water-colour, which he afterwards sold at five to ten guineas, his pupils being glad to secure the work they had seen in progress; by this means he realised much more than by the lessons only. The exhibition of the Society of Painters in Water Colours left but a small surplus in those days—not much more than two hundred pounds, and this was divided into sums of about thirty pounds each, which were balloted for by the members. This used to give about six prizes; and it was agreed between the members that those who obtained the money should spend it in making studies from nature, to be afterwards exhibited, and Cox was fortunate among others in drawing a prize. He still had many of his drawings returned unsold, and the former secretary of the society, Mr. George Fripp, has related to me that on one occasion he went to the gallery a few days before it closed, and, on looking round, he was pleased as well as surprised to find the blue ticket, indicating "sold," on all Cox's works; the more so, as although Copley Fielding, and one or two favourite artists of the day had sold a great many works, only one or two of Cox's had to within a week of that time been purchased. On remarking this to the keeper of the gallery, Mr. Abraham Worley, he replied, "Oh, that is Mr. Cox's own doing. On looking round the other day he appeared rather vexed, and said, 'Go at once and put a ticket of "sold" on all my drawings. They shall not have another chance now.'"

There is not the least doubt but that Cox, with all his modesty, well knew how much his drawings were underestimated by the public. He used to relate a story that, on one occasion he was quietly looking on at the exhibition, when an elderly lady was being wheeled in a chair round the gallery, accompanied by a young lady as companion, who read out the numbers. "Well, my dear, whose is that?" said the lady. Response: "By Copley Fielding." My Lady: "Oh, how very beautiful! what a lovely effect! And whose is that curious drawing, my dear, just above the other?" "Oh, that one is by David Cox." My Lady: "Oh, indeed; go on, if you please, go on!" Another lady is reported on one occasion to have said, "Pray, Mr. Cox, do you not think it would be worth while to take a few lessons from Mr. —— in *finish?*"

In 1827 Cox sent seventeen drawings, many of them views in North Wales and some near Birmingham, but there are no longer many subjects in the neighbourhood of Hereford or of the Wye. In 1828 he sent twenty-six drawings, and in 1829 thirty-five to the gallery of the Water Colour Society. Amongst the most noteworthy of those exhibited in the last-mentioned year are several views in France and Belgium, such as "The Entrance to Calais Harbour," "Calais Pier," "Fruit and Flower Market, Brussels," "Boats on the Scheldt," &c.

The journey which Cox made to Belgium and Holland in 1826 had, without doubt, stimulated his desire to see more of the Continent. The sketches and drawings that he made on that occasion had been successfully exhibited, and now, in the summer of 1829, he determined to give himself the relaxation of a more lengthened tour in France in company with his son. Their original intention was to work their way slowly to Paris, sketching *en route*, and from thence to Orleans, and along the banks of the Loire. They started from London in June, and crossed from Dover to Calais, where they remained about a week, as Cox found many subjects to sketch about Fort Rouge, the jetty and harbour, which pleased him very much. From these he afterwards made many beautiful pictures both in oil and water-colours. Luke Francia, an artist in water colours, who painted clever sea

CHAP. V. and coast views, had taken up his residence in Calais. In
1827—1835. 1826 he was still there, and Cox renewed his acquaintance with him. Cox and his son took the diligence from Calais to Amiens, remained there two days, sketched the cathedral from the citadel, the Rue de Condé, and other subjects. From Amiens they walked to Beauvais, and stopped there to sketch for three days. They had intended walking on to Paris, but the weather had become excessively hot, and finding the country in France near the high roads far from picturesque, they again took the diligence for Paris, where they put up at the Hôtel de Tours.

John Pye, the engraver, was living in Paris at that time. He made haste to welcome Cox and his son, and to offer his services as cicerone. The second day after their arrival Pye took them to see the Palais Royal, and, amongst other sights, they must needs go up and see rouge-et-noir played in one of the gambling saloons of the Palais. In descending the stairs Cox unfortunately sprained his ankle rather badly, and this incapacitated him from walking about Paris all the six weeks he remained there. This also put a stop to the projected tour along the banks of the Loire. He, however, was not to be baffled in his intention of sketching the monuments of Paris; so, with his usual spirit, especially when the pursuit of art was in question, he used to drive out in a fiacre, or cab, every day, and making it stop when he came to an interesting subject that took his fancy, he painted away indefatigably for many weeks, seated in the cab, or occasionally in a chair near the Seine or in some other not overcrowded spot. In this way he secured views of the Tuileries, Palais de Justice, Chambre de Deputies, Rue St. Honoré, Montmartre, the bridges over the Seine, and many others. Cox exhibited views of these places for some years afterwards in the Water Colour exhibition.

Cox only went abroad once more after this visit, and then only for about a week. King Charles X. had in the interval retired from France, and in his place his cousin Louis Philippe had been raised to the throne. A grand review was to take place not far from Boulogne, and Frederick Bruce, Cox's former pupil, persuaded him to accompany him thither. Cox was fond of describing this review, its dust and brilliancy, and the many scampers to get out of the way of the troops. He used also to relate as a joke that his young friend had partly beguiled him across the Channel by boasting how well he could speak French; but that at breakfast the first morning in a French hotel Bruce could not recollect the French word for eggs, and so Cox, with his readiness in pantomime, helped him out by showing how eggs were eaten with a spoon. They made an excursion as far as St. Omer, sketching in that neighbourhood before returning home. Cox also visited Dieppe, and made sketches of the pier and harbour there; one of a thunder-storm passing off, and reflections on the wet pier, is very beautiful. He was always fond of the banks of the Thames, and in 1829 he took lodgings for his family at Gravesend, Mrs. Cox's sister, Mrs. Hills, occupying apartments in the same street opposite to them, which made it more cheerful when Cox was absent on his frequent sketching excursions. Several drawings of views near Gravesend, and on the Thames, resulted from this visit. How moderate were the prices Cox still obtained for his drawings may be gathered from an entry made by him in an old account book of the following sale to Mr. Everitt, Birmingham :—

1830.
July 5. Five Water Colour Drawings, viz., Calais Pier, View in Ghent, Boat on the Scheldt near Dort, Minehead, and Landscape in Wales—price for the five, £12 0s. 0d.

In the year 1830 Cox made one of his first excursions into Yorkshire, and the following spring he exhibited for the first time a view on the river Wharf near Bolton Abbey; also scenes in Yorkshire, and many views in France, &c.

CHAP. V. 1827—1835. This year William Radclyffe, junior, of Birmingham, painted an oil portrait of Cox, which is now in his son's possession. The costume is very unbecoming, as he has a coat with the very broad stiff collar of that period. The face is represented as close shaven, which was his constant practice throughout life; it is rather full, but paler than in later years, when he had generally a good hale colour. The bright grey eyes look out very intelligently from beneath the full and rather bushy eyebrows, and are the most distinguishing feature of the face. Cox was of middle stature and active, though by no means robust. He was plain but neat in his dress, especially on Sundays, or if going out to dine with a friend. On such occasions he was anxious to look well dressed, and before going out he would often say, "Now *tell* me am I all right."

About the year 1830, or 1831, Cox made the acquaintance in London of Mr. William Stone Ellis, which shortly ripened into a warm and life-long friendship. Mr. Ellis had first become acquainted with the works of Cox, by seeing some of his sepias at Palser's, in the Strand, about 1825. Speaking of these in 1860, Mr. Ellis wrote—"They were very broad and beautiful; I would sooner meet with these than with the Turner sepias in Marlborough House." He had also purchased some drawings by Cox which he had seen in the shop window of a dealer in Ludgate Hill, of the name of Clay; some of them being very early ones. He had been taking lessons in water-colours from the well-known artist, George Robson, in 1829, and he told him what he had seen at Palser's, and described as well as he was able, and rather enthusiastically, the subjects and mode of treatment; but he did not *know* who had painted them. Robson exclaimed, "Ah! you mean Old Farmer Cox. Go and have lessons of him if you fancy it." This appellation of "Old Farmer," was without a doubt given to express the unsophisticated simplicity of Cox's manners and address. That Robson should recommend his pupil Ellis to go to David Cox for further advancement in art is interesting, as it shows the appreciation and esteem entertained for him at that period by a brother artist. Cox gave lessons in Russell Square to Mr. Ellis, who introduced him to another friend, Mr. Norman Wilkinson, who was a young man at that time, and a resident in London. Mr. Wilkinson also possessed a small cottage at Streatham, where many artists congregated at times, and at these pleasant gatherings Cox was ever a welcome guest. No one understood Cox's genial character or appreciated his genius better than this gentleman, and a life-long and warm friendship was formed between them.

On the 1st of August, 1831, the New London Bridge, which had taken seven years to build, was opened with great ceremony by King William IV. and Queen Adelaide. Cox, who had formerly painted the embarkation of George IV. at Greenwich for Scotland, went down to a coal wharf near St. Saviour's Church, Bankside, to sketch the preparations, &c., in water-colours. The gentleman who narrated this to me was a little boy at that time. He watched the artist all day at his work on the wharf, which was occupied by the boy's father. He had an early taste for art, and when the drawing (a very beautiful one) was finished, he asked for it for his own. "Oh! my lad," replied Cox, "do you know it is worth five pounds?" This drawing, I am informed, has since been sold for a hundred pounds.

Speaking of Greenwich reminds me that Greenwich Hospital was a subject of which Cox was very fond, and of which he has made a good many beautiful early drawings. I have seen one lately, showing the whole of one of the front porticoes and the side of the hospital; light in tone, very correctly drawn, and admirable as respects the arrangement of light and shade. In front of the building a number of pensioners are seen loitering about.

In the summer of 1831, Cox, accompanied by his son, went

CHAP. V. 1827—1835.

to stay at the Peacock, in Derbyshire, intending to make a series of drawings at Haddon Hall. The inn, in those days, was kept by some very kind people, Mr. and Mrs. Severn. The esteem between the hosts and their guests appears to have been mutual, and for many years after this Cox seized every opportunity of returning to the Peacock, and revisiting "dear old Haddon," as he always used to call it. Mr. William Roberts, of Birmingham, joined them there, and remained part of the time. Cox had made the acquaintance of Mr. Roberts about the year 1825, during his periodical visits to Birmingham, and that gentleman, who was an enthusiastic amateur, and a great admirer of Cox's genius, made many subsequent sketching excursions with him, and became one of his most intimate and very dear friends. The following letter, written at this time to Mr. Roberts, speaks for itself:—

From DAVID COX *to* W. ROBERTS, ESQ.

"Rowsley Inn, near Wirksworth, Derbyshire,
Sunday Evening, August 28th, 1831.

"MY DEAR SIR,—Thanks for your kind letter. It gave both myself and son great pleasure to learn that you got safe home. We should have been much gratified if it had been possible for you to have joined us again; but, as that cannot be at present, I hope by the end of the week to see you in Birmingham, there to show you a few additional sketches of this delightful old Haddon; and, as it will be utterly impossible for me to make all the subjects which I see and feel pleased with, I must defer it until another year. We have therefore resolved to take our leave on Tuesday or Wednesday morning towards Ashbourne and Dovedale, where we hope to meet with some little work for the pencil, and afterwards to work our way to Birmingham. We have visited the Hall each day since you left. To-day we had Mr. Severn's car and went to Chatsworth, and round by

Bakewell, but did not see anything striking; but I do not expect to be much pleased with anything this country can afford after my favourite old Haddon. Indeed, that alone is quite enough for one summer. The weather has been very fine until yesterday afternoon, when we had heavy rain and thunderstorm, but got home dry in the evening, and it afterwards turned out fine. To-day it has been beautiful for the *effects*. I shall expect when I have the pleasure of seeing you in Birmingham to find that you have begun several pictures from your sketches. Begin while the scenes are fresh in your memory. I shall also expect to see that Mr. Lines has several on the easel. Pray make my respects to him. I shall be happy to show him what I have done when I meet him in Birmingham. My son begs to join me in kind wishes, and believe me to remain, my dear sir, CHAP. V. 1827—1835.

"Yours very truly,
"DAVID COX."

Cox stayed several weeks with his son on this occasion, spending the whole day at Haddon, and having their mid-day dinner conveyed thither from Rowsley and spread out on the old table in the great hall. Cox loved, with the love of an artist and poet, the old terrace at Haddon, with its broad flight of old stone steps and balustrades, and yew-tree walk on the top; the interior of the grand old mansion, with its antique tapestries, panellings, and carvings; the quaint domestic arrangements of the time of Henry VII.; and, not least, the old park, full of ancestral forest trees, beneath which flows a broad trout stream fringed with water plants, with many a curve, as described in Tennyson's idyl, "The Brook:"—

"It winds about, and in and out,
With here a blossom sailing;
And here and there a lusty trout,
And here and there a grayling."

CHAP. V. 1827—1835.

Here Cox found a great variety of charming subjects for his rapid pencil. Of the series of water-colour sketches which he made on this visit, he sold twelve, some time afterwards, for a hundred pounds, to Mr. George Proctor. I have seen a letter from this gentleman to his brother, the Rev. Dr. Proctor, mentioning that he had just purchased this collection of drawings for that sum. It is dated in January, 1837. One of the finest, "An Interior of the Great Hall, Haddon," was exhibited in London in 1832, and "The Bedroom," "The Entrance," and "The Garden, Haddon," also appeared in the same exhibition. Cox likewise found some subjects at Rowsley, especially the picturesque water-mill, upwards of three hundred years old, with an undershot wheel, and quantities of willow herbs, candocks, and other wild plants growing about it, which he sketched several times. It cannot be seen from the road, and is, therefore, sometimes missed by tourists. He also went this year to the English Lake District, and made sketches of "Langdale Pikes," "Windermere during the Regalia," &c.

In the years 1830, 1831, and 1832, he exhibited respectively in the Water Colour Society's Gallery thirty, nineteen, and thirty-five drawings. The last-named year is especially rich in the variety of subjects. Besides views in France, Belgium, the Lake District, Yorkshire, Derbyshire, Westminster, and Windsor, it contains numerous views in North Wales, one being of a "Peat Moor." This subject is one of which he was particularly fond in his latter days, and it afforded scope for grand effects of approaching storm and gathering mists, the figures introduced being of peat gatherers hurrying home, and bending under their loads. Cox continued to give many lessons in London. In some cases he allowed his pupils to keep the drawing which he had made before them, and in a memorandum book of the year 1832 I find the following entries :—

Captain Rawdon, lessons in drawing (to keep the drawing) February to July, 1832, 18 lessons at one guinea each. Honourable Miss Leveson Gower, 9 lessons at half-a-guinea. Countess of Verulam, 4 lessons at half-a-guinea, &c. &c.

A year or two later he discontinued the plan of parting with the drawing, as he discovered it was more valuable than the extra price charged for the lesson.

It was in this year, 1832, that Cox made his last trip across the Channel, and he also went to North Wales, and many new views of different parts of the Principality were taken this year. It was of about this period that Mr. Henry Gastineau, one of the oldest members of the Water Colour Society, who resided at Camberwell, spoke to me of his having spent pleasant evenings occasionally at Cox's house in Foxley Road, where he was always kindly and hospitably received. He remarked that Cox's heart and hand were at all times in his work with unceasing industry—early and late, it was always the same—and that he cared but little for games or any description of amusement. In those days, too, Cox would encourage the younger members of the society, as related by Mr. G. Fripp. They often had to endure the disappointment of seeing all, or nearly all, their exhibited works returned unsold. Cox would say to the new associates and others, in the kindest manner possible, "Don't be discouraged; don't be cast down; have patience. The same thing has formerly happened to me many and many a time. I have had nearly all my drawings returned unsold; but it is better now than in those very early days, when the brunt and burden of the day had to be borne by the earliest members."

The Miss Hills, nieces of Mr. Cox, used often to come to Foxley Road, and one of them has related to me how very kindly their uncle David always behaved to them when they were children. He was ever ready to enter into all their games and little pleasures, which he had the knack of doing in a very diverting way. All his life he was fond of the

CHAP. V. 1827—1835. society of the young, and he would exert himself for their entertainment in various ways. For the amusement of children (who might be pleased with it) he would sometimes throw himself into whimsical pantomime positions, even down to a late period of his life. Sometimes, if he remarked that his nieces came into the parlour in a shy or awkward manner, he would take the trouble to get up and go out of the room himself, then open the door and enter, giving a lesson in deportment. On one occasion he presented his eldest niece with a beautiful water-colour, his own work, but, expecting something brighter, she did not express much pleasure at the gift. Cox evidently felt rather disappointed, but he only said, "Well, my dear, I think it is really a very nice drawing." Always gentle and kind, he never indulged in a cross word or sharp rebuke.

Although Cox was delighted with what he saw of the coast of France, and some of the rivers in Holland and Belgium, he did not at all admire the scenery of the interior of France, and he never expressed a wish to return again to the Continent in after life. He thoroughly believed in the superiority of English rural scenery to any other; he said he best understood English subjects. When any one showed him any Continental views he would exclaim—"Oh! that's *foreign*," which expression became a by-word. Boulogne and Calais, however, had special attractions for him, from the opportunity they afforded of displaying space over sands, with bright figures and reflections. On one occasion a gentleman who had travelled abroad a good deal tried to persuade Cox's son to go to Switzerland to paint, saying it was so much superior to anything at home. Cox listened quietly, and at the end of the conversation he remarked, "Don't try to induce David to go on the Continent in search of scenery. Wales, Yorkshire, and Derbyshire have been good enough for me, and I quite believe they may yet do for him."

In the year 1833 Cox exhibited at the Water Colour Society thirty-six drawings, thirteen of which were views in France, views at Calais predominating; namely, "Fort Rouge," "The Harbour," and "Pier." The forts and sands of Calais were also a favourite subject with J. M. W. Turner. Both these great artists have produced some of their finest effects of sea and sky, full of light and movement, on this part of the coast of France. There were also several views in Yorkshire and Wales, and of Haddon Hall, in this year's exhibition. Cox continued at this time to exhibit small drawings each year at the rooms of the Liverpool Academy and other provincial exhibitions, the prices obtained being about five to six guineas each.

At the end of July, 1834, Cox made another excursion to the north of England, visiting Lancaster and the adjoining sea-coast, where he made his first series of drawings of the broad expanse of Ulverstone Sands, a subject which he afterwards frequently repeated, and treated under a variety of effects, both early morning and at sundown. The Ulverstone and Lancaster drawings are generally enlivened with groups of market folk crossing the sands, sometimes stretching far away into the yellow haze of evening, their long shadows thrown across the wet sands, and their retreating forms at the same time reflected downwards. The flutter and shimmer of innumerable sea-birds often add life and movement to these subjects. This trip included visits to Bolsover Castle, Bolton Abbey, and other places in Derbyshire and Yorkshire. Cox was accompanied on this sketching tour for the first time by Mr. W. S. Ellis, of London, his son having gone by himself to Scotland. In after years Mr. Ellis, whose tastes and sympathies were quite at one with those of Cox, often accompanied him to these parts of England, and also to North Wales. The following letter, written just before starting, relates to this expedition :—

CHAP. V.
1827—1835.

"9, Foxley Road, Kennington Common,
London, June 8th, 1834.

"TO WILLIAM ROBERTS, ESQ.

"MY DEAR SIR,—I am much obliged by your kind and friendly letter, wherein you express a wish that Mrs. Cox and myself should join you and Mrs. Roberts in Yorkshire. I regret exceedingly that it will be quite out of my power to leave London until the middle of July; at all events not until I have sent home the drawings from the Exhibition, and I do not expect we shall close until the first week in July.

"I have made up my mind to visit Yorkshire again, and shall try to get as far as Barnard Castle; perhaps to Carlisle. My plan is to go to Manchester, where I expect to meet a young friend, who will accompany me from thence to Lancaster, Hornby Castle, Kirby Lonsdale, Hawes, Richmond, &c., &c. I may perhaps make some change in part of my plan. David is going to Scotland alone. He also starts in the middle of July.

"When you and Mrs. Roberts come to London, Mrs. Cox and myself and son will be delighted to see you in Foxley Road. If there should be any alteration in your plans, pray give me a line to say where you will be about the early part of August, as I think that the most likely time for my being in Yorkshire.

"Believe me to remain,
"Yours obliged and truly,
"DAVID COX."

There were twenty-four drawings exhibited by Cox this year, 1834, in London, amongst the most important of which were—"A Bridge on the Derwent, near Chatsworth," and a "Lane Scene in Staffordshire." There were also again views on the coast of France, and his favourite subjects in Wales.

The drawings which I have seen of this middle period are

pure in colour, with a considerable amount of finish. Those especially painted for albums are highly finished, and, although they have perhaps less breadth than those very early works which, in their neutral low tones and flat washes, resemble the works of John Varley and the early efforts of Prout, they gain on the other hand in brilliancy and atmosphere, or feeling of space, and were more liked by the public. Cox objected, even when finishing highly, to the use of body colour, and on the rare occasions where he transgressed this rule, it was merely for small and sparkling touches of light. He worked with a large swansquill brush, full of colour, putting on his tints very wet, so that they dried full and powerful, but without blackness. To give richness he hatched over again with repeated touches, but he avoided washing over the tints when once applied, as he considered that the plan of washing made the effect weak and poor. The range of his colour-box was of the simplest description, and the rarer pigments sometimes used by artists were unnecessary to him. When half-finished, or even when more advanced, his sketch or drawing would sometimes look flat and tame, as he reserved the full power of his pallet for the finishing, when his consummate knowledge enabled him with a few powerful touches on the figures, and a rather dry brush dragged over the foreground, to give point and force to the whole, and clear up the half-shadows, putting everything into its right place. It was not until a year or two later than the time we have described that Cox commenced to use the very rough Scotch paper, an account of which will be given by-and-by, on which his latest and finest drawings were generally painted, and which are more poetical, and partake of a deeper sympathy and feeling for nature. Indeed, I must repeat that Cox never went back, or even halted in his wonderful industry and constant practice, and this, added to his ever-increasing knowledge of and love for nature, made some of his latest works, like the "Welsh

CHAP. V. 1827—1835.

Funeral" and "On the Moors near Bettws," the finest of all. The depth of his poetical feeling may perhaps account for his occasional fits of melancholy and depression of spirits. On these occasions his wife, who was, as we have seen, a thoughtful woman, and an ever-ready helpmate to her husband, would manage him admirably. At times he would say, "Oh, Mary, I cannot go out this morning to teach—I feel I cannot do it." She would gently combat this notion with cheering words, and, putting on her bonnet and mantle, would offer to accompany him. The effort once more made, his spirits soon rose, and the work, when fairly commenced, generally went right. During the London season he had quite as much teaching as he wished. He used to relate with some amusement that on one occasion he went to teach the daughter of a lady of rank: she sat in the breakfast-room during the whole of the lesson, and when it was over, addressing the artist, she said, "Mr. Cox, I have been trying to imagine, but I cannot, where you sell all the pictures you paint." To this Cox replied that the merchants and manufacturers of London, Liverpool, Manchester, and Birmingham were the best patrons of art in those days, and purchased most of them. "Ah, indeed!" said the lady, "I suppose those merchants must be very rich." Sometimes when Cox saw a drawing by another artist that struck his imagination, he would make a study of it at home from recollection. In this way, the first time he visited Birmingham, after seeing J. Martin's picture of "Belshazzar's Feast," he sat down, and in an hour or two produced a slight but graphic representation of that celebrated picture, which he gave to Mr. Edward Everitt, who still possesses it. In the same way he reproduced Cattermole's "Battle of the Bridge," a drawing which was long valued by his friend Mr. Roberts, and which sold for thirty-two guineas when that gentleman's collection was brought to the hammer after his decease. At times, although rarely, Cox occupied himself in making a copy of some work which he particularly admired. Thus he obtained permission from Sir Robert Peel to copy the grand work by Meindert Hobbema, now in the National Gallery, representing an avenue of trees, with cultivated fields, and a Dutch village in the distance. He also copied two figure subjects by R. P. Bonnington, which I have seen at Brixton Hill. These of course were only for practice, and have never been offered for sale.

VI.

SECOND RESIDENCE IN LONDON—(*Continued*).

1835 TO 1840.

CHAP. VI.

1835—1840.

AT the end of July, 1835, Cox visited Lancaster, where he remained some time sketching the scenery of that neighbourhood—the river, with the bridge and tower rising up in the distance, and the picturesque and finely situated castle. But what again especially attracted him, as on preceding visits, was the expanse of the Lancaster and Ulverstone sands, with market people preparing to cross, or dimly seen in the distance, under various effects of weather, at sunset, or by the tender light of early morning. From these sketches he made several drawings, which were exhibited the following spring in London.

After quitting Lancaster he paid a short visit to Liverpool, and whilst there he stayed at the house of Mr. Samuel Eglington, secretary of the Liverpool Academy, with whom he was on very friendly terms. He arranged to send him some drawings, four of which were sold in the Exhibition for £23 10*s*. One of these was "Market People crossing Ulverstone Sands," which went for £5 10*s*.; and another, "Fish Market on the Coast," was purchased by Mr. William Lassells, the astronomer, for the same sum. On leaving Liverpool, he visited his sister, Mrs. Ward, at Manchester; and then proceeded to Derbyshire, where Mr. W. Roberts joined him. The following letter refers to this visit:—

"Lancaster, September 5th, 1835.

"To WILLIAM ROBERTS, ESQ.

"MY DEAR SIR,—I received your kind letter two days ago, and delayed answering until I could fix the time of our meeting. It is my intention to leave this for Liverpool on Monday morning, where I shall stop one day, and on Tuesday evening reach my sister's, at Manchester, where I shall spend Wednesday, and on Thursday will start for Bolsover, which I hope to reach by five o'clock. If you have not seen Bolsover, I think you will be pleased with the distant views of it. There is another castle within seven miles of it—Hardwick Hall, one part in ruins. It stands equally as fine as Bolsover, but there is no good inn near. However, we must contrive to see it. The interior is fine, and there are some good pictures. With regard to Conisborough, I am afraid it will be too far off for me, as I shall have only a week that I can remain, and I thought we might return either by way of Nottingham (distant view of castle, &c.), or else return by way of Rowsley, and spend one day at old Haddon; but this matter can be settled when we meet. My excursion hitherto has been a very pleasant one, though I have not coloured so much as I could have wished; the weather has been so excessively hot. I suppose my son has told you that my excursion has been principally to the Lancaster and Ulverstone sands.

"Believe me, my dear Sir,
"Yours most sincerely,
"DAVID COX.

"Please direct to me at Mr. Ward's, 55, Spring Gardens, Manchester."

Cox exhibited twenty drawings in 1835 at the Water Colour Exhibition, one of which was "Waiting for the Ferry-boat," afterwards repeated in oil. The scenery is that of the River Wye. The water, on which some ducks are swimming, forms the immediate foreground. On the left the river-bank rises up covered with candock and rushes, and a rough stone causeway leads down to the stream. At the top an old man on horseback, and another rustic figure with a basket, apparently in conversation with a woman, are waiting for the boat, the proximity of which is indicated by a rope wound round a primitive windlass, which, passing over a pulley, is thrown across the river. Near the figures are some trees, with cottages behind. In the distance there is a view of some precipitous hills, partly wooded, and a little peep of the bright river winding far off. The sky is quiet, and the whole picture is thoroughly imbued with quiet country life. Another drawing in the same exhibition, "Returning from Ploughing," has the same charm of rural seclusion and repose manifested especially in Cox's works during the latter years of his residence at Hereford.

It was in the year 1836 that Cox first met with the rough Scotch wrapping paper which on trial turned out to be very unabsorbent of colour when used for water-colours, producing a powerful effect. The surface is hard and firm, the paper being made from old linen sailcloth well bleached. Cox obtained the first few sheets by chance at Grosvenor and Chater's, and on showing it to S. and J. Fuller, their traveller ascertained from the Excise mark stamped upon it, 84B, that it was manufactured at a paper-mill at Dundee, North Britain. There a ream was ordered for Cox, and it was some time before it could be obtained. On its arrival he was rather surprised to find that it weighed two hundred and eighty pounds, and cost eleven pounds. However, Mr. Roberts was willing to share in the purchase, and after some years Cox rather regretted that the quantity ordered had not been larger, as he was never able to obtain the same quality of paper again. Whilst on the subject of paper it may be worth mentioning that when Mr. Gardener, who married Mrs. Cox's sister, had the sale of the Government Ordnance maps he was commissioned to get some superior paper made for them at the paper-mills at Uxbridge. He went there once or twice on this errand. Some sheets were made beyond the order, and these and some cuttings of the paper were obtained for Cox, who prized them as being superior and less absorbent of colour than any other kind. Some of Cox's most powerful studies and drawings after this period were painted on the rough Scotch paper. It gave the texture he required, and suited his peculiar mode of rapid work with a large brush, charged as full as possible with very wet though rich colour. It enabled him to obtain *power* at once. The paper was very thick, not quite white, with here and there little black or brown specks. In the landscape part these specks were of no consequence, but they looked out of place in the sky. On one occasion being asked what he did to get rid of them, he replied, "Oh, I just put wings to them, and then they fly away as birds!"

In the summer of 1836 Cox went to Rowsley with Mr. Roberts, Mr. Norman Wilkinson, and Mr. Ellis. Mrs. Roberts had preceded them there. It was an expedition for painting at Haddon Hall, and they spent two or three weeks very agreeably in that pretty neighbourhood. Cox used to get up very early to sketch before breakfast, and one of his friends relates with what raciness he used to expatiate on the sweetness of the air on a summer's morning in July. He had been suffering, however, from rheumatism, and his friend Wilkinson persuaded him to take a few baths at Buxton.

When he came back to Rowsley Mrs. Roberts and other friends went out to meet him and inquire how the baths had suited. His reply, equally unexpected and demonstrative, was to commence dancing and skipping about in a very lively fashion. In his early days Cox had been a good dancer; even in his latter years the sound of dance music

CHAP. VI. 1835—1840. appeared to reawaken the old feeling, and Mrs. Everitt has told me that she could generally make Cox begin to waltz, if she played one of his favourite old tunes on the piano.

Cox spent some time in North and South Wales in the autumn of 1836, making drawings for the illustrations to Roscoe's work. He also appears to have sketched in the neighbourhood of Birmingham, where he stayed at the house of Mr. W. Radclyffe (No. 6, George Street, Edgbaston, now George Road), who had undertaken to engrave all the illustrations for the work on Wales. The following letter, referring to this work, was written at this time:—

"6, George Street, Edgbaston, October 13, 1836.

"WILLIAM ROBERTS, ESQ.

"MY DEAR SIR,—I beg to thank you for your kind invitation to dine with you to-day, but I made an engagement to go out to dinner while I was in town this morning, which was when your messenger arrived with your note; and I find that the engravers are waiting for a drawing for the Welsh work. This will also prevent my seeing you to-morrow, which I very much regret, as I am anxious to receive your kind information in regard to oil painting; but I hope, as soon as I return from my friend Birch's, at Dudley, to call and benefit from your very kind assistance. Mrs. Cox is much better than when I saw you yesterday, though still weak. She hopes to call and sit an hour or two with you and Mrs. Roberts when we return.

"I beg to remain, dear Sir,

"Yours obliged and sincerely,

"DAVID COX."

It was about this time that on one occasion Mr. Charles Birch, who then lived at Burnt Tree, near Dudley, called at the Birmingham Society of Artists' Rooms, then situated in Temple Row, for Cox. They were to go over to Dudley to sketch, but on going out Cox saw before him such beautiful colour on the porch of St. Philip's Church, that he stopped and said that he hoped his friend Birch would excuse him, but that he really must make a study of it. He had his sketching materials with him, so he immediately set to work, and in a short time produced an "upright," very lovely in its variety of changing greys, and admirable as a specimen of correct and rapid work. This sketch, which is without figures, is now in the possession of Mr. J. Jaffray, of Park Road, Birmingham. That gentleman has also a still earlier but beautiful little drawing of St. Martin's Church, Birmingham, taken from the old Moat Lane, showing the water of the moat in front. The colour is true, tender, and delicate, and it is the more interesting from the circumstance that this part of the town was modernised, and the houses pulled down, many years ago.

Cox exhibited the unusual number of thirty-four drawings in the Water Colour Society's gallery this year, 1836, and of these four were views in Scotland, taken from sketches which his son had made during his tour in that country in the year 1834. Cox himself was never in Scotland until he went there to have his portrait painted in 1855. Amongst the more important drawings exhibited were "Ellerside Peat Moss, Lancashire," "Lancaster Sands—Market People returning from Ulverstone;" "Bolton Castle—Twilight;" and "Haddon Hall."

During the whole of his residence in Foxley Road, Cox continued to give lessons throughout the London seasons, chiefly to his old pupils. Copley Fielding did the same. It was almost a necessity in those days, as works of the highest excellence in water-colours used to produce such very small prices. Cox continued to lay by a little money each year, as he was careful and simple in his expenditure. The end of the summer and the autumn were always passed travelling in Wales and England, sketching from nature, and in the winter he made finished studies from his summer work ready for the spring exhibition. In this he was indefatigable, working late every evening by artificial light, with sepia, and sometimes in chalk and colours. Indeed, he has been known to make three sepia drawings after dinner, in one afternoon and evening.

He was, however, beginning to feel that it would be of advantage to him in his art-life to remove into the country. By so doing he would be able more easily to relinquish teaching, and turn his attention to larger works, especially in oil, and the sequel proved that in this he was quite right. He was also desirous to escape from the importunities of some of the London dealers—Roberts, of Henry Yard, Oxford Street; Houghton, in the Poultry; Hixon, a print-seller, and others—who were continually applying to him for more of his small drawings, which had a very ready sale at the low prices charged. Referring to a memorandum of the sale of his drawings at the exhibition, Pall Mall, in 1837, I observe that out of seven drawings sold, six guineas was the highest price obtained, with one exception, "A Mountain Road—Infantry on the March," which was purchased by Mr. J. H. Maw for thirty-five guineas—a large sum for Cox to receive in those days. This was a large drawing; the scene represented was the Vale of Nan Frangon. A grand mountain range towers up partly wreathed with mists. A stream is descending into a peaceful valley in the distance, near which a few cattle are grazing. This year twenty-three drawings were exhibited. One of them—"Gleaners returning at Evening"—suggested the subject for Cox's fine oil picture, with Dudley Castle in the distance, now in the collection of Mr. S. Mayou. There were also exhibited many views of the Ulverstone Sands, and of various parts of North Wales.

It was this year, 1837, I believe, that Cox first visited Powis Castle, the seat of Lord Clive, and made several sketches there. One, of the Garden Terrace, which I have seen, is beautifully fresh in colour. I have been told, with reference to this and other journeys, that at Powis Castle, Hardwick Hall, and similar places, Cox appeared to be quite at home, and well-known to the stewards, gardeners, &c., who all seemed pleased to see him. He was in the habit, too, of walking about, quite unattended, wherever he liked; but he was a good deal afraid of the bloodhounds at Hardwick Hall, and would go half-a-mile round to avoid them. The easy way in which he made friends with all classes of society throughout his life may be accounted for by his modest, unassuming bearing to all, his kindness and benevolence. I may mention amongst other instances of this unselfish disposition, that besides giving his father an annuity as mentioned, Cox always arranged to pay the old man's doctor's bill. Old Mr. Ledsam, a well-known doctor in Birmingham in those days, was the medical attendant, and, as he liked art, Cox gave him a drawing every year instead of money. Many years afterwards, upon seeing these drawings, he said they were only "pot-boilers," and insisted on changing them for better ones. This practice of squaring his debts by paying in drawings instead of money was one which appears to have been often followed by Cox, and rather to have increased with advancing years. No doubt it was a mistake, at least in a pecuniary point of view, but a very harmless one, by which he himself was the only sufferer. Cox also visited Bolton Abbey, Castleton, and Hardwick Hall in 1837. The celebrated drawing of "Returning from Hawking, Haddon Hall," was suggested on this occasion, and several others were from sketches made at the same place. On the 29th March, 1838, Cox accompanied his wife to Seabrook, near Hythe. They stopped there in a cottage called Mill-house, lent to them by Mr. Norman Wilkinson, and remained about six weeks. Mrs. Cox had been far from well, and the change was very beneficial to her, whilst it

CHAP. VI. 1835—1840.

afforded Cox the opportunity of sketching on the Kentish coast. He visited Dover, and made a drawing of the pier. The following is an extract from a letter written by him at this time to his son:—

"Seabrook, May 11th, 1838.

"I have been out sketching the last three or four days. I have been to Saltwood Castle, and made several sketches. To-day I have been about five miles to Lymne Castle.

"It is very small, but stands on a bold situation overlooking Romsey Marshes. The atmosphere has been very clear for more than a week, and we can see the French coast quite distinct. To-day it was more clear than I have before seen it, and the sea of a most beautiful colour.

(Signed) "DAVID COX."

The visit above mentioned to Lymne Castle gave the outline and first idea of the beautiful drawing afterwards painted of "Peace and War, with Yokels," now in Mr. Quilter's collection.

In August of this year he visited some of his Birmingham friends, and afterwards spent a month in Derbyshire.

On this occasion he went to Rowsley and also to Hardwick Hall, where he made the three celebrated drawings of the interior of the picture-gallery. The perspective, colour, and appearance of truth in these drawings are excellent; the more they are examined the better they appear.

This success is the more remarkable as the subject was rather foreign to Cox's usual style. He had, however, previously made some very admirable sketches of the interior of Haddon Hall. The resemblance, also, to the old masters on the walls is carefully adhered to, although the handling is free; the effect also is rich and very pleasing. The two following letters to Mr. Roberts relate to this visit to Derbyshire:—

"Rowsley, Monday, August 20th, 1838.

"MY DEAR SIR,—When I passed through Birmingham about a fortnight ago I learnt that you were on a journey, and would be absent there a fortnight. As it is about the time of your return, I send you a few lines to say how much pleasure it would give me to have your company for a few days or a week, or more if you like. I have been to one or two places in this neighbourhood, where I should like to accompany you. I think of paying a short visit to my sister in Manchester, No. 55, Spring Gardens, where I shall stay till the middle of the week, about the 28th, so that if you should not get this time enough to write here, a letter to Manchester would find me, so that we might arrange to meet, as I wish very much to go to Hardwick. Let me know by return of post, if possible, that I may go to Manchester, pay my visit, and return here by the end of this or beginning of next week, as time is drawing to a close when I must return to London. Give my kindest remembrances to Mrs. Roberts, and believe me, my dear Sir,

"Yours very truly,

"DAVID COX.

"P.S.—Cotman was to have accompanied me from London to Birmingham, but he failed in his engagement. Mr. and Mrs. Severn send kind regards."

"Manchester, August 29th, 1838.

"MY DEAR SIR,—After remaining at Rowsley eight days, the whole of which I had rain, so that I could do but very little, on Sunday morning last I left, and reached Manchester in the evening. I rather expected when I reached Birmingham that I should have tempted you to have gone with me, and I was much disappointed when I learnt you were not likely to return under a fortnight or three weeks, so I left Birmingham in rather a sulky mood. I went by Nottingham and Mans-

CHAP. VI. 1835—1840. field to Bolsover and Hardwick, and found some good sketching, but was rather uncomfortable at the time; and, as I had requested Mrs. Cox to write to me at Rowsley, I bent my way there: and it was so far fortunate, as I got to a comfortable house during a very rainy week. I was bound to come to see my sister here, and now intend returning by Hardwick, as I have several of my sketches to finish, and I intend to be in Birmingham about the 10th of September, where I really hope I may be fortunate enough to meet with you before you leave for Rowsley, as I shall not be able to return that way. I was in Birmingham with my son, and it was he who called at your house. He, his wife and child, and myself were in Birmingham. Mrs. Ward desires to be kindly remembered to you; and believe me, my dear Sir, to remain,

"Yours very truly,

"DAVID COX."

John Sell Cotman, the well-known artist of the Norwich School of Old Crome, who had thought of accompanying Cox on this occasion, was an associate exhibitor of the Water Colour Society. He was Professor of Drawing at King's College, and the originality, knowledge of composition, light, and shade displayed in his works were fully appreciated by Cox, who never lost an opportunity of speaking well of them.

In 1838 Cox exhibited thirty-two drawings, and twenty-six in 1839, in the Water Colour Society's gallery. The subjects are very varied. The usual favourite scenes in Lancashire, Derbyshire, and Yorkshire abound, and, for the first time, a picture appears with the title of "Going to the Hay-field." This was the subject of many fine works in oil, painted in later years; and, although so often repeated, there is a variety in the incidents of each. In 1839, amongst the sales of Cox's drawings at the Exhibition, were two purchased by the Marquis of Conynham for her Majesty, No. 280,

"Battersea Fields," and 297, "A Castle in the Olden Time." Cox used always to make a point, if possible, of being present on the private view day at the Water Colour Exhibition, as he met there so many of his friends. On one of these occasions a lady wanted to purchase a small drawing by Cox which he had marked as "sold," as not wishing to part with it, thinking it too slight. He said he had rather not sell it, it had so little finish he really could not put a price on it. And, when she still insisted, he made it part of the bargain that he should first put some more work into it, to make it what he considered more equivalent to the money paid.

In the year 1839 W. J. Müller returned to England from that long journey through Greece and Egypt, in which so many of his most celebrated works were painted. He determined to fix his abode in London, and, although at that time only twenty-seven years of age, he had attained to wonderful power and dignity in his works, which few could understand and appreciate so well as Cox did. Müller was on intimate terms with George Fripp the artist. They had known each other from boyhood, had sketched and travelled abroad together; and now Fripp, hearing from Cox that he was turning his thoughts to oil painting, spoke to him about Müller's style of manipulation, and offered to introduce him, so that he might see him paint. Cox gladly embraced this suggestion, which resulted in Müller's giving Cox a few lessons in oils. Cox afterwards told Fripp how much he had been pleased, and that his expectations had been even more than fulfilled. There is but little doubt that the experience he gained of Müller's work impressed him deeply, and assisted in forming his latest and best style of manipulation in oils. Müller was left-handed, but he could paint nearly equally well with his right hand, and, when interested in his work, he would paint with both hands at once. Cox related that the first lesson he had, Müller nearly painted a small

CHAP. VI. 1835—1840. picture at *one* sitting, painting all the time with great ease and rapidity. When he went for his second lesson Müller had *wiped out* this picture, saying that he was not satisfied with it. He then commenced another, the subject of which was "The Ammunition Waggon." He made great progress with this also; and, when Cox called the next time, he was surprised to find it nearly finished, the horses, soldiers, and other incidents having all been introduced, and the rest of the picture a good deal worked up. When Cox afterwards went to live at Birmingham he used often to urge his friends there to purchase Müller's paintings. They followed his advice, and, in consequence, acquired some of his most beautiful works; but the fact that Cox gave this advice proves, if any proof were wanting, how far he was removed from any feeling of jealousy. Indeed, I believe he did not know what professional jealousy was.

Mr. William Roberts, of Harborne, was fond of painting in oil, and he urged Cox to paint some pictures to be exhibited in London, and gave him some hints about the use of vehicles. The following letters refer to these subjects:—

"9, Foxley Road, Kennington Common, London,
May 20th, 1840.

"To W. ROBERTS, ESQ.

"MY DEAR SIR,—I have delayed answering your letter several days in expectation of receiving some information respecting Blackpool from a gentleman at Liverpool, as I have no knowledge of it myself. Should I hear anything worth communicating, I will write again.

"I have so many things on hand at present that I cannot say at what time I shall be able to leave London, but I think most likely about the *end of July*, and, as I must go to Manchester to spend a short time with my sister, I should like, if it were possible, for us to meet, as I should be most happy to go with you a short trip. For the reasons

I have stated respecting my professional engagements, I must decline entering into any engagement to make drawings for your friend, the Rev. Mr. Kennedy, to whom you have kindly recommended me, and, in fact, I have no sketches in Shropshire. My son has sketches in the neighbourhood of Shrewsbury, Buildwas, &c., &c., which he made last year when on a visit to a friend there.

"I am making preparations to sketch in oil, and also to paint, and it is my intention to spend most of my time in Birmingham for the purpose of practice, when I hope to avail myself of your guidance and instruction.

"I expect to see Mr. Birch in London very soon, and will then mention to him your plan for us three to make an excursion, and I really and sincerely hope I may be allowed that pleasure.

"Mrs. Cox, my son, and his wife, join me in very kind remembrances to yourself and Mrs. Roberts.

"I remain, dear Sir,
"Yours very sincerely,
"DAVID COX."

From DAVID COX *to* W. ROBERTS, ESQ.

"9, Foxley Road, Kennington Common, London,
June 2nd, 1840.

"MY DEAR SIR,—I cannot sufficiently thank you for your very friendly and kind invitation to your house, and, although I am very far from ceremonious, yet to know that I am not in any way disturbing Mrs. Roberts's family arrangements would be an additional inducement to visit you, and I hope to spend a week or nine days with you. I have also promised my friend, Mr. Birch, I would spend some time with him, and, as I am determined to make a fair trial in oil painting, I expect to gain a good deal of information by having his pictures to look at, and with your instruction in the vehicle and use of the oils, I hope to produce some-

CHAP. VI. 1835—1840.

thing which may encourage me to pursue the study. It is also my intention to practise from Nature as much as possible, and I am getting a small contrivance to hold the millboard whilst I paint. It is very simple, and may be made to hold large or small millboard, or even a stretcher, with canvas, (at least two feet). I do not know whether I can describe it, but will endeavour. The box to carry my colours is what they sell at the shops, and I believe there cannot be anything better; a tin japanned box, with divisions for the bladders and bottles.

"I shall be most happy to join you at Blackpool for the purpose of having a short ramble, sketching, and shall be glad to go as far as Derby Dale with you. I wish also to get several good views of Lancaster, though after all I am fearful my time will not suit yours, as I cannot leave London till towards the 20th of July, as I must wait to send home the drawings I have sold in the exhibition, and we shall not close until the 11th of July. Perhaps you will write again and tell me more of your plans, as to the time you will be at Blackpool. I here send you a short account of Blackpool, which my friend at Liverpool has sent me. He has copied it from Gorton's 'Topographical Dictionary.' This description has been written in a very great hurry, but pray excuse it, and believe me to remain

"Yours very sincerely,

"DAVID COX."

NOTE.—The description of Blackpool was copied out by Cox in this letter, and occupied an entire page.

VII.

PROGRESS IN ART AND REMOVAL FROM LONDON.

1840 TO 1841.

I AM now entering on that period in the life of David Cox when it may be said that he attained to the height of his power in technical knowledge and manipulation as a painter in water-colours. After his return to London, in 1827, he soon freed himself from all conventional ideas in his foliage and foregrounds, attaining perfect looseness in the former and a rough, varied surface in the latter. The transparent shadows full of reflected lights, and the dewy sparkle which characterize his landscapes of the middle period, appear to have been produced with the easiest possible sweep and dash of his brush, and this charm is to some extent missed in his earlier works. At the same time he got rid of a somewhat fettered manner, into which he was probably led by the habit of making a great many drawings for young pupils.

I have seen a good many drawings, principally small ones, of the dates between 1820 and 1826, in which there is a good deal of delicate finish, but often the foliage is rather stiff and constrained, and the high lights on the trees are occasionally touched in with body-colour: this method Cox discarded in after years; the lights, if not left, being taken out with the brush or handkerchief. The figures also in the drawings of the early period now referred to, are brighter in the colours of their dress, they have less depth of shadow, and are deficient in the movement and action, which are so admirable in the incidents and figures of his more mature works.

After 1834 and 1835 especially, his exhibited works had a well-marked character and originality of their own, different from his earlier drawings, and very distinctive of Cox's works as compared with those of any other artist. These works of his middle period are clear, fresh, full of play, and delicate in execution; no touch but has its meaning, whilst his choice of subjects, his knowledge of means to produce a beautiful or striking effect, and his power of concentrating the interest, are probably equal to anything in the whole range of landscape art. But his later works, especially those of the last few years, although less defined and looser in the handling, are grander and fuller of a deep feeling for Nature in her most solemn moods and phases. Those exhibited in 1857, 1858, and 1859, above all others, are endowed with a pathos and a power to touch the heart, and awaken the higher sympathies of man, which to kindred minds is altogether irresistible.

He had, however, in this middle period of which I am now treating, nothing to learn, either in composition or in breadth of light and shade. He had, moreover, attained to that rare power retained by him to the last, of investing the simplest subject with a poetic charm which speaks directly to our feelings, because its truth, thoroughly broad and unconventional, has been transmitted through a true artist's mind. For instance, a meadow with a gate and a few trees, a hay-field with a low range of distant hills, or a country lane with cottages, in which most people would see little but what was commonplace, become transformed, by the magic touch of Cox's genius, into a true pastoral poem, simple, yet full of pleasant country life, "nothing consciously sought for, but the nature of the man speaking out in his works." The series of drawings which he made about this period in North and South Wales—the coast near Penmaenmawr, the passes of Nant Frangon and Aber-Glaslyn, the falls of the Llugwy and Ogwen, the Vale and Castle of Conway, the Castles of Carreg-Cennen and Harlech—are rich in subject and beautiful in their treatment and colour. The pastoral scenes too, in which Cox especially excelled, where flocks of sheep are seen *crunching* through turnip fields, or meadows are represented with cows knee-deep in the rich grasses, may be cited as thoroughly characteristic of his best and most frequent work. The same may be said of his often-repeated views of the Ulverstone and Lancaster Sands, his lanes in Warwickshire, and his sketches at Haddon Hall, Bolton Abbey, Barden Tower, and other places in Derbyshire and Yorkshire. These bring at once to the eye and mind not only what is most beautiful in the scenery of our islands, but by the representation of sunshine breaking through the drifting clouds, the movement of the wind bending the boughs of trees, or passing over the long grass, the scenes are clothed with an individual charm and meaning which are altogether the creation of the genius of the artist himself. This ray of genius which had originally fallen on the young Birmingham scene-painter, had been cherished and developed by incessant self-culture, until it shone out well defined and unmistakable in the works of his middle and later period; quite as much in his rapid sketches as in his more finished productions.

The pre-eminence of Cox is at last beginning to be understood and acknowledged; hereafter, I believe, this will be more fully the case even than it is at present. This cannot but exercise a healthy influence on the School of Landscape Art, as his works are so free from trick and false sentiment, and so true to Nature in their broad, simple mode of treatment.

At the risk of repeating what has been to some extent previously expressed, I have felt compelled to offer these remarks, believing as I do, that in insisting on the *truths*

CHAP. VII. 1840–1841. here referred to consists the chief usefulness of bringing prominently before the public an account of the works and art-life of David Cox.

As I intend to describe many of his representative and celebrated drawings in a separate chapter, I shall for the most part postpone until then any detailed account of these works. A chapter will also be devoted to the consideration of his more important works in oil—works which are rivalling in public estimation his finest drawings, and which are realising very large prices. A gentleman, who has lately been purchasing many of Cox's finest oil paintings, and has for many years past been a collector of his drawings, remarked to me the other day that although he often parted with the works of other artists, he never liked to sell anything by David Cox that had once come into his possession, for this simple reason, that although he often got tired of other pictures, he *never tired* of Cox's, but liked them better the more he looked at them.

One of the secrets of the pleasure conveyed by the drawings and sketches of Cox consists, I believe, in the way in which he always introduced his incidents and figures, so naturally, and so appropriate to the place. He never lost an opportunity of making a rapid sketch or memorandum of any groups or figures which struck his fancy and imagination, and these he worked up a little, always adding the right colours as soon as he got home. Thus in a sketch of a village in North Wales, which I have lately seen, an Italian organ-grinder is leading a bear, which is being saluted by the village curs, and gazed at by the wondering natives; the bear is true to Bruin's nature, and the whole is very natural and easy. It impresses you, too, as being a real scene.

I must now proceed to give my readers some account of the remaining years which Cox passed at his residence in Foxley Road. In July, 1840, Cox paid a short visit to Birmingham, and then proceeded to his sister's house, at Sale, near

Manchester. Mr. and Mrs. Roberts were staying at the same time at Blackpool, and he had promised to join them there, with the intention of having some sketching. The following is an extract from a letter written at this time to his son :— CHAP. VII. 1840—1841.

"Sale, July 29th, 1840.

"This is certainly a very pleasant place to live at. The country is country, and the walks quite rural—green lanes and cornfields in great abundance. The land hereabout, and for several miles around, is entirely wheat and other corn, and quantities of vegetables; indeed, the country for six or eight miles is the corn and market garden of Manchester. The scenery for sketching is not very picturesque; but three miles beyond is wood, rather picturesque, and some very extensive views. I have not been to Manchester yet, nor have I a wish, as this place is so delightful. We have the best bread you ever eat, equal to the potatoes; meat and coal cheap—the former sevenpence-halfpenny all joints—coal eleven shillings per ton, and then, to make the comfortable more comfortable, we have plenty of PEAT. I wish you and Fanny could enjoy it with us.

"DAVID COX."

The reference in the above letter to peat is characteristic, as it illustrates the love Cox always felt for the smell of peat, which reminded him of North Wales. While living in the Foxley Road he would occasionally buy turf or peat from the Addington Hills brought to the door by hawkers' carts, and placing a block on the fire, when the blue curling smoke sent out its peaty perfume, he appeared to feel quite happy.

Early in August he went to Blackpool, and was the guest of Mr. and Mrs. Roberts. He complained that he could find nothing there worth painting, and that the scenery in the neighbourhood of Manchester was far prettier. He made two sketches, however, in front of the town with the seashore and some houses, which included a view of the lodgings they

CHAP. VII. 1840—1841.

occupied. He presented these to Mrs. Roberts, and they were afterwards mounted and framed. Blackpool was a very primitive place at that time, and with nothing going on in the way of amusement, so after three days Cox and Mr. Roberts started on a sketching excursion to Dent Dale and other places, which does not appear to have prospered very well, judging from the account which he wrote of it to his son after his return to Sale. This letter, from which the following is an extract, gives an amusing and graphic account of the difficulties artists have to encounter in their sketching expeditions:—

"Sale, August 10th, 1840.

"I returned a day or two since from my excursion. Mr. Roberts and I met at Blackpool as agreed, and started for the long-talked-of Dent Dale. But what a disappointment! I never saw so uninteresting a place for sketching. I was almost miserable to think I had been waiting for my friend a fortnight, and, after travelling nearly one hundred miles from Sale, to meet with nothing but green hills; rivers dried up; trees not larger than our pear-trees; no oak excepting three small ones at the entrance of a very poor, ill-built village. I was out of spirits; I really could not sketch, nor, in fact, was there anything worth going two miles for. I made one coloured sketch in water-colours of some dock leaves. You will wonder I did not go further, but I had no wish to go so far out, and so decided on returning; but, unfortunately, we had promised our friend Birch to wait at Dent, as he had promised to meet us there. But on the Tuesday afternoon a letter came from him to say he was detained on business, and could not leave home. We then immediately returned to Kirby Lonsdale, where I made a sketch. We spent two days there; it rained most of the time, so we made up our minds to go to Hest Bank, on the Lancaster Sands. The inn there was so full of visitors we could not have beds, and again we moved on to Lancaster. There also we were disappointed.

The judges were sitting in assize, and every room at respectable inns was crowded to the roof; so there was no alternative but to take the railroad and get back to Manchester the same day, and Mr. Roberts went to Blackpool to Mrs. R. and the children. I assure you I am greatly put out, as my sketching is done up entirely for the season unless I go to Wales or return to Lancaster Sands as soon as the assizes are over. To Wales it would be nearly one hundred miles, and a great deal by coach; to Lancaster the railroad would take me in three hours. I have promised we will be in Birmingham in a fortnight, when I hope to sit and make a picture or two in oil.

"DAVID COX."

He did not return to Birmingham, except for a few days about the 21st of August, till the latter end of September. However, on 8th of October, 1840, he wrote from thence to his son :—

"I am, thank God, very well, and am happy to say going on well with my oil painting. Mr. Roberts gives me much praise for my late picture, 'A Woody Lane near Hardwicke,' about twenty inches, a tolerable size for me, a young beginner. It is not yet finished; but I myself think it is pretty good.

"DAVID COX."

He always, in his early days of oil-painting, consulted Mr. Roberts as to the mediums to be used, method of putting on the colours, &c., as he thought a good deal of his experience and judgment. When they were in the neighbourhood of Lancaster he made the sketch this year for a picture which he afterwards painted very successfully in oil. The subject chosen was "Market People crossing Ulverstone Sands." On a subsequent occasion, when Cox and Mr. Roberts were staying at the inn at Lancaster, two commercial travellers, overpowered with fatigue (as the weather was very hot), fell asleep after dinner, and Cox, struck with the drollness of the subject, and urged on by his friend, made the two sketches which were sold in 1867, and are now in the possession of Mr. Thrupp. The elder traveller, with the handkerchief over his head, woke up when the sketching was partly finished, and opening one eye, looked out for a minute or two amused at what was going on, and then relapsed into a profound slumber.

Amongst the oil pictures which Cox painted in 1840 was a clever landscape with a waggon on the road, and a peasant crossing a rustic bridge. This was purchased by Mr. E. Bullock, at whose sale, in May, 1870, it produced two hundred and forty-five pounds. Mr. Bullock was one of Cox's earliest patrons for his works in oil; amongst those in his collection was one dated as far back as 1831, the subject, "Carrying Vetches."

In 1840 Cox exhibited at the Water Colour Society's Gallery eighteen drawings, but only ten in 1841. The small number exhibited in the latter year may be accounted for by the fact that he had now begun to devote a good deal of his time to working in oil, and he sent some pictures that year to the British Institution, as well as to Suffolk Street, and he also commenced a picture for the Royal Academy.

He had been thinking for some time of leaving the neighbourhood of London, as already mentioned in the last chapter. His son was now married, and settled as an artist in London, and Cox thought he would certainly be able to take charge of some of his pupils; besides, he had never liked the bustle of London, and this feeling had increased very much as he grew older. He desired also to be nearer to Nature, which he loved so well. Towards the close of 1840, therefore, he determined to look out for a house in the neighbourhood of Birmingham, his native town. There many of his oldest and dearest friends resided, and there he turned with the feelings not unusual to many true-hearted men, who desire to return in the evening of life to that spot which is associated with the bright aspirations of youth, and where their earliest days have been spent. He also had some idea that he might benefit in his practice in oil by painting in the gallery of Mr. Charles Birch, at Harborne, surrounded by the works in oil of many distinguished artists. The following letters, dated the 1st and 12th January, of which I give fac-simile copies at the end of this chapter, and those of the 26th February, and 28th March, 1841, refer to his progress in oil painting, and also to his proposed removal to the neighbourhood of Birmingham:—

CHAP. VII.

1840—1841.

"9, Foxley Road, Kennington Common, London,
February 26th, 1841.

"MY DEAR FRIEND ROBERTS,—Your letter, which contained more than a brother's kindness, I duly received. I have no words to express the gratitude I feel for the assistance you have afforded me in acquiring some knowledge in that delightful branch of the arts—oil painting. So far from being discouraged, I like it better every day, and feel I really now make some progress, though I know I do not paint in that regular way a professional would; I mean I cannot keep the shadowed part of some objects quite free from opaque colour, so that I am obliged to paint it to look transparent. I perceive this in many of the old masters—Claude, for instance. I have improved the small picture of the 'Heath,' but it is not one at all to my mind. It was really very unfinished when I sent it to the Institution, and the directors have therefore done me a kindness. I shall send the 'Heath' and 'Water Mill' to the Suffolk Street Gallery on Monday. I wish you could see them. Your wish to purchase the 'Heath' is very kind, and I estimate your kindness much, but really I cannot consent to your purchasing a picture unseen; and if it should sell I am sure I could paint

CHAP. VII. 1840–1841. something *much better*, and more worthy of your patronage, which will be more agreeable to my feelings. After the Monday I shall commence a picture for the Royal Academy, 26 × 38; there will be just a clear month for me. I have two or three subjects, and I have sent two in a letter by this post to our friend Birch, who I hope will show them to you. I hope to have a letter from you when you have seen them. The third subject is the 'Lane,' with oak-trees, near Coleshill, like the small one I painted for Mrs. Roberts. I have introduced gipsies, &c. My friend Birch has written me a long letter, and mentions a cottage he has seen half-way along the flat to Harborne, but from what I can recollect of it I do not like the situation. I do not see how it will be likely that my good friend can quite fix on a house; it will therefore be as well that I should pay a short visit to Birmingham, for the purpose of walking round with you both to look out for one. However much I may wish to be living near to you, I should have been very sorry to have dropped in on the day of your dinner party, as my enjoyment would have been something like dear Mrs. Roberts's.

"Mrs. Cox desires her kind love to Mrs. Roberts, and joins with me in sincere wishes for your health, happiness, and comfort.

"My dear friend, very faithfully,

"DAVID COX.

"You do not mention the Tots. I hope they are both quite well."

From DAVID COX *to* W. ROBERTS, ESQ.

"9, Foxley Road, Kennington Common, London,
March 28th, 1841.

"MY DEAR FRIEND ROBERTS,—I am much gratified by your very friendly and kind letter. The weather turning out so unfavourable last Sunday afternoon was a great disappointment for me, as it prevented you and Mrs. R. from coming to Harborne. I should have liked much to have spent a few hours with you in talking over matters before I left, and it was my intention at one time to have driven round by your house as I came off to the railroad, but feared you might not be up so early; and it was lucky I did not, as I was only just in time to get seated before we were off. I arrived in town at a quarter past one, found all quite well, and much pleased with the description of my cottage at Harborne. David and Hannah are much pleased with the idea of removing into my house, though not with the thought of our being so far apart. David has given notice to leave his house, and it is my intention to remove to the country at Midsummer, or as soon after as possible. We are busily employed in our plans of what goods to take with us. And here I will presume to encroach on your kindness in allowing me to purchase at your warehouse a few articles of hardware goods, as it will not be advisable to take with us such heavy things as fire-irons, pots, fenders, &c. Your kindness on a former occasion served me very much, but, as I know it must be rather against your rules in business, I am rather reluctant to make the request: and if your partner should make the least objection, I beg you, my dear friend, will not scruple to let me know. I have only my poor thanks to offer you for the kindness in undertaking to speak to Messrs. Pickford respecting the conveyance of goods to Birmingham. Long ere this you will have seen our friend Birch, who would inform you what I thought of my pictures in the Suffolk Gallery. 'They look chalky for want of glazing,' &c., which could not be done, as the day appointed for the purpose of touching, &c., was during my short visit to Birmingham. However, I am prepared for some disappointments, and therefore shall not hurry my present picture to send it to the Royal Academy, having had some teaching since my return, and having several drawings to finish, which have been begun for some weeks. Notwithstanding, I hope to see

CHAP. VII. 1840—1841.

you in town, as you give me hope to expect when the exhibitions are open. I have not seen Cattermole since my return to town, but as soon as I can procure the exact materials for the vehicle he mentioned, I will send it. I hope you will not suppose that I am at all discouraged by my pictures not looking well. On the contrary, I feel the more anxious to follow it up, as I now see more of what I wanted to produce —*richness*. I have done but little to my picture since my return, and, as I do not intend to exhibit it at the Academy, it will be all the better I should take more time; and as I hear of several gentlemen very anxious to see what I have done, I shall have a much better opportunity of showing it to them at my own house or at theirs. I cannot sufficiently return my thanks to dear Mrs. Wilmot for her great kindness in sending such a very bountiful present of biscuits—a hamper sufficient to feed half-a-dozen children for six weeks. David and his wife beg I will give their grateful thanks to Mrs. Edward, and also beg to join my wife in kind love to Mrs. Roberts; and pray give my kind remembrances to them, and tell them they, with the young folks, must come to my cottage and eat raspberries and cream. Indeed, it will give both Mrs. Cox and myself much pleasure to have them in our humble way as often as they possibly can come; and I fully expect you will come and see me, and spend some of your hours with me. Indeed, it will be one of the enjoyments I have calculated on in living in the country. When I left, our friend Birch gave me some expectations he should come up to London on the 3rd of April; if so, I shall have only a few days to wait. I shall impatiently wait the time. If he does not come, pray ask him to write me a letter, and tell me all about the house, if the person is gone out, and whether the repairs are begun. With kind regards to dear Mrs. Roberts, believe me to remain, my dear Friend,

"Yours very sincerely,

"DAVID COX.

"I have a great deal more to say on the subject of my moving, and on the subject of painting, and of the time we may hope to spend together. Pray write me a few lines soon." CHAP. VII. 1840—1841.

The desire to become an oil-painter as well as a water-colour painter, had now taken full possession of Cox's mind, and I think the letter of the 1st of January is especially interesting as showing the energy with which he had taken up this comparatively new branch of art. It appears that Mr. Birch was rather anxious that Cox should confine himself to water-colour painting, as that in which he was so pre-eminent; and he (Mr. Birch) had said to Mr. Roberts that he was incurring great responsibility, in his opinion, by urging their friend to take up oil-painting. Referring to this in his letter, Cox writes, with his usual ardour, "*I will succeed!*"

In the visit which Cox made to Birmingham in March, 1841, he arranged to take a lease of Greenfield House, situated in Greenfield Lane, in the village of Harborne, about two miles from Birmingham, and not far from the residences of his friends Birch and Roberts. The house was an old one, and wanted a good deal doing. The landlord, however, undertook the repairs, and also agreed to put a good-sized bow-window into the principal sitting-room, which would then command a pleasant view of the garden. This was to be all finished before Midsummer, and on the 20th of June, 1848, David Cox and his wife took leave of their relations in Kennington, and accompanied by their trusty servant, Ann Fowler, started by train for Birmingham. They had spent fourteen years in Foxley Road, successful ones on the whole, but Cox felt very happy at the idea of living in the country again, and having more leisure for painting.

They spent the first few days at the house of Mr. Birch, on arriving at Harborne, and then removed into Greenfield

CHAP. VII. 1840–1841. House. I purpose giving a description of their new home in my next chapter.

Cox liked his change of residence very much, and he continued to carry on his labours there for many years with unwearied industry and with increasing success. It may indeed be said with truth that it was only after his removal to Harborne that he attained to the height of his fame as an artist, the feeling and knowledge displayed in his latest works excelling all his earlier efforts.

9 Hoxley Road Kennington Cross [illegible]
London Jany 1st 10[illegible]

My Dear Friend Roberts

A Happy New Year to you and
to Mrs Roberts and the dear Tots, and indeed to
all your family — pray in your next say how
Miss Wilmot is — I believe she is mending
fast. — Mr Lord surprised me at your
kind present of Magnificent Bird in which arrived the
day — for which I return you my best thanks, you are
too kind. Why give yourself so much trouble
I feel greatly obliged for all favours and for the
great interest you take in my welfare and permit
me to assure you that
in oil painting. — and now let me assure you that
whatever my good friend Birch says about your
responsibility — in my succeeding or not you shall
have nothing to answer for. — I will succeed

and am happy to say I am in much better spirits
than when I wrote last — tho' I have given up the
picture I had began and have taken up two smaller
viz. — Lane nr Coleshill line Mr R.. and water mill. I hope
to succeed better as they are much less than the one
I described to you last .33.23.. I am going on now
pretty well... I ought to have continued my practice as
soon as I returned to London.. instead of which I was
six weeks and did not touch my oils. and when I began
it was too large a picture but I hope to finish it at
my leisure it is a pleasing subject but rather cloudy
and perhaps rather dark tho' the Rocks on the right
side are light — but I find the water a very difficult
part to paint. I wish you could see it.

Thanks for your hints about Megilph — but
I have not had occasion ~~to~~ make any yet —
Mrs Cox sends her love to dear Mrs Roberts — with every
kind wish to yourself for health and happiness. for a many
new years — and believe me very truly — yours

David Cox

The subject of my large picture but now given up for the present

4 Hoxley Road Kennington Lane. London Jan 9 1841

My Dear Friend Roberts

I am just returned from taking two small oil pictures to the Institution. One a Heath Scene the other. (I hope you will excuse the liberty I have taken) a Bank with an old Oak Tree — the one I painted for you. I could not finish the Water Mill to my mind and therefore shall finish it at my leisure. Several of my friends were very urgent I should send the Sandy and the Chelsea Pensioners. But I am quite satisfied with sending only two, and I feel certain you would like the Heath Scene pretty much. It was very slight — but if it should be received I shall have an opportunity of doing a little to it. Glazing &c. I think I perfectly understand you with regard to the

Magylph. It certainly works most pleasantly I wish I could have shown you those I have painted I am afraid they are too thin in the mode of painting and several who saw them think them too thick. but I hope to do better and will lead the colour more upon my next — I quite calculate on going out with you some short excursions this summer when I will attempt in oil from nature. indeed our friend Birch wishes me to go and spend three or four months at his house. and I think it not improbable but I may go down in the Spring. to prepare a Still for the country exhibition I wrote to Mr Birch a few weeks ago — to enquire if the little Cottage near his gates was to let — if so I think I should take it and reside there half the year — and then I could have Mrs Cox and the Servant — and should be near both yourself and Mr Birch I think I might do a great deal in painting as I have so many calls — and hinderances. that I really do little or nothing — but to end all this the Cottage

is not to be had.. and I had presumed very much ... in Mr B. gallery. – I am quite happy to hear that Mr Wilmot is so much better pray make my kind remembrances to her. also pray give my kindest respect to Mrs Roberts and say that having finished my pictures I will now turn my thoughts to finishing the two views of Blackheath I will also as soon as possible do something more to the portrait and send all back that you were so good as send for my friends to see. ... Mrs ... sends her love to Mrs Roberts and most sincerely wishes you both health and every happiness to enjoy many new years ...

also remember me to Mr & Mrs Edward and Mrs Wilmot and all & love to the tots. – I have ... ...

[illegible]

HELIOTYPE

now. I must conclude hoping you will write to me again soon. and if you have no particular subject pray write to me as a letter from you is really quite necessary to my Comfort if you see Mr Bush tell [illegible] write very soon. and now God bless you All and believe me very sincerely & truly Yours Cox

[illegible] news none but as I may write again to you soon if I have neglected anything I can remember it in my next. Many thanks for sending to Hardwick. I do not know yet what I may wish to send I have not yet received the Pig Pudding that Mrs Piggott promised me -

VIII.

FIRST YEARS AT HARBORNE.

1841 TO 1844.

GREENFIELD HOUSE, which was destined henceforth to be the home of David Cox, was pleasantly situated in the village of Harborne, about two miles and a-half from Birmingham. It soon became truly a home to him: he had chosen it after many changes and wanderings, and he loved its quiet situation, which contrasted pleasantly with the populous London suburb, Kennington, in which he had passed so many preceding years. With increase of years, his love and preference for the country, as compared with the bustle of cities, took a deeper and firmer hold on his mind. CHAP. VIII. 1841—1844.

His house stood in a lane leading to Harborne Church, beyond which meadows and open country stretched out in the direction of Hagley. There were also many trees and undulating hills on this side, which became a sort of "home preserve" where Cox could always find subjects for sketches near at hand and without fatigue.

Greenfield was rather an old-fashioned place when he went to live there. From a desire to be very quiet and retired, he kept the front door facing the road always fastened up, and all comers entered by the garden-door at the back—the one shown in the view of the house given in the book. All this is altered now, and a street divides the garden. On the ground-floor was the parlour or dining-room, with the bow-

CHAP. VIII. 1841—1844. window mentioned in the last chapter, the other two windows in that room having been converted into blanks. On the other side of the passage was a small smoke-room, a front and back kitchen; and up-stairs there were two or three bed-rooms, and a long room used as a studio. This was lighted by a skylight and by one window facing the north. The approach to the studio was by a back staircase leading out of the kitchen. In this studio Cox kept a great many portfolios full of old sketches and studies of various kinds. His easel was a large mahogany one, rather solid, and strongly constructed, and one or two simple tables and old chairs completed the furniture. No bric-à-brac or elaborate carvings of any kind. In the winter this studio was very cold. He therefore at that time of year generally transferred his easel and painting apparatus to the dining-room. The house also was very simply furnished, but in his dining-room he had several oil-pictures on the walls. Two of these were by Anthony, one of them being a representation of "Ennis Cathedral;" a large unfinished painting by J. W. Müller, a "Mill and Salmon Trap," and "An Interior of a Welsh Cottage;" also an early landscape, by R. Lee; a head of St. Cecilia—being a present from Mr. Hollingsworth—a portrait of a Persian prince (I have not been able to ascertain the name of the artist who painted the two last), and several of his own works in oil, some being rather unfinished. The interior by Müller was a very picturesque one of a cottage in the Lledr valley, which Cox afterwards painted himself.

The garden was a large one surrounded with trees, and he took great interest in it, often working there himself. He planted a good many young forest trees, which he preferred to any others. These grew well and made the place rather bushy, but they have since been cut down. There was also an avenue of filberts and nut-trees in the garden, and a large willow-bush, of which Cox was immensely proud, having been originally a cutting from *the* willow which grew over Napoleon's tomb at St. Helena. A friend going to India sent him two or three cuttings of that willow, and one of these grew and had thriven well under his constant care. CHAP. VIII. 1841—1844.

Cox cultivated broad-leaved plants in his garden, such as rhubarb and different kinds of docks; also Scotch thistles, of which, as well as of hollyhocks, he was especially fond. He had always a beautiful variety of hollyhocks, and one year he made a study of them in blossom, which I have seen. It is very successful and charming in colour, showing how well flowers may be treated *en masse* in water colours, with a full-flowing brush, when handled by a master. He had many of the old-fashioned herbaceous and cottage-garden flowers also, and a variety of tulips, which last he was fond of exchanging with his friends.

On arriving in Birmingham, before going to Mr. Birch's house, where they were invited to spend a few days whilst their furniture was being arranged, Mr. and Mrs. Cox drove direct to Greenfield House. Cox was eager to show the house he had taken to his wife, and to set to work immediately the trusty carpenter, Lewis, who had accompanied him down from London.

In his first letter to his son he told him how much pleased they were with the cheerful appearance of the large old-fashioned kitchen, and especially with his painting-room, although it had not yet been papered. One of the recommendations of the kitchen which he remarked upon, was that there were "plenty of hooks on which to hang up bacon and hams." One of the inmates of the house was a cat, a great favourite, but they kept no dog, for the reason, Cox said, that they liked to be very quiet and undisturbed. They had several old congenial friends living in the neighbourhood; to be near them had been one of the inducements to remove to Harborne and their society, and their sympathy in his work was a source of constant interest and pleasure. Cox's wants were few and simple; his ambition took no flight beyond the

CHAP. VIII. 1841–1844. constant aim of his life, namely, to excel in the practice of his art. The inexhaustible wealth of nature, his genius and the love of his family and friends sufficed to fill his cup with more happiness than is allotted to most men; even when his steps were fast approaching that goal to which all human efforts tend, he was still serene and generally cheerful. Among the first things to which Cox turned his attention after he and Mrs. Cox had got comfortably settled in their new home, was to prepare some work to be sent off to the Manchester Exhibition. The most important of these were his three drawings of the interior of Hardwick Hall, which were afterwards purchased by Mr. Bullock. He also began to sketch in the green lanes and neighbouring fields, which—simple subjects as they were—treated after his swift and peculiar manner, and enriched with foreground plants and the broad shadows he loved, became delightful pictures of English midland scenery.

Although full of years when he came to Harborne, Cox was yet in the full maturity of his powers, in which for many years there was no appearance of failing. His works, I think, prove that it was even rather the other way, and his medical attendant, Mr. Bindley, has told me that when in good spirits Cox used sometimes to exclaim that he felt still quite young. After they were settled at Greenfield House, Mrs. Cox again resumed the long-established practice of reading out loud to her husband, whilst he painted, articles from newspapers and occasionally from books. He had ceased, as I have already mentioned, to take much interest in politics; indeed I do not find that he had taken any active part in them since he was living at Hereford, but the *Examiner*, which he took in, was still favourite reading with him, for he never quitted the "liberal camp," but afterwards he took in the *Illustrated London News* instead.

Mrs. Cox was now rather advanced in years, and far from strong. Mrs. Roberts, who lived near her at Metchly, relates what a kind old lady she was. She often went to see her, and on those occasions Mrs. Cox was very glad of her arm to walk round the garden. Cox would then sometimes ask his wife to sit down or stand as a model for a figure to be introduced into one of his pictures, and for this purpose he would throw a shawl or a cloak round her so as to obtain the form and mass of colour and shadow which he required. CHAP. VIII. 1841—1844.

She had been conversant with art all her life, and Cox had a high opinion of her judgment. He used always to show her his work in progress, and, after she had passed her remarks on it, he would say, "Oh, Mary, you are *too hard* on me; no one else criticizes my pictures as you do." "Yes," she replied, "I always tell you of your faults, and the whole truth to the best of my judgment, which others do not like to do if unfavourable." He never left home, even to go into Birmingham, without first going to take leave of his wife; and, on her side, she would exert herself to get her household duties all finished whilst he was out, so that she might be quite at leisure to read to him and companionise him when he returned. A lady, who knew Mrs. Cox, has mentioned to me that she used often to receive letters from her at the time of the London exhibitions containing very clever criticisms on the pictures, and also that Cox himself was never quite satisfied with any picture he had painted until his wife had approved of it. When he had got his drawings ready to send up to the Water Colour Exhibition, he used to show them to Mr. Roberts and other friends, and tell them the prices he was going to put on them. These were often much below their value, but it was generally with much difficulty that he was persuaded to put an increased price on them. Mr. William Holmes, of Birmingham, who sold many of Cox's drawings and pictures after he came to live at Greenfield House, however, says that Cox was not unconscious of the value of his works, and that he was often rather reluctant to part with them, especially in later years, as he wished to

CHAP. VIII. 1841–1844. bequeath some of the best to his son. Many times he has said to Mr. Holmes, "Oh, I wish they would not want all my drawings; I should much rather keep them." On one occasion, after looking over a portfolio of drawings and sketches in the studio at Greenfield, Mr. Holmes picked out five or six, and said, "Pray, Mr. Cox, will you name a price for these? I should so much like to buy them." He replied, "I had rather not part with them;" but shortly, selecting two out of the lot, he added, "I should like to present you with these two, if you will accept of them, instead of selling you the others, which I should prefer to keep." This reminds me of another anecdote showing the same simple-hearted kindness. An artist in Birmingham had asked Cox to paint an oil picture for him. The price was fixed at ten pounds; it was a very successful work, but, when the purchaser put down the two notes to pay for it, Cox said, "I think I have charged you too much; you must take back a sovereign," which being declined on the ground that the picture was worth much more, Cox insisted, and put the sovereign into the artist's waistcoat pocket. Such facts as these tend to disprove an assertion which has been made, and for which I believe there is no just ground, that Cox was very fond of money.

After he got matters somewhat straight at Greenfield House, he commenced painting in oil very assiduously. He wrote, on the 5th of July, to his son, "Lewis, the carpenter, is making my easel." On the 5th of August, 1841, Mrs. Cox writes to her son, "Your dear father is getting on with his large painting of 'The Sands' to his satisfaction—it is the size of the old 'Cader Idris'—and is having the old frame regilt for it to exhibit at the Birmingham Exhibition."

In the middle of September of this year he started, with Mr. Birch and another friend, on a sketching expedition to Bolton Abbey. Some account of this is given in the following extract from a letter to his son:—

"Otley, Yorkshire, September 17th, 1841. CHAP. VIII. 1841—1844.

"We arrived at this very beautiful country yesterday at six o'clock, all quite well, and, whilst dinner was getting ready, we strolled out, and before breakfast this morning I made several small sketches. We are now about to start for Bolton Abbey, twelve miles. We have a most beautiful morning and fine scenery, which gives all three most excellent spirits, and the change of air very great appetites. I expect we shall remain at Bolton until Tuesday or Wednesday, when Mr. Birch and myself shall most likely go on our way for Manchester.

"DAVID COX."

Directly after he returned home he recommenced painting in oil. At this time he did not possess any painting by Müller, and we shall see in the following letter how much he desired to possess one of Müller's works to look at, and how much he admired them. It is written to his son.

"Greenfield House, October 15th, 1841.

"If you can make it *convenient* to call on Mr. Rought and remind him, he said he would procure me a picture by Müller before he left for Egypt. I should certainly *wish and like* to have one, if he (Mr. Rought) can oblige me, and take it out in drawings. I very much admire Mr. Müller's style, it is quite to my feeling, both in breadth and colour. I should much prefer a scene with some trees and water, with a distance seen, &c. Perhaps Mr. Rought may have one by him which he would have no objection to let me have. Please try to go to him *as soon as you can*. I have this day began oil-painting again, so hope to paint a few pictures which have been ordered.

"DAVID COX."

The following letters from Cox and his wife, to their son,

CHAP. VIII. 1841—1844. also refer to oil-painting, and to a picture by Müller which he had just obtained.

From MRS. COX *to her* SON.

"Greenfield House, October 24th, 1841.

"I am glad to hear my dear David spoke of painting. I hope in seven weeks on Tuesday to show him a small painting by Müller, his father has got by exchange for drawings. It is quite David's subject—the figures are clumsy, but the background and colouring are beautiful. I think you will like to copy it. Your father has three pictures in hand, of middle size, of good *promise*. The Gallery (in Birmingham) will be closed when you come, but the best pictures, except those you have seen in London, have been purchased by friends, and you will see them."

From DAVID COX *to his* SON.

"Greenfield House, October 24th, 1841.

"I believe I may say we are all very happy. I, at least, can answer for myself. I like my painting, too, very much, and I hope it may please God to give me health to practise for a few years to enable me to enjoy the practice.

"Your mother has told you that I have purchased a small picture by Müller, but *I do not wish to prevent* your calling again on Mr. Rought, as I still wish him to send me one by Müller; nor do I wish you to tell him that I have one, as that might prevent his sending. I have several pictures in hand, and hope to finish one or two soon, as Mr. Darby is anxious to possess one. I have also several to paint for Mr. Roberts, but I am particular what I let go out of my hands.

"DAVID COX."

On the 31st December, 1841, he again writes to his son:—

"I have finished Mr. Darby's picture, and have begun

another small one for him. I have also *dead coloured* one, about two feet, the best thing I have ever made." CHAP. VIII. 1841—1844.

Soon after Cox had got settled at Greenfield House, he wrote to his son to send him from London a water-colour sketch, which he had left there, of Wyndcliff, near Chepstow, as he intended painting a large oil picture of it for the Birmingham Exhibition. It did not, however, progress very fast, and was not finished by the end of the year. On the 22nd of January, 1842, he thus writes to his son :—

"The gentleman who purchased my 'Lancaster Sands,' has given me permission to exhibit it at Suffolk Street, and I am endeavouring to finish the 'Wyndcliff,' to send with it.

"D. Cox."

After Cox had sent one of these pictures to London for the Suffolk Street Exhibition, he began to wish he had retained it in Birmingham, the more so as the last he had sent there had not been well hung. The following extract from a letter from Mrs. Cox to her son refers to this subject :—

"Greenfield House, February 14th, 1842.

"Your father regrets sending his picture, and wishes he could see it with others to judge for himself, and is in doubt if he will send to the Academy. Mr. Birch is sorry it should be *scandalized;* he is convinced it is a good picture, and persuaded him not to send another picture."

On the 31st March, 1842, Cox writes to his son :—

"I am gratefully obliged for your letter, with an account of the Suffolk Street Gallery. I find it will not do to send pictures to the 'British Artists' any more."

On the 18th April, 1842, Mrs. Cox again writes to her son :—

CHAP. VIII. 1841—1844.

"Your father spent the day at Mrs. Roberts's yesterday to meet a gentleman from Worcester, to whom he is giving lessons, and he went again this morning before breakfast to give him another lesson before he returns to Worcester."

The gentleman referred to was Mr. Taunton, a solicitor at Worcester, who had great admiration for Cox and love for art. Although Cox had determined not to give any more lessons after he left London, he was persuaded to make an exception in favour of Mr. Taunton, and these he continued for some years. In April of that year Cox went up to London as usual to stay with his son and arrange his drawings for the Water Colour Exhibition. He exhibited eighteen drawings this year in Pall Mall. The following were the most important:—"Lancaster," "Distant View of Kenilworth Castle," "The Old Holyhead Road near Penmachno," "Twilight," "Bolsover Castle," and "Powis Castle." Whilst staying on this visit in London he wrote as follows to his wife:—

"June 19th, 1842.

"Oh, how much I should like to take you into Wales! I hope to do so yet. It is the pleasantest country to go to for quiet and grand scenery; but it is in the truly rural simple state of nature—that is one of the great delights of going there, not forgetting the dear PEAT."

And again, on the 3rd of July, just before leaving London, he writes to his wife:—

"I have agreed to go with Mr. Roberts into Yorkshire—Bolton Bridge. We shall be absent about nine days or a fortnight."

This time Cox took a portable easel and materials for painting in oil to Yorkshire, and worked from nature in oils, besides making many sketches in water-colours. Some of the subjects painted on this occasion were—"On the Wharf, near Bolton Abbey;" "Wharton Hall, Yorkshire," "Sherwood Forest," "Bolsover Castle," &c.

He gives the following account in a letter to his son:—

"Bolton Bridge, July 17th, 1842.

"We arrived here last Thursday. We work hard, and have had five days in the last week most excellent weather for our pursuits. I have been at work in oil, and Mr. Roberts tells me I have succeeded extremely well. I feel myself that what I have done is much better than anything I ever made yet, and will assist me very much in making a picture. Indeed, I feel I know more about it than I should have done in three years' painting in a room, as I have had a subject before me which has assisted me in the knowledge when to use the transparent and half-transparent colours when required."

Towards the end of July Cox returned home, and he then asked his son to accompany him to North Wales, as he said that Wales, besides being nearer home, afforded him "more matter" than any other place; besides, he was anxious to keep up his practice from nature in oils, as he considered he had got quite a start, and been really successful with his sketches in that medium in Yorkshire.

They started from Birmingham about the middle of August, halted for a day or two at Rhyl, and were at Conway on the 20th August, on their way to Bettws-y-Coed. Cox made several sketches in Wales, and returned to Greenfield House on the 27th August. The weather had been unusually hot, and this helped to turn their steps homewards sooner than they had intended. On the 4th September he again left home for Kenilworth, where he passed a fortnight hard at work. On the 5th he writes to his wife: "I made one sketch on my way here (Kenilworth), and have made two since

CHAP. VIII. 1841—1844. dinner." He was exceedingly fond of Kenilworth, and often took an opportunity of going there for a few days. Whilst staying there this time he wrote a note of congratulation to a little girl on her birthday, which was accompanied by two sweet little sketches in water-colours as a present—one of a blacksmith's forge, and one of the Castle, which I have seen, thus showing his ever-ready wish to give pleasure to children.

Cox now settled down to his autumn work at home, making occasionally short excursions to sketch in the neighbourhood of Birmingham, when the weather permitted. Thus I find as late as the 2nd November, it is recorded that he went to Bromsgrove by railroad to sketch a water-mill, accompanied by Mr. Birch and by Mr. Roberts. After a hard day's work he felt great relief to his spirits in the occasional society of these friends, who lived very near. He used often to stroll in and spend an hour or two with one or the other in their gardens, smoking a cigar; or, if in winter, by their firesides, talking over the wide domain of art, an inexhaustible topic of interest; or planning future excursions for sketching and painting. The following letter about practice, in charcoal, and colours, appears to have been written to his son in consequence partly of Mr. Norman Wilkinson having written to Cox that he thought his son's recent drawings "were more black, but had less force from contrast;" hence the advice as to the use of colours and method of leaving lights :—

To his SON.

"Greenfield House, Harborne, November 18th, 1842.

"Yesterday was so fine I went to Birmingham, and afterwards called and dined with my good friend Roberts. I got home by five to tea, and worked at a coloured drawing by lamplight. I find that what I do by lamplight in general turns out better by daylight than what I do by daylight. I am speaking now more of the effect, but I have been very lucky in my colouring. I have in many of my late studies been most fortunate in mountainous scenes; they certainly afford scope for more effect, and sentiment in the effect; and I have been three nights in studying one subject. In a short time I may alter my feeling, and be altogether as much pleased with very extensive views, as a short time ago I was for lane scenes. All are good, but each requires a good deal of thought. Try by lamplight a subject in charcoal, and don't be afraid of darks, and work the subject throughout with charcoal in the darks, middle tint and half, and with some very spirited touches in parts to give a marking. When you have done all this, have your colours quite soft, and colour upon the charcoal. Get all the depth of the charcoal, and be not afraid of the colour.

"When you look at it by daylight, and clean it with bread, you will find a number of light parts which have been left when the colour would not exactly adhere over the charcoal. For a distant mountain I have used cobalt and vermilion, and in the greyer part I mix a little lake and a small quantity of yellow ochre with the cobalt. In the middle distance I work each part separately, in fact, something like mosaic work. The foreground the same, taking care to leave the reflected lights clear for a distant cool or bluish tint. I use very similar colours for the middle distance as for the three (query, foreground), for green, indigo, lake, and gamboge, with its varieties; occasionally for the rocks, cobalt, vermilion, and yellow ochre, and sometimes lake instead of the vermilion. In the foreground I use indigo and van-brown, and indigo and brown-pink. Sometimes add sepia to the indigo and brown-pink. I use for the grey in the sky cobalt and vermilion, and for the more neutral, grey, cobalt, and light red.

"DAVID COX."

He also mentioned at this time that he was hard at work on an oil picture of Harlech Castle.

Early in the year 1843 Cox was getting forward with a

large picture of the outskirts of a forest, which he was thinking of sending to the Academy, but for some reason he does not appear to have done so. In the spring of this year he exhibited fifteen drawings at the Water Colour Society:— "Sands at Rhyl," "Penmawr Mawr," "Cader Idris," "Stubble Field, with Gleaners," and "Bolsover Castle," were some of the most important.

Mr. Roberts was thinking about this time of making a tour in North Wales with his family, and Cox not only drew for his friend a coloured map, or plan of the country, which I have seen, with all the roads, towns, villages, waterfalls, watermills, and the places of interest marked on it, with remarks as to which was the most beautiful, but he also made a list of all the distances, and of the probable cost of travelling from place to place. The tour proposed was to Bala, Dolgelly, Barmouth, Machynlleth, Towyn, Aberdovy, Aberystwith, Beddgelert, Capel Curig, &c., including a visit to all the lakes and waterfalls. A more interesting document it is difficult to imagine.

In the summer of 1843 Cox had rather a serious attack of illness. This left him less strong than usual, and in the autumn he went to stay at Sale, near Manchester, with his sister, in order to recruit, and make sketches in different parts of Lancashire. The following letter to Mr. Roberts, whilst on this visit, appears to have been written when he was rather out of spirits:—

"TO WILLIAM ROBERTS, ESQ.

"Sale, near Manchester, October 12th, 1843.

"MY DEAR FRIEND ROBERTS,—I began writing to you yesterday, but felt so poorly I gave up the idea; but when I read your very kind letter it roused me again, and I cannot help expressing the great pleasure it gave me, and telling you how much I feel indebted for your kindness in writing and thinking of me. The information you received of the death of your old master, together with the loss of two other dear friends, all within a very few weeks, must have been a shock indeed. These events, I have no doubt, are ordered for our good, to warn us of the precarious nature of our poor frames. Since my little illness at Greenfield I have not been the same as I used. I feel feeble, and all at once get very old. Indeed, I have been but poorly ever since I have been here, and the weather has been so rainy and unfavourable for going out. Only once I have gone out sketching, and was then driven back by rain; but thanks to my dear sister's good nursing, and a little medicine, I feel much better this morning.

"I have visited Manchester twice since I came, one day to the exhibition, which is a very poor one—not any picture as a striking feature. Their Art Union took place last week; they had upwards of £700, £100 of which was laid out in a print, leaving £600 for the lottery; there was besides about £600 made in purchases. Times have been bad, or it was expected there would have been a much larger sum subscribed. I wish I had sent a picture here; it is really one of the most spirited places I ever knew. I have not been to Liverpool, nor do I think of going now, though I am told their exhibition is a very good one. I must think of returning about Tuesday next, or Wednesday at the latest, when I hope to find you and dear Mrs. R. and the two dear little girls all quite well. I have not said anything to Mrs. Cox about my being poorly—as it has not been anything serious—to alarm her, and I believe my spirits have been very low. I have not been able to go out, nor to do much painting; all tends to make me *down*.

"Pray, my dear friend, believe me, ever faithfully,

"DAVID COX.

"P.S.—I will endeavour to write to Mr. Birch; but if he is in London it will not meet him, so must write to my wife. Direct to me as before."

CHAP. VIII. 1841—1844.

In 1843 Mr. Charles Birch received a letter from J. W. Müller, which is still preserved; it contains a message for Cox which is interesting, as it shows the kindly feeling which was still subsisting between these two artists. Müller wrote—"Give my kind regards to Mr. David Cox, and tell him if he will call on me I shall be very glad to show him my 'Lycia' and my sketches." Two years after this Müller died.

It is a matter of great regret to me that since Mr. Birch's death any letters or papers that he may once have possessed relating to art and to his friend, David Cox, have been either lost or dispersed. There were probably many that might have proved of interest in this memoir. In 1843 Cox painted more oil-pictures, I believe, than in any preceding year; indeed, he was already beginning to like oils better than water-colour, a fact which he expressed in a subsequent letter. One of his best works in oil this year, and which produced at Mr. Gillott's sale nine hundred guineas, was called "Washing Day," and represented two women at a pool of water, and a cottage in the distance with clothes hanging out to dry. It was painted for Mr. Froggett. Another beautiful oil-picture was painted this year for Mr. W. Roberts, "Outskirts of a Wood, with Gipsies." The scenery represented was that of Sherwood Forest, sketched some years before, and this picture was so much admired that Cox subsequently repeated it many times.

Cox sent eleven drawings to the Water Colour Exhibition in the spring of 1844; the following were the most important:—"Scene in Bolton Park, Yorkshire;" "A Mill near Bromsgrove;" "Summons to the Noonday Meal, North Wales," a girl blowing a cow-horn in the foreground, and two or three other subjects in North Wales.

The following extracts from letters written early in 1844 will, I think, be read with interest:—

"*From* MRS. COX *to her* SON'S WIFE.

"Greenfield House, February 8th, 1844.

"David will remember the picture he persuaded his father to alter—the subject, 'Carreg-Cennen Castle;' he will be glad to learn that it is considered by himself and friends the best subject and work he has done yet. It is entirely repainted, and he hopes to finish it this week. We have received a long letter, and a very kind one, from Norman Wilkinson; he is very indignant with the hanging committee for not receiving your father's picture, especially as they have rejected one of Smyth's. He tells us also that Lewis has sent a picture of Grand Cairo."

The above picture referred to as being rejected was a small one which Cox had sent to the British Institution, Pall Mall, and was a beautiful little work, the subject, "Going to the Hayfield." He received it back on the 12th February, and I do not find that he sent many pictures there afterwards. On the 14th March, 1844, he wrote to his son:—

"I begin to fear I shall not have so much to exhibit in large drawings as I expected. I get on but slowly. I have had one subject which has been a *teaser* to me, and I don't know whether I shall not give it up yet. I begin to feel quite furious, and, therefore, hope to succeed much better."

And again Mrs. Cox writes, March 18th, 1844, to her son:—

"Mr. Birch did not return until Saturday evening. He brings a bad account of the gallery pictures except Danby's and Webster's. He thinks the former very grand. He says your father's 'Going to the Hayfield' would have been a little gem amongst them. Your father's *furiousness* ended in washing out part of a large subject, 'The Wyndcliffs,'

CHAP. VIII. 1841—1844. (junction of the Wye and Severn), which we all thought very promising. He has taken up the *rich* oil sketch in Bolton Park which you so much admired, and Mr. Birch says if he finishes it as well as he has began, he saw no drawing in London that equals it. He has also finished the 'Bala Lake,' which was begun for last year, and which you, David, saw. He has taken out the cows and put in a bolder foreground, and that is all that is done at present."

The drawing referred to in the foregoing letter as having been partly spunged out became afterwards one of his most noted works, and was exhibited at the Manchester Art Treasures Exhibition in 1857, and at the Great Exhibition in London, 1862.

Mrs. Cox again writes to her son about the progress of her husband's work:—

"Greenfield House, March 25th, 1844.

"I trust your father will return in good spirits, for with him much depends on his spirits. Both Birch and Roberts think so highly of his works that he can't want encouragements; but if they suggest the slightest alteration, he begins to sponge away and then fancies he has destroyed the spirit. However, he has three good-sized ones (drawings) rich in colour, that I should hope are so forward as to be out of danger; one from the Bolton oil sketch, 'Bala Lake,' and 'The Mountain Path;' but your letter so animated him, that he seems determined at present to try to finish the 'Carreg-Cennen,' which is considered the finest subject and best work of anything he has attempted in oil, and was put by to be finished at leisure; but your description of what is done has given him much encouragement."

On the 3rd of April Cox sent off two pictures in oil for the Royal Academy to the care of Ford. The subjects were

"Carreg-Cennen," and a small one of "Going to the Hay-field." I believe the former is now in Miss Phipson's collection at Edgbaston. Shortly after that he went up to London, as usual, to stay with his son at Brixton, to see the exhibitions, and finish his drawings for the Water Colour Society. Cattermole's celebrated drawing of the "Battle of the Bridge" was exhibited there this year; that is the one referred to in the following letter to his friend Roberts:— CHAP. VIII. 1841—1844.

"Streatham Place, Brixton Hill, London,
April 25th, 1844.

"Your letter gave me very great pleasure to learn that you are all well. I shall be very glad when the time arrives for my return; the bustle here is too much for me. I hope I may not have created too great expectation with regard to Cattermole's drawing, and have, therefore, sent you a rough sketch from recollection. It gives but a poor idea of the beautiful work and drawing. This morning I took David to see Turner's picture at Mr. Griffith's, also several of Cattermole's. I told Mr. Griffith I hoped you would be in town, and that you should go and see them. He was expecting Mr. Gibbons this day. I will go the first opportunity. I have seen a box which was made at Messrs. Robson and Miller's, Long Acre, with moist colours in *bottles*, and India-rubber stoppers. We will go and select one when you come. Please, both you and Mrs. Roberts, accept sincere thanks for kind attentions to my dear wife. I must conclude, for the post leaves Brixton Hill at four o'clock.

"Yours ever faithfully,
"DAVID COX."

N.B.—This letter accompanied the drawing from memory, by David Cox, after the one by Cattermole, "Battle of the Bridge," sold at Mr. Roberts's sale for thirty-two guineas.

He soon returned home, and towards the end of June he

CHAP. VIII. 1841—1844.

set out on a journey to North Wales, in company with a young friend, Mr. Harry Johnson, an artist who has since attained to considerable eminence. Johnson had worked in Müller's studio, and was a great favourite with Cox. On this occasion they became more fully acquainted with the fine scenery of the Vale of Clwyd, and Cox made sketches for the beautiful pictures he afterwards painted of this subject. After visiting Ruthin, Denbigh, St. Asaph, and Conway, and sketching in all these parts, he proceeded to Bettws-y-Coed. Mr. David Cox, junior, has in his possession two of his father's large sketches, rather slight, of the "River Conway, from Llanyfrwd." They show the rapidity of Cox's work from nature at this time, and are both dated the 2nd July, 1844. The following letter, dated the 1st of July, gives some account of this journey into North Wales:—

"Ruthin, half-past six, morning,
July 1st, 1844.

"MY DEAR FRIEND ROBERTS,—I write a few lines to tell you that I and my fellow-traveller are quite well and in high spirits. We reached this place on Saturday evening about eight. We had one hour in Chester and I made one sketch, and a second I made on my reaching this place. Yesterday morning to church; after dinner a long walk. This morning we are going out to make two little hand-book bits in the town; then breakfast, after which a car to Denbigh. In the afternoon to Abergele, where we most likely shall sleep, and to-morrow to Conway, and there spend Wednesday and Thursday. So if you write a line by return of post just to say how you all are, and, if you please, tell me how my folks are getting on at *my mansion*, you will greatly oblige. The weather is, as usual, delightfully fine, and the atmosphere very clear. I shall not go to Rhyl, so shall not see Mrs. Roberts. My young friend Johnson is a very agreeable travelling companion; he begs to send his kind regards to you. I will expect a line from you directed for me, Post Office, Conway, North Wales.

"Ever yours faithfully,

"DAVID COX.

"Eight o'clock. Just returned from making two sketches, one of them a mill. Now to breakfast, and then off to Denbigh."

I also give on the next page a facsimile of a letter written ten days afterwards, containing a graphic sketch of the little Welsh inn where Cox and his young friend were staying in order to sketch the beautiful scenery of this part of Carnarvonshire. The original is firmly outlined in black chalk, with just a wash or two of colour. It is very rough, but it breathes the atmosphere of North Wales most unmistakably. The "Mill, near Conway," which is referred to in this letter, was exhibited the next year in London, as also "Cottages in Cheshire," sketched during this trip.

Cox and his companion stayed at Llanbeder a week, and then proceeded to Bettws-y-Coed, where he spent between a fortnight and three weeks at the Royal Oak, and made good use of his time. His visit to Bettws impressed him very much, so much so that from this time forth he was never happy unless he paid an annual visit to that favourite spot. He also formed the project of purchasing a freehold cottage there. Cox arrived at his home in Harborne at the end of July, having, as he said, exceedingly enjoyed the whole of this trip. I must remark here that when out on a sketching excursion, Cox by no means confined his work to grand subjects, such as mountains, moors, and rocky streams. He was very fond of sketching old houses, picturesque bits of street architecture, and interiors of Welsh cottages. Quaint figures in the costume of Wales were also often jotted down in his pocket sketch-book.

CHAP. VIII. 1841—1844.

I have seen several drawings by him of curious Welsh kitchens, with the broad, open fireplace, clothes hanging from the walls, three-legged stools, and marvellously old dressers. Streets in Conway, too, with gabled houses, dating back almost to the time of King Edward III., and figures, unmistakably Welsh in their costume and gait, walking along the causeway.

HELIOTYPE

Tynllan Llanbedr near Conway

My Dear Friend Roberts. I trouble you with a line to say we moved from Conway yesterday to this (the above inn) and as we are in the immediate neighbourhood of [illegible] [illegible] [illegible] [illegible] scenery in other respects very beautiful. ~~so that~~ we shall most likely stay here a week and therefore if you have not written please direct as above. Our accomodation is very limited as you may suppose from the outward appearance of the house. we [illegible] with breakfast and at tea but I am afraid dinner will be but so so. however we will make the best of it and the scenery will do the rest. I think we may go to [illegible] in the course of next week. and if you have written ~~to~~ already [illegible] [illegible] [illegible] as soon as I can. I will conclude [illegible] [illegible] [illegible] and a request that you will write soon

ever Yours David Cox

[illegible] steel pen

HELIOTYPE.

IX.

LIFE AT HARBORNE TILL DEATH OF HIS WIFE.

1844 TO 1846.

COX did not remain long at Harborne after his return from North Wales, but set off again on a painting expedition at the beginning of September. This time he bent his steps to the Devonshire Arms, near Bolton Abbey, where his companions were Mr. Roberts and some other friends, all fond of art. He wrote as follows from this place on the 5th of September, 1844, to his son :— CHAP. IX. 1844—1846.

"MY DEAR DAVID,—Our party here seem all to enjoy themselves very much, but to-morrow three are to leave for Malham, and on Saturday Mr. Roberts, Mr. Spiers, and myself are to leave for Knaresborough. When we have been there a day or two we shall decide upon our further move. The weather has been most delightful, and we work until six and seven in the evening from nature. I am sorry to say I cannot please myself with my oils, but have been looking over one of our party, and I have gained a good deal of the practical knowledge, and now I must put it into practice.

"*Saturday, September 7th.*—We left Bolton Bridge yesterday, and arrived at this place (Knaresborough) safe at seven at night. I went out and made a chalk sketch, and this morning another. I think it will afford several good subjects. We think of remaining here until Wednesday next.

"DAVID COX."

CHAP. IX.

1844—1846.

The large drawing of Knaresborough Castle exhibited in London in 1845 was the result of this expedition, and several other views in the north of England. The excursion to Yorkshire referred to in the preceding letters was much enjoyed, I have heard, by all parties. The plan at Bolton was to engage boys to carry out their painting traps after breakfast, when each went his separate way, to meet again for the mid-day lunch at some place previously agreed upon. In the evening, when congregated in the parlour at the Devonshire Arms after the day's work was done, they compared and criticized each other's work. On one of these occasions Nesfield the artist, who was one of the party, felt so dissatisfied with his own performance that he crumpled it up in his hand and threw it towards the fire. Cox, who was present, started up exclaiming that it was a really fine work, and that he would rescue it, which he did. After carefully damping the drawing and getting out all the creases, it was mounted, and eventually Cox gave it to Mr. Roberts. It was framed and hung up in Mr. Roberts's house, and at the sale after his death it was disposed of under the title of "A Landscape (by Nesfield) near Bolton Abbey."

After Cox's return from Yorkshire in September, 1844, he set to work again immediately at his oil-paintings. The following letter, written to his son, refers to his projected work:—

"Greenfield House, October 5th, 1844.

"I have received my unsold drawings from Mr. Foord, with the exception of the 'Summons to the Noonday Meal,' which he understood was intended for you; but as I think of doing something from it for next year, I will write for him to send it down to me. What subject for an oil-picture shall I think of for the Institution? Tell me, and for the Royal Academy also. I have one subject which I think good, Knaresborough Castle; but I have not yet studied for an effect. Mr. Birch wants me to begin a large picture from the old drawing of Cader Idris. Mr. Roberts wishes me to make one from Knaresborough. The worst is, I cannot finish. By-the-bye, I am told my 'Carreg-Cennen' looks very well in our exhibition, and is thought the best landscape there; it is on the line."

Mrs. Cox wrote to her son as follows from Harborne on the 9th of October, 1844:—

"Your father can't make up his mind about going to London. He is finishing the 'Calais Pier,' and wants to see the sea. He talks of going to Liverpool. He has sold in that exhibition a small oil-painting, 'Young Anglers,' for £20 the first week."

There is no doubt that Cox used to feel at this time very sensitive about the position his oil-pictures would take in the estimation of the public; and whenever he sent off a work he was nervous until he had heard how it looked when hung in juxtaposition with other pictures. Many were put away in the cupboard under his studio staircase, as he would only send out those with which he was satisfied.

The following are extracts from letters written to his son:—

"Greenfield House, February 9th, 1845.

"I have not yet begun any of my drawings for the Exhibition, but keep making studies. One or two small ones upon your sized paper are full in tone, and bear out the colour most beautifully. I wish I could have some larger paper. I have made a trial with a piece of the sized paper and a piece of my old favourite cartridge joined together in one drawing, and the same tint washed over both papers is not at all the same.

"DAVID COX."

CHAP. IX.

1844—1846.

"Greenfield House, February 14th, 1845.

"I feel a great wish to see what others are doing, and am frightened to think when my pictures are exhibited that they will look all wrong. I am finishing one, Kit-Cat size, which you saw (mountain rather dark), which I intend for the Royal Academy. I hope it may not disappoint you and my friends.

"DAVID COX."

"Greenfield House, March 30th, 1845.

"I have four large drawings in hand. One, Knaresbrough, one distant view of Brough, one Garden Terrace, Haddon, and one distant view of Kenilworth; the two former 23 by 33, the two latter 25½ by 30. I have six small ones, 10 by 14½, but all unfinished, so what I may be able to send I do not know. I have my oil-picture packed up, and shall send to Foord's the day before I leave, so that I may have it up at your house to finish, as I mean to send it to the Manchester Exhibition by the 16th of May."

The winter of 1844-5 had been a hard one in England, and Cox suffered from a severe cold on the chest in the spring. This did not prevent his paying his usual visit to London before the opening of the Water Colour Exhibition, to which he sent sixteen drawings. In the following letter he describes how some of these were hung; several do not appear to have been at all favourably placed, but he makes no complaint:—

"Streatham Place, Brixton Hill, London,
April 23rd, 1845.

"TO WILLIAM ROBERTS, ESQ.

"MY DEAR FRIEND ROBERTS,—Thank you for your kind letter of this morning. It was my intention to have written to you before this, but really I have nothing to tell you worth the trouble of your reading. You do me great kindness in talking of me so frequently with my friend Birch, and I have no doubt all are anxious about my health and welfare, for which I thank you. My chest has been very sore and bad for the last two or three days; indeed, I do not think I shall ever get quite well. I am thankful I am able to go about; and when I can get off into Wales I hope to breathe the sweet mountain air. I have made some inquiries about the little property in Wales, and hope in a week or nine days to hear more, as it is necessary for the person to write down for all particulars. I have seen one or two who have resided there in the winter, *artists*, who agree that it is a great deal warmer in Bettws than in London. I have also been introduced to a lady who was born in the neighbourhood of Bettws, and she tells me how much warmer it is at Bettws than in London. This all tends to give me a better idea of the place, and I hope I may be able to purchase the place I wish for within a moderate sum; but land about Llanrwst fetches £120 to £130 per acre. A gentleman I have seen has purchased some, and gave more than £100 per acre. He is now about building a house there. But why do I speak so much of this matter? I finished my drawings last evening, and am quite dissatisfied with them. They are too slight, and I hope and wish I may never make another large drawing; I cannot finish to please the public. 'The Garden Terrace, Haddon,' is on the row above the line; 'Kenilworth' up quite at the top, consequently only a bold sketch, and I have put prices accordingly; 'Knaresborough' is in the next place; 'Brough' next. These two I have done but little to. My 'Haddon' is the best work. If it could have been hung upon the floor it would have had the light falling upon it. As it is, it hangs forward a little, and this causes it to look gloomy; whereas, upon the floor, it looks bright, I was going to say beautiful. The Exhibition is not a striking one. Cattermole has a drawing the size of the one I sold to Mr. Ellis, the subject very like it in composition, Holy Men coming down from a Monastery to meet

CHAP. IX. 1844—1846.

Crusaders, or something of that kind, I do not know his title, but, as usual, it is worth hanging in the very first collection in the kingdom; and I very much wonder some gentlemen who are lovers of the art do not beset him and procure a fine drawing, for they will never get oil paintings from him, for he is so particular about his oils going forth to the public. His water-colours are more under his command. I shall see Birch on Friday or Saturday, I expect, but you I shall expect when I see you, as I know you are some time making up your mind. With best and kindest wishes to Mrs. Roberts and the young ladies, I remain,

"Ever faithfully yours,

"DAVID COX."

I have seen a memorandum which he made respecting two pictures in oil which were painted for Mr. Birch in 1845, one being a large view of "Carnarvon Bay," for which he received nineteen pounds, and a small "Lane Scene," eight pounds. He also made a powerful drawing of large size on the rough Scotch paper, full of colour, with an exceedingly beautiful windy sky, for Mr. Birch for twenty-five pounds. "The Stubble Field" is the title of this drawing, which is one of his most celebrated ones.

After Cox returned from London, towards the middle of May, he again went to stay at Rowsley, accompanied by his friend Ellis. They spent a fortnight sketching there, principally at Haddon Hall; and on his way home he again visited Hardwick Hall and also Sherwood Forest. The following letter refers to this visit to Derbyshire:—

"Severn's Rowsley Hotel, near Bakewell, Derbyshire,
May 26th, 1845.

"MY DEAR FRIEND ROBERTS,—Did you ever know of two poor fellows being so unfortunate in the weather for a fortnight's sketching excursion? Rain all day Saturday, yesterday, and now this morning promises to be quite equal!

"We had three days last week rather fine, but severely cold. Notwithstanding, I made a number of hand-book sketches, which I have coloured. Painting in oil has been quite out of the question, though I take my colours with me every day in the hope I might be fortunate in having a fine day for effects. My friend Ellis begins to despair of having it fine or warmer than it now is, and he must be in London on Saturday, and has agreed to start from this on Thursday afternoon. We intend spending one clear day between Matlock and Ambergate, and think of sleeping at Birley's Hotel, Stanwell Bridge, which is two miles from Ambergate. Severn says it is a very clean comfortable house. Hope for our having better weather, then I wish it may tempt you to come to us. We occupy the same quarters as to rooms at the Rowsley inn, and the house will be quite to ourselves, as the only family remaining are going by mail to Manchester at eleven. I wish you could come and help up with our drooping spirits. We should be mightily glad to see you; pop in and surprise us. Then you and I could go to Hardwick, where I fancy the weather must make a change by that time. I shall be very dull there by myself, and you are aware that Mrs. Riggott is poor company. However, I hope to be well occupied, as I wish to make several sketches in the Hall, and that will not be quite so bad as sitting at the inn all day. I am happy to learn from my wife that you are *all* well, and that dear Mrs. Roberts has been so kind in going to see her every day; for such kindness I am sure my wife and myself are greatly obliged. So, with every sincere and the best wishes, I conclude, as heretofore,

"DAVID COX."

He also wrote the following letter to his son:—

"Severn's Rowsley Hotel, May 25th, 1845.

"MY DEAR DAVID,—The weather has been wretchedly cold, although it has not deterred us from going up to the

CHAP. IX. 1844—1846. old Hall each day and sketching till four o'clock, until yesterday, which was raining the whole day, and we sat indoors; I working upon my sketches which I have been making for my friend W. Ellis.

"Mr. Ellis must be in London on Saturday, and it is his wish to go for one day into the neighbourhood of Ambergate Station for the purpose of sketching, where we shall separate—he for London, and I to spend two or three days at Hardwick. I believe, from what Mr. Ellis says, that Norman Wilkinson will like two or three interiors at Hardwick."

Although Cox complains of the weather in the two preceding letters, he must have made excellent use of his time during the fortnight he spent at Rowsley and Haddon, judging from the beautiful series of sketches which I have seen in Mr. Ellis's portfolios, all made on this occasion; several were sketched before breakfast at Rowsley on the banks of the old mill-stream, very powerful and admirable in arrangement and colour, also front and side views of the Peacock inn; the latter, a late sunset effect, is very poetical in its treatment. The series of Haddon Hall sketches, especially that of the Monk's Bridge and the old steps leading up to the courtyard, are as fine as possible, evidently very rapid, but nothing is wanting, except more finish, to make very lovely and powerful drawings.

Later in the summer of 1845 Cox made a journey into North Wales, and stayed for some time at the Royal Oak, Bettws-y-Coed.

This was the second of his annual visits to this favourite spot. In his latter years the name of David Cox was completely identified with Bettws, through the series of drawings and paintings made by him, year after year, of its varied and beautiful scenery, and each succeeding visit he appeared to cling to it with increasing affection. I intend to devote a future chapter to a description of Bettws and his visits there.

This year he made drawings of Bettws Mill, Vale of Dolwyddelan, cottages at Bettws, &c. After his return home to Greenfield House, he wrote to his son, October 14th, 1845, a letter of home news chiefly; but from which the following is an extract:— CHAP. IX. 1844–1846.

"I went over to Dudley yesterday for the purpose of making a sketch of the castle for an oil-picture for Mr. Twamley. Mr. and Mrs. Birch and Mr. and Mrs. Roberts also went. We had a delightful day. I must conclude, as I am anxious to get all Mr. Wilkinson's sketches ready before Mr. Ellis comes.

"DAVID COX."

The oil-picture referred to in the preceding letter was very successful; it represents Dudley Castle in the distance, with meadows in front in which cows are feeding. It is still in the possession of Mr. Charles Twamley.

This year, 1845, closed in great sorrow and gloom for David Cox. His wife's strength had been gradually failing for some time, and her death took place on the 23rd November, at the age of seventy-four years. She was buried under a chestnut-tree in the parish churchyard of Harborne. Cox deeply felt his loss, but, being a truly religious man, he did not mourn as one without hope. The following letter, written to his son and daughter-in-law about a month after this event, describes to some extent his feelings at this epoch of his life:—

"Greenfield House, Harborne, December 21st, 1845.

"MY DEAR DAVID AND HANNAH,—Your two letters, also the one I received this morning, have been the greatest comfort and gratification to me. I learn that you are all in good health. I certainly was very much out of spirits when I wrote on Thursday, but I am much better now; and I believe I have no real cause to be otherwise, for all things I

CHAP. IX. 1844—1846.

feel are ordained for the very best for my good. I have been at my work with more calmness, and shall, I have no doubt, do better and be better in all ways, with God's grace and assistance. Your letter was of the most encouraging kind, too, with regard to my work, and yesterday I took your advice and immediately took up a canvas to begin in oil for the Institution. I hope I may be able to please myself and get ready with my picture for the Institution, which I believe ought to be delivered there on the 12th or 13th of January. If there is any alteration in the day for taking pictures, perhaps you will let me know, &c.

"DAVID COX."

Shortly afterwards he wrote the two following letters:—

"Greenfield House, Harborne, January 21st, 1846.

"MY DEAR DAVID,—I want you to do me a kindness, which is to call at the British Institution, and learn whether my picture is hung up. Perhaps it will be as well to ask to see Mr. Barnard, who will best be able to tell you; and, if it should be hung, request him to ticket it as sold to Norman Wilkinson, Esq. I will now give you my reasons for wishing you to make this inquiry. Mr. Wilkinson has written to me to say he had seen my picture at Rought's, and had bought it, and wished me to write to Mr. Barnard, giving the necessary directions. The parcel is not yet come, but I hope to receive it this evening, as I may see Mr. Bullock to-morrow; he sometimes comes over to dine with Mr. Roberts. I also want the sketch of Rhyl Castle and the Valley, for a picture I want to begin. Love to all.

"Your affectionate Father,

"DAVID COX."

"Greenfield House, January 7th, 1846.

"MY DEAR DAVID,—I have finished my picture except a little more glazing, which, if it is quite dry enough, I shall do to-morrow. I fear it will look very queer among such high-finished works as are usually sent to the Institution. CHAP. IX. 1844—1846.

"I call my picture 'Wind, Rain, and Sunshine;' the size about 26 inches by 18 (canvas). I intend asking thirty guineas for it, and if it does not sell I don't care, but perhaps they will not receive it. . . . . .

"Your affectionate Father,

"DAVID COX."

The picture referred to above was a very successful one. It represented a woman on horseback holding an umbrella bent over against the pelting rain; a stormy sky, and trees bending before the blast, and gleams of sunshine on the distant hills. The title was suggested without doubt by Turner's impressive picture of "Rain, Steam, and Speed," exhibited at the Royal Academy in 1844, and now in the Turner Gallery of our national collection. Cox admired that picture very much, but it was almost the last of that great artist's works that he did thoroughly admire. Before commencing the next chapter it may be worth while to pause for a few moments to consider which, of all the great qualities in which Turner excelled, had most impressed and influenced Cox in the treatment and the selection of his subjects. Although I have shown that the large drawing of "Æneas approaching Carthage," painted by Cox in 1825, after Turner's manner, was not altogether a success, I think probably that this work, and the careful study of Turner's pictures, led the way to a more careful selection by Cox of objects, and their combination in such a manner that they should be thoroughly in harmony with each other. In other words, that the detail of every part should be entirely at one with the feeling and ideal intended to be conveyed by the work as a whole.

Turner, perhaps more than any other landscape artist, looked on his subject as a whole, and disregarded minute

CHAP. IX. 1844–1846.

details and accidental forms if they interfered with the *mass* of cool or warm colour. He sought at all times all that was most poetical by a comprehensive and generalising treatment. He was most careful, nevertheless, in his selection and arrangement of colour, and the blending of light and shadow, so as to obtain those difficult, but, to a painter, most invaluable qualities—light and mystery.

I think by comparing Cox's later works with his earlier ones, we may trace some of this influence and feeling for mystery in his works, the same as in Turner's; but as Cox's mind and character were very dissimilar to those of the great painter of light and mystery, there is naturally a very marked and great difference in their work. This is the more pronounced probably from the fact that Cox relied always more on a close and truthful imitation of nature than on the teachings and refinements of art, much as he valued the important aids which art affords to painters. Without doubt Cox was strongly impressed early in his career with the great importance of cultivating the *imitative* faculty as the real basis of all true excellence in art. His early study of flowers, still-life subjects, shipping, and architecture, prove that he felt that *this* was the only safe road to success.

X.

LIFE AT HARBORNE, AND SUCCESS IN OIL-PAINTING.

1846 TO 1849.

ALTHOUGH the shock caused by the death of his wife paralyzed for a time Cox's interest in painting, that state of feeling did not long prevail; and, after he had been induced to resume his usual occupation, he followed it with renewed ardour.

I consider 1846 and the ten following years as those in which the artistic power of Cox may be said to have culminated. A great majority of his most celebrated works were produced within that period, especially in oils. His first large oil-picture of the "Vale of Clwyd" was painted in 1846, also the "Peace and War, with Troops marching towards the Town of Lancaster," for which the competition at Mr. Gillott's sale was so keen, that, although rather a small picture, it produced the large sum of £3,601 10s. "Gipsies crossing a Common" and "Going to the Mill" may also be cited among the successful and well-known oil-paintings of this year. Although these works have much richness and finish, the handling is rather less free than those painted a few years later. Cox also made many large water-colour drawings this year—"Caer-Cennen Castle," the "Vale of Clwyd," and several others, were much admired.

The following is extracted from a letter written to his son and daughter-in-law:—

CHAP. X.

1846—1849.

"Greenfield House, February 12th, 1846.

"My work has not plagued me so much as sometimes. I have begun for the Water Colour Exhibition, and have two tolerable size ones nearly finished. I have also begun a large oil-picture, 4½ feet by 3 feet. I hope to get it finished ready for the Royal Academy.

"I suppose David knows that my picture is rejected at the Institution, but they must have a great many much worse there. If it is unfairness on their part in not hanging my picture, I am terribly vexed.

"DAVID COX."

And again he writes February 15th, 1846:—

"I am greatly pleased to hear —— say what he does of my picture. I conclude he has seen it. Tell him also that encouragement spurs me on, and he shall see a better if please God I am spared to finish what I have begun. I have better ideas for subjects than ever."

He also writes from Greenfield House:—

"March 29th, 1846.

"I find the time draws near for sending my oil-picture (if I can get it finished) into the Royal Academy. I almost wish I had to paint it over again; I am sure *I could improve upon it.* However, I have of course done my best; we all try to do that, but cannot always succeed. It is a bold scene, and the work is also bold, or rather coarse. I keep on at my water-colours a little each morning while my room is getting warmed, and then work at my oil until dusk. At lamplight, at my water-colours again.

"DAVID COX."

The above letter shows how indefatigably he worked even in the winter season, the studio up-stairs being reserved for his work in oil, and the parlour on the ground-floor, which was warmer, for his water-colour. When on his usual spring visit of about six weeks' duration to London, he made arrangements with Mr. Ellis and other friends to go to Bolton Abbey in May. The party put up as usual at the Devonshire Arms. Mrs. Wilson was the name of the landlady at that time. She and her niece, Miss Wyatt, were very desirous to do all in their power for the comfort of their guests, and Cox entertained a very friendly feeling for them. He made Mrs. Wilson a present of several of his water-colour sketches. Some of these were originally in the Visitor's Book, but they have long adorned the walls of the hotel. The following letter describes this visit:—

"Devonshire Arms, Bolton Bridge, near Otley, Yorkshire,
May 30th, 1846.

"MY DEAR FRIEND ROBERTS,—I ought to have written to thank you for sending me the spectacles. One pair suits very well; the others I will return when I see you. I have no doubt you and our friend Birch have often thought how lucky I and my companions have been in the weather; indeed, it could not have been finer. Of course we have been a great deal of our time in the open air. My friend Ellis is as tough as any one I ever knew. He is out early and late, and has made a great number of coloured sketches. For myself, I cannot say so much, as I do not go out at all before breakfast, nor in the evening, as my breathing has been very much tried in walking up some of the hills. But Mr. Ellis is very kind, and has had the car out most days. We have been to Bardon three times, and last Monday we went to Malham, and did not return till nine at night. I have made a number of hand-book sketches, but few of a larger size. I cannot find out much that is new to interest me very much, though the country is very beautiful, and I have quite made up my mind that there is nothing like being out a great deal in the country. We purpose leaving this on our return

CHAP. X. 1846—1849.

on Thursday next, the 4th, and I hope to be at home at seven that evening.

"Ever truly yours,

"DAVID COX."

On the 12th of July, 1846, he wrote to his son from Greenfield House, "My landlord is going to send some workmen to repair the roof of the house, paint, &c., so I cannot leave home till the middle of July. I am not able to finish the 'Vale of Clwyd' for the Birmingham Exhibition, as they take in pictures on Tuesday next." The picture mentioned here was the large one sent to Liverpool this year. On the 17th July he writes, "I have just sent off my picture ('Vale of Clwyd') to Liverpool."

Cox exhibited twelve drawings this year (1846) in the Water Colour Society's Gallery. The subjects were very varied, and the "Outskirts of the Forest" was the finest. He again went to Bettws-y-Coed this year, and also visited his sister in Manchester. At the latter end of October his friend, Mr. Ellis, came to stay with him at Greenfield House, and, as the season was fine, they were enabled to go out for a good deal of sketching together. Mr. Ellis describes that on one occasion they had been out soon after breakfast, and were walking home to dinner, which was always ready punctually at one. It was past the time, but Cox, after looking up, stopped suddenly, exclaiming, "Look there!" and turning round, drew with the end of his stick the outline of a large picture in the *dust* of the road, and commenced rapidly filling in the details of the effect which had arrested his attention. Generally he was very particular to get to his mid-day meal, and would leave his work incomplete, trusting to his memory to finish it at home, when his companions would gladly have remained longer on the spot. On another occasion, when Mr. Ellis and David Cox and his son were walking near Harborne, Cox, who was always on the look-out for "an effect," suddenly exclaimed, "Look, look, David!" and pointed to an effect of sky reflected in a window near them. When out he would often stop short, and sketch any instantaneous effect of sky, or anything else which struck him. Indeed, he always had a small sketch-book and a piece of chalk or pencil in his pocket wherever he went. His attention and interest in the aspect of nature appeared never to flag or slumber. On one occasion, his sketching companions missing Cox from his place, found that he had turned round and was engaged sketching a donkey that had been looking over their heads. The following letters, dated September 10th and November 26th, 1846, written to his son, are not without interest, as showing the happy frame of mind he was in, and his thought for others:—

"Greenfield House, September 10th, 1846.

"MY DEAR DAVID AND HANNAH,—Your letter gave much pleasure to learn that you were all quite well, and enjoying yourselves with the scenery around you, and that my sister Hills enjoys herself. I sincerely hope she will gain strength and benefit by the change. Please take care of yourselves. We have had rather a bad accident on the Liverpool line; several persons hurt severely. I received a letter from Ann this morning. She tells me it is the music meeting at Hereford, and she fears she may not get a place by coach on Saturday morning, so I have written to say I will not expect her till Monday or Tuesday. Tom is very busy planting the garden with a winter crop. I think of going to see my sister some day towards the middle or latter end of next week. Mr. Birch and his young family are all quite well, but Miss —— is in rather delicate health. I think she has too much on her hand, and too much care. She would like to go out, but has no one to go with her. I received a letter from my dear friend Ellis on Sunday, and he tells me he is going to Sevenoaks to see his brothers and

CHAP. X. 1846—1849. sisters, and shall write to ask you to meet him at Chilham. And now, with love to all, and may God bless you, is the prayer of

"Your affectionate Father,

"D. Cox."

"Greenfield, Harborne, November 26th, 1846.

"MY DEAR DAVID AND HANNAH,—I could not let the day pass by and not write a few lines, although I expect you will see my kind and dear friend William Ellis this evening, who will tell you more about me and what I am doing than I could think of. He was kind enough to take a basket of our home-made bread, and would send you the half. I hope you will like it, and that my dear little darlings will eat very plentifully of it, especially of the brown. I am now calculating on seeing my dear David at Christmas, when we shall have a pleasant, happy chat. I rather think Norman Wilkinson will come down before Christmas, as he promised two months back that he would come. It is now very delightful weather, and it tempts me to go out sketching, for I hardly know how to tackle to work after the pleasant days William Ellis and I have had this week; though I have a great deal more to do than I can get through before the exhibition, so will finish, with love and affection, ever

"DAVID COX."

With reference to the home-made bread mentioned in the preceding letter I ought, perhaps, to remark that the bread made at Greenfield House had quite a reputation amongst Cox's friends for being better than any other. Mr. George Briscoe especially used to say it was the sweetest bread he ever tasted.

In 1847 Cox continued to work very industriously in oils, and produced many fine pictures, one of the most successful being "Counting the Flock." With reference to this exquisite picture a friend relates that, after looking at it for some time with admiration, he turned round and asked Cox whether he himself did not think it was very successful; to which Cox replied, with a quiet, amused smile on his face, "Well, I did rather feel as if my hand was in it."

The following are extracts from letters written to his son, from Greenfield House, in the early part of this year:—

"January 21st, 1847.

"Mr. Ellis says you wish me to paint the 'Flood in North Wales,' but I believe the 'Mountain Top' is to my mind more suitable to my feeling, as I wish to have something like the 'Dolwyddelan.' Everybody likes it better than anything I show them."

"February 4th, 1847.

"I have bought another Müller—an unfinished one; it was sold at the sale of his works. I have given one picture for it, and my parlour is pretty well hung with drawings and paintings."

"May 13th, 1847.

"To-morrow I am going with Mr. Hall to spend the day at Mr. Briscoe's, near Wolverhampton. He is one of my patrons, and has ordered three large pictures of me, and is very anxious to see one of them in hand."

Mr. Briscoe resided in a fine old country house called Old Fallings, about three miles beyond Wolverhampton; such a place as Cox would take a fancy to, as it was surrounded by lofty trees. Mr. Birch, Mr. Roberts, and Mr. Bullock were also invited to meet him.

"The Old Mill at Bettws-y-Coed," with geese in the foreground, was painted this year for Mr. Carritt, who paid forty pounds for it. It is a beautiful picture, and was sold in 1872 for fifteen hundred and seventy-five pounds.

CHAP. X.

1846—1849.

"Going to the Mill" is another of the celebrated oil-pictures painted this year; also "The Hayfield," with a man riding and leading a white horse, which the late Mr. James Bagnall purchased from Cox for forty pounds, and which, at the sale of that gentleman's pictures in 1872, sold for fifteen hundred and fifty guineas. The following characteristic letter, dated from his son's house at Brixton Hill, gives some account of the Water Colour Exhibition this year, and describes the disappointment Cox felt at the absence of Cattermole's works, which he felt the more because he had great admiration for the originality and talent of this artist, and used often to express the pleasure he derived from seeing his works:—

"Laurel Cottage, Streatham Place, Brixton Hill,
London, April 30th, 1847.

"MY DEAR FRIEND ROBERTS,—I dare say you have ere this expected a letter from me; but, having seen but little and heard but little in the way of the Arts, I have delayed writing till I received a letter. The latter part of last week and the beginning of this I have been occupied in touching up my drawings. I have done but little to them, however, and the members were very anxious I should do but little—do nothing to my 'Bolton Abbey,' which they all seem to agree is the very best drawing I have ever made, and they have used the most expressive words of praise I have ever received. I do not expect the newspapers will have the same feeling. The great man, Cattermole, has behaved rather shabby; he has not sent one drawing, and from all I can learn his excuse is the most lame. I think his conduct is unfeeling towards his brother members; for what use is it for a body of men agreeing to unite their strength and abilities to assist each other, and be deceived at the very last moment—that he could not send one drawing! We all think very highly of his talent, and if four, or half-a-dozen, were to act in the same way, where would be the stability of a society? But, notwithstanding, we shall have a fair exhibition; but his pictures were a feature that created interest, and he must know that. I think his treatment will be the cause of most of the other members uniting to exert themselves next year, not relying upon men who can deceive. You will excuse me taking up so much of my note on the above subject; but knowing his ability, and rapidity in work, I, for one, feel his treatment the more vexatious. The other members have contributed their usual numbers—De Wint rather better; Fielding much the same; one picture very good—quite a Claude; Hunt as usual; Nesfield the same; Evans, of Eton, two very large drawings, very interesting, but too much white body colour; Bentley, Callow, Gastineau, and all the rest, seem to have done well; but we want works of figure subjects. I went to Suffolk Street, and I think, on the whole, it was not a good exhibition. Pine is the best, but very papery, and nothing solid in them; Anthony characteristic; one small morning scene good in grey effect; Holland several small pictures, but not so good as I have seen. I have not yet been to the British Institution, and I hear it is no loss, but next week I intend paying a visit to them and the National; the Monday following the Royal Academy, and on the Wednesday or Thursday to home, quiet home. London is quite Babylon; the WHIRLING of carriages quite bewilders me, and makes me giddy. I learn that Bond is about to come to London, but whether to take up his abode I don't know. He has sold an oil picture at the British Institution for fifty guineas. Creswick, I hear, is giving dinners to his friends. I suppose this is preparatory to the election for academician. I hear of a number of artists going into Wales this summer. I understand from Ann she has received notice to pay the tithe on Monday. Will you have the goodness to let your man-servant take it to the Bell, as I think Ann will not like to go? How is my friend Birch? Has he any more pictures? Pray write me a letter, and tell me all the news

CHAP. X. — 1846—1849.

you can think of, and say when I may expect to see you in London. Receive the best and sincere wishes for you, Mrs. Roberts, and children.

"D. Cox."

The large drawing of "Bolton Abbey," mentioned in the foregoing letter, is very highly finished, and is unusually brilliant in colour. There are few more picturesque remains in England than those of this fine old abbey, which was founded in 1151, and was held by monks of the order of St. Augustine, at the time of its dissolution by Henry VIII., in 1540. The abbey is represented surrounded by trees, and reflected in a large pool of water, towards which cattle are descending, as is their habit on a hot summer's day. The sky is a bright cerulean blue with fleecy clouds, and on the left hand is a grand group of trees. It is now in the collection of Mr. H. T. Broadhurst, of Manchester, and by his kind permission I give a photographic copy of it, at the commencement of this chapter.

Cox sent thirteen drawings to the Water Colour Exhibition this year. The most interesting, besides "Bolton Abbey," were "Caer Cennen Castle," "Windsor Park," "Vale of Dolwyddelan," and "The River Llugwy, from Pont-y-Kefyn." There was also one of a very unusual subject, "George's Dock, Liverpool."

In the autumn he spent some time again at Bettws, making sketches. This visit will be noticed in the chapter on Bettws, at which place Mr. Hall joined him. The following is from a letter to his son, written after his return from London:—

"Greenfield House, June 4th, 1847.

"MY DEAR DAVID,—When the Exhibition in Westminster Hall is opened, tell me what is thought of a picture by Dobson. . . . He was late member of the School of Design here in Birmingham, and has been painting some pictures for a gentleman in the town. The one sent to Westminster is one of them, and is spoken of very highly.

"DAVID COX."

After his return home from Bettws, he wrote as follows to his son:—

"Greenfield House, Harborne, August 30th, 1847.

"My friends here tell me I have brought home some very good sketches, but I fear very deficient in many respects, and I must not lose sight of Nature, and therefore intend to follow up my practice as long as the weather holds fair."

Again he wrote from Sale, where he had gone on a visit to Mrs. Ward; the incident referred to, of his being up the ladder painting the sign is one that has been much spoken about.

"September 6th, 1847.

"I suppose it was Mrs. Ashley who told you she saw me upon the ladder painting the sign of the Royal Oak. The sign was in so bad a state I thought I could not damage it much, and I set to work, and in a very short time made a tree much fresher in its looks than it was before."

"Greenfield House, October 12th, 1847.

"I had Mr. Froggatt here on Saturday. He came down on purpose to see me and my works; he was very much delighted with what he saw, and wished to purchase one of my Welsh sketches in oil, but I had declined selling any of them at present. He says Mr. Lucas talked of coming down with him, but he has no doubt he will come, as he would like to mezotint from some of my works."

"Greenfield House, December 17th, 1847.

"I have lately received more orders for pictures, one for seventy guineas; besides which, I have to make three large,

CHAP. X. 1846—1849.

3 ft. 6 in. by 2 ft. 6 in. for Mr. Gillott. He also bought six small *bits* I had begun by lamplight, but they will take me some time to finish by daylight. You will be astonished to see how well I succeed by lamplight. I do not know whether you recollect the two Müllers I had. One a 'Cottage Scene,' the other 'Pandy Mill, Penmachno.' The former I sold for £70. I gave £35 in drawings for it; the latter, the Mill, I gave £30, and sold it for £90, and a frame into the bargain. Last week I bought a Müller, and gave one of my oil pictures for it. I think of keeping this, as it is quite an artist's *bit*, though I have been offered £30 for it; but I won't take it.

"DAVID COX."

In the first months of 1848 Cox was much occupied in preparing his drawings for the Water Colour Exhibition, to which he contributed fourteen drawings this year.

The following is from a letter written to his son, and referring to those drawings:—

"Greenfield House, March 16th, 1848.

"You wished to know what my subjects were I was doing for the Exhibition; but, as I have only three in hand, and two are very backward, I do not like to make too sure, but I feel pretty certain to-day that I may finish them. One, 'The Skylark;' second, 'Gipsies in a Wood Scene;' third, 'Peace and War,' though I don't think I shall call it by that name; 'Dungeness Bay' is the real view. I have several small ones, but they are unfinished.

"DAVID COX."

Besides those mentioned in the preceding letter was the "Lower End of the Vale of Clwyd," which was purchased by Mr. Joseph Parrington, of Croom's Hill, for forty guineas. This gentleman also purchased "A Green Lane, Staffordshire," one of Cox's very powerful and celebrated drawings. "Going to the Hayfield," was another fine drawing exhibited this year; the one referred to by Cox as "Gipsies in a Wood Scene," appears in the catalogue under the title of "Sherwood Forest." The drawing mentioned above as "A Green Lane, Staffordshire," is now in Mr. Quilter's collection; he also possesses a note written by Cox to Mr. J. Parrington on the subject of this drawing, of which the following is a copy:—

"Bettws-y-Coed, North Wales, August 13th, 1848.

"DEAR SIR,—I have received your kind note, and beg to thank you for the liberal patronage you have shown me. I feel most happy to have you the purchaser of my drawings. I have sent notice to my home to have the drawing of 'Green Lane' carefully packed, and sent directed as you requested, and hope you will be pleased with it. It was my favourite of all my own drawings. I must also beg to thank you for paying the amount to Mr. Ellis, who has given me notice of the same. I have had very bad weather since I have been here (a month) until yesterday it was fine the the whole of the day, and to all appearance the weather is looking 'as taking up,' and I hope to make a few sketches in the remaining fortnight I think of staying. I beg to subscribe myself

"Your most obedient servant,

"DAVID COX.

"J. PARRINGTON, Esq., 20, Croom's Hill, Greenwich."

The drawing of "The Skylark," which Cox exhibited this year, is now in Mr. Albert Levy's collection. It is one of the most delightful in feeling, for, like the oil picture of the same subject (painted in 1849), it conveys the sense of perfect repose, so characteristic of English rural life. The aspect of the country is bright and cheerful, but the interest is

CHAP. X.

1846—1849.

concentrated on the group of children, who appear to be listening with delight to the song of the skylark hovering above them. It would be difficult to imagine a scene more suggestive of Shelley's beautiful lines commencing—

"Hail to thee, blithe spirit!
Bird thou never wert,
That from heaven or near it
Pourest thy full heart
In profuse strains of unpremeditated art!

"Higher still, and higher,
From the earth thou springest;
Like a cloud of fire
The blue deep thou wingest—
And singing still dost soar, and soaring ever singest."

I have fully described these pictures in the chapters on oil-pictures and water-colour drawings.

The following is from a letter written to his son whilst on the visit to Wales this year:—

"Royal Oak, Bettws-y-Coed, August 16th, 1848.

"We have very wet weather, and I am fearful we shall not have it better during my stay in Wales, as I think we shall have it raining during the moon. I have made fewer sketches this year than any former year, and I give it up as a lost summer, as I think of returning home towards the end of next week or early the week following. You must know that with the sales of my drawings in the exhibition, my July dividend, and the sale of my 'Green Lane,' altogether enabled me to buy £200 stock. The parting with the drawing of 'Green Lane' was the most unpleasant part of the transaction, but I hope to do better things some day.

"DAVID COX."

He painted a great deal in oil this year. Among the more important works was the large one of "The Vale of

Clwyd," for Mr. George Briscoe, for which he received £95, but which has lately been sold for £2,500. Also "Dudley Castle, with Gleaners returning Home, Sunset," a highly finished and beautiful picture, rich in subject and colour. These are more fully referred to in the chapter on oils.

The following are extracts from letters written to his son in the autumn of this year:—

"Greenfield House, September 29th, 1848.

"I think —— will like to see my sketches which I made in Wales. I have one or two oil sketches which are better than anything I have hitherto done. One I have sold, but it is not yet sent home, and I half repent having parted with it. I have also painted a picture in oil since my return from Wales, but it is not a Welsh subject; it is one of my very best. My friend Birch says the above pictures are the best I have yet painted, and he, you know, is a good judge.

"DAVID COX."

"October 20th, 1848.

"I am happy to tell you my work goes on very well. I have nearly finished the large 'Mountainous Scene.' I thought to have finished it by to-morrow night, but there is always something to require a little more finish or alteration. Mr. Bullock came over yesterday to see it, and was quite delighted with it; so also was Mr. Roberts and Mr. Birch. Indeed, I never had so much praise for any oil-picture, notwithstanding I must be careful how I receive so much praise from friends; three other gentlemen would be anxious to have had it.

"DAVID COX."

"November 3rd, 1848.

"I am ashamed to say I have not *quite* finished my large picture, owing in a great degree to the very dark days; however, it is nearly finished, but I have been taken from

CHAP. X. it, to paint two small pictures which I hope to have out of
1846—1849. hand on Monday."

"November 16th, 1848.

"I finished a picture for Mr. Froggatt, which I sent off to him last Monday. I think it was one of the best I have painted, and I am happy to say I go on much more rapidly in my painting than I did, and if I have my health I shall get my orders a little under."

"November 24th, 1848.

"My work goes on as well as I can expect in these dark days, and, if there is a bright day, I am sure to have some one or more call to look at what I am about. I have done but little by lamplight; the FIT has not come yet, and what little I have done has been of the same feeling, that is, rather of the heavy style."

Cox used occasionally to go to dine, quite without ceremony, at the houses of his friends at Harborne. He took but little wine, and, as soon as he had smoked his *half* cigar, it was his happiness to have his colour-box out, or, if by artificial light, generally his sepia, and, setting to work would make one or two spirited drawings in the course of the evening. Whilst so employed, if any one would play to him on the piano, he was delighted, as he always could get on much better whilst music was going on. He was never happier than when at work; and in this constant practice, as already remarked, we may discover one of the secrets of his success. When advice was offered to Cox that he did not wish to act upon, he would turn it off with a joke. Thus, on one occasion, whilst working in his studio at a drawing for Mr. Birch, that gentleman came in to see it. "Now," said Cox to him, "will that do?" "Yes," replied Mr. Birch; "only I think just a few more ripples in the water would be an improvement." Cox immediately handed him the brush with which he was working, and said, "Do it, do it!" But Mr. Birch wisely declined the honour. On another occasion he had painted a "Landscape near Coventry," with some figures in it, for a gentleman, who, when he came to see the picture, remarked that he thought the figures wanted just a little more of the artist's spirit and *fire* in them. Cox merely replied, pointing to the grate, "Pray put it in, and then they will have plenty of fire."

Cox was in the habit for several years of entrusting a good many of his works for sale to Mr. William Holmes, the dealer in Birmingham. He was fond, when he went there, of strolling into Holmes's rooms and looking at the pictures which were exhibited there, and on one or two occasions, when standing in front of his own works, he has been overheard, saying in a low voice, as if addressing himself, "Not very bad, either, David. Not very bad, David."

Mr. Holmes knew the market value of Cox's paintings in those days probably better than any one. During several years a great many of his works, both in oil and water colour, had passed through his hands; and, in the early days of his oil-painting, they had frequently found no purchasers, and had to be returned to Greenfield House. Cox, however, never appeared to regret having a picture sext back to him: indeed, he often expressed regret at parting with one, especially if it was at all a favourite.

The next chapter will be devoted to an account of Bettws-y-Coed, and I shall then proceed with an account of his method of oil-painting, and with the promised description of his pictures.

XI.

BETTWS-Y-COED.

CHAP. XI.

DURING many years David Cox made Bettws his head-quarters in North Wales. He had, from his youth upwards, traversed repeatedly almost every foot of the wild scenery of this part of the country, but in his latter years he quite made up his mind that Bettws bore the palm over all other spots.

It is situated in a valley in Carnarvonshire, on the banks of the Llugwy, close to the picturesque bridge of Pont-y-Pair, and not far from its junction with the river Conway. The scenery is unusually varied and beautiful, and it has long been chosen as the favourite rendezvous of English landscape-painters in the summer and autumn months. It is surrounded by rocky glens and deep wooded valleys, which open out occasionally into broad fields and meadows, shaded by a variety of trees. Through these the mountain streams, the Machno, the Lledr, and the Llugwy, flow on towards their junction with the Conway, now sleeping in dark, deep salmon pools, and now foaming and fretting over huge boulders, pent in between lofty walls of rock. All these streams are spanned by old and picturesque bridges, well known to lovers of art and Welsh scenery, and their banks also adorned by several ancient water-mills; of these, Pandy Mill, on the Machno, is the chief, on account of its romantic situation and the fine old oaks which surround

it. Starting from the vicinity of the beautiful Beaver Pool and the Beaver Bridge on the Conway, the old Holyhead road follows upwards the banks of the river at some distance below the new road. You look down on one side into a deep rocky and richly-wooded pass of the Conway, not far from its celebrated falls. This is the Faiëry Glen, of which the foliage is very varied and luxuriant; ferns and mosses also clothe the tops of the rocks, which are worn into many fantastic shapes and hollows by the constant action of the running stream. The views from the upper part of the road are unsurpassed for grandeur and extent, by anything in North Wales. The whole of the wild and beautiful valley of the Lledr and Dolwyddelan is spread out before you, guarded on one side by the giant form of Moel Siabod, and beyond these the peaks of the Glyder mountains and Snowdon may be seen in the far distance in fine weather.

Close to the village of Bettws is its little Welsh church, old as the venerable yew-trees which nearly encircle it. A vignette of this appears on the title-page. Formerly there was a chancel, but this was destroyed many years ago by the encroachments of the river Conway, which runs at the foot of a very steep bank close to the churchyard. In this chancel was the tomb of Gruffydd Gôch, a descendant of the Welsh princes, who died in the fourteenth century, and who was a nephew of Llewellyn, the last prince of North Wales. His effigy, which surmounted the tomb, is still preserved in the church; it is well carved in stone, of life-size; he is represented as a knight in a full suit of armour, and underneath is the following inscription: "Hic jacet Gruffyd ap Davyd Gôch, agnus Dei miserere mei."

The old road leading to this church started from the turnpike road almost exactly opposite the Royal Oak, it also led to the old farmhouse belonging to the inn and its large and pleasant garden; but of late years this road has been swept away, or, at least, the greater part of it, as well as the farm-

CHAP. XI. house, by the new railway station and its approaches; the fine old "Big Meadow," too, has been cut up, and may be said to exist no longer. The village, as it existed in Cox's time, with its picturesque cottages and primitive inhabitants, is much changed; indeed, it is scarcely to be recognised, so much has it been "modernised."

This remark applies also to the old water-mill which stood close to the farm, and which has lately been rebuilt. A very favourite subject this used to be with the artists stopping at the Oak, who generally chose it as their first essay after arriving. The falls of the Conway have been already referred to; the beauty of this spot has of late been rather marred by the construction of an ugly stone salmon-ladder, which greatly detracts from its former wild aspect. Many other fine waterfalls exist in the neighbourhood of Bettws, the chief being the Rhaidr-y-Wenol, or Swallow Falls, a mile and a half on the road to Capel Curig, also those of the Llugwy and the Machno. After heavy rain the water comes foaming down, dyed of a deep amber colour from the peat bogs through which it has passed. The mountainous road behind the Oak leads upwards to a high tract of wild and rather desolate moorland: here peat bogs abound, and here Cox drew his inspiration for some of his most impressive works. Following along in the direction of the Dolwyddelan valley, you arrive at a high and lonely mountain tarn, named Llyn Elsi; it is almost destitute of trees, but there are fine rocky banks, which compose well with the distant peak of Moel Siabod, seen towering high above them.

The subjects which Cox most frequently chose for his pictures were views of the rocks behind the Royal Oak, the heights above the valley, the mill at Bettws and the salmon trap, Bettws Church, the river Lledr, Beaver Pool, Pont-y-Pant, Pont-y-Kefyn, Pont-y-Pair (or the Cauldron Bridge), the Machno and Pandy Mill, also views from the old Holyhead road, of which subject he painted one or two fine finished drawings. Of late years he worked a great deal out of doors at Bettws with oils. Cox used to say he could find any number of subjects close to the Royal Oak, and of these the "Big Meadow" was, perhaps, the one in which he delighted the most. These views, when transferred to the paper or canvas of Cox, were generally powerful, and always thoroughly broad and truthful pictures; they give not only the outward forms, but the exact sentiment and feeling of the spot, so that, in looking at them, you feel for the time that you are really face to face with the wild scenery of North Wales.

In the numerous excursions Cox made through Wales during the long period of years whilst he resided at Hereford and London, Capel Curig, Bettws-y-Coed, and the neighbourhood of Conway were occasionally visited; but it was not until the year 1845, after he had come to live at Harborne, that he made this district regularly his head-quarters in North Wales, and took up his residence for some weeks every autumn at the Royal Oak. When he first knew Bettws, that inn did not exist, far less the present large hotel of that name, which was erected fourteen years ago on the exact spot once occupied by the old inn, and which was pulled down to make room for its more ambitious successor.

The little inn at which Cox first stayed was the Swan, represented in Creswick's picture of Bettws, and situated on the west side of the Bettws turnpike. An old Welsh woman, who lived to be ninety, of the name of Owen, was the land-lady in those days, assisted by her daughter. The former used to relate that Cox when young stayed there with other artists, and started a sketching club. He used to get any artists staying in the neighbourhood to come, and all worked together on wet days and exchanged drawings, a word being given as the subject of the day's work. The excursion Cox made to North Wales in July, 1844, with his young friend Harry Johnston, led him to Bettws-y-Coed, which was the

CHAP. XI. first of the series of his annual visits there. On this occasion he wrote the following letter to his son :—

"Bettws-y-Coed, July 15th, 1844.

"I cannot be at home under a fortnight from this time, and it is possible I may stay a few days longer. I find so much to do at every place I go to, I really believe Wales grows more beautiful and romantic every time I see it. We stayed at Llanbedr a week and one day, and when we went had planned only two or three days at most, and now we are at Bettws, where we arrived on Friday evening. We agree to stop a week; there is no end of the fine river scenery and rocks and mountains.

"Creswick is here; he is a very agreeable companion; he is communicative, and I wish he was going to stay longer, but expect he will go in a day or two, as he is going into Switzerland. I very much regret my friend Roberts cannot be with us, as I feel quite sure he has no idea at all of North Wales. In rocky-bedded rivers there is nothing I have seen can come up to them.

"DAVID COX."

The sketching excursions Cox had hitherto made with his friends, Roberts, Birch, Ellis, and Norman Wilkinson, had been almost exclusively in Derbyshire, Lancashire, Yorkshire, and Cumberland, or only just to the border country of Wales; but now he was impressed with the fact that Bettws was of all others *the place* for good and impressive subjects, and he never lost sight of this. The pleasure of congenial companionship undoubtedly gave zest and spirit to his work during this journey in 1844, and, indeed, Cox always liked to have a companion to travel with him when going to Bettws. He used to leave Birmingham in July or at the beginning of August by the old Grand Junction Railway (the Stour Valley line did not exist in those days) and travel by way of Chester and Rhyl to Conway. At the latter place he was generally met by an open Welsh car sent down on purpose from the Royal Oak, and in this he proceeded up the valley of the Conway. Whenever the opportunity offered, Cox preferred these Welsh jaunting cars to any other mode of conveyance, as the scenery could be seen so well whilst driving along the road, and he could stop when he wished to admire a view or make memoranda. Stage coaches he never liked, and always avoided if possible. Tunnels in railways were especially distasteful to him. The landlord of the Royal Oak, Mr. Edward Roberts, was delighted to honour David Cox, and he was assisted by his daughter, Miss Mary Roberts, whose arrangements gave great satisfaction. The inn was a small quiet one in those days, and the large bedroom was always reserved for him. There were two beds in it, and on wet days he would often work there, having four or five drawings or more in hand at once, which he used to spread out on the beds to dry whilst he worked at others. If the sky looked overcast, he would sometimes say, "I think it will rain to-day, so I shall only go down to the 'Big Meadow,' and do a sky or two." If an effect of clouds struck him when out of doors, he would dash away with chalk and colours, leaving the sketch to be finished afterwards at home, with a streak of blue distance, and a few trees and plants in the foreground. He was always ready to give advice to any young artist who might be out sketching at Bettws. If he saw one working timidly, with little colour and small brushes, he would exclaim, "Don't be afraid; dab, *dab*, DAB it!" Once it happened that a young artist unknown to fame came to study at Bettws. Cox, pleased with his assiduity, asked him to go out sketching with him, but, after a short time, the young man said he must leave at the end of the week; he was evidently getting on well, but could not be persuaded to stay. Cox, hearing this, seized an opportunity of taking him quietly aside, and said that if the state of his purse was

CHAP. XI. the cause of his resolution to leave, he hoped his young friend would allow him to become his banker, and to defray the cost of his board and lodging at the Royal Oak. In those days many artists came to that quiet Welsh inn for real work, and the old parlour was the common ground where all met in the evening to talk over their day's work and to compare notes. At these gatherings Cox was looked up to as the great ruling spirit of the place, although always kind and unassuming to all. The inn parlour had a door in it, fastened up and plastered over, but not papered; Cox thought this could be improved, so one wet day he set to work and painted a fresco on the plaster, the subject being Redgrave's cartoon, Catherine Douglas securing the door of the bed-chamber of her sovereign with her bare arm against murderers. The following letter written by Cox from Bettws in August, 1846, refers to the time when the waterspout broke over the Vale of Corwen, and did considerable damage. He had arrived in July, and his friends Edwin Bullock, Dr. Kittermaster, and William Roberts were with him, but the latter had left at the end of that month.

"Royal Oak, Bettws-y-Coed, Llanrwst, North Wales,
August 13th, 1846.

"MY DEAR FRIEND ROBERTS,—I received your welcome letter, and am glad to tell you I also received the stool on Friday last, after I had sent my last letter to you. It had been sent to Bangor, where it was for several days. If you had sent me a letter by post I should have got it the next day after you had written it, though the newspaper you talked of sending off on Monday has not yet come to hand, but, as my friend Birch sent me two, we have amused ourselves during a wet day or two. I suppose you have heard of the very awful storms of rain we have had. The road at Corwen has been completely stopped from the large stones washed down from the mountains at the back of the inn there. It has filled the road for some distance, a quarter of a mile at least, and it has buried carts, and covered the walls on the sides of the roads more than two yards deep. Many of the houses opposite the inn Owen Glendour have heaps of stone up to the bedroom windows. One poor woman was killed by a stone washed against her, and swept away in the flood. I was most agreeably surprised and pleased on Tuesday evening to see Mr. Coleman and Mr. Hall, artists, arrive. There was no room for them that night, so they went on to Llanrwst to sleep. Next morning, Wednesday, I went over and breakfasted with them, and we took a car, and have made arrangements for them to sleep at the Royal Oak. In the afternoon we went to Pandy Mill, and returned to dinner at five. We had a most delightful day. I should have told you, on our return from Llanrwst we found Mr. Gillott and his two daughters were waiting to see me. We were all of us, of course, very much pleased to meet. We stopped about half an hour. This morning, Thursday, we had the most heavy rain I ever witnessed. The river Llugwy has risen nearly three yards. It is much higher than I ever saw it. All the rocks at the fall above the bridge are completely hidden, and I fear we shall hear of more serious effects at Corwen. I have done but little in painting since you left; the weather has been so bad. I have received a very kind letter from Mr. Sherrington, wherein he expresses a wish I would make him a sketch as large as the one I made at the Stepping Stones, up in Dolwyddelan Vale; but I do not think the weather will permit, if I should stay long enough; but if I don't travel with Messrs. Coleman and Hall to Beddgelert, and round by Carnarvon, Menai, Bangor, Conway, and so through the Vale of Clwyd to Chester (if they cannot return by Saturday, 22nd), I will return in a car by myself on Monday. I beg to thank dear Mrs. Roberts and Miss Wilmot for their kind remembrances of me. Mr. Coleman is painting Mr. Hoyle's portrait, the weather being quite unfit to go

CHAP. XI. out. Mr. Hoyle hopes you will send him Ibbotson by next mail. I must now conclude, and believe me ever,

"Yours truly,

"D. Cox."

This letter was sealed with a black seal, engraved with a bundle of sticks, and the motto "Union is strength." Mr. William Hall, the artist referred to above, has related to me his recollections of this journey. He says that he and his friend Coleman slept at Llangollen on their way to Bettws. All night it blew "great guns," and rained in torrents. They, however, pursued their journey next morning up the valley, but on arriving at Corwen they witnessed an extraordinary scene. A waterspout had burst on the mountains, and torrents were rushing down the hills on each side, sweeping rocks and earth before them, knocking down cottages, and covering the road with spoil. They had great difficulty in getting on to Bettws, where Cox met them at the door of the Royal Oak. He came out and told them there was no room just then, but directed them to comfortable quarters at Llanrwst. The next morning the inn servant knocked at their door before they were up, and said a gentleman was waiting to see them down-stairs. On descending they found David Cox, who had walked over from Bettws, across the fields, quite three miles, to breakfast with them; and he told them they could now be accommodated at the Royal Oak. Having related to Cox what had happened in consequence of the waterspout, a day or two afterwards, on his way home, he made one or two sketches of the effect of the storm, from which he painted pictures on arriving at Harborne. It was in such weather as this, though a few years later, that he was told that the River Llugwy had swollen with the heavy rain to a great height, and was rushing and boiling grandly under the bridge. Cox, who had always a number of small pieces of drawing-paper ready, hurried to the spot, and made a rapid sketch of the torrent. The subject pleased him so well that he went on adding bit after bit, until he had achieved a considerable work. Arrived at home, the pieces, four in number, were carefully joined together, and, when mounted on a board, became an interesting and very effective drawing, which was afterwards exhibited, the joinings hardly showing at all at a little distance. It was whilst staying at Bettws in 1846 that Cox made a lovely drawing from the window of the Royal Oak, looking towards Pont-y-Pair Bridge, and up the valley in the direction of Capel-Curig, with cattle, ducks, and geese in the foreground. There were not nearly so many houses in the village at that time, so that the view was much less obstructed than at present, and it was one of his best and most characteristic works of this year. I am informed that he made a present of this to Mr. Bond, the artist, who afterwards sold it, and at the sale of Mr. Bullock's collection, in 1870, it went for the sum of £230.

During the long visit of more than a month which Cox made at Bettws in 1847, he wrote several letters to his son, from which I shall now present my readers with some extracts :—

"Royal Oak, July 21st, 1847.

"MY DEAR DAVID,—I left home on Monday at ten, and arrived at Chester at 2.30. An omnibus took the passengers about two miles beyond Chester to the railway beyond the bridge which broke down. I went on by rail to Rhuabon, and there a coach took me to Llangollen, where I immediately took a car to Corwen. None of my friends from Birmingham went with me, but when I arrived at Corwen I was agreeably surprised to meet with Messrs. McKewan, Bennett, and Price. We all agreed to take two cars to Pentre-Foelas, and reached there at ten at night. The following morning Mr. Price and I took a car on to Bettws. We were fortunate enough to find an empty house, and occupied their four beds.

CHAP. XI.

"The weather is very fine—too fine and hot to sit out in the middle of the day; but we have each done something.

"DAVID COX."

"Royal Oak, July 25th, 1847.

"We all intend to go to Festiniog on Tuesday morning, where we shall stay until Saturday, as Bennett, McKewan, and Price wish to reach Liverpool on that day, so I shall join one of them in a car to Pentre-Foelas. I shall there leave them, and walk to Bettws, as I may have by that time Mr. Roberts, and Mr. Sherrington from Yarmouth, a gentleman who was with us last year.

"DAVID COX."

"Royal Oak, August 6th, 1847.

"I was very agreeably surprised yesterday, after a wet morning's sketching, to find my friend Birch at the inn. He had no engagement with me, but good-naturedly thought I should not be disappointed of all my Birmingham friends.

"DAVID COX."

In the year 1847 Cox painted a sign-board in oil colours for the Royal Oak Inn—the subject, King Charles in the tree at Boscobel, with cavaliers on horseback galloping beneath, and dogs in the distance. An old sign previously existed, which hung up in front of the inn, and Cox mounted up on a ladder to repaint the same in the way described. Whilst he was busily employed in this position, a lady drove up—Mrs. Ashley, an old pupil and acquaintance. Stopping her carriage, she greeted our artist, much to his astonishment, thus: "Oh, Mr. Cox, is it really you! I hardly expected to see you here, mounted up so high on the ladder of fame." This sign-board is now carefully varnished, and framed with twisted branches of oak from which the bark has been removed, and hangs on the right-hand side, in the entrance-hall of the new Royal Oak Hotel. Cox's pallet, which has been gilded, and brush, are placed over it. It has long been considered too precious for any other position. Two years after the sign was painted it wanted varnishing, and Cox, with his usual kindness, again mounted up on the ladder for this object.

As the following letter refers to this sign, I think it may interest my readers if I insert it here :—

To WILLIAM ROBERTS, ESQ., *Rhyl, North Wales.*

"Greenfield, Harborne, Birmingham, July 15th, 1849.

". . . . . Pray go to Bettws and sketch, and on Saturday, the 28th, or Monday, the 30th, I hope to be with you. I do not yet know whether my son will be able to come down to go into Wales, as he has received summonses to go elsewhere. I hope to receive a letter from you to say you are safe, and comfortably seated at the Royal Oak at dear old Bettws; and remember and look at the sign, as painted by myself. I expect now it will want retouching (two years since I painted it). Give my kind remembrances to Mrs. Roberts, and believe me, my dear friend,

"Very sincerely,

"DAVID COX."

When Cox visited Bettws he used generally to paint a good many pictures out of doors in oil. The privilege of carrying his painting traps and easel was one for which there was keen competition amongst the village lads, who coveted this post of honour. He was universally respected and beloved by the poor Welsh people, and many were the little gifts he bestowed on them, the old women being often employed by him in knitting worsted stockings. On one occasion he was out in a field at Bettws, painting in oils, accompanied by an artist. His companion, hearing him throw his pallet down with a dash, and exclaiming, "It's no

CHAP. XI. use, I *can't* do it!" hurried to Cox, and found him about to wipe his picture off the canvas. "Mr. Cox!" he exclaimed, "what are you doing?" "Oh," he replied, "I can't manage it at all to my satisfaction, and must wipe out my work." The picture was a very nice one; so after some further remonstrances, Cox said, "Well, I want a tube of Indian yellow, and if you have one to spare, and will give it me in exchange for my picture, you shall have it." As may be supposed, the bargain was soon made. Besides painting the sign of the Royal Oak, Cox presented the landlord with a visitors' book. He walked over one morning by the old road over Pont-y-Pair Bridge to Llanrwst, and ordered a handsome one, bound in dark leather, and when it arrived he was the first to sign his name and address, with the date July 27th, 1846. He also made a water-colour sketch in the book for the sign of the Royal Oak, which he painted next year on panel. This sketch has since been taken out, and is now pasted inside the cover of a more recent visitors' book. The old book, although rather dilapidated, is still preserved in the Royal Oak, as a relic of the olden times.

An artist who resided for many years at Plas Myria, near Bettws-y-Coed, where Cox was an annual visitor then, Mr. George P. Popkin, has favoured me with the following reminiscences of David Cox and Bettws in the olden time:—

"I first knew David Cox in 1846 or 1847, and from that date till within one or two years of his death, hardly one passed that he did not spend a few weeks at Bettws—always at the Royal Oak except the last two visits; the last but one he came accompanied by an old housekeeper. But artist-life at the Oak had entered on a new phase; the old faces were missing; the house was in new hands; the snug but seedy old parlour had disappeared; the 'inn' had become an 'hotel;' the new race of artists were rollicking, and 'knew not Cox.' The old ideas and manners had departed with the old faces, and the failing strength of the old man could not endure the new régime; so he took lodgings at the farm-house close by the church in the fields where he had so often sketched; it is in the lane which supplied him with materials for his 'Welsh Funeral,' one of the last and most solemn and impressive of his works. Old David's feeling for Nature was so intense, that the materials he used made no difference. I have seen mere charcoal outlines made by him before commencing to colour, which suggested to the mind's eye of any one familiar with his works exactly what the drawing would be when finished. I think I have seen it remarked, by-the-bye, that it is impossible to visit North Wales and not 'see Cox' in every bit of its scenery. He so entered into the spirit of its character, that *Cox* and *Wales* are synonymous terms. And no other artist has ever, or can ever, represent its moods and phases unless he adopts the peculiar style and method he practised, and to do this *successfully* one must have a considerable degree of talent and boldness in using it.

"Cox had no preconceived ideas of his own, no *master always present in his mind;* Nature was before him, and time was an object. *He* had none to waste in high and laborious finish; he must get the effect as quick as he could, and by the readiest and simplest means, and it was thus that he became quite independent of artists' colourmen, and proved the possibility of representing Nature in her every mood without having recourse to the glaring, glittering, dangerous inventions so much in use in these days. I do not mean to say that he would not have used any means *at hand* to produce what he wanted; but he never relied on them, never went out of his way to obtain them. To the end his colour-box contained the same simple list of colours which he had used from the beginning; no Chinese white, no chromes, no aurelian Viridian, *et id genus omne.* I did not even see cadmium there. I know he had emerald green, for I recollect once seeing him use it for a mossy rock on which he stood at the time (it was down in the ravine called Foss Nowddin, below the Conway

CHAP. XI. Falls), which rock he had placed in the foreground of his sketch. And here I should observe that he made a great distinction between sketches and drawings. When before Nature he was too ardent and impulsive to consider the *means;* he got the nearest tint and texture he could, and as *quick* as he could. 'I don't care *what* I use,' he said to me, when I expressed surprise at his using emerald green, 'if I can but get the colour I want and see; it is time enough to *think* when one is working at home.' I was told by an old friend of his that he worked at home by candle or lamplight till bed-time, seeming happier so. Work was enjoyment to him—he needed no 'rest.' His habits at Bettws were exceedingly simple and primitive. In the evening he sat on the sofa in the parlour of the Royal Oak inn, which in those days was an artists' club *pur et simple.* Here he took his cigar (he smoked no pipe) and his pint of ale, with one or two cronies by his side, willing to listen and willing to teach. There was no racket, no shouting, no fastness or slang; it was an intelligent, rational, pleasant evening's amusement, and I have heard French, German, Hungarian, English, and Welsh flowing on like a polyglot stream at the same time in that same dingy parlour. Then on Sunday morning, as regular as Sunday came, there was Mr. Cox's car to take him and any friend to Llanrwst Church; at that time there was no nearer English service. He was a sincerely religious man, with no show but great earnestness; in fact, this *earnestness* was a great feature in his character in all that he did, and so great was his influence, that the most roistering son of the brush that ever ventured from Cockagne never attempted to dispute his dictum. Nevertheless, he was a mild and kind despot, and ruled more by love and esteem than by any other means. The desecration of the Sabbath was the only way of raising his indignation; he banished his favourite colour-box and brushes totally, and dressed distinctly different on this day. As for this said colour-box, it contained, as already stated, only the usual list of colours. He was well aware that it was not the material that made the artist, neither was it talent only; nothing but constant and unceasing practice could in his opinion, obtain success. Even when he had reached the highest rank in art he continued to be the most earnest student of Nature; indeed, I never met a man with a more humble opinion of his own works. I have frequently been out sketching with him, when mere tyros have come up to see him at work, and get some 'wrinkles' from the good old man, who never showed the least objection to their presence, or testified the slightest approach to jealousy or dislike to having what I have heard artists of half his genius and position term, 'having their brains sucked,' that is, having their secrets or mode of work watched. Dear old Cox had no secrets, he knew well enough that his genius could not be copied, though his manner might. So far from showing dislike to their presence, I have often heard him say over his shoulder, 'If you see anything wrong I wish you would tell me;' and if one said they had come to learn and not to *teach*, he would say, 'Ah, Mr. ——, it is a difficult business, a difficult business; one has never done learning at it. After all the years I have been working I only know very little.' On one occasion I asked him if he would allow me to become his regular pupil. He replied that he had given up teaching, but that I was heartily welcome to see him work and ask any questions which occurred to me, saying at the same time, 'But really you do not want lessons; all you require now is practice, practice, practice, and that you will require, as we all do, to the end of our lives.' At another time he called at my house with an old acquaintance, Dr. Kittermaster, and said, 'Popkin, you asked me about lessons the other day; here is Dr. Kittermaster has just asked me the same thing. If you like I will come in and show you both at the same time how I always sketch.' Of course we were delighted, and in two minutes we were settled at the table. The process was simple in the extreme. He worked with a large swan quill brush, and *slopped* his colours with water (he used the old-fashioned *hard* cake colours, but of extra size, in the usual japanned tin sketching box). He was jealous of wearing his brush, and if any colour was obstinate from having been baked in the sun, he rubbed it with his finger. His tints were very fluid, but not watery, and he explained that, by working with a full brush, the colours never dried *dark*, as they would do if the brush were half dry. I noticed that tints which looked very dark dried quite light. His system was constant *repetition of touches* till the effect was produced, being very careful that the preceding touches *were dry*. He seldom washed his tints after laying on, as he liked to see each touch defined, not softened off; he said it gave spirit and character to the sketch. 'But mind,' he said, 'I am only showing you how I *sketch*. These are three sketches I have just done for you, they are not *drawings*. I have done the same thing for other people, and they have sold them afterwards as my drawings.' And yet he was not rendered cynical or less kind-hearted by this ungrateful conduct; indeed, he was as simple and trusting in his nature as a child until the end approached, and his powers of sight and memory began to give way.

"I have the three little rough examples by me still, and I value them highly. They are quite unfinished, but they recall old times—the days that are gone for ever, and the noble-minded old David Cox.

"G. P. P."

Whilst Cox was staying at the Royal Oak, in the autumn, I believe, of 1849, a Miss Roberts, some relative of the landlord, died. She was quite young, and the event excited much sorrow in the little community. Cox attended the funeral, which, according to the habits in North Wales, took place in the evening, and the ceremony gave rise to his impressive and celebrated drawing of "The Welsh Funeral," now in the possession of Mr. F. Craven, and of which I give a copy, photographed from the original, in this book.

It has been remarked that Cox was always a very regular attendant at church, and, although no bigot, as mentioned by Mr. Popkin, he had a strong feeling that it was right "to keep holy the sabbath-day;" he also desired to pay respect to all religious observances, as well as to the clergy themselves. Some gay young artists, who had come down to stay at the Royal Oak in the summer of 1849, or 1850, in the exuberance of their spirits, had amused themselves with painting some caricatures on the walls under the Lych-gate porch, such as the parson thundering from his pulpit in an undignified attitude, the clerk fast asleep below, &c., &c. This much offended Cox's sense of propriety and decorum, so one evening soon afterwards, just at the close of the day, he called for a lanthorn, and said, "I am going off to Bettws Church to-night." A young friend, Mr. Edwin Butler, jun., who was present, said, "What for, Mr. Cox?" "Oh!" he replied, "I am going to wash off all those unseemly drawings." The young man volunteered to accompany him, and presently they sallied forth in the dark, one carrying a lanthorn and the other a large basin of water. Cox worked away in his usual energetic style until he had removed the whole of the offending sketches which had been the cause of his nocturnal expedition. Many a worse subject might be chosen for a picture than this earnest and venerable old man, with his youthful companion, approaching the church porch, bent on their pious mission, and the fine old yew-tree spreading round them. I am informed, in reference to the above incident, that Dr. Eagles was the clergyman who used to officiate at Bettws Church occasionally, reading the service in English; but he generally gave rather long sermons, which were not always liked by his audience. As the following two letters addressed to Mr. Roberts, who was then at Rhyl, and dated

CHAP. XI. 6th and 12th July, 1849, refer to journeys to Bettws, I think they will not be out of place if inserted here:—

"Greenfield, Harborne, July 6th, 1849.

"MY DEAR FRIEND ROBERTS, Rhyl, North Wales,—Many thanks for your kindness in writing to me so soon. I was also pleased to learn you were not altogether disappointed with the place, and that provisions, &c., were to be had reasonably cheap. Write again as soon as you get to Bettws, and tell me all the news. You tell me the climate is like Naples. How much I started with a desire to join you, and to receive a little benefit from the pure air of the sea and the mountains of Bettws; for I cannot help thinking that the smell of the oil paints has disagreed with me; and, as the time for sending my picture draws near, I am the more anxious, which makes me nervous, and then the work does not go on well. If you go to Bettws you may, if you please, ask Mary to let me have a bed in the house. I expect my son and Mr. Hall will accompany me, but I cannot at all see my way until the 20th, or thereabouts. I have not seen Mr. Bullock since you left, but I suppose, from what he said on Monday evening, he will join you next week. I have not seen Mr. B.; indeed, he went to London last morning. I received a letter from my friend, Mr. Barber, who wishes me to join him in Wales (Bala), as he starts to-morrow, (Saturday). When I go I shall most likely stop at Abergele for a night, or perhaps go on at once. I must be guided in part by my companions. I hope at all events we shall meet, and believe me,

"Very truly,

"DAVID COX."

"Greenfield, Harborne, Birmingham, July 12th, 1849.

"MY DEAR FRIEND ROBERTS,—I am glad you are about to visit dear old Bettws, and only wish I could be there with you, but I may probably yet get my paintings finished and be able to start in about a fortnight, or about the 28th or 30th, but I fear not before. My old friend Barber, of Liverpool, is at Bettws, with two of his daughters, and a brother of Mr. Pritt's, our curate. They write in great spirits, and are delighted with the neighbourhood, and glad they have made the change from Bala, where they all first went to. I have not seen Mr. Bullock since you left, and therefore I suppose he is with you. My son is coming to see me next week, and will very likely accompany me into Wales. At all events Mr. Hall will be ready to accompany me by the end of this month, and he will have his pupil with him (a son of Mr. Butler's). They are to come to my house to-morrow evening, to make further arrangements. I have nearly finished my picture for the Birmingham Exhibition, and have got on very well with one ('Kit Cat') for Liverpool. I do not like working to a fixed time. I think in all probability Mr. Ellis will join me in Wales about the second week in August, but of this I shall hear more. If you should go to Bettws, please mention to Miss Roberts of the time of my intended visit, and also of that of Mr. Hall, &c. Please give my sincere regards to Mrs. Roberts, and love to the young ladies, in which my sister begs to join, and believe me, sincerely,

"DAVID COX."

In 1850 Mr. Hall, Mr. Coleman, and other friends, stayed with Cox at the Royal Oak for several weeks in August and September. It proved unfortunately an exceedingly wet autumn, and the greater part of this visit had to be spent indoors, much to the mortification of the artists, who could only snatch occasional sketches between the continual storms of rain and wind. In spite of the weather, however, Cox continued this year to make some of his most effective and grand drawings in the neighbourhood of Bettws, among

CHAP. XI. which the following may be especially noticed:—"Rocky Scene near Capel Curig," "Vale of Dolwyddelan," "Beaver Grove, Bettws," "Moel Siabod, near Capel-Curig."

After a serious illness, which at one time threatened David Cox's life, and to which I shall refer more at length in another chapter, he only made a few more journeys to Bettws, the last being in the year 1856. On these latter occasions he was always accompanied by his housekeeper, Ann Fowler, and by an attendant, George Priest, a picture-mounter and manufacturer of frames, stretchers, &c., who lived at Birmingham, and for whom Cox felt a good deal of friendship—as appears, moreover, by some notes preserved by his widow. Mr. Priest knew Cox's ways, and was able to do much for his comfort on these journeys, for although age and infirmity were then fast overtaking the venerable artist, his heart was still in his work, and his love for the scenery of North Wales was unabated.

In 1852, 1853, 1854, 1855, and 1856, Cox put up at the farmhouse belonging to the landlord of the Royal Oak, situated in the lane leading to the church, and about a hundred yards from the inn. In 1852 he was accompanied by his grand-daughter as well as by Mrs. Fowler. They stayed at the farm, but used to walk across to the Royal Oak for meals. Dr. James Kittermaster, a physician who was very fond of sketching, was at Bettws at the same time, and used to be a good deal with his friend, David Cox. Miss Cox describes her grandfather on this occasion as usually walking only a little way along the road, and making sketches or studies of the valley and hills of Bettws, near the river, and of effects of light and shade, without going many paces away from home. One day they all went in a car as far as Llanberris and back. Cox made the car stop twice on the road on this occasion, to take rapid sketches.

He used to get up at eight to breakfast, and if fine he would go out sketching till dinner, at one o'clock. After dinner, a good rest and a nap, followed by an early cup of tea, quite refreshed him, and he would then sally out again to see and take notes of the evening effects, and especially the sunsets, which he never liked to miss. At eight, or sooner, he returned home to a light supper, and then to bed, about nine o'clock.

In 1853, at the end of August, Cox was sufficiently recovered from his illness, which occurred on the 12th of June, to undertake a journey to Bettws. He went there this time accompanied by another grand-daughter, and also by Mrs. Fowler, and for the first time by Priest. Again, in 1854, he left Harborne on the 4th of August with his son, Mr. Ellis, and Mrs. Fowler. They went to Rhyl, Abergele, and on to Pentrefoilas, and afterwards to Capel Curig, not very far from Bettws. They were away some weeks on this trip, and Cox, although feeble, was able to go on with his work as usual. Later in the autumn Cox felt rather restless, regretting that he had not been to stay at dear old Bettws, so he made a second journey into Wales, accompanied only by Mrs. Fowler and Priest, and put up as usual at the farmhouse belonging to the Royal Oak. This time he had all his meals sent across to the farm, instead of taking them at the inn, as the bustle there was now too much for him. This was also the arrangement in the autumns of 1855 and 1856, when he went to Bettws for the last time. Just before leaving Bettws, in 1855, he painted an interesting oil-picture out of doors of the rocks and hills behind the Royal Oak, with a rocky foreground, much heather, and a little bit of blue distance. The day was very fine, and the effect excellent. When Cox had finished he turned to Priest, and said that that was his last picture of Bettws that he should paint from nature. He felt that the journey was becoming too fatiguing for him, and he was doubtful if he should be able to come again. Early in September, 1856, however, he again arrived at Bettws, accompanied by Mrs. Fowler and Priest.

On the 11th September he writes to his son:—

"I must tell you how glad I am to be at old Bettws-y-Coed, but I cannot paint out of doors; but I walk a small distance, and talk to some of the old travellers. I hope you are still pleased with your drawings. I am going out with a car for a ride, so must finish a short letter. Love and affection to my dear children, and I remain

"Your old,

"DAVID COX."

The ride in the car was to Capel Curig, to see Dr. Kittermaster and Mr. and Mrs. Collingwood Smith, who wanted also to come to Bettws, but could not get accommodated.

Cox's old friend, Mr. Roberts, was staying at Bettws at this time, and also Sir Charles Eastlake. Cox lodged as usual at the old farmhouse near the Royal Oak, and every one was delighted to see him there again. Mr. Coleman, who was also at Bettws, used to call to take little walks, and although Cox found he could not make sketches from nature, he appears to have enjoyed himself very much indeed. He said that being at Bettws had done him "so much good." A day or two before he left he wrote: "I and Ann (Mrs. Fowler) are better than when we left Harborne, and we like the air so well." Fortunately, the weather was unusually fine. Just before leaving this year, he again signed his name in the visitors'-book at the Royal Oak—"David Cox, September 22, 1856."

This was the last time, for he never came to "dear old Bettws" again.

XII.

PAINTING IN OIL-COLOURS.

AS an introduction to the account I am shortly intending to give of the most important works in oil painted by David Cox, after he came to reside at Harborne, and of the prices obtained for these pictures during the last few years, I propose to relate in the present chapter some particulars of his progress and method in oil-painting. I shall briefly notice, also, the subjects selected, and the names of the original purchasers of these works.

There are oil-pictures painted by Cox as far back as 1812, and others dated in 1830; but it was between the years 1842 and 1857 that the best pictures were produced.

Before the first of these dates the handling was somewhat timid, hard, and dry, and they were painted at longer intervals. After 1845, he displayed a more thorough grasp and knowledge of the material, and as years went on his power and ease in the production of the desired effects greatly increased. Without doubt his best period was from 1845 to 1856. I believe he never painted anything finer than his large and grand picture of Bettws Church, now in Mr. A. Levy's collection, and which bears the date of 1856.

It is, I think, deserving of a passing remark, that before the first of these dates Cox had entered on his sixty-second year. How few men, even at a less advanced period of life, would have thrown themselves, with the enthusiasm and ardour of this veteran, into a comparatively new branch of

CHAP. XII. art! Cox had removed to Birmingham with the fixed determination of following up the pursuit of oil-painting, and it was among his friends there that he found purchasers for most of his early works. How little his fame as an oil-painter had spread, or become known at a distance, even many years later, is proved by the fact that there was not a single example of David Cox's work in oil in the Manchester Art-Treasures Exhibition of 1857, nor in the Great International Exhibition of 1862, and only one small one in the Leeds National Fine-Arts Exhibition of 1868, although all these exhibitions professed to contain the works of all our best modern landscape-painters in oil. They all, however, comprised a collection of some of his choicest works in water-colours. For several years after Cox took up his residence at Harborne, he devoted his time and thoughts much more to oil-painting than he did to water-colours, and his full energies were concentrated on that, to him, comparatively new branch of art. He loved oil-painting so heartily that it appeared to give him new life and spirit; and considering this, we shall perhaps wonder less at the extraordinary progress he made in knowledge of the material, and in the handling. By comparing the pictures painted by him in successive years, this progress is very apparent, and easily recognised.

Those friends who had helped to persuade Cox to remove to Birmingham—Mr. W. Roberts, Mr. E. Bullock, and Mr. C. Birch—were amongst the first to give commissions to him. They were soon followed by other gentlemen in the same neighbourhood—Mr. Darby, Mr. W. Tarratt, Mr. George Briscoe, Mr. Marshall Carritt, and a few local dealers. They purchased the pictures generally direct from the easel, but at very low prices, as will be hereafter related.

It is a fact that many canvases and panels in the studio at Greenfield House were marked on the back with the initials of the would-be purchaser of the picture not yet painted, so eager were some of these collectors to secure more of these simple yet charming transcripts of nature. Mr. William Holmes relates that in a large cupboard under the staircase leading to the studio many of these oil-pictures were deposited, and there he used to select out whatever he fancied would sell at the prices then current. Of the original collections referred to, that of Mr. Birch was sold by auction in 1857, Mr. Briscoe's in 1860, Mr. Roberts's in 1867, Mr. Bullock's in 1870, and Mr. Darby's some years earlier, but by private treaty. Of those who made collections at second hand, I may mention Messrs. J. Gillott, W. H. Dawes, J. Bagnall, F. Timmins, H. Fletcher, S. Mayou, P. Allen Sydney Cartwright, T. M. Whitehouse, T. Page, &c. Recently many of the finest of these works have passed into the collections of the Messrs. Nettlefold, De Murietta, A. Levy, F. Huth, and others, at continually advancing prices. Mr. David Cox, jun., possesses many works in oil of the highest excellence by his father, which were bequeathed to him.

The prices which Cox himself received for oil-pictures varied from £5 and upwards to about £50, reaching in one case £95, and in one only £100—the highest ever paid to him for one of his works. It is a trite, though true remark, that the public are often too slow to appreciate true genius in an artist during his lifetime. As with Cox, so also with Müller, their great merits, alas! were only fully recognised after they were gone.

Cox felt that his handling in his oil-painting was not quite equal to that in water-colours. Without doubt for several years there was a certain hardness and stiffness which he afterwards corrected, and he used to say that he did not fully understand all the technical resources of the art, such as scumbling, glazing, and hatching, as well as some oil-painters did. So he did not like people to go very close to examine what he had just painted; on such occasions he would say, "Well, what do

CHAP. XII. you see amiss? You must understand I am no great hand at oil-painting; it is not the work I have been used to." He never used a maulstick when at work, but preferred to rest his right hand on his left in those parts that required great accuracy of outline. Cox was a great admirer of Müller's, Linnell's, and Constable's landscapes, and also of some of the works of Gainsborough. I think no apology will be deemed necessary for quoting the following observations on Gainsborough by Sir Joshua Reynolds, as they are so truly applicable to Cox also:—

"We can hardly refuse acknowledging the full effect of diligence under the appearance of chance and hasty negligence. However they appear to superficial observers, painters know very well that a steady attention to the general effect takes up more time and is more laborious to the mind than any mode of high finish or smoothness without much attention. Whatever he attempted he carried to a high degree of excellence. His handling, the manner of leaving the colour, or, in other words, the method he used for producing the effect, have very much the appearance of the work of an artist who had never learned from others the usual and regular practice belonging to the art, but still, like a man of strong intuitive perception of what was required, he found out a way of his own to accomplish his purpose."

Cox's oil-pictures have stood well; they were generally painted rapidly, as Müller used to paint his, producing the local colour and effect as far as possible at once, instead of going over the same ground many times. The mediums he relied on were very simple, chiefly linseed-oil, turpentine, and gum copal, and occasionally plaster of Paris. The following extract from a letter written to his son—to whom he was recommending a trial of oil-painting—will be interesting to many, and may be introduced here with advantage, I believe, as showing Cox's method, and the colours he used in oil-painting. It is dated from Harborne, December 21st, 1845:—

"In your dark you will use the transparent colours, and if you were to procure a pot of some fine powder of plaster of Paris to mix with the transparent colours, it assists to give them a substance without making them look opaque. In your greens or half lights also use a little of the plaster of Paris, and so on, till you come to the high lights, when you may use Naples yellow, lemon yellow, and also yellow ochre. White, I think, must be cautiously used, only in such sparkling touches as Constable did; but there are occasions where white must be used, in very pale greens, upon dock leaves, &c., &c., but in a little time you will discover all the properties and uses of each colour. I find that by using the same colour, or nearly the same, for oil as in water, for instance, light red and cobalt for extreme distances, and so on towards the middle distance, where I should begin with a light Prussian blue and light red, and in the nearer part Prussian blue and burnt sienna and a light red, all three together, and in the foreground bitumen and Prussian blue. The second green or half lights with Prussian blue, light red, and yellow ochre, and vary it with raw sienna; the high lights with an addition of lemon yellow and Naples yellow, but you will find terra vert and ivory black, or terra vert and raw umber very good. Terra vert is a most useful colour.

"Do not use Indian red in your greens; as I said before, use light red, and work in the compounding of your tints in a very similar way to what you would in water-colour painting. There are perhaps many other observations which I may think of in some future letter, but I cannot use the chrome yellows without a great risk of throwing everything out of harmony. I therefore use it very sparingly, and sometimes not at all."

The colour of Cox's oil-pictures resembles his water-colours in many respects; they are equal to them in brilliancy and truth of tone. What they lose in tenderness and *atmosphere* they gain in power. There is not quite the

CHAP. XII. same ease and freedom of handling in *all* of them as in most of his water-colours, but after a careful examination of many of his finest works of his best period in oil, I am led to the conclusion that they lose little or nothing in this respect in comparison with his best water-colours, and they have undoubtedly the advantage of greater durability. The colour also of his oils is very agreeable; they abound in cool greens and silver greys, and are never foxy. Bitumen, although named in his letter to his son, is a colour which he used very sparingly, especially in his best works. It is to be remembered that when Cox took up oil-painting he had arrived at the maturity of his art-knowledge and power of handling in water-colours, having had forty years' practice as an artist—indefatigable practice, I may truly say; but his feeling for nature and his broad and impulsive method of treatment continued to advance for many years.

After Cox had got over the early difficulties and had begun to *feel* his strength in the new material, he appears to have derived more pleasure from working in oil than in water-colour. On the 2nd April, 1843, he addressed a letter from Harborne to his son, in which, after advising him to try painting in oil from nature, he goes on to say:—

"There is not half the trouble with oil as with water-colours. I should never again touch water-colours only for my honour and duty to the society I belong to. I have had more plague with two of my large drawings this year than I should with twenty in oil.

"In oil you may make alterations, but in water-colours you are subject to spots in the paper, and if you alter, the paper becomes so rough that you lose all atmosphere. Small drawings may be made very well in water. Give me oil. I only wish I had begun earlier in life; the pleasure in painting in oil is so very satisfactory.

"DAVID COX."

In 1843 and the two following years especially, he painted a good deal from nature in oil. These were almost always on small canvases, but by degrees he increased the size of his works until in 1846 he produced his first very large picture, "The Vale of Clwyd," 3 ft. 3 in. by 4 ft. 8 in. The approach of winter hardly interfered at all with his work, as he painted a great deal by lamplight, and his long experience generally enabled him to avoid mistakes in the colour. He used always to like to finish his pictures by daylight, but with respect to the effect, he has repeatedly said that he could manage that and the light and shade quite as well or better by artificial light than he could in the daytime.

The subject which Cox chose for his oil-pictures were almost always those which he had previously painted successfully in water-colour, and by which he felt his sympathies had been most deeply moved. In looking through the catalogues of the Water Colour Exhibition after 1841, the date when he came to reside at Harborne, I generally find that several of his most representative drawings of one year were chosen the next for works to be painted in oil. Thus views at Bettws such as "The Rocks behind the Royal Oak," "The Old Mill, Bettws," "Bettws Church," "Peat Gatherers Returning," "Besom Gatherers," "Cutting Vetches," "Calais Pier," "Asking the Way," and "A Hayfield," were very favourite subjects in oil, some of them being painted many times over; but his most representative works were "Changing the Pasture," "The Vale of Clwyd," "The Skirts of the Forest," "The Welsh Funeral," "The Big Meadow, Bettws," and above all, "Going to the Hayfield." His friends all wanted a copy of these pictures, and no one who has ever seen them will wonder at this. It is, however, deserving of remark that in no case is there an exact replica. He always varied the "incidents," grouping the figures in a different way each time, and also making some change in the sky, the trees, or the foreground. One of his best works,

"The Skylark," was, however, only once painted in oil. Most of these pictures are painted in a free, vigorous, and rather loose manner, and require to be looked at from a certain distance to obtain the best point of view and the most complete effect. Some are painted on the back or reverse side of the canvas, as by this method Cox considered a more loose and free effect was obtained.

There is, I think, as much or more simplicity and unity in the late oil-pictures painted by Cox as in those of an earlier date. In the middle period I find more richness and fulness, and in the latest more solemnity and sacrifice of accessories to the one leading idea. In other words, he concentrated his powers as years advanced, being more entirely penetrated with the true meaning and life of the subject he sought to represent. This was what he termed painting with *the mind.* I could apply these remarks equally to his water-colours, which are often nearly identical in subject.

In concluding these observations I must add that in nearly all Cox's pictures we can recognise the same truth, the same love for simple, rural life, devoid of all false sentiment and exaggeration, and the same quick and discriminating appreciation of natural scenery. In the earlier, as in the latest works, there is much of the same power of seizing on the most salient and interesting points in a subject, and then dashing them with apparently little effort on to his canvas. He forgot himself in his work, and such was his ardour that I fear he often injured his health by over-exertion, especially when painting large pictures. I must not, however, any longer delay giving the promised account of the works themselves.

XIII.

OIL-PICTURES.

THIS chapter will contain an account of Cox's most celebrated works in oil, and the prices at which they have been sold. As many have no dates attached, and others are replicas, I shall not attempt to follow an exact chronological order, but I will first take some of the best-known pictures, and then touch on a few of the original collections, giving all the dates and the sizes, as far as I have been able to ascertain them.

THE VALE OF CLWYD. 1846. 3 ft. 3 in. by 4 ft. 8 in.

The spot chosen for the subject of this picture is near St. Asaph, about half way between Rhyl and Denbigh. It is solidly paintèd and very effective. A grand group of oaks on the right shelters some figures journeying along the road. On the left a yellow harvest-field with woods and distant hills beyond. The sky is full of light breezy clouds, and shadows alternate with sparkling lights on the distant hills and mountains. The handling is rather less free than in many of his later works. Not being ready for the Birmingham Exhibition, for which it was intended, Cox sent it to Liverpool, July 17th, 1846, catalogue price eighty guineas, and it was returned unsold in March, 1847. This is from a memorandum in his own handwriting.

Not having obtained any satisfactory offer after a few months, he parted with it to a Mr. Nixon, in exchange for a

CHAP. XIII. large, but unfinished painting by W. S. Müller, very fine in colour: the subject represented was a salmon trap, with rocks, trees, and a water-mill, which used to hang in the parlour of Greenfield House. This "Vale of Clwyd" was sold by Mr. Nixon for £70; it changed hands once or twice before Mr. Holmes purchased it in 1868 for £480. Mr. Sharp then purchased it for £580, and for many years it hung in his house at Handsworth. Early in 1872 Mr. McClean gave £2,000 for this picture, and resold it for £2,200 to Mr. de Murietta. The two "Vales of Clwyd," and the "Collecting the Flocks," from the late Mr. Bullock's collection, are the only ones of this large size, 3 ft. 3 in. by 4 ft. 8 in., ever, I believe, painted by Cox.

VALE OF CLWYD. 1848. 3 ft. 3 in. by 4 ft. 8 in.

Painted for Mr. George Briscoe, who paid Cox £95 for it. In many respects it is like the one described above, but the trees have more vigour, and rooks are wheeling round about them, which adds to the windy effect. It has more play of light and shade, the texture is rougher, and there is rather more freedom in the handling. The colour also is brilliant and powerful. At Mr. Briscoe's sale, May, 1860, Mr. Frederick Timmins bought it for £250; it was sold in 1872 for £2,500, making with two small works, estimated at £1,500, the sum of £4,000. Mr. de Murietta has this picture also, I am informed. It is one of Cox's finest works in oil.

PEACE AND WAR. 1846. 18½ by 24 in. A harvest-field, and troops marching towards the town of Lancaster.

This celebrated picture has great richness of colour and more finish than some of his later works; it has an excellently arranged foreground, and is full of subject and interest. The chromatic effect, light and shade, composition, and general feeling, are very pleasing and truthful.

It was originally made a present of to a friend of the artist's, a clergyman, at Bromyard. This gentleman, being subsequently in want of funds, asked Cox "*if he would mind his selling it.*" Cox offered at once to buy it himself, which he did for £20; and he shortly resold it for the same sum to Mr. Darby.

Mr. W. H. Dawes purchased it from Mr. Darby for £25. Some years after this, it passed to Mr. Gillott, with another picture, "A Pass in Wales," for £650.

At the sale of Mr. Gillott's collection, in 1872, the "Peace and War" went for the large sum of £3,601 10*s*. Mr. Agnew eagerly competed for it on behalf of a client of his, but it was ultimately knocked down to Mr. Gillott's son.

COUNTING THE FLOCK. 1847. 24 by 36 in.

For all the qualities that go to make up a complete work of art this is perhaps unsurpassed by anything Cox ever painted. A shepherd stands by an open gate through which a numerous flock of sheep, full of movement, appear to have just passed, and are wending their way down a sloping hollow, with a range of low hills beyond. The road is rough and broken in the foreground; greenish greys prevail in the landscape, and the pure silvery tones of the sky are very charming. This, and the companion picture of the same size and date, viz., "Haymaking," which is also beautiful and full of atmosphere and summer sunshine, were purchased direct from Cox for £28 each by Mr. Thomas Darby. Mr. W. H. Dawes purchased them from Mr. Darby, in 1858, for £250, and he also purchased from him at the same time several smaller ones at very low prices compared with their present value, of which he sold five, together with the "Counting the Flock," and "Haymaking," in 1871, to Mr. Agnew for 4,000 guineas.

CHAP. XIII. The subjects of the other small pictures. which are all very pleasing and quiet, and which Mr. Darby bought direct from Cox's easel, at prices varying from £10 to £14, were :—

ASKING THE WAY. 1848. 20 by 30 in.
· THE FERRY ON THE WYE. 1848. 20 by 30 in.
RETURNING FROM LABOUR. 14 by 18 in.
GOING TO PLOUGH, MORNING. 14 by 18 in.
HARLECH CASTLE, an upright, and several others.

THE SALMON TRAP. 1850. 18 by 24 in.

This fine picture, which was painted for the late Mr. George Briscoe, is remarkable for its grand and solemn truth. The subject is twilight, according to Cox's own description on the back, or early morning. The scene is near Moel Siabod, North Wales; mountains are seen on all sides, with a deep ravine running into the heart of the range, and a broad stream in the foreground. The water in the salmon pool is still, and reflects a large tree and dark mountains; it flows thence under foliage into the salmon trap, from which it rushes surging over a rocky bed. The contrast of the half daylight with the tumult of the mountain stream is finely given. Two figures appear to be quietly searching the trap for fish, one having placed a basket on the stones close by. In the middle distance some cows are at rest, and a few scattered sheep are dimly seen feeding on the mountain side. The rays from the sun about to rise are thrown on to the Western mountains, and this light is again reflected in a few streaks on the water. Some fine bluish, purple, and orange clouds, just above the mountain tops, appear as if rolling away before the influence of the coming day. The whole conception is full of a fine poetical feeling and the treatment admirable. Mr. Briscoe paid Cox £14 for this picture as soon as it was finished, in 1850. At the sale of this gentleman's collection at Christie's, in May, 1860, it sold for

47 guineas, and for many years it adorned the collection of Mr. T. M. Whitehouse. In 1871 it was sold with one or two others, and produced the sum of £400. It is now the property of Mr. de Murietta, who paid £500 for it, I believe. Its present value is undoubtedly much higher.

SOLITUDE. 1850. About 24 by 36 in.

A rather gloomy but very impressive picture of a wild rocky glen, with large boulders in the foreground and two herons; some leafless trees hang across the centre, and in the distance is part of a dark mountain gorge. The subject and treatment somewhat resemble Salvator Rosa, and the colouring is quite as powerful as that of Velasquez. It was commenced a year or two before Cox's attack of illness, and never quite finished till afterwards. The late Mr. Reeves, of Birmingham, was the original purchaser of this work, and at his sale in 1865 it passed for 80 guineas into the hands of Mr. T. M. Whitehouse, who lent it to the Wolverhampton Fine-Arts Exhibition in 1869. It has lately been purchased by Mr. A. Levy, in whose collection it now is.

WASHING DAY. 1843. 18 by 25 in.

Painted originally for Mr. Froggett, an old pupil of Cox's, who paid £15 for it. A year or two afterwards Mr. Carritt bought it for £55. It then passed through Mr. W. Hall's hands to Mr. Gillott, who gave for it 150 guineas; at his sale in 1872 it produced the sum of £945. This picture represents two women at a pool of water; a cottage with clothes hanging out to dry, and flapping in the wind. Trees, with a bit of distance, and a fresh, breezy sky complete the subject. The colour is admirable, especially that of the foreground.

THE SKYLARK. 1849. 28 by 36 in.

This picture was exhibited in the Birmingham Exhibition.

CHAP. XIII. It is of the highest quality; the light and shade are admirably arranged and very broad. It is one of those subjects where the artist has concentrated all his thoughts and power on an idea which is so thoroughly realised that the spectator feels carried into the scene itself. The foreground consists of a luxuriant growth of leaf plants and grass, with a path leading to a stile, near Harborne. On the left is a group of fine trees growing out of the hedgerow, and these are again supported by some bushy trees farther off. On and round about the stile are five country children in various attitudes, eagerly looking up at a skylark seen far above in the air. The uppermost of the group is a little child extending both its arms towards the lark; she is upheld on the topmost rail by an elder girl, whilst another, seated on the grass, leans over on her hand in an attitude of perfect ease and enjoyment. Some broken rails and bushes complete the line across the picture. Beyond is a meadow of long grass, in which cows are quietly feeding here and there, but so disposed as to carry the eye towards the far distance. The sky is unusually tender and full of *space*, and so is the distant landscape which stretches far away and melts into the sky at the horizon. The feeling conveyed is that of early summer, with perfect repose and enjoyment of out-door country life.

This picture was, unfortunately, never repeated by Cox. It was originally purchased by Mr. Butler, of High Street, Birmingham, from Cox for £40, and resold by him to Mr. MacCarthy for £125. This gentleman is said to have repented of his bargain, so Mr. Butler took it back and then sold it for £150 to Mr. Thomas Darby. He exchanged it for some other pictures with Mr. Holmes, who parted with it in August, 1859, to Mr. Mayou for £50, and some water-colour drawings valued at £100. It remained in Mr. Mayou's collection till 1872, when Mr. Nettlefold purchased it for £2,300, and he is now its fortunate possessor.

THE SEA-SHORE AT RHYL, with distant View of the Town. Dated 1854-55. 29 by 53 in. CHAP. XIII.

This picture was lent by Mr. R. Adams, of Birmingham, to the Loan Exhibition of Pictures and Drawings, the works of David Cox, in 1859, at 168, New Bond Street. It was No. 1 in the catalogue, and attracted much attention from its large size and high quality. It was thus noticed at the time in the *Art-Journal*:—"A marvellously fresh and life-like representation. The subject little else than a large open bay with a line of sands traversed by a few figures, and the small town in the distance; but the effect of light, the motion of the silvery clouds, and the clear grey waves, form one of the most beautiful representations we have ever seen. It is painted in a remarkably free manner, and must be looked at from a distance."

It was exhibited in Liverpool, and sold by the artist to Mr. Croft for £100. It passed through several hands, amongst others those of Mr. Agnew, being sold in 1864 for £150. Ultimately it went back to Mr. William Agnew, of Manchester, who retained it for many years, and in 1872 he parted with it to Mr. Levy, of London, for £2,300. It is undoubtedly one of the finest pictures painted by Cox. The sky and waves are so full of movement, and on the left a broad shadow is cast by the clouds over the sea, which adds greatly to the effect of light on the sandy shore; the figures seem to be blown about by the wind, and even the bathing machines are so massed together and treated as to add rather than detract from the general effect. Some sea-gulls skimming above the waves help to carry the light over the picture.

Mr. Charles Birch's collection of oil pictures, sold 27th February, 1857, comprised a beautiful example of the "Welsh Funeral," very freshly painted in 1850, and now belonging to Mr. Bett's, also

CHAP. XIII.

COAST SCENE—SEA-SHORE WITH SHRIMPERS. 1845. 14 by 18 in.

This represents part of Carnarvon Bay, and is a very beautiful picture. Bought from the easel for £19.

THE BIG MEADOW, BETTWS. 1849. 18 by 24½ in.

A powerful work with figures.

ROAD SCENE. 1845. 9½ by 14½ in.

This fresh little picture was also purchased from the easel for £8.

GOING TO THE HAYFIELD. 1849. 2 ft. 4 in. by 3 ft. Mr. Briscoe's picture, now Mr. Page's.

This well-known and most natural picture is painted on the wrong side of the canvas. The silvery grey sky is very luminous; foreground, an abundance of docks and other leaf plants, cool and fresh in colour. A countryman, in a white vest or jacket, is riding a grey horse and leading another towards the hayfield, preceded by a rough terrier dog. In the middle distance are the usual hay-waggons and hay-makers, with a range of low, bluish hills beyond. Several trees on the right hand assist the general effect. It was purchased direct from David Cox by Mr. Briscoe for £20, and at Mr. Briscoe's sale ten years afterwards Mr. W. Holmes purchased it for £90. He resold it at a small profit to Mr. Hall, who, in 1859, sold it to Mr. Howard Fletcher for £130. After that gentleman's death it was purchased in September, 1861, by Mr. Page, of Great Barr, for £162 15s. Mr. Page has since refused £2,500 for it.

THE OLD MILL AT BETTWS-Y-COED. 1847. 2 ft. 4½ in. by 3 ft., with geese in the foreground.

This mill exists no longer. It is a powerful picture, and

an exact representation of the spot and of the scenery at Bettws; painted for Mr. Carritt, who paid £40 for it. At his sale it went for 60 guineas; and, after changing hands several times, Mr. Holmes purchased it for 180 guineas, and resold it to Mr. Gillott, in July, 1865, for 200 guineas. At Mr. Gillott's sale, April, 1872, it fetched £1,575. CHAP. XIII.

GOING TO THE MILL. 1847. 2 ft. 5 in. by 3 ft.

Figures approaching a windmill; an excellent subject, often repeated by Cox. It was painted for Mr. W. Holmes, price £30. The picture wanted more sky, so a piece was added by Cox to the top, and it was sold to Mr. Butler, who resold it to Mr. Bickerstaff, of Preston, for £100. Mr. Gillott purchased it in 1859 (the year Cox died) for the same sum, and at the Gillott sale, in 1872, it went for £1,575.

The three following oil-pictures are in Mr. Mayou's collection at Edgbaston:—

GOING TO THE HAYFIELD. 1849. 28 by 34 in.

The print at the commencement of the chapter is from this picture—one of the finest, if not the very finest, of this favourite subject. The atmospheric effect of the sky in this picture is wonderful; it is full of very light clouds, which appear to be gliding away. The meadow is being mowed by two or three men, and the long grass seems all in movement bending before the breeze. In a distant field are some haymakers turning the hay, and an empty hay wain with horses and drivers approaching. In the immediate foreground are broad-leaved plants, some in flower, and on the right some trees grouped together, rather bare of foliage and the stems standing dark against the sky. On a rough bit of road a man on a white horse (without his jacket to show the heat of the day) is carrying a basket and leaning over to talk to two country women, one of whom is carrying a hay-fork

CHAP. XIII. and the other a basket. The man is followed by a white terrier, true to life. I give, through the kindness of Mr. Mayou, a photograph of this beautiful work. He purchased it about twenty years ago from Mr. Butler, of Birmingham, for £120, and for many years hung it as a companion to the "Skylark." 2,000 guineas have, I understand, been offered for it lately.

DUDLEY CASTLE, WITH GLEANERS APPROACHING. 1848. 18½ by 24 in.

This picture is rich in colour, highly finished, and full of subject. A number of dark trees rise up on the left, as if growing on a sloping bank. On a path leading through a stubble field are several figures carrying bundles of corn. Beyond this field the ground appears to dip into a hollow, and rising again, shows a steep hill in the distance covered with shocks of wheat, and many figures busily gleaning. At the top the castle rises up against an evening sky. The treatment is something like the "Peace and War." It was purchased at the late Mr. W. Barrows' sale at Himley for £80 by Mr. Mayou.

GOING TO THE MILL. 1847. 8½ by 12 in.

The sun is setting near a windmill situated on a hill; some women and lads are winding their way up a road towards it. The handling is free, and the colour warm and pleasing.

A STREAM, WITH FIGURES FISHING. 1850. 14 by 18 in.

An upright, with some fine trees in dark green summer foliage, very fresh and cool in colour, and masterly in its treatment. The water is especially fine, and appears to be gently running under a bank, as trout streams do. The effect is particularly pleasing, as it abounds in greys and low-toned greens. There is no high finish, but it is an eminently successful work, and very characteristic of the artist. Mr. Marshall Carritt paid Cox £14 for this picture in 1850, and some time afterwards Mr. Holmes purchased it for £30, and sold it to Mr. Rodgett, of Preston, for £40. At Mr. Rodgett's sale it was bought by Mr. Sidney Cartwright, of the Leasowes, near Whampton, for 80 guineas; he has since refused 400 guineas for it. Mr. Cartwright has two other very fresh little oil-paintings of fine quality by Cox; a Hayfield with hay wains, and the often-repeated subject, a Cottage on Dulwich Common, with clothes hanging out to dry. CHAP. XIII.

A GRAND MOUNTAIN LANDSCAPE. 1847.

The scenery is somewhere in the neighbourhood of Bettws. It was originally painted for Mr. G. Briscoe, who, not caring to keep it, sent it to Mr. W. Hall, who parted with it to Mr. James Bagnall, of Meyrick House, West Bromwich, for £30. After his death it was sold at Christie's, 4th June, 1872, for 830 guineas.

A HAYFIELD, with a man riding and leading a white horse, and a boy and dog in the foreground. 1847.

This is one of the numerous examples of "Going to the Hayfield," and a very beautiful and successful picture, although not quite equal in feeling and handling to that in Mr. Thomas Page's collection, painted two years later. Mr. Bagnall purchased this picture from Cox, soon after it was painted, for £40; at the sale after his death in June, 1872, it was sold for 1,550 guineas.

FROLIC IN THE HAYFIELD. 1852. 19 by 28½ in.

A number of young women, boys, and girls are tossing hay in the foreground, and a young girl holds a bundle aloft on the end of her hay-fork; a man on a dark horse is leading a white one, and a hay waggon in the distance make up the

CHAP. XIII. incidents. It is a fresh breezy picture, full of movement. There is a beautiful blue distance streaked with light, and a summer sky with grey and white clouds. It is now in Mr. A. Levy's collection.

GOING TO THE HAYFIELD. 1852. 19 by 28½ in.

This is the usual subject of a man on horseback approaching the haymakers, with a few trees and a silvery sky. The treatment is free and the colour pure.

These companion pictures were painted by Cox for a young friend who lived with him at Harborne, Mr. Thomas Welsh, junior, who was going to be married. They were only finished just in time on the day of the wedding, and sent, it is said, when the newly married couple were getting into their carriage. The price charged for them was £25 each. Recently (in 1872) they were purchased by Mr. Agnew for £3,200. They are beautiful works of the best period.

THE WELSH FUNERAL. 1850. 28 by 36 in.

This impressive picture, one of the grandest Cox ever painted, was purchased by Mr. Thomas Darby in 1850, and presented shortly afterwards to his friend Mr. David Jones, of Birmingham, whose widow parted with it and the "Skirts of the Forest," in 1872, to Mr. Nettlefold for 3,000 guineas. It is unusually full of subject, and the trees which border the road are remarkably fine and full of rich shadows.

I have given a full account of this subject in the chapter on water-colour drawings, when describing Mr. Craven's drawing of the "Welsh Funeral," by Cox, a photographic copy of which appears in this book, and I shall not now refer to it further except to remark that the same subject was painted for Mr. Charles Birch, and sold by him to Mr. H. H. Betts: also a smaller copy, in Mr. E. Bullock's collection, was sold in May, 1870.

THE SKIRTS OF THE FOREST. 1853. 28 by 36 in.

Cox painted this picture for Mr. David Jones; the price charged was only £40. As stated above, it has been recently sold with the "Welsh Funeral" for £3,300.

It represents part of old Sherwood Forest, a wild and grand subject, finely treated. There is a group of wide-spreading oaks on the left-hand side, one with a noble grey stem in the immediate foreground. A woman underneath it is apparently hurrying after some travellers along the edge of the forest, one of whom is seated on a donkey; a purple distance is seen rather high up in the picture, and the sky is low toned and grey; it is not so brilliant as some of his earlier works, but it is free and impressive. Many copies by Cox of this subject exist, some of a smaller size.

GIPSIES CROSSING A COMMON. 1846. 14 by 18 in.

GOING TO THE MILL. 1846. 14 by 20 in.

The above two little pictures were purchased by Mr. Jesson, of Walsall, soon after they were painted, for £10 each. In 1865 he sold them for £100 each to Mr. William Hall, who obtained £150 each for them from Mr. Frederick Timmins; that gentleman parted with the pair for £1,500, in 1872, when he sold the "Vale of Clwyd."

THE BIG MEADOW AT BETTWS. 1849. 19 by 28½ in.

A beautiful peaceful landscape, a herd of cows grazing in a large meadow, with two countrymen in the foreground stretched at full length in the long grass. Some fine trees in the middle distance, and the rocky hills of Bettws rise up beyond; the sky is full of blowing clouds, but not gloomy; the feeling conveyed is that of breezy freshness on a fine summer's day. This picture was many years in the possession of Mr. Howard Fletcher. At his sale at Walsall, September,

CHAP. XIII. 1861, it was purchased by Mr. Thomas Page for 33 guineas. This gentleman also possesses the following two pictures, which he purchased at the same sale, in 1861 :—

PEAT GATHERERS. 1850. 14 by 18 in.

Grand effect; dark purple hills and lowering, stormy sky, and figures approaching with baskets of peat—price paid, 29 guineas—rocks and heather make up the foreground.

PASS OF DOLWYDDELAN, WITH MOEL SIABOD. 1849. 18 by 24 in.

This is a beautiful subject and pleasant in colour, but rather deficient in shadow; not so effective as most of the works painted about this time by the artist. Price paid, £26.

PONT-Y-PAIR. 1849.

Cows crossing the stream. A very sweet little picture, which Mr. Benjamin Urwick bought from the easel for £15. Sold at this sale also for 27 guineas.

MR. WILLIAM ROBERTS'S COLLECTION, ALL PURCHASED DIRECT FROM DAVID COX, AT HARBORNE.

OUTSKIRTS OF A WOOD, WITH GIPSIES. 1843. 28½ by 36½ in.

This picture, like the one afterwards painted for Mr. David Jones, represents the scenery of Sherwood Forest. The effect is wild though pleasing, and the figures well introduced. It was painted for Mr. Roberts, who paid £40 for it. Mr. Roberts did not retain it very long, but sold it to Mr. Marshall Carritt for £45; it then passed to a Mr. Cooper, of Lynn, and was eventually purchased by Mr. Gillott for 350 guineas. At Mr. Gillott's sale, in 1872, it went for £2,315 5s.

CUTTING HIS STICK, *alias* DRIVING THE FLOCK. 1850. 10 by 8 in.

This is an effective little picture of the best period. The lad who is driving a flock of sheep is occupied in cutting a stick; there are a few cottages and a blue distance, a summer sky, of which the colour is very brilliant and the atmospheric effect unusually fine. At Mr. Roberts's sale, in May, 1867, it went for £84. It is now in Mr. A. Levy's collection.

GOING TO THE HAYFIELD. 14 by 8 in.

As successful as any Cox has painted of this favourite subject. The incidents are the usual two grey horses with the waggoner riding one of them, a little girl carrying a beer barrel to the hayfield, which is seen in the distance, with hay-carts and figures. The foreground and grey sky are, as usual, very beautiful. Sold for £273 in 1867.

FRIGHTENING THE GEESE. 14 by 8 in.

An interesting picture of the best period. A stream is in the foreground, with a rustic bridge, across which an old woman is hurrying along, shaking her stick at some children who are driving the geese down the opposite bank; in the distance a cottage with trees, and a fresh breezy sky. Sold in May, 1867, for £137 11*s.*, and resold shortly afterwards for £250.

CROSSING LANCASTER SANDS.

A celebrated picture, full of atmospheric effect and beautiful in colour. Sold for £131 5*s.* This was rather an early picture, date about 1843, and was given by Cox to Mr. Wilmot in exchange for half a fat pig and a silver watch.

BATHERS ALARMED. Date about 1852.

A black bull has just rushed into the water, and some lads,

CHAP. XIII. partly dressed, are taking shelter from his fury behind a clump of trees which are growing on the bank; the incident well expressed, but it is rather slight in the painting. Sold 21st May, 1867, for £52 10*s*.

GOING TO SCHOOL.

A lane scene with a cottage in the distance; some poor children are loitering along the path; very happy in its treatment. Sold for £32 11*s*.

BESOM MAKERS. Date about 1853. 10 by 7 in.

A view on Chatmoss, the heather in full blossom. A group of figures are collecting and carrying heather, some loading bundles of it on a donkey; a very bright effective little picture. Sold for £53 11*s*.

LANE SCENE WITH FIGURES. 5 by 11 in.

Purchased for Mr. J. Gillott at the sale of Mr. Roberts's pictures for £69 6*s*., resold at Mr. J. Gillott's sale, April, 1872, for £160 13*s*.

Besides, the following small pictures were disposed of at the sale:—

LANCASTER SANDS. Price £33 12*s*.

CHELSEA PENSIONERS. Price £17 17*s*.

A LANE SCENE, near Maxtock, Warwickshire. Price £38 17*s*.

A RIVER SCENE—AUTUMN. Price £24 14*s*. 6*d*.

AN UPRIGHT LANDSCAPE, with sheep. Price £28 18*s*.

I must now give some account of the late Mr. Edwin Bullock's collection at Harborne House, Harborne, which was the most numerous, and one of the most interesting of the works in oil by David Cox. These pictures were sold by Messrs. Christie, Manson, and Co., in May, 1870, and the prices realised were small as compared with those obtained two years later, when the Gillott sale took place. I shall not attempt to describe all these pictures, but will give a list of them and the prices obtained. All these works were obtained direct from the artist by Mr. Bullock; they were on very friendly terms, and when Cox painted a successful picture in oil, Mr. Bullock generally had the offer of the original, or else of a duplicate copy.

"Collecting the Flocks," in North Wales, 3 ft. 3 in. by 4 ft. 8 in., is a remarkable work of the best period, and is one of the three largest pictures ever painted by Cox. There is no doubt he found these large works in oil very fatiguing, and he used to complain sometimes very much of this, especially when on the verge of seventy, which was his age when this picture was painted. In some respects it is less vigorous in the treatment than others of his works, and less bright, but the feeling is fine and the arrangement admirable. I understand that since the sale, in 1870, 1,500 guineas have been offered for it. I believe it is now in the possession of Mr. Thomas Walker.

"Going to the Hayfield" is very cool and fresh in colour, the silvery grey sky being remarkably fine and the usual incidents of the horses and figures equal to anything Cox has painted. It was a slight drawback to this picture when I saw that the frame had the corners rounded. It is not quite so large as the one belonging to Mr. Thomas Page, but was painted in the same year, 1849.

The "Churchyard, Darby Dale," 14 by 18 in. is a delightful work, as showing how much Cox could make out of a subject which in other hands would have been commonplace. His genius invested with the charm of poetry almost everything it touched. This picture is rather slightly painted, but the feeling is solemn and impressive. The yew-trees and the figures add to the effect, and make it a complete work.

"Landscape with Peasants, a White Horse, and a Dog." Although only 6 by 8 in., this picture is of the highest quality, being particularly bright and beautiful in colour. It excited the keenest competition among the bidders at the sale.

The following were the prices obtained for some of the most important pictures at Mr. Bullock's sale: "Going to the Hayfield, 1849, 20 by 30 in., £425; "Going to the Hayfield," 1853, a very fine work, £400; "Landscape with Peasants," 6 by 8 in., £413; "Collecting the Flocks, in North Wales," the large picture, £400; a landscape, with a waggon on a road, and a peasant crossing a rustic bridge, date 1840, £245; "Windsor Castle," from the forest, with deer, £240; a river scene, with a church tower, and a peasant funeral crossing a rustic bridge, a solemn evening effect, date 1840, £170; a landscape, with peasants, and a white horse and a dog, beside a gate in the country, £225; a river scene, with horses watering, early morning effect, £200; a river scene in North Wales, on the Lledr, with anglers, £150; the original sketch for the "Welsh Funeral at Bettws-y-Coed," date 1850, a very powerful little work, 8 by 10 in., £155; a landscape, with two mounted peasants, and a dog on a country road, date 1852, £120; "Dudley Castle," evening effect, with limekilns, and barges on the canal basin in the foreground, a very effective work, like the celebrated drawing of the same subject, £125; a river scene, with boys on the bank angling, £145; a view on the sea-coast, with a man and boy and fishing nets, date 1846, £100; a river scene, with boys and cows, early morning, date 1849, £105; "Carrying Vetches," one of his earliest oil-pictures, dated 1831, £90; a landscape, with some peasants and a white horse passing along a road, £160.

Besides the above, there were sixteen oil-pictures by Cox disposed of at this sale, many of them small works of less interest than those already named: several of these were landscapes with sheep, reapers, gleaners, anglers, gipsies, cows asleep, &c., all natural and thoroughly characteristic of the artist; in all thirty-four pictures, besides "The Salmon Trap," a late work, partly painted by Cox and finished by Bond. CHAP. XIII.

The following were painted by Cox to decorate the summer house at Hawthorne House, in 1849, and were sold for about £50 each: four allegorical female figures, freely painted, representing Spring, Summer, Autumn, and Winter.

COLLECTION OF PICTURES BY DAVID COX, BEQUEATHED TO HIS SON, AND NOW AT HIS RESIDENCE, PARK ROAD, BRIXTON HILL.

THE WELSH FUNERAL. 1850. 1 ft. 9½ in. by 2 ft. 5 in.

Painted on the thick Scotch paper; a grand and impressive picture, the figures very natural and effective, and in its general arrangement like the large water-colour drawing in the possession of Mr. F. Craven, although less brilliant in colour.

DISTANT VIEW OF CONWAY CASTLE, with mountains rising up behind, and the estuary of the river. 1848. 2 ft. 4½ in. by 3 ft. 6½ in.

The effect is that of very early morning, tender, yet rather warm and harmonious in colour. In the foreground is a cart and horse with Welsh market women in it, and close by another woman on horseback, and several sheep grazing near. The figures are well introduced, but the foreground wants a little more finish.

CHAP. XIII.

GOING TO THE HAYFIELD. 2 ft. 4 in. by 3 ft. 6½ in. 1854.

A grand picture of this often-repeated subject. It is full of movement and beautiful in colour, but not quite finished. The silvery grey sky, the woody foreground, and distant hay-waggons, are all excellent, as well as the man with the two grey horses, and a lad near carrying a bundle. There is also a pool of water in the foreground. The handling is particularly free.

SOLITUDE. 1 ft. 8½. in. by 2 ft. 6 in. 1854.

The subject of this picture is the bridge over the Lledr, a mass of rocks with running water and without any figures. The effect is sombre and impressive.

ROCKS AND HILLS AT THE BACK OF THE ROYAL OAK, BETTWS. 1850. 17½ by 24 in.

This is one of the rather late grand and most vigorous of Cox's landscapes. He used to say that he thought it had something of the feeling and treatment which Velasquez would have put into it. It was entirely painted on the spot, and was a great favourite of the artists. The rocks and hills with heather, &c., in the foreground, are dark and powerfully painted.

IN BOLTON PARK. About 1843. 18 by 24½ in.

A very effective picture. This was a sketch entirely painted on the spot.

COTTAGE AT HARBORNE. 1844. 13½ by 17 in.

This represents a broad road leading towards a cottage, and some fine trees. Children are at play not far off, and the effect of light on the road and on the clouds is very pleasing.

CALAIS PIER. 1846. 18 by 28 in.

The sea is rough and full of movement, and of a light grey colour, as when the water is churned into foam. On the pier are a good many figures picturesquely grouped. The sky is stormy and effective. This picture was a great favourite with Cox, and used to hang in his parlour at Greenfield House. Although it was painted in his studio from a sketch, it has all the appearance of having been painted out of doors, being very true and fresh, though quiet in colour.

RHYL. About 1848. 11 by 16 in.

A wide sandy shore, with a strip of dark sea breaking on the distant sands. The figure of a Welsh woman on horseback and some shrimpers with nets give character to the scene. Grey clouds cover the sky, which has rather a threatening aspect.

LANCASTER SANDS. 1850. 10 by 15 in.

The distance is delicate and aëreal, with small receding figures. The sky is unusually tender, and this is brought into relief by a great flight of sea-birds, full of flutter and movement. A broad expanse of sand with scarcely any detail, forms the foreground. This is a very successful little picture.

HILLS AT BETTWS-Y-COED. 1852. 13 by 16 in.

The subject represented is part of the river-bed of the Llugwy with some fine boulders and rocks, and a man fishing in the act of throwing his line; the trees are rather dark in colour. It was painted on the spot, and is broad and vigorous in treatment.

CHAP. XIII.

SKIRTS OF THE FOREST. About 1854. $10\frac{3}{4}$ by 14 in.

Two women—one having a red cloak and seated on a donkey—are passing near some fine trees, with a bank of weeds and wild-flowers below. The usual peep of blue distance and a grey "blowing" sky, make up this little picture.

GOING TO THE HAYFIELD. About 1850. $11\frac{3}{4}$ by $15\frac{3}{4}$ in.

The arrangement is the same as in Mr. Mayou's large picture of this subject, of which I give the photograph. The mowers are, however, rather more prominent, and the hay-waggon is wanting. This picture appears to have been painted rapidly and slightly, without much finish. The colour, especially that of the sky, is very agreeable, and there is a remarkable appearance of wind.

BOY FLINGING AT WILD DUCKS. About 1848. $10\frac{3}{4}$ by 14 in.

A boy carrying a large basket is descending a path near a pool fringed with rushes, and appears in the act of throwing a stone. On a bank just above some women laden with baskets, &c., are returning from market. Beyond is a flat, distant sweep of country, and a sky full of rolling clouds and birds. It is fresh and bright in colour, and more finished than many of his later pictures.

THE OLD CHURCH AT BETTWS. About 1854. 14 by 20 in.

An upright, without much detail, but fine in effect. The last glow of evening lights up the distant hills, and also illumines the road leading to the church, of which but a small part is seen. Some tall trees nearly conceal the church, and these are dark and grandly massed together.

OLD WOMAN WITH A STICK DRIVING GEESE. 10 by 14 in.

The time chosen for this picture is late evening, and a reflected light falls on some low hills. In the foreground is a pool of water and rushes, near which the woman and geese are passing. The whole effect is rather quaint and weird.

WHITE HORSE WITH CART. 1852. 9 by 12 in.

A clever sketch of an old horse, very free and agreeable in colour. This cart and horse had brought a load of coals to Greenfield House, and Cox engaged the man to stop whilst he painted it.

MOORLAND SCENE. About 1856. 12 by 16 in.

A late and rather gloomy but impressive picture. A group of cattle standing on some rising ground in the middle distance are relieved against the sky, which is strong and rather dark.

OLD WINDMILL. About 1857. 14 by 18 in.

Two figures are approaching the mill. The sky is grey and pleasing, but the general effect is marred by the want of rather more finish, especially in the foreground.

WALK IN THE HAGLEY ROAD. 14 by 18 in.

A number of figures representing a young ladies' school are walking down a road, which is bordered by trees on the right. The effect is sketchy, but fresh and bright in colour.

Mr. David Cox, junior, has also two large pictures in oil left unfinished by his father. One of them, "The Lost Sheep," is a grand, rocky subject, 25 by 36 in. Some stems of trees are thrown diagonally across the foreground rocks. A

CHAP. XIII. woman is resting her arm on one of them, and at the bottom of a deep fissure a poor sheep is seen huddled up. A bright light from above strikes on some of the rocks. The other one is still larger—2 ft. 4 in. by 3 ft. 6 in. The subject is, "Keep the Left Road." A man and horse and other figures are on the right hand, and in the centre a lad driving a flock of sheep. It is, however, only sketched in, and the sky is not commenced, which is much to be regretted, as it has all the promise of a fine work.

I have already described some of the pictures in Mr. A. Levy's collection, but he has also the following :—

BETTWS CHURCHYARD. 1857. 30 by 42 in.

A picture of unrivalled beauty both in treatment, colour, and composition; very solidly painted, yet as fresh, pure, and brilliant as any of the water-colours of his best period. Bettws Church is partly seen on the extreme right, and some seven or eight figures are ascending the steps towards the door or gateway through which an elderly man is just passing. Another old man has hold of a boy's hand, and is pointing to him "the right way to go." A woman and girl are seen approaching on the left, and near to them is a magnificent group of trees. This picture was formerly in Mr. Norman Wilkinson's collection.

COUNTING THE FLOCK. 1852. 23 by 33 in.

A man and lad, accompanied by a dog, are standing near the open gate through which the sheep are passing. The sky is very pleasing, grey in tone, and full of wind; the colour and handling are of the highest quality.

SUN, WIND, AND RAIN. 1845. 18 by 25 in.

A wild sky, with a storm of rain just coming down, and

gleams of sunshine in the distance, give the name to this clever picture. A woman, on a white horse, holds up a green umbrella to shelter herself, and a boy steadies himself by some palings close by. The broad dock leaves in the foreground are full of freshness, and appear turned back and crumpled by the high wind; on the right are some thin, tall trees, with birds wheeling round their tops, and a few cows in the distance.

HADDON HALL. 1845. 14 by 18 in.

Two figures on horseback are riding towards the old hall, and dogs are seen far off in front; some fine trees are grouped all along the left side as far as the hall, and a wide extent of wooded distance spreads across to the right. The sky is very tender, and of a light grey colour.

HARLECH CASTLE. 1845. 10 by 18 in.

A remarkably tender blue sky, against which the distant castle is clearly defined. In front of it is a strip of blue sea, and a narrow, sandy shore. Nearer still, a sloping cornfield, with stacks of corn and reapers, adds warmth and colour; and on the left hand a bank rises above the corn, and on this bank some tall trees are relieved against the sky. It is a sweet, peaceful scene, soft and quiet in effect.

RAINBOW ON THE THAMES, BELOW GRAVESEND. Date, 1857. 16 by 26 in.

The sky is wonderfully full of rain, and is entirely spanned by a low and perfect rainbow, indicating the winter solstice. A low, flat shore, without much incident, assists very much the effect, as great quietness in the rest of the picture is rendered necessary by the brilliant colouring of the bow. On the meadow in the foreground two lads are stretched at full length on the grass.

CHAP. XIII.

CARREG-CENNEN CASTLE, SOUTH WALES. 1844. 32 by 26 in.

An upright; quiet, and rather low in tone and broad in treatment. The castle, which has a warm glow on it, rises up against the sky in the distance, being situated on a high hill. Some fine trees border a country lane, down which a man and dog are driving some sheep. It is a fine work of the early period in oils, and was originally purchased by Miss Phipson, of Edgbaston, in whose possession it now is.

GATE-HOUSE OF KENILWORTH CASTLE. Date, about 1844. 10 by 16 in.

This picture, which is an upright, is well arranged, quiet, and pleasing. The gate-house had been turned into a farm-house, which is indicated by some poultry in the foreground. It is also in Miss Phipson's collection.

Before concluding this chapter I should mention that there are several fine oil pictures at Ludlow, in the possession of Mrs. Joseph Tarratt. Of these a fine upright, entitled "Milking Time," and a small, bright little picture, "Landscape, with Sheep," were lent to the Wolverhampton Fine-Art Exhibition in 1869. "Milking Time" represents a country lane, with fine trees on one side, and a number of milch cows standing under their shelter. Some women are engaged in milking them, and the immediate foreground is enlivened by poultry. This picture is of the middle period, about 1848, and is very vigorous and fresh in colour, but it required to have been carried a little further as respects the finish, which is but slight. I must also mention a fine Welsh landscape, painted about 1849. The view which is represented was taken from a field near the Conway Falls, in the neighbourhood of Bettws-y-Coed. You look down a wooded valley towards the huge, rugged Trifaen Mountain. On one side are some trees, with a meadow in front, in which some men are lying down at rest in the long grass. It is one of his very characteristic and truthful works. The size is about 16 by 24 in.

Mr. William Hall, the artist, was present with Cox when he painted this picture from nature. He was also with him a few days afterwards, when he painted a very excellent picture, 18 by 24 in., of the end of Bettws-y-Coed old church, with the old trees, and part of the Conway River.

I must not conclude this chapter without referring to a fine oil-picture painted by Cox in 1850, "View of Darley Church," about 20 by 30 in. A large yew occupies the centre, tomb-stones are clustered around its base, some in deep shadow, and some in half light, which give breadth to the composition. On the left some steps lead up to the church, the upper part being illumined by the glow of evening. Some girls seated on these steps assist cleverly in carrying the light across. The sky is bright, yet powerful. *Power* and brilliancy are the chief characteristics of this picture, as, indeed, of all his best works. He loved power almost beyond everything else. This picture, after passing through several hands, is now, I believe, in the possession of Mr. Agnew.

Besides the pictures I have noticed, I have seen several smaller ones scattered about various parts of England, especially in Lancashire, Birmingham, and a few in London. The subjects, however, are nearly always similar to some of those I have already described, and I believe enough has been written in this chapter to give a good general idea of what Cox achieved as an oil-painter.

XIV.

LIFE AT HARBORNE (*continued*).

1849 TO 1855.

Chap. XIV.
1849—1855.

IN the tenth chapter, at the end of 1848, I left David Cox hard at work with his oil-painting. That he made no vain boast when writing to his friend on the 1st January, 1841, "I will succeed," no one can doubt who has had an opportunity of seeing the beautiful pictures completed by him during the ten years following that date. I have endeavoured, as far as lay within my power, to compress a description of the most important of these works into the last chapter. That some have been omitted from notice is, I fear, certain, and probably a few fine ones; collections of his oil-pictures, as well as water-colour, have repeatedly been sold, and have necessarily become widely separated, within the last half dozen years.

It has been remarked that Cox put a very low price upon his oil-pictures, especially on his earlier works, and that he sometimes made presents of choice little bits to his friends. In illustration of this I may mention that, having promised to paint a picture for Miss Wilmot, the sister-in-law of Mrs. W. Roberts, for £5, he painted two of the same size, and gave her the choice. One represented a heath scene with trees and some figures, and was a beautiful

fresh little work, full of movement; the other was a view from the terrace in front of the hotel at Llangollen, with houses and figures—a subject which Cox had been requested to paint. This he complied with at once, saying, however, that the subject was "too pretty and artificial to please him." Both Mr. Birch and Mr. Roberts were charmed with the "Heath Scene," and wished to purchase it for £15. Cox said, "No, Miss Wilmot was to have the choice first." This she accordingly had; and, without much hesitation, she selected the "Heath Scene" for the £5 originally named. The following are extracts from letters written to his son in the early part of this year:— CHAP. XIV. 1849—1855.

"Greenfield House, March 15th, 1849.

"I went to a sale of pictures on Tuesday at Mr. Butler's, at Handsworth, his country house; they were all modern, and nearly all by Birmingham artists. There were five of mine: they fetched more than the price they cost him, even with the frames.

"DAVID COX."

Note.—Mr. Butler had been a picture dealer for many years in Birmingham, and had purchased many of Cox's early works in oil.

"Greenfield House, May 20th, 1849.

"I feel a very great desire to lay out a sum of money in a picture by Linnell, which I can have for £160; but the person will take nearly half in my drawings. The picture was in the Institution two years ago, and it was bought by Mr. Gillott for £125. It will appear a great sum for me to give, but I feel quite sure it will be of service to me, in my having it by me while at work.

"DAVID COX."

Cox had gone to London, as usual, in April, and sent

CHAP. XIV. — 1849—1855.

fifteen drawings to the Water Colour Exhibition, among which was the large and very poetical one of "Beeston Castle, Cheshire," now in Mr. F. Craven's collection, of which he has kindly enabled me to give a copy; also "Barden Tower, Yorkshire," "Shepherds collecting their Flocks," "Cross Roads," and the "Missing Flock"—these are all well-known representative drawings, and very characteristic of the artist's feeling and manner. Some interesting drawings of subjects in the neighbourhood of Bettws were also exhibited.

Cox returned to Harborne, from London, about the 10th of May, and immediately set to work with renewed zeal at his oil-painting. Of the celebrated oil-pictures painted this year I have to record "The Skylark," first exhibited in Birmingham; four with the title of "Going to the Hayfield"—namely, those painted for Mr. Briscoe, Mr. Roberts, Mr. Bullock, and Mr. Butler; two of the "Big Meadow, Bettws;" a "River Scene with Boys and Cows," and some others. The following extract from a letter written to his son refers to the progress of his work:—

"Greenfield House, June 29, 1849.

"I do not expect to be very much hurried, as I have learnt to take things more patiently and can paint much quicker than formerly; and you will say so when I tell you I have painted eleven small oil-pictures nearly all complete, besides the large one sent to the Manchester Exhibition; and I have one now as large in hand for Liverpool, in all making thirteen pictures in the seven weeks since my return from London.

"DAVID COX."

The completion of various works in oil detained Cox later than usual at Harborne this summer, and he did not start until quite the end of July for Bettws, whither Mr. W. Hall and young Butler accompanied him; it proved a very wet season in Wales, but in spite of the weather he brought home many sketches and studies, both in water-colour and oil—indeed, he never allowed any difficulties to stand in the way of his work. The following short extract from a letter to his son describes this visit:— CHAP. XIV. 1849—1855.

"Royal Oak, Bettws-y-Coed, August 17th, 1849.

"I have not had much to say, except about the weather. I have never done so little, excepting going out in the cars four miles and beginning sketching, when the rain has come down so heavily I have packed up or covered up as well as I could, and at the day's end walked home wet through.

"DAVID COX."

Later in this year he writes again to his son:—

"Greenfield House, Nov. 16th, 1849.

"In an evening I go to oil-painting by lamplight (small pictures). I wish I could finish them by lamplight as well as I can make the beginning, for I find when I paint in oil or water-colours by lamplight, my picture is always broader in effect and more brilliant, and often better and more pure in the colour of the tints.

"DAVID COX."

In the early months of 1850 Cox worked very industriously at the drawings he was preparing for the Water Colour Exhibition. On the 15th of March he wrote to his son, "My drawing upon the Scotch paper is so rough I fear I shall bring down all against me, but the paper has plagued me so that I am very nervous." He always *felt* himself that his drawings on the rough paper were his best ones; but he deprecated the criticisms of the majority of the public, who then, as now, frequently disliked what was not smooth and

CHAP. XIV. 1849—1855.

highly finished. Cox was on the hanging committee of the Water Colour Society this spring. In the following letter he gives some account of this exhibition, to which he had contributed thirteen drawings. The most important were, "Changing the Pasture," "Blackberry Gatherers," "A Rocky Glen," and the "Vale of Conway." He also sent "Beaver Grove," "Pandy Mill," and other Bettws subjects.

"Laurel Cottage, Streatham Place, Brixton Hill, London,
April 30th, 1850.

"My dear friend Roberts will perhaps wonder at not having heard from me ere this, but I am just returned from my duties as one of the committee, as the arrangement occupied us rather more time than we at first thought it would. I will give you a short account of our own exhibition, as I have only had time to see one other (the New Water Colour) for half an hour. I think our exhibition, on the whole, a very good one. J. Lewis's picture of the 'Harem in Cairo' is very attractive: the master, with his three or four wives upon ottomans with a newly purchased slave (a Nubian); but you must see it, for to describe the very high finish will be quite out of my power. Cattermole has some brilliant small drawings, but no large one; Tayler only five, all small. G. Fripp has some very carefully finished landscapes, which are very good and are much liked. My own drawings are much liked. 'The Funeral' has not found a purchaser yet. You will be glad to hear that my dear son has sold half what he sent in, and his drawings are much better than any he has done before.

"I have an engagement for to-morrow to spend the day with Mr. Ellis. On Thursday I hope to visit some of the great number of exhibitions which are now open, and towards the end of the week I expect you and Mr. Bullock will be in town. I quite long to return to my dear home, and I think of leaving London next Wednesday.

"I am, my dear Friend,

"Yours sincerely,

"D. Cox."

The preceding letter is the more interesting from the circumstance that it refers to his "Welsh Funeral" not having found a purchaser. No drawing has ever added more to the reputation of an artist than this one has done, and yet it was only through the recommendation of a brother artist, Mr. Topham, that it was eventually chosen as an Art-Union prize. On his return home, this year, Cox painted one or two oil-pictures of the "Welsh Funeral;" also the "Salmon Trap," for Mr. Briscoe—a very grand work; "Peat Gatherers inquiring at the Cross Roads," "River Scene, with a Peasant Funeral crossing a rustic Bridge," and several other fine works in oil were also painted this year. In the summer he again stayed at the Peacock, Rowsley, with several friends, Mr. Bullock, Mr. Charles Birch, Mr. W. Roberts, &c., and had a pleasant time making many sketches. The same friends accompanied him to Rhyl early in September, where they spent a week, and he thence proceeded on his usual visit to Bettws-y-Coed. Sometime after his return home to Harborne, his friend, Mr. Norman Wilkinson, persuaded him to give a few lessons in water-colour to a friend of his, about which he writes as follows to his son:—

"Greenfield House, November 8th, 1850.

"I am about to receive Colonel D'Aguilar down here to take a few lessons of me. My good friend Norman introduces him, and I could not refuse my old friend Norman; else I am quite frightened to give a lesson now, and I sincerely wish it was over."

CHAP. XIV.
1849—1855.

The year 1851 was that in which the first great International Exhibition was opened in Hyde Park, and Cox, anxious to show attention to foreign artists, wrote the following letter to his son:—

"Greenfield House, Feb. 14th, 1851.

"I have lately been thinking that it would be a friendly thing if our society would give free admission tickets to all the continental artists who will visit London this summer. I do not know how to bring such a thing before the society, but I could wish you to call and name it to Mr. Cattermole, and hear what he says. I must leave the mode, or plan, as to how the tickets are to be distributed to the different artists; but Dominic Colnaghe would know all the leading foreign members of the academies, and I have no doubt he would assist in the plan. If you can call and name it to Mr. Cattermole I should very much like it, as it would be doing a friendly act, and just what we should all like done to us, and indeed what I feel the French would do.

"DAVID COX."

Just before starting on his usual visit to London, before the opening of the exhibition, he wrote to his son a letter, from which the following is an extract:—

"Greenfield House, April 10th, 1851.

"I have been woefully mistaken in my calculation about my drawings, and have been obliged to put aside my largest, although I have procured a frame and glass for it; but I must not mind trifles, it was quite advisable I should leave off as I was getting very nervous. I shall have four 24 by 34 in., and some small. I have had sixteen visitors this day, and am expecting four or five others; for the last three days I have been hindered most of each day. It seems quite a pleasant walk and lounge; all regret having taken up my time, but words are easily spoken. I have been the principal loser.

"DAVID COX."

There were eleven drawings of Cox's at the Water Colour Exhibition in 1851. Most of these were views in North Wales, but we also find the favourite subject of "Going to the Hayfield," also "Cutting Green Rye," a charming scene several times repeated, and "Morning." He painted again a great many oil-pictures, but not so many large ones as previously, as he was beginning to find that the size of the canvases, if large, increased the fatigue of painting very much. He visited his sister at Sale, near Manchester, and also spent a month at Bettws-y-Coed. After his return home from Wales he wrote a note to G. Priest, which I give as it refers to the size of the canvases he was then using:—

"Greenfield, Harborne, Sept. 22nd, 1851.

"DEAR PRIEST,—It is very kind of you to think of making any return for the small picture which is what I had no idea of taking anything for in return. But as you so handsomely wish to send me a dozen canvases, I will have the pleasure of accepting of half-a-dozen, at your leisure, the size 11 by 14½ in. I remain, dear Priest, yours very truly.

"DAVID COX.

"P.S.—I shall not be able to go to Manchester till the end of this week."

On another occasion on their return from Bettws, after a visit of four or five weeks, when Priest had accompanied him, he said he feared he had suffered in his business by being away so long, and to compensate he made him a present of four little drawings, which he told him he could sell for five or six pounds each; but they readily sold at the rate of ten pounds each. Cox had made a drawing of Sherwood Forest,

CHAP. XIV. 1849—1855. with grand oak-trees, 2 by 3 ft., one of his best works, and this he let Priest have for £50, which was below its value; but he said "it was enough for him to pay." Priest parted with it to Mr. Banner for £100, who exhibited it for some time in his rooms, and then sold it to Mrs. Eberhard, for £140. I believe it is still in the possession of that lady.

When he was last at Bettws, Cox had made two sketches out of doors, on each side of a sheet of the thick Scotch paper, a landscape, and a figure subject—a Welsh woman resting with a bundle of sticks by her side. Both sketches were very natural, and full of character. He showed them to Priest and said, "Now, if you can separate these drawings I will make you a present of one." Priest was of course delighted to try. He had a damp cellar at home, on the brick floor of which he placed the drawings till the paper was so saturated with moisture that he succeeded easily in splitting them with a sharp knife. Cox was pleased with his success, and gave him the figure subject, which he afterwards sold for £40.

The year 1852 did not pass without his usual visit to London. He exhibited thirteen drawings at the Water Colour Society. The most noteworthy were—"Bettws-y-Coed Church," "On the River Conway," "On the Llugwy, near Bettws," and "Besom Makers gathering Heather on Carrington Moss, Cheshire." This last-named subject was from a sketch he had made when staying at Sale. It was a beautiful drawing, and he afterwards repeated it several times with a variety in the incidents; having a low horizon, there was ample space for a grand effect of sky, and the powerful rendering of great atmospheric space in sky is one of the charms of all Cox's drawings of moors, commons, and sea-shores.

After his return from London, in June, Mr. W. S. Ellis joined him, and they made an excursion to Ludlow, Stoke-Say, and other places in the neighbourhood, and also visited Powis Castle. The weather was unusually bad, but I have seen many beautiful sketches made by Cox on this occasion, although, judging from the following letter to his son, he was not himself satisfied with his work:— CHAP. XIV. 1849—1855.

"Feathers Inn, Ludlow, June 20th, 1852.

"MY DEAR DAVID,—I write a few lines to thank you for your kind letter come to hand this morning. We have now been here nearly a week, and it has rained every day, and some days it has been very heavy. Of course, I have not done much in the way of sketching, though Mr. E. and myself have been out in some of the most heavy torrents, and the lanes and roads are very muddy. The castle is not at all, to my ideas, a good one; there is only one view which is passable. The country around is chiefly meadow, bounded by distant hills, in form long and round. The principal beauty is the look of the meadows, varied in tint, when there happens to be a gleam of sunshine. Yesterday we had a car, and went to Lentwerdine. The scenery about the hills on the Downton Castle estate is very woody; but in such rainy weather I cannot do anything; indeed, the few sketches which I have made are the veriest *daubs* ever made by any poor painter. I am quite disgusted with my bad success, and think of returning on Wednesday. I hope to have better luck in the weather when I go into Wales.

"DAVID COX."

The drawing of Stoke-Say, of which I give a copy, was made from a sketch taken on this occasion. The sky is unusually threatening, and looks as portentous of continued rain as it is possible to imagine.

Soon after this excursion to Ludlow, Cox left home again for Bettws. The autumn was passed at Harborne, hard at work, as usual, both in oil and water colours. His life at Greenfield House was very uneventful, one day being spent almost like another. His habits, when breakfast was over,

CHAP. XIV.

1849—1855.

was to go up to his studio, and work for an hour or two at any picture in hand, or turn over his folios of sketches for a subject for a new work to be commenced. After this he went out into his pleasant garden, which would find him occupation for half an hour or more, whilst he smoked his favourite *half* cigar. Then again he resumed the work at his easel till dinner time, which was at half-past one. The same in the afternoon, with the exception of a short nap, and at tea time, or a little later, he received the visits of his friends. Commissions for pictures were often given, and future sketching expeditions were arranged, at these evening meetings. Cox was always pleased to paint a picture for a friend, but it has been truly remarked that he had his "likings" and the reverse, and that he would not part with his works to any one who attempted to patronise him. Mr. W. Hall has described that, if alone, or nearly so, and the evenings were long, "he lighted his lamp and went to work again; this time down-stairs in his sitting-room, where, taking up a sheet of rough paper, which he delighted to paint on, and striking out some grand effect of sunshine or shadow, of cloud and tempest, which his quickened fancy enabled him to conceive, he produced what he called a cartoon; a subject to be treated with greater care, and in another form, on a future occasion. Many of these cartoons were made during the long nights of autumn and winter, and were exceedingly fine things, requiring but slight alteration of their colour, by the light of day, to render them perfect works of art." After the death of his wife, Cox spent his Christmas Day either with Mr. Birch or Mr. Roberts, and about New Year's Day his son generally paid him a short visit. When the inclement season came round, the wants of the poor in his immediate neighbourhood were never overlooked. He did not know how to turn a deaf ear to those who asked for help, and without doubt he was occasionally imposed upon by the undeserving. Often has he cut the best slice out of a leg of mutton to send to aged and infirm villagers. It was his practice also to make many presents on St. Thomas's Day, the 21st December, of raisins, sugar, meat, and occasionally of money. On the Queen's birthday, too, every summer, he sent his housekeeper round with little gifts to the poorest and oldest inhabitants.

Early in the year 1853 Cox painted several important works in oil. "The Skirts of the Forest," for Mr. David Jones; "Going to the Hayfield," for Mr. Bullock and others. The following are extracts from letters to his son of this date:—

"Greenfield House, February 17th, 1853.

"Several of my small pictures, 9 by 14 in., which I have sold for £5, have been sold for £15, and others at the same proportions; other pictures which I received £40 each for, sold for £75. I have given notice to one or two friends that I would not take any more commissions at the price I have hitherto had.

"DAVID COX."

"Greenfield House, March 9th, 1853.

"I am now confined to my bedroom—a most violent attack of bronchitis, which nearly suffocates me at times. If I should be spared, I will get rid of some commissions, and make no more promises, but merely go out when I please and paint what I please. It is of no use my working for some; they are rather too selfish, and hurry me to paint faster than it is possible. Perhaps they are aware that if I should die they will not be able to procure any more. Some who have not set that value upon my small bits have parted with them at an advance of two hundred per cent., and in some cases more.

"DAVID COX."

He also refers to this serious attack of bronchitis in the following note to George Priest:—

"Greenfield, Harborne, March 11th, 1853.

"DEAR PRIEST,—I feel greatly obliged by your kindness in sending to inquire about me. I am happy to say I have had two good nights, having slept four hours each night. I have not left my room yet, as my doctor wished me to keep myself quiet, as talking brought on my cough; and as I feel getting better, it is safe to be on the sure side. Thank Mrs. Priest for her call. I shall hope to be better soon.

"Yours very truly,

"DAVID COX."

This illness prevented his going up to London as early as usual this spring. On the 15th of April he wrote to his son:—

"I suppose you are aware I sent four large drawings and nine small to the exhibition—two of the small ones were painted in the last ten hours.

"D. C."

Of these drawings, "Barden Castle," the "Summit of a Mountain," and "The Challenge," were among the most important. The last-named is a picture of a wild, barren waste, amidst mountain tops, with a fierce-looking bull, with tail extended, bellowing at one far way on the opposite hills; the sky is dark and lowering, and the treatment and colouring powerful and impressive. It was hung in the place of honour at the end of the room. The following is from a very interesting letter to his son written before he had seen this exhibition:—

"Greenfield House, April 18th, 1853.

"MY DEAR DAVID,—I feel very much obliged to Mr. Tayler for touching upon my Eagle. I wish now I had taken Mr. Roberts's advice and sent my drawings in without a price, as it strikes me the committee think them too rough; they forget they are *the work of the mind*, which I consider very far before portraits of places (views). I also think the committee ought not to hang my principal drawings by the door, as my drawing of 'Penmaen Mawr' of last year, and my drawing of 'Bettws Church, with the Funeral,' also hung at that end of the room; so also did Hägg's large upright, and one of Richardson's large drawings—so that it is like showing the public that we are fixed to those particular places. I certainly have said that I will remain with them as long as I am able to paint for them, but perhaps I may not live to send any more, and if I should be spared, I think I shall not be able to contribute much. I hope to be in London on the 3rd of May, and then I will take out of the price-book the sums I have asked for my four large drawings, and if there are those of the public who appreciate mind before mechanism, they will write to me to learn how I estimate them. I may be wrong, but the world has yet to be taught. Perhaps I am made vain by some here who think my 'Summit of a Mountain' worth—I am almost afraid to say—£100, and if I could paint it in oil, I shall some day, with D. V., get that sum. I am now getting more myself again. I have been this day by omnibus to Birmingham, and have walked a great deal. This is the first visit to Birmingham for ten weeks. God bless you all is the prayer of your affectionate father,

"DAVID COX."

After arriving in London, he wrote the following letter:—

"Laurel Cottage, Streatham Place, Brixton Hill, London,
May 18th, 1852.

"MY DEAR FRIEND ROBERTS,—In a letter I received from Ann (his housekeeper) she informs me that you had kindly answered a letter which came from Mr. Pritt of Preston. I beg you will accept my very best thanks for obliging me so much. I was disappointed in not meeting you at the station

CHAP. XIV. 1849—1855.

on the morning I left Birmingham for London, but I concluded business matters prevented you. Mr. Holmes and I had the carriage to ourselves all the way. The weather since I left has not been very tempting until lately, I therefore have not been often to town. A few days ago I called at the 'Craven' to inquire. My visit to London is now drawing near the end, and I shall return next week. I have seen but few of the exhibitions, therefore can say but little about them. I do not think very well of the Royal Academy; Millais is very good—perhaps the best picture in the exhibition, but this I ought to be careful in saying. ——'s large tree is a failure. I must leave all other remarks until I have the pleasure of seeing you. There is one bit of news I must tell you because you will be well pleased—that is, I I have sold my large drawing, 'The Challenge,' for £80. It is purchased for, and is to be sent to, America. I have also a commission to paint another, same size, as a companion.

"Yours very faithfully,

"DAVID COX."

He returned to Harborne in the last week of May, and soon after wrote the following letter:—

To W. S. ELLIS, ESQ.

"Greenfield, Harborne, June 3rd, 1853.

"MY DEAR FRIEND ELLIS,—I daresay you expected a letter from me before this, and also to receive the drawing of 'Windy Day,' which I am glad to say is so nearly finished that I have *determined to leave off*, and will send it on Monday, for if I had it by me for a month I should be finding out something that I might fancy could improve it. However, I hope your friend or yourself will like it. I will direct it to you, 11, Birchin Lane, unless I hear to the contrary. You will, I expect, be wishing to learn what I have thought of or where to go on our sketching trip. I cannot learn much that is very satisfactory about Beaudesert or neighbourhood, but have seen a gentleman who comes from the neighbourhood of Bridgnorth. He speaks of the scenery near there, and of Apley Terrace and Wenlock Abbey; now I think we might go to these places for three or four days, and then take a car to Ludlow. You must know I have a great wish to go to Ludlow again, having heard of one fine scene four miles on the road to Leominster; it has been described to me as one of the finest subjects in England—finer than the view from Richmond Hill. Besides which, the drawings I borrowed from you have given me a fresh start, and I should like to see a little more of that country; and who knows but I may come out quite astonishingly fine next year? So I think you will indulge me with this wish. We can spend a fortnight, or perhaps a little more; but I must tell you I shall not be ready to start for a fortnight, as Ann is going to see her mother on Monday, and will most likely be absent a fortnight. Let me hear from you soon.

"God bless you, ever affectionately,

"DAVID COX."

The plan suggested in the foregoing letter of a visit to Bridgnorth and Ludlow was never carried out, as in little more than a week after writing it, Cox was seized with a very serious attack of illness, which at one time put his life in great danger, and left him much enfeebled; indeed, he never entirely recovered from the effects of this attack. It was soon after breakfast on Sunday, the 12th of June, that he went into his garden to cut some asparagus for dinner, and whilst stooping down, thus occupied, the blood rushed apparently to his head, and he fell almost senseless.

Ann Fowler was unfortunately absent at Hereford, but Mrs. Roberts hearing, from the maid Mercie, what had happened, drove off for his usual medical attendant, Mr. Bindley. He was sent for out of church, and was quickly in

CHAP. XIV. 1849—1855. attendance. Cox's son also arrived the next morning to help nurse his father. He had been telegraphed for, and there being no passenger train he had travelled down by a goods train in the night, and he remained at Greenfield till the 27th June; being then replaced by one of his daughters. The attack partook somewhat of the nature of paralysis, but he recovered sufficiently by the end of six weeks to go out in the fields behind Harborne, and make a water-colour sketch; although he was so feeble that he required two persons to assist him to walk. When once seated to his work, his mind appeared to re-assert all its former vigour, and he produced a broad, rapid, and very beautiful sketch, which is now in Mr. Ellis's collection, where I have lately seen it. The sky is stormy and particularly fine, a path leads through a field, the long grass of which appears as if blown by the wind, and some fine trees rise up on the right-hand side of the drawing. About two months after this attack he was able to make his usual journey to North Wales. He stayed at the Farm House, at Bettws, and was accompanied by his grand-daughter as well as by his housekeeper, and by Priest. His hand, by degrees, grew tolerably steady again, and he had the same perception and feeling for nature as ever; but his eyesight was affected, especially that of one of his eyes, over which a drooping of the lid had taken place.

By the beginning of 1854 Cox had very much got over the effects of his illness of the preceding summer, and he painted during this year many admirable oil-pictures and impressive drawings in water-colour. Of the former I may mention several in Mr. Bullock's collection—"Keep the Left Road," "Peat Gatherers," and "Cutting his Stick." He only sent seven drawings to the Water Colour Gallery in 1854. Some of these were the same subjects as he had chosen for his works in oil; but there were also two views from Capel Curig, one of them being a particularly fine and impressive view of Snowdon; also "Ludford Bridge," and "Crossing the

Downs." It was in 1854 that he made his celebrated drawing of "Besom Makers collecting Heather on Chat Moss," now in Mr. Craven's collection, of which I give a copy. It was not exhibited in London till the following year.

Cox visited London this spring as usual, also Bettws, where Mr. Ellis and his son accompanied him, and where he painted from nature both in oil and water colours.

Cox felt the winter of 1854-55 a good deal, and he suffered in his health during the spring. This did not, however, interfere much with his work, and he sent thirteen drawings again this year, 1855, to the Water Colour Society. "Skirts of a Forest," "Snowdon from Capel Curig," "A Hayfield," "The Coming Gale," and "Flint Castle," were the most interesting. There was also a drawing called "The Old London Stage," which attracted a good deal of notice, and was deservedly popular. A very good critique on these drawings appeared in the *Spectator* in May, 1855, for the insertion of which in this place I hope no apology will be deemed necessary. The *Spectator* says:—

"How far the contributions of Cox may be the doings of the past year, we are unable to say. We recognise one or two of the designs of former seasons. We only hope that any of the remainder belong to the present; for if they do this noble veteran of art is still in the vigour which has long rendered him a king of water-colour landscape. There is the same deep grand gloom as ever, the same penetration beneath the surface of things to their meaning and life, the same impatient power, whose play and carelessness throws off in a twist, or a spirt of the brush, that which talent, age, and faultlessly educated talent, shall strive for its life long with all labour and appliance, and *never attain*. 'Flint Castle, Snowdon,' 'The Coming Gale,' 'Crossing the Heath,' 'Moon Rise,' and 'The Old London Stage,' are conspicuously fine, where every one bears the mint-mark of genius."

CHAP. XIV.

1849—1855.

It was after Cox had returned from his usual visit to London that his friends at Birmingham proposed that a subscription should be entered into to obtain a portrait of David Cox, to be painted by some eminent artist, and afterwards to be presented as a testimonial of their regard to him. The idea originated in the minds of one or two near friends; but when made known, it was warmly responded to, and it resulted in the well-known portrait painted by Sir John Watson Gordon, now in the public gallery at Birmingham. A full account of this will be given in the next chapter, and I shall, after that, introduce the promised one on water-colour drawings.

XV.

PORTRAIT OF DAVID COX, BY SIR J. WATSON GORDON.

EARLY in 1855 the friends and admirers of David Cox in Birmingham, after consulting together, determined to take steps to get a good portrait of him painted by some eminent artist. It was also proposed to present it to him as a testimonial of the general esteem in which he was held in the town. For this purpose a circular, to which many influential names were attached, was issued convening a meeting. This took place in the rooms of the Birmingham Society of Artists on the 31st May, 1855. A committee was there formed—Mr. Charles Birch being elected chairman, and Mr. J. B. Hebbert and Mr. John Jaffray, honorary secretaries; and a subscription for carrying out the proposed object was originated. CHAP. XV.

Referring to this meeting, the *Midland Counties Herald* of that date published an article, from which the following is an extract:—

"To the truth of the proverb about the esteem in which a prophet is held in his own country, there are, we are sometimes gratified to find, exceptions. Birmingham, we have much pleasure in learning, is about to furnish one of these exceptions to established rule.

"She owes much to art, and she is about to acknowledge her obligations in a graceful and appropriate manner by paying a richly-merited tribute of respect to one of the most

CHAP. XV. gifted members of the English school, and one, moreover, whom she has the privilege—a distinction of which she is justly proud—to number among her citizens. We allude to Mr. David Cox. To enter at this period of his lengthened and honourable career into any elaborate and formal eulogy of his works would be a needless expenditure of time and space. Not, however, to professional talents of the highest order alone, is the compliment we allude to about to be paid. It is intended as a token of the esteem in which Mr. David Cox is held—for the personal worth, the kindliness of heart, and unobtrusive virtues which have marked his modest and laborious life."

After communicating their wishes to Mr. David Cox, and after careful consideration, the committee decided to apply to Sir John Watson Gordon, then resident at Edinburgh, as the artist who would be best qualified to do justice to the thoughtful character and noble though rather tried expression of David Cox at this period of his life. The only difficulty lay in the length of the journey to Scotland, which in the infirm state of his health at this time was a matter of anxiety to all parties concerned. Cox himself dreaded so long a journey very much, and at first declined to go; but after consulting with Dr. Bell Fletcher and Mr. Bindley, he was persuaded to alter his mind, and on the 23rd July, 1855, he wrote thus to his son :—

"MY DEAR DAVID,—The committee wrote again to me yesterday, after I had written to Mr. Ellis, and four of them have most particularly; and two of the doctors write that there can be no risk of my health, and most particularly urge me to start in nine days. So I feel ready to go. Be ready to go with me to Edinburgh. So I wish you to tell Mr. Ellis I should like him to go with me, as we are not to be detained more than five or six sittings, and shall make it a very quiet journey—three days up and three back. I should like Mr.

Ellis to accompany me, if possible—Messrs. Bullock, Birch, yourself, and me. If Mr. Ellis cannot go with me, I can go with him for a short trip for nine days. God bless you and Mr. Ellis, and accept my love.

"Yours,

"DAVID COX."

Cox's writing was less legible than usual at this time, and in a letter to Mr. Ellis he says that writing had made him feel quite giddy.

After Cox, with the sanction of his medical advisers, had consented to make the effort, everything being arranged, he left Birmingham for the north on the 13th August, accompanied by his son and by Mr. William Hall. They reached Carlisle the first evening, and slept at an hotel. The next morning they all went out to see the place, and soon found their way on to the ramparts of Carlisle Castle, from which there is a good view, as it is situated on an eminence between the town and the river Eden. Cox was much struck with the appearance of the old keep, and immediately set to work to make a sketch of it. His son also followed his example. The castle was at that time maintained as a garrison fortress, and on the ramparts a sentinel was walking up and down. The only notice he took of the sketchers was to cast occasionally a wondering glance at their work as he walked up and down. Before long, however, an officer made his appearance. He went up to the sentinel, and desired him to request the sketchers to leave off immediately, as it was not to be endured, he added, that in time of war people should be allowed to make drawings of one of Her Majesty's fortresses (it happened to be the time of the Russian War). Cox was rather indignant, and shut up his book rather in dudgeon. Whilst putting up his box, &c., the officer withdrew; whereupon the sentinel came by again, and, remarking it was all humbug, said that if they would tip him with half-a-crown, they

CHAP. XV. might continue their work. Cox, however, refused rather abruptly, and having shortly adjourned to the banks of the Eden, they obtained an excellent view of the castle, of which Cox made a graphic sketch. They arrived the same evening at Edinburgh, namely, on the 14th, and stopped the first night at an hotel.

The following letter, addressed by Mr. David Cox, jun., to his daughters, describes this journey :—

"Edinburgh, August 15th, 1855.

"We arrived here on the 14th, at the Royal Hotel, Princes Street, and have since moved into lodgings at No. 10, Albyn Place. We travelled seven hours on Monday to Carlisle, and next day came on to this place. The hotel was rather noisy, and my father complained that it disturbed him. Mr. Hall is with us, and we are enjoying ourselves very much."

Mr. Hall described that when they arrived at the hotel, a waiter in full dress came in, and asked what they would please to order for dinner. Cox, who wanted something to take very much, and did not care how simple it was, appeared rather vexed when he was made to understand that he was expected to order a grand dinner of soup, fish, &c.

The following is an extract from a letter written by David Cox, jun., three days after they had removed into the lodgings in Albyn Place :—

"My father has been for a first sitting, and I think it all goes on well. I expect he will not be wanted above five times. Yesterday we took a drive round by the Queen's Drive, a new road from Holyrood Palace round Arthur's Seat.

"Sir W. Gordon is affable and entertaining, with a grave and dignified carriage, An active man, too, for his years. Our lodgings are in a very good part of the town. Sir

J. W. G. lives just round the corner. I don't think lodgings are at a premium, although we pay 50*s*. a week.

"*Monday, 20th August.*—Mr. Birch arrived early this morning, and we shall be sight-seeing perhaps all day. It is fixed that we are to go to Mr. Reeve's cottage, at Bolton-le-Sands, near Lancaster, and return with him to Birmingham.

"Sir John has finished the portrait. My father is delighted with it. It is as real as can be, and a very pleasing portrait. Mr. Birch is equally satisfied, and indeed I think Sir J. W. Gordon expects it will bring him credit in the Academy next year."

Mr. William Hall has informed me that there were five sittings in all. He describes their first introduction at Sir J. W. Gordon's house thus:—They were ushered into a parlour, and the artist came out promptly from his painting-room, and accosting Cox, with a broad Scotch accent, said, "Welcome to Scotland, Mistair Cox!" When the sitting commenced, Cox was placed in an easy arm-chair, on a sort of rostrum. Once he happened to fall asleep in this chair, when Sir Watson exclaimed, "Rouse up now, Mr. Cox; I am going to do your expression." This had the desired effect, when turning to his son, Cox said, "Eh! David; what is it he is now talking about?" Sir Watson was delighted with his subject. He said he had formerly painted Sir Walter Scott, and that the form of his head and that of David Cox were very similar, and that the lower part of his face was like Lord Brougham's.

Cox himself, however, rather demurred to this, and he used often jokingly to remark afterwards that he was sure he never had such a *long Scotch head* as Sir Watson Gordon had given him. Before leaving Edinburgh they all went to dine at this artist's country house, and were very hospitably entertained by him. He was evidently highly pleased with his guest, and desired to show him all the attention in his power. The country house was at a place called Newhaven, close to the sea. During the drive thither Cox was much amused seeing the Scotch fish-wives, with their quaint costumes and brawny arms, almost like men. Miss Watson, the sister of Sir J. W. Gordon, received them, and his nephew, Mr. Watson, was also of the party. Cox was sufficiently well to see something of the neighbourhood of Edinburgh during his visit, and to take a drive round Arthur's Seat, all which interested him very much.

When the portrait arrived at Birmingham from Edinburgh, it was placed in Mr. E. Everitt's rooms in New Street, and there Cox went to see it, on the 9th November, accompanied by his housekeeper. On his return home that day, after seeing it, he wrote thus to his son :—

"November 9th, 1855.

"MY DEAR DAVID,—The portrait is the finest ever seen, and Mr. Birch thinks it worth one of his Turners. The weather is very dark, so God bless you all. Write to me often. Love to all.

"DAVID COX."

Again, on the 14th of November, he wrote the following letter to his son about the forthcoming presentation :—

"MY DEAR DAVID,—I do not know what Mr. Birch wrote to you; and *now* I would tell you that I should not wish you to come down, as I know it would be an unpleasant irksome feeling, and it is for that reason.

"We shall do very well, I hope, as Dr. Fletcher has said that he will just say a few words. My love to Mr. Ellis, and tell him I shall be very glad to see him at any time at my house. Thank God, I am much better, and my cough is nearly gone. God bless you, and love to all.

"DAVID COX."

The presentation of the portrait to Mr. Cox took place on

Monday, the 19th November, 1855, at Metchley Abbey, Harborne, the residence of the Chairman of the Committee, Mr. Charles Birch. That gentleman had invited the acting members of the committee, some of the principal subscribers, and other friends, sixty-two in all, including fourteen ladies, to be present on this occasion, and to partake of a collation served in the picture-gallery. This apartment contained several pictures by Cox himself, one being the "Welsh Funeral" (now possessed by Mr. Betts), also choice examples of Constable, Turner, Etty, Müller, Danby, Maclise, Cooper, and others, all well selected, as Mr. Birch had good judgment and true feeling for art. Among those present were the Rev. J. Garbett, Rev. J. Blackburn, and several other clergymen, Dr. Bell Fletcher, Messrs. W. Roberts, E. Bullock, William Sharpe, Hyla Betts, C. Cope, Arthur Ryland, R. G. Reeves, J. Pemberton Gwyther, R. Wright, H. Wiggin, J. Feeney, J. Jaffray, Bracey Henshaw Hallam, R. Chattock, W. Tarratt, A. E. Everitt, J. D. Hebbert, W. Hall, and several other friends.

The portrait, surmounted by a wreath of laurel, occupied the end of the drawing room.

After the repast, at which a good many ladies were present, the chairman rose to make the presentation. David Cox sat on his right hand; he had arrived rather late, leaning on the arm of Dr. Bell Fletcher. Mr. Birch briefly referred to the object of their meeting, to the artistic genius and private worth of his honoured guest, with whom he said it had been his good fortune to enjoy an uninterrupted friendship of more than thirty years. He spoke of his intense devotion to his profession, and enumerated several of the principal works of Mr. Cox, which had made his name famous throughout the whole world of art. Whilst expressing his admiration for the professional talents of his friend, he adverted to his early struggles with adverse times, to his simple and sincere love of Nature, to his transparent truth-

CHAP. XV. fulness at all times, his readiness to oblige others, his patient devotion to study, the simplicity of his character, the purity of his life, and his Christian charity and benevolence. He heartily congratulated the subscribers to the testimonial, upon the truly magnificent work of art and faithful portrait which they had obtained from Sir J. Watson Gordon, adding that the feelings which had inspired the subscribers were better expressed than his humble abilities allowed, in an address prepared by the committee, which one of the secretaries, Mr. Jaffray, would now read. The address was then read, as follows:—

"TO MR. DAVID COX.

"DEAR SIR,—Several old friends, who for many years have enjoyed the pleasure of intimate communion with you, and a few others who only know you by your professional works, having a desire to express to you their admiration of your genius and their respect for your private character, have entered into a subscription, the result of which is the portrait now presented to you in the name of the subscribers.

"In thus expressing their feelings they were also influenced by the desire of preserving in your native town a memorial of one who already holds a high place in the estimation of all who can distinguish between the meretricious and true in art, and who will yet be held in higher repute as an able teacher in a genial, manly school of landscape-painting. For, disregarding the mere outward prettiness of Nature, you seized the true essence of her grandeur, and the spirit of her beauty, and became her faithful and therefore her famous exponent.

"It has been said of those who patiently and with a single mind love virtue for her own sake, that the very act of self-denial is happiness. The same may be said of the patient, modest, unselfish student of Nature. To him she reveals her secrets and lays bare her beauty; the very act of self-sacrifice is the passport to fame. CHAP. XV.

"Such we believe to be the spirit in which you entered upon and pursued your half century of study. Beginning in a humble way, neither aided by patronage, nor buoyed up by applause, you have won a high place amongst contemporary artists, have made your name famous in many lands, and, better still, have surrounded your declining years with troops of friends who not only admire your genius, but reverence and love you. To the man as well as to the artist we offer this mark of respect.

"Like many who have climbed to the highest pinnacles of fame, you tasted adversity. In the two extremes you have shown the same high qualities of mind; bearing obscurity with manly fortitude, and, what is still more difficult, acquiring fame without losing the simplicity of your character. These are rare qualities always, very rare in an age of showy accomplishment and restless action, and by preserving in some public building in your native town this record of you —a record as true and unaffected as the man it represents— we seek to perpetuate the example of your private virtues as well as the remembrance of your professional fame.

"Accept then, dear Sir, this expression of the admiration and love of your friends; and they are sure that you will value the gift more highly as being the work of an artist kindred to yourself in spirit, who in a different walk of art has won an honourable reputation, and who by this portrait has added another to the list of his professional successes.

"We fervently hope that you may long be spared to wear the laurels you have so well won, to give more evidence of the unabated freshness of your thoughts and the vigour of your pencil, and to enjoy the serene repose of a virtuous and honoured old age.

"BIRMINGHAM, November 19th, 1855."

CHAP. XV.

The address was very handsomely bound in vellum, with illuminated title and borders, and bore the signature of one hundred and six subscribers, including all his oldest friends, also the Rev. John Garbett, Vicar, W. C. Macready, David Roberts, R.A.; Tom Taylor, M.A.; T. Creswick, R.A.; Mark Anthony, John Pye, and Samuel Bellin, the engravers, and many other men of distinction. Besides letters from Mr. John Ruskin, Mr. Boddington, and other friends who could not attend, and which were read by the secretary, was one from Mr. Horsley, the then newly elected Associate of the Royal Academy, who, whilst begging to add his name to the list of subscribers, expressed his regret that he could not be present to pay homage to the "royal supremacy" of David Cox.

After the reading of the document, which was heartily applauded, David Cox merely bowed his thanks, and Dr. Bell Fletcher, who, on account of his aged friend's very delicate health at the time, had undertaken the office, then rose and in a few appropriate words expressed Mr. Cox's grateful sense of the mark of esteem and regard which he had received. Many toasts were afterwards proposed and cordially received, including the health of Sir John Watson Gordon, which was proposed by Mr. Hyla Betts. The gathering at Metchley Abbey, which was one of true friendship and cordiality, did not separate till late in the evening.

In the course of the afternoon, a clergyman, who was present, told a gentleman who sat next to him, that he had travelled from a considerable distance in the north of England to be present on the occasion. He said he had been the curate of Harborne Church for several years, and had learned to love and venerate David Cox. He added that he had almost always found, when sent for to a cottager's sick-bed in the village of Harborne to administer to their spiritual wants, that Cox had preceded him in his visits, and had fully cared for their temporal comforts and requirements. Cox had presented him with a drawing before he left, and this remembrance of the old man, he said, he valued more than anything he possessed. CHAP. XV.

At the time the portrait was presented it was arranged that it should eventually be placed in some conspicuous public building or gallery in Birmingham. This has been carried out within the last few years, when the public Fine Art Gallery for the town was opened in the building of the Midland Institute, and the picture painted by Sir J. W. Gordon may now be seen gratis. It is in most respects a very successful work of art, and very like David Cox, but having been painted after his serious illness, which happened two years before, the expression of the features is more grave and pensive than was the case a few years previously.

This portrait has been well engraved by S. Bellin, and being published only for the benefit of subscribers is rather scarce. I give a copy from this engraving by the Heliotype process at the commencement of this chapter. On the 20th November, the day after the presentation, Cox wrote a short but cheerful letter to his son, giving some account of the presentation, which he says "went off very well," and expressing his gratification at the kindness of his friends. The portrait had been placed in his parlour in Greenfield House, and, referring to it, he says "the portrait is very much liked."

In the following spring, that of 1856, the portrait of Cox was exhibited in the Royal Academy, and there it attracted a great deal of notice, both on account of the artist who was represented and the artist who had painted the picture.

XVI.

WATER-COLOUR DRAWINGS.

CHAP. XVI.

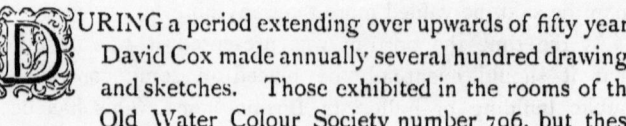

DURING a period extending over upwards of fifty years David Cox made annually several hundred drawings and sketches. Those exhibited in the rooms of the Old Water Colour Society number 796, but these form only a very small proportion of the drawings he produced. As to his sketches, they are beyond calculation. Although a change in his manner of viewing nature and powers of expression, appears gradually, and I may add almost unceasingly to have taken place during all the lapse of years, yet in each period there are many points of resemblance, and much of the same originality of feeling and treatment.

When Cox began to draw in water-colours at the commencement of the present century, this branch of art was in a state of transition. During the preceding thirty or forty years, although water-colour landscapes had been produced by such early pioneers in the art as J. Webber, J. Cozens, W. Gilpin, Paul Sandby, and W. Hearne, they were little else than outlines, tinted with low-toned flat washes, the shadows being frequently put in first with neutral tint. This was the approved method taught in the earliest treatises. This was improved upon by Girtin, J. J. Chalon, and one or two others, but the modern art of water-colours, as now practised in England, with its delicacy, purity, and yet depth of colour, its pearly lights, rich tones, and powerful shadows,

may be said to have taken its rise with the formation of the old Society of Painters in Water Colours.

Their first exhibition was held at 20, Lower Brook Street, in 1805. It started with sixteen members, all good men, who have left their mark in their various walks of the art, but George Barrett, J. Glover, Joshua Cristall, William Havell, Robert Hills, F. Nicholson, and John Varley are the best-known names to all collectors of early water-colours. Body colour has of late been a good deal used, especially when high finish is required. W. Hunt, the great still-life painter, was one of the first to carry this method to perfection, and many distinguished artists now follow in the same track.

Some of the best early water-colour painters considered that the use of body colour was illegitimate in the practice of their art, except on rare and very special occasions, and this was Cox's opinion. Many of his finest drawings have scarcely a touch of body colour, but, on the other hand, he laid on an immense deal of colour at once with an abundance of water, which dried *sharp* and pure in tone, giving the appearance of finish, especially when worked up with repeated touches and hatchings.

With a view to distinguish Cox's changes of style, and to classify his drawings, I propose to divide them into four classes or periods. Taking the first as that between 1804 and 1814, the date of his removal to Hereford, we may recognise the influence exerted by the study of the old masters, and by the works of Girtin, Barrett, and Varley. They are generally good in composition, but the colour, although not inharmonious, is wanting in variety and sometimes in freshness. It is flat, low-toned, and often rather dull and dark. This last remark applies especially to the foliage of his early trees. These works generally show much painstaking care and labour, but at the same time a fine eye for *effect*. In that most important quality Cox was indeed never wanting.

I take the second period as between 1814 and 1829. These are careful, but less conventional. The colouring is brighter, and the finish, although not more elaborate, is more telling. The small delicate drawings for albums of this period are, however, sometimes very highly finished, and the high lights occasionally touched in with body colour. These are exceedingly different from the grand rough works of his latest period, but the subjects are always pleasing, especially those on the Wye and in the neighbourhood of Hereford, and indicate refinement and a careful study of nature. The figures are well put in, but have less life and action than in his more advanced works. In the first period there is more art and less nature, and in the second more nature and less art, or at least the art is better concealed.

The third period, which may be said to extend from about 1830 to 1850, comprises without doubt most of Cox's important representative drawings. In these there is a visible increase of breadth, more vigour and rapidity in the handling, more insight and penetration into the deeper meaning and mystery of nature, more movement, more sparkle and brilliancy, and a more mature knowledge of effect, and of the forms and treatment of sky and clouds. There is also a more decided character in the figures introduced. The well-known series of views of Lancaster and Ulverstone Sands, delicate and refined in colour almost beyond any others, are of this period. So are also the large and highly-finished drawings of Hardwick Hall, Bolsover Castle, the Vale of Clwyd, Bolton Abbey, Berden Tower, Sherwood Forest, &c. The last period, from 1850 to 1859, comprises many of his pastoral subjects, and those grand pathetic works, "The Welsh Funeral," "The Moors near Bettws-y-Coed," "Peat Gatherers returning," "The Missing Flock," "Snowdon, from Capel Curig," "The Mountain Top," and many more. In these there is the deepest sympathy with nature, and greater power than in any others, being even more the work of the artist's mind than of his hand. The supreme excellence of these drawings must be *felt;* it cannot be described. CHAP. XVI.

During the last few years in which Cox's eyesight was somewhat affected by his illness, his feeling and love for grand and solemn subjects was extraordinarily vivid, but the power of carrying out his ideas was somewhat impaired, making the handling loose, and to some extent "blotty." For this reason many persons prefer the drawings of what I have termed the third period to any others.

I shall describe some of the most important collections of Cox's drawings which now exist, and which comprise some of almost every date. It is to me a matter of regret that so many of the collections purchased direct from the artist, namely, those of Messrs. W. Roberts, Edwin Bullock, Norman Wilkinson, and Charles Birch, have been dispersed. However, the extremely choice collection belonging to Mr. W. S. Ellis is intact, and also the very interesting drawings and sketches bequeathed by Cox to his son. These comprise some which were especial favourites of the artist himself. Many of Cox's most important, truthful, and spirited drawings, after being exhibited at the Water Colour Society, have appeared in later years in other great representative exhibitions. For instance, in the Manchester Art Treasures of 1857, there were eighteen very choice drawings by David Cox. In the Great International Exhibition in London of 1862, "The Welsh Funeral," "The Junction of the Severn and the Wye," were exhibited; also "Beaumaris," "Fern Gatherers," "Beeston Castle," "The Horse Fair," "Going to the Hayfield," &c.

F. T. Palgrave, in his handbook to the Fine Arts Collection in the International Exhibition, 1862, makes the following remarks on the drawings by David Cox exhibited there:—

"The poetry of David Cox, within its peculiar range, and whenever he choose to express it, is pure and perfect. His

CHAP. XVI. feeling for certain aspects of English landscape has all the strange irresistible force of true passion. When a man views his art in this spirit, it must be left to tell its own story to those who share the emotions which animated it. Such will recognise in specimens here shown the intense imagination which penetrates his work; what majesty he saw in the common field or cottage; with what an inner eye of sympathy he watched the wreathings of the stream beneath the gloom of forest greenery; the visionary sadness of wide horizons and dreary heaths, or the last red gleam that ebbed away from the heights of Craig-y-Dinas. In the 'Welsh Funeral,' 'Bolsover,' 'Beeston,' 'Fern Gatherers,' 'Wye,' and many of the small scenes, as 975 and 976, these high qualities are especially shown. They belong peculiarly to the artist's later style, in which his often blurred and imperfectly realised execution is a severe lesson to the lovers of the neat and the conventional. Yet this seemingly slight and hasty touch conceals a thoughtfulness and a delicacy in handling which is more like Turner's than any other man's work. The sweet gradation of colour and beauty of form in the breaking wave of the 'Beaumaris' (1010) seem to me of unsurpassed excellence."

And again he says further on :—

"All truths of the highest order are separated from those of average precision by points of extreme delicacy, which none but the cultivated eye can in the least feel, and to express which all words are absolutely meaningless and useless."

At the Leeds International Exhibition thirty-two drawings of the highest quality were again exhibited. The titles comprise three of the Hayfield, three of Views in Windsor Park, two of Bettws-y-Coed, "Bolton Abbey," "Bolton Wood," "Fording the Stream," "Kenilworth," "The Golden Vale," "The Haystack," "Passing Shower," "Going to the Hayfield," "Sunrise on the Beach," "Landscape and Bridge,"

"Harlech Castle," "On the Thames," "On the Severn," "A Welsh Lane," "The Welsh Funeral," "Richmond, Yorkshire," "The Besom Gatherers," "Summer-time," "Landscape and Figures," "Wind and Rain," "Classical Landscape," "The Vale of Clwyd," "Near Hereford and Bolsover Castle." This gathering of Cox's drawings at Leeds was one of the most important that has ever taken place, and as some of his best works of nearly every period were represented there, it was unusually interesting and instructive. The principal collectors who lent these works were Mr. G. W. Moss, Mr. Peter Allen, Mr. F. Craven, and Mr. W. Quilter.

Several of the above works will be described as I proceed, since they are included in the collections I am about to pass in review.

MR. F. CRAVEN'S COLLECTION, HIGH BROUGHTON, MANCHESTER.

THE WELSH FUNERAL. 1850. 2 ft. 6 in. by 3 ft. 3 in.

This is the original drawing exhibited in 1850. This grand work represents the hills and crags on the eastern side of the Vale of Bettws-y-Coed; at their foot is the belfry of the old church, in which the bell is seen swinging. The greater part of the sacred edifice is concealed by some fine yews and other trees, whilst the road leading towards it is occupied by the mournful procession. It is chiefly composed of poor women in long cloaks, with handkerchiefs to their eyes indicating their deep grief. An old man with a stick and hat-band, to represent the artist himself, and a girl and boy—the latter with head bent forward and hat in hand—all express the reverential and solemn feelings of the moment.

Bordering the road on either side are stone walls, or dykes, partly overgrown with brambles, and on the right two children are leaning over the top dropping flowers into the uplifted

CHAP. XVI. apron of another child. Near this group is an elder bush in full bloom to indicate the sweet season of summer. Cox remarked, when showing this picture, "You must not think that those are common field flowers. Oh, no! they are poppies, symbolical of the sleep of death." The golden evening light falls on the upper part of the church, a type of the bright home in heaven; it also illumines that portion of the hills not shaded by the rising mists. A wild and stony tract they look, and form a striking contrast with the verdure of the vale below. The subject of this touching picture was suggested to Cox by his being present at the funeral of a young Welsh girl, a relative of the landlord of the Royal Oak, whilst he was staying there. It took place in the evening, as was often the custom in North Wales. This drawing not being sold when it was exhibited in London, in 1850, Mr. F. W. Topham, the artist who admired it exceedingly, persuaded the holder of a £50 Art-Union prize to select it. The owner did not appear to have appreciated the treasure he possessed, and Mr. Topham repurchased it from him, and he lent it to the Art-Treasures Exhibition at Manchester in 1857. By the kind permission of Mr. Craven I am able to present my readers with a photographic copy of this celebrated drawing.

SHEEP ASTRAY, OR THE MISSING FLOCK. 1849. 2 ft. by 3 ft. 9 in.

A very poetical drawing of the best period, and one which Cox thought highly of himself. He bequeathed a drawing to his friend Charles Birch, and this was the one selected. The scene represented is a wild valley near the high moorlands of Kirby Lonsdale, in Cumberland. The sky is stormy and lowering, and the drifting clouds throw dark shadows over a grand range of blue hills. A man leading a mountain pony, and with outstretched arm, is descending a rocky path towards a flock of frightened sheep, who appear to be rushing wildly along. The rocks and boulders in the foreground are large and broken, and are light in colour, forming a pleasant contrast with the dark and gloomy distance. The handling is peculiarly vigorous and free.

BEESTON CASTLE. 1849. 2 ft. by 2 ft. 10 in.

This beautiful drawing is full of play of light and shade, and was particularly admired when exhibited in the Water Colour Exhibition in 1849. The castle stands up grandly with a fine light on it, although mists are gathering around its top, and a storm is approaching in the distance. The lower part of the hill is clothed with trees, and on the plain below a group of cattle, preceded by a bull, are being driven along by a peasant woman. In the immediate foreground there is a pool of water, fringed with water plants and swallows skimming low over the surface, thus indicating the approach of rain. There is a beautiful range of distance, with some low bright clouds. This is one of his most perfect drawings, and I am very glad to be able to give a photographic copy of it in this book.

BOLSOVER CASTLE. Date about 1843. 1 ft. 11 in. by 3 ft. 1 in.

The sky is especially beautiful, and the old trees on the right very picturesque in form and character. The colour also is very pleasing. A knight and a lady on two palfreys, followed by some dogs, are cantering towards the castle, which stands out brightly against the sky. The distance is tender, with a good deal of finish; the sentiment of the figures is less satisfactory than in most of the later works. I also give a copy of this drawing.

WINDSOR CASTLE. The Queen is coming. Date about 1853. 2 ft. 4 in. by 3 ft. 3 in.

One of the largest and most important drawings; full of

CHAP. XVI. subject and well arranged. Windsor Castle rises dark against the horizon. The forest trees of the great park massed together, and a retreating herd of deer form the middle distance. Immediately in front, on the right, four gnarled and giant oaks throw their broad shade over nearly half the picture. Underneath these a woman, holding the hand of a little boy, leans forward, and pointing towards a distant group of horsemen, is supposed to be exclaiming (as Cox himself explained), "There, there, the Queen is coming!" The figures of the Queen and Prince Consort in front of the escort are very easily distinguished. The sky indicates wind, with large rolling clouds and numerous birds. The handling is loose and powerful.

VALE OF CLWYD. 1848. 1 ft. 11 in. by 3 ft. 1 in.

A finely-wooded range of hills in the distance, with a variety of incidents and light and shade. The sky is rather bright, and the whole effect cheerful. In the middle distance a house, partly concealed by trees, is sending up curling wreaths of smoke. In the foreground are figures and a waggon and horses descending a road. On the left is a cornfield, where shocks of yellow corn are standing. It is an eminently bright pleasing drawing, very rich in subject, and with a good deal of finish.

BROOM GATHERERS ON CHAT MOSS. 1854. 2 ft. by 3 ft. 2 in.

This well-known drawing is on the rough paper, and represents a common, with heather in full blossom. On the left two figures are bending under the burden of large bundles of heather, and in the centre several figures of men, women, and boys are loading some donkeys with the same material. The attitude and costumes of these figures are very picturesque. In the distance are some cattle, and rooks wheeling about in the sky,—the latter indicates fine weather,—with light grey clouds passing over the blue expanse. The sky is a grand feature in this drawing; the horizon is low, it is full of movement, and in his latest manner. This drawing was originally exhibited at Manchester, where it did not sell, and was for many years in the possession of Mr. S. Mayou, of Birmingham, who sold it to Mr. F. Craven. Through the kindness of this gentleman, I am able to give a photograph of it herewith.

A HILLY LANDSCAPE, WITH A WINDMILL AND COTTAGES IN THE DISTANCE. Not dated. 1 ft. 11 in. by 2 ft. 8½ in.

In the foreground a road leads upwards on the right, on which is a cart and two horses, led by a carter; and immediately behind, two men are stooping down in the act of loading it. The light on the front horse, which is white, and on the smock frock of the carter, gives point to the whole. The sky is silvery in tone, the handling rather slight in parts and sketchy, but masterly, and the whole effect pleasing.

A STORM ON THE NORTH-WELSH COAST. Date about 1838.

The spot chosen for this drawing is near Penmaen Mawr. The clouds are drifting along in dark masses, and the waves beat wildly on the shore. A wreck appears to have just taken place in the neighbourhood, as groups on the shore are helping to save many figures of men and women out of the treacherous sea. It is a work of the middle period, and not so free in the handling as most of the later works.

MR. W. QUILTER'S COLLECTION, UPPER NORWOOD.

This very important collection contains drawings by David Cox of nearly every period, many of them being representative

CHAP. XVI. works of his best years. I will give an account of some of these which are framed, in the order of their date, and then just glance at the contents of the folios.

THE OLD BRIDGE AT BRIDGNORTH. About 1809. Long and narrow.

This early drawing is much worked upon, and very carefully finished. There is a good deal of effect and power noticeable, but it is somewhat too dark and heavy. It is a good specimen drawing of his first style, and was exhibited in the Bond Street Exhibition. The bridge has some curious old buildings on it, and the houses of the old town in the distance have a foreign aspect.

THE HAYFIELD, NEAR HEREFORD. 1819. 12 by 16½ in.

This pleasing, quiet and low-toned drawing was exhibited in the great rooms in Spring Gardens in 1819. A waggon and horses, with some figures, give interest to the foreground. The hayfield occupies the middle of the picture, beyond which are some trees and hills near Hereford. A smooth sky, very quiet in colour, completes the picture. As an example of Cox's early Hereford work, it is interesting.

CARTHAGE—ÆNEAS AND ACHATES. 1825. 2 ft. 5 in. by 3 ft. 7 in.

This drawing was exhibited in the Water Colour Gallery in 1825, under the above title; it has since been described as a "Classical Landscape." Without doubt, admiration for some of the works of Claude and Turner led Cox to make this experiment, which is very unlike most of his other works. It is highly finished throughout, and shows a good eye for colour, and some imaginative power; but, as a whole, it looks too laboured, and cannot be pronounced a complete success. The distant buildings of Carthage have a good deal the character of some of the creations of Martin. They are admirably drawn, and have a grand and imposing appearance.

THE PICTURE GALLERY AT HARDWICK HALL. 1839.

These two upright drawings, with the long one as a centre (now belonging to the Duke of Devonshire), formed the celebrated series of interior views at Hardwick Hall, for many years one of the chief ornaments of Mr. Bullock's collection. The effect is very real, and the perspective excellent, not only of the building itself, but also of the collection of old portraits and other pictures which adorn the walls. These pictures have so much character, that the painter of the originals, whether Rubens, Rembrandt, or Vandyke, may be easily guessed.

HOP GARDEN IN KENT. Date about 1840. 10 in. by 1 ft. 2½ in.

The sketch for this drawing was made from the window of an inn, on a hill, near Sevenoaks. The hops are seen hanging in clusters from the poles, which are being stripped by a group of girls; near them a farming man on a white horse has pulled up, and appears to be engaged in conversation. The trees in the middle distance are low in tone, and beyond them a rich plain extends far away. The sky is bright and fresh, and the whole drawing is carefully finished. It is more of a figure subject than most of Cox's landscapes, and is a fairly good example of this period.

VALE OF CLWYD. 1845. 1 ft. 7 in. by 2 ft. 3½ in.

Very full of power and brilliant in colour, with a good deal of finish. A blue sky is seen through rough rolling clouds,

CHAP. XVI. and the grand oak-trees on the right appear to be tossing their branches in the wind. Beneath these, women are carrying bundles of gleaned corn, and close by is a man on a white horse. The distance is very fine, being well wooded, with a beautiful range of purple hills beyond, and streaks of sunshine breaking through the clouds. This drawing was recently sent by Mr. Quilter to one of the loan collections of drawings exhibited in Pall Mall.

DRWSLLYN CASTLE, VALE OF TOWY, NEAR CARMARTHEN. 1845. 10 by 14½ in.

A reposeful drawing, rather highly finished. Some broad meadows, with cattle, occupy the middle of the picture; a range of hills rises up beyond, on which are some groups of trees and a mansion house. Jeremy Taylor resided there in olden times. It is a verdant rural scene, but not at all grand as a composition.

THE GREEN LANES, STAFFORDSHIRE. Dated Aug. 13, 1848. 2 ft. 1½ in. by 2 ft. 7 in.

This is an impressive drawing of the highest quality and best period, and one which was much esteemed by the artist himself. It also attracted much attention when exhibited in the Water Colour Society's Rooms. An avenue of fine dark trees forms the principal subject. The feeling conveyed is one of country seclusion and repose. On the right are some figures, and a flock of sheep feeding at leisure, and scattered along a wide green country lane. The handling of the foreground is remarkably free, and the colour and light and shade powerful and very harmonious. This drawing, sold by Cox originally for £45, re-sold for £105; and after changing hands once or twice, was purchased by Mr. Quilter for 350 guineas.

PEACE AND WAR, AND "YOKELS." 1848. 1 ft. 11 in. by 2 ft. 10 in.

The subject of this drawing is said to have been suggested to Cox by seeing Müller's painting of the "Baggage Waggon and Troopers." The scene represents the heights above Lymne Castle and Hythe, looking over a flat sea-shore on which there are numerous martello towers, with a wide expanse of sea in the distance. A company of soldiers are marching down a gorge towards the coast, and on the left are some rustic figures—"Yokels"—two men, a boy, and little girl, gazing in "vacant wonder" at the soldiers, and tending a flock of sheep. The effect is rather dark, but the light and shade are powerfully contrasted. The handling is free and rapid. It was exhibited in the Water Colour Society.

COTTAGE IN STAFFORDSHIRE. 1849.

A small and characteristic drawing, representing some men ploughing in a field, and women approaching them carrying a basket. In the distance is a cottage and rising ground. The treatment is broad.

GOING TO THE HAYFIELD. 1850. 2 ft. 1½ in. by 2 ft. 7 in.

A fine breezy summer's day is here represented. In the foreground a farming man on a white horse appears to be leading another horse towards the hayfield. Several women are tossing the hay about, full of movement and frolic, and a lad is trying to save his hat, which appears to have just blown off. The foreground is enriched with many broad-leaved plants. There is a grand summer sky, with clouds drifting before the wind. The colour is beautiful, and the treatment loose and free. This is one of Cox's most characteristic drawings.

CHAP. XVI.

BETTWS-Y-COED MEADOW. 1853. 19 by 28 in.

A group of fine trees occupies the left of the drawing, with the Bettws hills and rocks in the distance. It is the great meadow near the Royal Oak (now destroyed by the railway), with some figures and sheep scattered about. Very beautiful, and complete both in feeling, composition, and colour. Such drawings as this of Bettws Meadow, the "Going to the Hayfield," and the "Green Lanes," are very representative of the genius of Cox, and differ widely from the works of other artists.

DRIVING THE FLOCK. 1855. 19 by 28 in.

This drawing was exhibited in 1856, and much admired at the time. It represents a broad valley near Capel Curig, along which a flock of sheep are being driven in a leisurely sort of way. They are thorough Welsh sheep, and contrast well with the grey and purple tones of the distance. The hills and mountains are grand in form, as is also the sky. The harmony of colour and vigour of handling are equal to any of his earlier works.

THE BIRMINGHAM HORSE FAIR.

This very effective sketch on rough paper must be looked at from a distance to get an idea of its full character and meaning. The colour is very pleasing—the rich browns, blacks, and chestnuts contrasting well with the cool greys. The principal group, where a jockey is showing the mouth of a white horse to a would-be customer, is very cleverly arranged. The patient, resigned aspect of the poor old horse, and the eager, inquiring attitude of the purchaser, are admirably indicated. Considering that it is merely a rapid sketch, it is very powerful and complete, and was much admired by Mademoiselle Rosa Bonheur, who saw it in Cox's studio when she visited Birmingham.

By the kindness of Mr. Quilter I am enabled to present a copy, by the Autotype Company, of this sketch.

Although the preceding description comprises many of the most important drawings in Mr. Quilter's collection, I must not omit to mention "Crossing the Sands," "Calais Pier," "Mill at Bettws," "Windy Day," and the "Terrace, Powis Castle" (date, 1838), which have been all recently exhibited in the Loan Exhibition, November, 1870, at 53, Pall Mall. I feel it necessary, also, to refer to a drawing of the "Red House and Battersea Mill, on the Thames," rather an early work, but lovely in colour. Cox is said to have painted this in imitation of C. Stanfield's feeling and manner. He made one or two drawings about this time, also in representation of Turner's style and treatment. Besides the water-colours, Mr. Quilter possesses a great variety of admirable sepias by Cox, of various dates and degrees of finish; but to refer to these in detail would take up too much space. He has also all the original pencil sketches and drawings, being the subjects which Cox afterwards etched on copper for his illustrated drawing-book, published about 1846. These were lately purchased from Messrs. R. and S. Fuller, and are the same which have been described by me in the chapter on "Works illustrated by Cox."

MR. A. LEVY'S COLLECTION OF WATER-COLOURS.

LANCASTER SANDS. 1835. 24 by 34 in.

A highly finished drawing, on smooth paper, and one of the most perfect of this delightful subject, full of atmosphere and movement. On the left many country people returning from market are grouped together, waiting to start on their perilous journey across the sands—a cart and horse, men and women on horseback, some riding "pillion;" full of life, action, and gesticulation. On the right some horsemen are

CHAP. XVI. hurrying across the sands, whilst in the distance a heavy shower is seen approaching, and a flight of sea-gulls adds to the feeling of the unsettled and treacherous state of the weather. The foreground is free in treatment, and is formed of sandbanks and masses of wiry grass. The colour throughout is clear and beautiful.

CROSS ROADS. 1849. 24 by 34 in.

A work on rough paper, of the highest quality, imaginative and yet truthful. The scenery is that of Carrington Moss, near Sale, Manchester. Two rough-looking old men on horseback have met on the edge of the Moss; behind them is a white dog, and on the left are a few tall, ragged Scotch firs. One of the men is pointing with his whip to a signpost in the distance. A flock of sheep, and waggons, are also seen afar off, with blue hills beyond. The sky is full of grey clouds, and has the appearance of wind, which is added to by the movement of birds.

CHANGING THE PASTURE. 1845. 24 by 36 in.

A beautiful drawing, with sheep scattered over the hill, a man and boy in the foreground, and grey masses of clouds blowing over the hills; very pure and fresh in colour, with cool greys and greens.

LANCASTER—MORNING. 1835.

A very sunny and tender drawing, of medium size, and very highly finished. In the distance is a bright gleaming river, spanned by the Bridge of Lancaster, with the town and castle towering up beyond, and hills in the far distance. On the right is a small ravine, with a stream and trees, and a rich foreground of plants and weeds. A man on a chestnut horse is leading a white one along the road, and you perceive other figures farther off. The effect is that of a fine summer's evening.

THE SKYLARK. 1848. 24 by 34 in.

This drawing, exhibited at the Water Colour Society's Gallery, suggested the subject for the oil-picture already described. It is full of dignity and repose. Some hedgerow trees on the right, with bushes underneath; a foreground full of crumpled, broad-leaved plants; cows descending a bank, with others in the fields beyond; a dark-blue distance, with banks of low white clouds, and blue sky above—form this delightful drawing. Near the trees on the left some children are grouped together in easy attitudes, gazing upwards at the skylark in the heavens. The light on the girl's sun-bonnet, contrasted with the dark purple distance, focusses the light, and gives point to the whole.

SHEEP-SHEARING. 1850. 10 by 14½ in.

The scene represented is near Bettws, with rocky hills rising above some well-wooded banks. In the foreground three women and a man are shearing a sheep, whilst another is being held ready by a second man, and a quantity of fleecy wool helps to light up the foreground. The light strikes on some of the figures, and is carried across the drawing in a masterly manner. The whole is very sketchy, but lively in colour and admirable in feeling, and the perfect ease with which it has evidently been thrown off adds very much to the charm.

CORNFIELD AND HILLS. About 1812. 10 by 14 in.

This very early drawing represents a valley with cornfields, hills, and trees, rising up on the left, underneath which a country house is snugly sheltered. The colouring is exceedingly quiet and low in tone, having evidently been laid on in flat broad washes, like some of De Wint's very early work.

POYNTON PARK. 1834.

A small drawing, with slender, upright trees against the sky; very quiet in colour. On the back it was marked, "From D. Cox to his niece, Margaret Hills, on her birthday, April 29, 1834." This view is on the way from Stockport to Derbyshire, but the neighbourhood is now much cut up with coal-mines.

LEITH WOOD, OR MERIVALE. 1846. 18 by 24 in.

A waggon is descending a road, with trees on a bank. Admirable in colour, and free in the handling.

THE MISSING FLOCK. About 1858. 2 ft. 4 in. by 2 ft. 6 in.

A fine wild rocky foreground, with some sheep crowding together in a deep hollow, and a woman looking down in search of them from a bank above, a mountainous distance and rather gloomy sky—not at all highly finished, but grand in conception and treatment. This drawing, although not dated, may be considered one of the latest period. Cox left an unfinished oil-picture of the same subject.

Sketches not framed:—

THE TERRACE OF POWIS CASTLE, with figures, very beautiful in colour.

LOCH IN WESTMORELAND, near Patterdale, very tender and bright in colour.

PONT-Y-PANT, a fine wild scene, very vigorous, but only slightly finished.

BROOK NEAR BALA, with lads fishing on the bank, and some fine trees. 8 by 12 in.

WIND AND RAIN, a dreary moorland scene, with rain descending, and a man on horseback hastening away in the distance.

A YELLOW BANK OF RAGWORT, near Sale, Lancashire, very beautiful in colour, although slight.

A SKETCH, two miles from Atherston, clear distance, very fresh, blue sky. 1846.

THE STUBBLE FIELD, a sketch at the back of Metchley Abbey; the subject of the admirable large drawing painted for Mr. Birch, now Mr. Hawkins's, very slight, but exquisite in colour.

Some very beautiful sepia drawings are also framed, which formerly belonged to Mr. D. Cox, junior. Of these, "Caer Cennen Castle," with a drove of cattle descending a hill, and a "Lane Scene, near Matlock," with trees hanging over it, are the most interesting.

MR. W. S. ELLIS'S COLLECTION, AT STREATHAM COMMON.

CADER IDRIS. 1828. 2 ft. 6 in. by 3 ft. 8 in.

This celebrated drawing, bequeathed by Cox to Mr. Ellis, his executor, may be looked upon as one of the finest and most important works of his early-middle period; it is rather dark, and there are rich masses of herbage in the foreground, which has evidently been a good deal worked upon. The view is taken from the vale of Dolgelly, which is richly wooded; a grand range of mountains rises up on the far side, crowned by the peaks of Cader Idris. Near the centre of the drawing are some dogs, and also a man leading greyhounds; the effect is that of evening with a great breadth of shadow.

CHAP. XVI.

SMUGGLERS—SUNSET. 1854. 10½ by 14½ in.

The effect is twilight, with a narrow streak of reddish light over the distant sea close to the horizon; the same light is repeated on one or two clouds in the upper part of the sky, which in other respects is dark and threatening. On a rough road in the foreground some figures are seen hurrying along with a donkey, over whose back a large sack or bundle has been thrown. In the middle distance is a dark ravine, with low hills beyond on which some scattered sheep are feeding. This drawing is on the rough Scotch paper, powerful and sombre in tone; it is admirable in feeling, but very loose and rapid in the handling.

STOKE-SAY, NEAR LUDLOW. 1852. 11 by 15 in.

This is also on the rough paper, with a lowering, murky sky unusually grand in form. Low-toned green hills on one side recede towards a narrow ridge of dark blue moorlands, and in the distance are seen the church and manor-house of Stoke. A pathway leads through long grass or unripe corn, along which two peasant women are approaching; some birds in the sky add to the effect of windy and rainy weather; the colour is particularly harmonious, indeed, a delicate harmony of broken greens and greys pervades the whole drawing.

OVER THE MOORS. 1854. 9½ by 14¾ in.

An expanse of yellow and green hills, with soft grey clouds above and rain descending in the distance; a cart and figures are approaching over the rising ground; it is rather slight and sketchy, but pure and pleasing in colour and full of truth.

LUD CHURCHYARD, LUDLOW. 1852. 11 by 14½ in.

An old country churchyard is seen surrounded by yew-trees; broad shadows are relieved by scattered lights on the village tombstones, and by the powerful colours of the ivy-clad church; in the corner an old sexton, with bent head and spade in hand, completes the composition. The handling, like that of a rapid sketch, is very rough, but the feeling is full of pathos, and the colours are excellent.

SOLITUDE. 1851. 14 by 21 in.

This powerful drawing is on rough paper: two figures are reclining on a rocky bank beneath some dark trees; a ray of light touches parts of their dress, and is carried across the picture by some sheep feeding near; broad deep shadows are thrown over the foreground, and also over the middle distance, in which a narrow strip of blue water is seen and a mass of foliage. Rugged grey and purple mountains rise in the distance, and close to the mountain-tops some white clouds are rolling along; the rest of the sky is of light grey clouds with streaks of blue.

OLD CHURCH AT LUDLOW—SCENE DURING THE PLAGUE. 1852.

This is an upright representing an old church doorway, and part of the tower of an ancient gothic church, with a group of poor and aged people, some kneeling and others stooping forward, in attitudes of deep reverence, to receive the sacrament, which, according to tradition, was administered by the Roman Catholic priests at the church door during the prevalence of the plague. It is grimly impressive, both in feeling and in the mode of treatment, the handling being swift and vigorous.

THE HULKS, SHEERNESS, with shipping in the distance.

A large drawing, very fine both in colour and light and shade. There is the appearance of wind in the movement of the waves, and the scud and forms of the clouds, but withal it is bright and cheerful in effect, and very truthful.

ROCKS NEAR BETTWS, man driving a horse.

Very free in the handling and true in colour.

A FIELD, WITH GROUPS OF TREES. 1851.

This drawing was commenced and completed on the day the first Great International Exhibition of 1851 was opened. The view is taken from a field near Streatham Common, and is a most successful representation of quiet English scenery.

EARLY MORNING, NEAR HARBORNE.

The effect is that of a hazy October morning, rather grey and tender in colour, especially on the left, where a man is ploughing an upland field, with grey trees in the distance; on the other side a woody lane leads towards a brook, with a rustic bridge, on which some girls are passing; the sky is quiet and the colour is true and natural. The general effect is rather dreamy and poetical.

VALLEY IN YORKSHIRE.

A hill covered with trees rises upon the right, and in front is a deep vale with distant hills. The lights and darks are well focussed, and the grey and neutral tone of the greens is very pleasing. The truth of tone and the feeling of space in this drawing are very remarkable.

AN ISLAND AT THE JUNCTION OF THE LLUGWY AND CONWAY RIVERS, NEAR BETTWS.

The water is pent between rocks, with picturesque overhanging trees. This spot has lost much of its wild character of late years. The sky is grand in form and colour.

Besides the drawings described above, Mr. Ellis has a large folio full of sketches taken at Haddon Hall and at Rowsley in 1845, which comprise two views of the Peacock inn. several of the village at Rowsley, of the old water mill there, and on the banks of the mill-stream. These views at Rowsley were generally sketched before breakfast. Cox made sometimes two drawings *before* breakfast, and began a third, and then spent the day afterwards sketching at Haddon Hall; this was in the month of May, 1845, when he was still in his full vigour. In Mr. Ellis's collection there are also several very beautiful sketches of the Terrace at Haddon Hall, of the old steps leading to the garden, the Monk's Bridge, the gateway of Haddon Hall, general views above the Hall, and in the Park, &c., &c. These are all free in the handling, and fresh and beautiful in colour. Also a portfolio full of very lovely drawings and sketches made in Yorkshire, Lancashire, and Derbyshire, at Bolton Abbey, Baden tower and church, Bolsover Castle, Hardwick Hall, Powis Castle, and in the neighbourhood of Lancaster; there are likewise three or four views of the Ulverston and Lancaster Sands especially deserving of notice as being of the highest quality, untouched and fresh, as when the sketch was first made. These perhaps give a higher idea of Cox's wonderful ease, truth, and refinement of colour in water-colours than anything I have seen, and it is well known that his friend Ellis always had the choice of his best sketches. I have still to describe a portfolio full of choice little drawings and *ideas* (some rather visionary), for pictures called "Gems." Many of them well deserve the name; they are very varied in subject, and comprise sketches of nearly all dates, from very early ones on the banks of the Thames and at Hastings, before Cox went to Hereford, until some of his latest memoranda of out-of-doors effects at Harborne. Many of them are evidently cut out of small sketch-books, and others are rather larger and have all the appearance of having been carefully finished at home.

CHAP. XVI. One of the most interesting represents an old woman on the border of Dulwich Common driving geese by twilight. There is also a drawing, the first that Cox made after his illness, at Greenfield, in 1853, a field with trees and a stormy sky, very interesting in itself as a work of art, and especially so considering when it was painted. Some of the sea-coast views are particularly beautiful; an unusually fine one represents a figure on a bank, boats on a rough sea and distant cliffs; the aërial tone of the distance and sky is very lovely and cannot be described. Also another view near Hastings; the moon just rising, a man on horseback, and fishing boats, dark and full of mystery. "Calais Pier," with boats and a rough sea; "Dieppe Pier," with figures and a thunderstorm passing off, and sparkling reflections, also a wide stretch of sea, with dark rolling waves and a distant shore: all these would make fine subjects for paintings.

In addition, there is a particularly powerful early sketch, date about 1808, the arrangement of light and shade resembles one of the old masters; a cottage on the banks of the Thames, near Battersea, also very early; and the side of a common with sheep climbing up a bank to feed. This last, although slight, is as fine in feeling as anything I have seen by the artist.

In addition to these treasures in water-colour, Mr. Ellis's collection of Cox's works contains many beautiful sepias in folios. I have only just referred to some of the finest of the sketches in the folios, as it would take up too much space to attempt a full account of them.

MR. DAVID COX'S (JUN.) COLLECTION, AT BRIXTON HILL.

SKIRTS OF A FOREST. 18½ by 25½ in.

This drawing conveys the impression of a stormy wind driving the clouds along and bending before it the limbs of the grand oak-trees. Dark masses of foliage form the middle distance, beyond which streaks of light pierce through the clouds near the horizon. A man in the foreground is hastening along with his hand to his mouth, as if to throw his voice in a tone of encouragement towards the sheep-dog seen in the distance collecting the distant flock. Cox was very partial to this drawing himself, and after it had been sold bought it back at an enhanced price from Agnew. It is powerful and striking in effect, of the best period, and is drawn on rough paper. Through the kindness of Mr. Cox, I give a photograph of it in this book.

STAFFORD CASTLE. About 1852. 10½ by 14½ in.

A dark wooded hill rises against an overcast sky relieved by a few light clouds, and in the long grass of a meadow some mowers appear about to commence their work. A woman with a basket is going towards them. It is a successful drawing, very powerful and characteristic.

THE PARK AT HADDON HALL. 1853. 1 ft. 9 in. by 2 ft. 6 in.

The old baronial mansion is seen in the distance rising above the woods, with a gleam of white clouds behind. Some fine trees on both sides overshadow a wide green glade, along which a man on horseback and shepherd are passing. Sheep are also seen scattered about the hillside and on the grassy path. The sky is grey with rooks wheeling about in the air, and the effect is solemn and sombre.

KENILWORTH CASTLE WITH HARVEST FIELD. 1848. 13½ by 18½ in.

The castle and a group of dark trees are relieved against a bright summer's sky; in the foreground are shocks of corn. This drawing is on the rough paper, and is brilliant in tone.

CHAP. XVI.

THREATENING WEATHER. About 1857. 11 by 15 in.

The sky is dark and stormy; on the right are a few stunted rough trees, and towards the centre a shepherd, a flock of sheep, and a dog, approaching a wild tract of moorland. It is loose in the handling, but very impressive. Cox, some time before, had made a large drawing of the same subject, which he liked particularly, and he borrowed it in order to make this copy.

INTERIOR AT HARDWICK HALL. 1845. 18 by 23 in.

This drawing is an upright, and represents part of the picture gallery at Hardwick, with old portraits on the walls, which are partly concealed by some effective long red curtains. The colour is rich and powerful, like the series of interiors which formed part of Mr. Bullock's collection.

ASKING THE WAY. 1854. 14 by 21 in.

The scene represented is a common near Sale covered with heather in blossom. An old farmer on a white horse is pointing across the common with his whip, whilst apparently asking the way of a gipsy woman in a red cloak, who is driving a donkey. She has her arm out in the same direction, as if telling the way to go. The sky is rather bright and fine in form; the colour of the purple "heather bells" contrasts pleasantly with the prevailing grey tones of other parts of the drawing.

DARLEY CHURCHYARD, DERBYSHIRE. About 1858. 12 by 21 in.

A small, dark, and impressive drawing on rough paper, in the latest manner. The moon is seen just rising, and sheds a faint light on some wide-spreading yews, and on the old sexton, who is seen digging a grave in the churchyard. On one side are some rough irregular stone steps leading up to the church, of which a very small part only is seen. This church is situated between Rowsley and Matlock. This was one of the last drawings exhibited by Cox in the rooms of the Old Water Colour Society. CHAP. XVI.

THE BIG MEADOW, BETTWS. Late. 1 ft. 10 in. by 2 ft. 9 in.

A pastoral scene, with sheep scattered about the meadow, a fine group of trees on the left, and the rocky hills above Bettws in the distance. The sheep are left light in colour, and the drawing is sketchy and not finished; but the effect is excellent, and it is interesting as showing Cox's method of work. Some fine docks, and other leaf plants, are indicated in the foreground.

CARNARVON CASTLE. Date rather late. 13 by 18 in.

The castle, with its massive walls and numerous towers, looks very imposing. It is of a yellowish grey colour, and stands on the banks of the Menai Straits, in which it is slightly reflected. A group of small vessels and boats assists the composition. Behind the castle are a bank of clouds and a light sky. The drawing and finish are careful, and the colour is agreeable, but it is rather wanting in power.

Besides the drawings described above, Mr. Cox possesses the large and important one of "Peat Gatherers," date 1856, size 19 by 29½ inches, of which, by his kind permission, I give a copy. He has also an extensive and interesting collection in portfolios of his father's studies and sketches of all periods, some in pencil, others in sepia and chalk, but chiefly in water-colours. Amongst these I may mention a remarkably fine out-of-doors sketch of a "Mountain Top," I believe the subject is Cader Idris; also a "View

CHAP. XVI. of Brough Castle," a wild and grand study of a "Salmon Trap in North Wales," "Kirby Steven Church," with a beautiful valley beyond, "Llyn-Tal-y-Llyn," "The Large Meadow, Bettws," and "Flint Castle;" likewise a large study in chalk and charcoal of the "Vale between Gwynant and Beddgelert," in which the effect of storm and mist is grandly portrayed. There are also several books and folios full of little bits from Nature; scraps containing the first ideas for larger works, and sketches of figures to be introduced. These are what Cox used to call his "stock in trade," and are very interesting, especially to artists.

MR. FREDERICK TIMMINS'S COLLECTION, EDGBASTON.

CARREG-CENNEN CASTLE, SOUTH WALES. 1847.

This large and beautiful drawing, sometimes called the "Rain Cloud," represents undulating hills seen through the dropping rain. The grey sky is unusually fine in form and colour. The castle rises on a high eminence in the middle distance, and in the foreground is a girl tending a flock of goats; the foremost one is in high light, and being brought against the deep shade of a ravine, give the greatest point of contrast. This subject has been fully described at the end of the fourth chapter.

VIEW FROM THE UPPER PART OF THE OLD HOLYHEAD ROAD. 1840.

A highly-finished and important drawing of the middle period, representing the full extent of the Lledr valley and part of that of the Conway valley nearest to Bettws. In the distance are Moel Siabod, the Glyder mountains, and the peaks of Snowdon; and a grand mass of rocks rises up on the right. Some cattle are being driven up the road, which, I understand, were put in by Frederick Tayler. The colour is less fresh and the handling less free than in his later works; the blues have slightly faded, but the whole effect is harmonious. CHAP. XVI.

CROSSING THE BROOK, OR GOING TO THE HAYFIELD.

A small drawing, very fresh in colour, with a tender, pearly sky, against which one or two slender trees stand out in relief. In the distance are hayfields, with the usual incidents of waggon and figures. The quality of this drawing is very fine, and resembles some of the Ulverstone Sand sketches made between 1834 and 1840.

THE MOUNTAIN TOP—MORNING.

This very beautiful painting represents mists clearing off the summit of Cader Idris, and between the rocks of the foreground are the figures of two men. It is on rough paper, and is grand both in form and colour. Cox related that whilst making this sketch, two travellers stopped to ask him their way to the top of Cader, and he immediately put them into his drawing.

OLD HOUSES AT HEREFORD.

An early drawing of about 1815, very like some of Prout's early works, quiet and low in tone, but forcible. The scene represented is a lane in the old part of the town, with two quaint-looking figures.

BEESTON CASTLE, CHESHIRE.

A very large and powerful drawing, on rough paper, with a fine group of trees on the right-hand side, and some horses and figures employed in agriculture. The tone of this drawing is rather low, and without much variety in the colour. It was lent to the Birmingham Exhibition in 1864.

FORT ROYAL, CALAIS.

A small, careful drawing, quiet and rather subdued in

CHAP XVI. colour, but full of aerial perspective. A vessel is approaching, and some fishing-boats are beautifully introduced in the distance. The sea is excellent both in form and colour. Date about 1835.

HARLECH CASTLE.

The castle is in deep shadow, with the sea behind; the sky also is dark, with an evening glow on the upper part of the clouds. Great breadth and repose are the chief characteristics of this very early drawing.

PENMAEN-MAWR, AND ENTRANCE TO THE MENAI STRAITS. 1849.

The woods and hills of the Isle of Anglesea, near Beaumaris, form the foreground and middle distance of this charming drawing, which is pure in tone, as well as very rich in colour. It is of Cox's best period, and is more highly finished than most of his later works.

CONWAY CASTLE. Date about 1844.

A small drawing of the estuary of the Conway river at sunrise, slight and hazy, but tender and pleasing in colour. Some cattle are seen standing about on the wet sands in the distance. It is very suggestive, but wants rather more finish to make it a complete work.

Besides the above, Mr. Timmins possesses a large and very impressive but rather unfinished sketch of a snowstorm in the Lledr valley; it is grand in feeling and of the best period. A man is seen collecting a flock of sheep, surrounded by rocks and beetling crags.

Also a fine sea-shore view, with a very effective sky, full of drifting clouds; and several other drawings of the middle and latest period.

MR. H. T. BROADHURST'S COLLECTION, NEAR MANCHESTER.

BOLTON ABBEY. 1847. 2 ft. by 3 ft.

This grand drawing was pronounced by the members of the Water Colour Society, when it was exhibited in Pall Mall, as the finest Cox had ever painted. There is much splendour of colour, the yellows and blues, which abound, being less neutralised than in most of his later works. The abbey and some trees are reflected in a large pool of water, towards which some cows are descending, as is their wont on a hot midsummer's day. On the left is a grand group of trees, full of dark shadows. The handling is very easy and free. A copy of this important drawing appears in the book.

BATHERS FRIGHTENED BY A BULL. 1853.

Two or three lads about to bathe are taking refuge near a tree from a wicked-looking bull, who has intruded himself into the middle of a pool of water, and is putting down his head in rather a threatening attitude. There is a great appearance of reality, although the handling is slight, and rather unfinished. It is on the rough paper, and was once in Mr. Roberts's collection.

By the kindness of Mr. Broadhurst I am enabled to give a copy of this drawing. In this collection are also many beautiful water-colour sketches, in folio chiefly, of the middle period.

THE STUBBLE-FIELD. 1845.

This is the large drawing on rough paper which Cox made for Mr. Charles Birch, and for which he received £25. It was exhibited in the Water Colour Society, and was considered at the time one of the best he had ever painted, as it undoubtedly was. The sky is marvellously full of movement, and beautiful in colour. The stubble is suggested rather than drawn, but seen at the right distance everything takes its proper place. When lent a few years ago to the Birmingham Water Colour Exhibition, it was hung in the place of honour, and dwarfed everything else in the room by its great power, brilliancy, and truth to nature. It is now, I believe, in the possession of Mr. John Hawkins, of Park Road, Edgbaston. Several smaller drawings of this subject by Cox exist.

MR. J. JAFFRAY'S COLLECTION, PARK ROAD, BRISTOL ROAD, BIRMINGHAM.

ST. MARTIN'S CHURCH. Date about 1825.

This early upright drawing represents the entrance to Smithfield from Moat Lane, and part of the old moat and the spire of the church and old buildings rising up beyond. The colour is quiet and tender, and the reflections in the water very successful. This part of the town of Birmingham has been greatly altered of late years, and these buildings have been swept away.

POWIS CASTLE. Date about 1831.

A small and successful drawing of the garden at Powis Castle; also a rapid sketch of the same subject, very beautiful in colour.

RETURNING FROM THE MOORS. 1855. 10 by 14 in.

A repetition of the favourite subject of peat gatherers returning from labour; broad and powerful in the treatment, with a dark sky, and a storm approaching.

SEED TIME. 1855. 10 by 14 in.

A ploughed field, in which some horses are drawing a harrow guided by a husbandman. The sky indicates wind, and many birds are hovering about. The colour is fresh and full, and the effect of movement is admirably given. This and the preceding drawing are on rough paper, without much finish.

The Porch of St. Philip's Church, Birmingham.

An upright sketch, very rapid and lovely in its light-grey colour. This has been previously described.

A hill scene, with cattle descending a road, and some other sketches—one of meadows with cows, date about 1820, low in tone, and rather highly finished; and one late one, with a dark sky, and grand energy in the feeling—are comprised also in this collection.

MR. PETER ALLEN'S COLLECTION.

The Lugg Meadows. Date about 1817. 17 by 26½ in.

This early low-toned drawing is of the finest quality; it represents a still summer's afternoon with a flock of sheep at rest in a wide tract of meadow land, under the shadows projected by a fine group of trees on the left. The light is rather subdued, and the feeling is one of complete repose. No figure breaks the dreamy stillness which pervades the entire scene. This sentiment is heightened by the arrangement of the principal lines, which are parallel with the horizon. I have seen no more perfect example of this period of Cox's work, and I am glad to be able to give a photograph of it at the commencement of the Hereford chapter.

Peat Gatherers Returning from the Moors. Date about 1854. Size 20¾ by 29 in.

An upright on the rough paper. A rocky glen occupies the middle of the drawing, with moorland and mountains above. In the foreground two women are bending beneath

CHAP. XVI. their creels loaded with peat. The colour is very true, and the treatment free and effective.

STOKE-SAY, NEAR LUDLOW. 1853. 11 by 15 in.

This drawing is very similar to the one dated 1852 in Mr. Ellis's collection already described. The same wonderful sky, storm-tossed and full of rain, is the leading feature of the scene. A photograph of this drawing also appears by the kindness of Mr. Allen.

BOLSOVER CASTLE. 1837. 15½ by 22½ in.

This highly-finished drawing on smooth paper is in the possession of Mr. Agar, of Brixton Hill. The colour is brilliant; the sky is a summer one with light grey clouds, and on the road leading to the castle and church a man on horseback, in a white smock, is seen leading another horse. On the left are some fine trees and leaf plants in the foreground. This drawing was exhibited two years ago in the Loan Collection in Pall Mall. It formerly belonged to Canon Greening, of Durham, and was purchased ten years ago for 100 guineas. It is an excellent example of the middle period.

WELSH LANDSCAPE, THE SALMON TRAP.

This drawing is on rough paper in the latest style, and was lent to the London International Exhibition in 1872 by F. Pender, Esq., M.P. The scenery is that of Bettws-y-Coed. Some grand rocks and mountains form the middle distance, at the base of which is a belt of dark trees, and a stream flowing through a salmon trap. A woman is holding up a salmon in her hand, and close by a man is kneeling down occupied with the sport. An elderly figure is seen approaching on the left near some fine dark trees. The light is carried across the picture on the figures, and on some railings, and on the traps; but the general effect is dark and rather gloomy, although powerful and impressive.

Of the fine collection of drawings possessed by the late Mr. Edwin Bullock, twenty-three fine ones still remain unsold, and are the property of Mrs. Bullock, having been discovered, I am informed, some time after Mr. Bullock's death. Of these I should specially mention the following:—

THE BROOKSIDE. 10 by $16\frac{1}{2}$. Sometimes called the "Stump and the Magpie."

This celebrated drawing is very powerful and truthful. A stream reflects a dark fringe of rushes. The colour and handling are fresh and vigorous. Also "Mosely Common with an old Windmill," $11\frac{3}{4}$ by 18 in., an early drawing, very pleasing from its great breadth and simplicity.

DUDLEY CASTLE, WITH LIME-KILNS. $12\frac{3}{4}$ by $17\frac{1}{4}$ in.

A warm evening glow lights up the sky and castle hill, the latter being clothed with low-toned green trees. On the left of the drawing grey curling pillars of smoke rise from the lime-kilns and drift across the scene, thus adding to the composition and also conveying a feeling of mystery. Some water forms the foreground, on which dark canal boats are cleverly massed together. They are very powerful in colour, and assist in imparting a luminous quality to the rest of the drawing.

A FARMYARD. $6\frac{3}{4}$ by $9\frac{3}{4}$ in. Date 1850.

A bright little drawing, slight and sketchy, yet powerful in effect. The sky is a tender grey, as of the early morning; some cattle are grouped in a farmyard, as if waiting to be milked, behind which are some farm buildings and trees, and the outline of faint hills in the distance.

CHAP. XVI.

WARWICK CASTLE, EVENING.

A very fine large drawing. The castle appears to be lighted up, as if a fête was going on. The sky is dark, with a streak of light near the horizon. The water underneath the castle reflects downwards the light and dark masses of shadow from the castle, to which the Broken Bridge adds additional force.

VIEW NEAR ATHERSTON.

A grand drawing of the best period. The house is seen in the distance between some fine trees, which appear to be tossing and bending before a powerful wind; the sky is stormy, with rain approaching. It is one of those wild effects in which Cox delighted, and which show his mastery and rapid power. The oft-repeated drawing of the "Mill near Lichfield" is another in this collection.

I have endeavoured, in the preceding account of Cox's drawings, to describe some of the important and most celebrated ones of every period.

In 1870 an interesting collection of four hundred and thirty-five water-colour drawings was exhibited in Manchester, being chiefly loans from gentlemen in that neighbourhood. It comprised twenty-six drawings by David Cox, some very beautiful ones; for instance, "Lancaster Sands," "Evening Repose," "Vale of Llanrwst," "Landscape with Man and Horse" (two), "Bolton Abbey," "Bettws-y-Coed Church," "Calais Pier," and "Landscape with Sheep." Such subjects as "Landscape with Sheep," and "With a Man and Horse," were peculiarly those in which Cox excelled. Plenty of weeds and rough herbage in the foreground, a few ragged trees, the man and horse cutting in strong relief against the distant green, "windy" sky, and the sheep all in movement, were the characteristics of these fresh, swift, and very powerful drawings, the form and colour of the cloudy sky, and the feeling of space, being one of their great charms. In order thoroughly to appreciate all their fine, strong, and unusual qualities, Cox's drawings, especially those on the rough Scotch paper, *must be looked at from a distance;* then everything takes its right place, with a wonderful appearance of finish, which is almost entirely lost when viewed close.

I give in the Appendix No. II. a list of the *original* and important collections of drawings by Cox which belonged to Mr. Charles Birch, Mr. Norman Wilkinson, Mr. William Roberts, and Mr. Edwin Bullock. The prices which they produced at the sales by auction are also given in most cases.

I have included in this Appendix an account of some other important sales of Cox's drawings which have taken place of late years. In the Appendix No. I. will be found a list of all the drawings exhibited by David Cox in the Old Water Colour Society, in London, between 1813 and 1859 inclusive.

XVII.

LAST YEARS AT HARBORNE.

1855 TO 1859.

CHAP. XVII. — 1855—1859.

IN the winter of 1855-56 Cox worked steadily and successfully, and produced many works both in oil and water colour, and although there was not the same finish, there was a grander feeling than in earlier days.

From the sketches made at Bettws and Capel Curig the preceding autumn he finished some admirable drawings, and these—eleven works in all—were exhibited in Pall Mall in the spring of 1856. The largest and most important were "Driving the Flock," "On the Moors near Bettws," "Peat Gatherers, North Wales," and "A Hayfield." Besides these, "Dover—Wind and Rain," and "Twilight," were very successful drawings. "The Peat Gatherers," with a dark sky and women bending in patient advance under the Welsh creels or baskets full of peat, and a wild moorland losing itself in the mist, was a complete poem in itself. "On the Moors," a pelting storm is descending, and in the midst a wild-looking bull is bellowing with extended tail. The artist has thrown into this drawing his deepest and most incommunicable quality.

On the 24th May Cox travelled up to London and remained there a few weeks on a visit to his son. It had been previously arranged that Mr., now Sir William, Boxall, R.A.,

should paint a likeness of Cox on this occasion, and on the 6th of June he went, accompanied by his grand-daughter, to that artist's studio, where the portrait was commenced. He appears to have enjoyed the sitting, as he said that Boxall conversed with him very pleasantly all the time. He went again on the 12th, and he was also able to pay visits to his old friends Mr. Ellis and Mr. Norman Wilkinson. Few men had friends more attached to him than Cox had; a friendship once formed was rarely or never broken, and the word indifference was not in his vocabulary. The portrait by Sir W. Boxall is in the possession of Mr. David Cox, jun., at Brixton Hill, and was lent by him to the Dublin Fine Art Exhibition in 1872. It is satisfactory as a work of art, but is not considered quite so good a likeness as the one painted the preceding year by Sir J. W. Gordon, exhibited in 1856 in the Royal Academy. He went to see the Academy and the other exhibitions during his visit.

Cox returned home to Greenfield House about the middle of June, and he does not appear to have been at all the worse for this journey, as he was able to undertake another one at the end of August to Bettws-y-Coed.

The following letters, written to him by one of his most intimate friends just before and just after this visit to London, will, I think, be read with interest as showing what was thought of the works which he exhibited this year by this gentleman, who was a good judge, what others also thought, and how much Cox was loved by his friends :—

"May 10th, 1856.

"DEAR COX,—I ought to have been allowed to see your drawings before they went into the Water Colour Exhibition this year. I wonder who bought the 'Peat Gatherers,' which is the grandest picture I have ever seen by you or any one. How you came to give such a high character to those two women with the black hair I cannot conceive, except that, as

CHAP. XVII. 1855—1859. I have often said, you don't draw with your fingers, but with *your mind.*

"The landscape is as wild and as true to nature as anything Turner, or Poussin, or Salvator ever did. What is the use of your being an invalid every now and then? It don't spoil your painting a bit. 'The Peat Gatherers' does really outdo everything that was ever hung up in that room. It made the tears come into my eyes to think that you had done such a good thing. The bull with his tail up in the storm made me laugh with pleasure; and the little sketch of Dover, although so slight, was being talked about all over the room when I arrived, and I kept hearing of it before I could find it. It seems as if you had become famous to the world all of a sudden, whereas you have been famous to me and other friends I could name from our young days. But now everybody is talking of you, and I hear no complaints of your want of finish.

"When I dined with Ward, the Academician, who has painted the pictures about Marie Antoinette, he said to me, 'I consider David Cox is a great man, and the finest landscape-painter living,' and Ward did not know how much I loved you. But the best of all things which was said of you is what poor dear little —— said one day, that what he complained of was, that when once people began to buy old Cox's drawings they never bought any one else's.

"Your portrait by Sir J. W. Gordon I have only seen on one dark day, and I could not see the eyes; the mouth appeared very like, but the head seemed too small for the body. The portrait is too high to be seen well. It does not represent you as speaking, but as if you were listening. Now we all like to be listening to you, and you look best when you are talking.

"You have got the place of honour in the Academy, as Ward says. He declares it to be the finest thing that Watson Gordon has done.

"I am afraid you do not mean to come to see me this year, but I hope you will; it will never be summer if I do not see you.

"Believe me, your affectionate."

"June 29th, 1856.

"DEAR COX,—This last small picture shows me you can work and paint as well as you did ten years ago, and although I think it is very natural that at your age you should only paint what you yourself happen to fancy, yet I hope you will make the exertion to paint me a common with a low horizon, and hardly a tree anywhere. Oh, if you knew how I walk up and down before your large picture of 'Bettws Church,' and how often I walk into the room where it is just to see how it looks, you would envy me the pleasure I have. I wonder you could ever part with it. I see now how very carefully you painted it, so many tints so carefully put on. When I compare it with all the modern landscapes in the exhibition, to me they are all poor.

"Now pray jump out of your chair and put on your hat and go out to the common, and help me to enjoy life by looking at nature through Cox.

"Your affectionate."

On the 16th August, 1856, Cox wrote to his son a short letter, from which the following is an extract:—

"We have the lady, Rosa Bonheur, here. I had the honour to see her at Mr. Birch's. She afterwards went to Mr. Bullock's. I am very well, and should like to go out for a short painting. I have finished two paintings, and sent them into the Birmingham Exhibition.

"DAVID COX."

Mr. Birch gave a grand dinner in honour of his guest,

CHAP. XVII. 1855—1859.

Mademoiselle Rosa Bonheur. He invited literary men, artists, and patrons of art to it, as he said he wished to make the company assembled as "representative" as he could. I am informed that she called at Cox's house and visited his studio, being much interested in what she saw there. Cox had in his possession his sketch of the Birmingham Horse Fair; he produced it from his portfolio, saying that he also was an animal painter, and the lady expressed her admiration of it. This, I believe, is the same identical drawing as the one now possessed by Mr. Quilter, of which the print (by the Autotype Company) is given in this book. There was also a large dinner party the following day at Mr. Bullock's to meet Rosa Bonheur.

Cox found the journey he made to Bettws this autumn very fatiguing, and although the Welsh air had refreshed him, he never returned. He was the better reconciled to this as he found that he was not equal to sketching out of doors on this last visit. The winter tried him a good deal, and his eyesight was weaker, which gave a rather loose and blotty appearance to many of the works painted after this date. At the beginning of March, 1857, he sold a picture, which he had recently painted, of Rhyl, for £50, and one of the "Night Train" for £40; also the "Bull," for £15, which is the one now in the South Kensington Museum, I believe. On the 2nd April, 1857, he wrote to his son a letter, from which the following is an extract:—

"My subjects are very slight and unfinished, but my eyes are so bad in the finishing that all my friends cannot like them. I fear I cannot paint any more, and my doctor wishes me to go into fresh air, but I fear I cannot go to London yet for some time.

"DAVID COX."

Again he wrote to his son on the 20th April, 1857:—

"I wish you to thank my brother artists for their good wishes towards me. I thought them so very kind. Tell them so, with my kind regards.

"DAVID COX."

In spite of failing health Cox was able to complete and exhibit fourteen drawings this year in the Water Colour Exhibition: "Near Capel Curig," "Gordal Scar," "Warwick Castle," "On the Llugwy," "Carnarvon Castle," "Forest Scene," "Bolton Abbey," and several views near Capel Curig, were the principal ones. On the 20th May, 1857, he wrote thus to his son about his intended journey to London:—

"It is my intention to go on Monday by the Great Western line, and Mr. Deakin (the artist) and I start by half-past seven, so that we may arrive by eleven. My friend Deakin will not stay longer than the one day, so as to see the Exhibitions, and back at night. I hope it will be convenient to you to meet me at the station by eleven.

"DAVID COX."

The simplicity and seriousness of the drawings which had been sent to London by Cox this year made a great impression on the public. It was known that the state of his health prevented his bestowing the same amount of labour as formerly on the "finishing" of his works, and they were regarded as the last expressions of a great mind in harmony with nature and at rest with itself. The "Carnarvon Castle," which forms part of Mr. David Cox's, junior, collection, has been described in the chapter on water-colours. The warm light on the grey walls is very beautiful. The same may be said of the "Bolton Abbey," which is very subdued, but harmonious in colour. The views near Capel Curig excel almost any others in power and grand feeling, with the exception, perhaps, of the "Forest Scene."

CHAP. XVII. 1855—1859.

Cox arrived safely in London, escorted by Mr. Peter Deakin, on the 25th May. He appears to have enjoyed himself as usual on this visit, taking short walks in the neighbourhood of Brixton Hill. On the 29th he went to Sir William Boxall's to have his portrait (which had been painted the year before) revised, and the same day he also visited the Academy, and another day the Water Colour Exhibition. Every Sunday he spent with his friend Ellis at Streatham Common.

At the beginning of June he was taken very unwell, and was attended by Mr. Kingdom, an old friend and former medical attendant. He did not visit London again, but as soon as he was sufficiently recovered he returned to Harborne, which was on the 13th June. His son accompanied him home on this occasion.

With the return of summer Cox's health and strength revived, and he again set to work with much energy, especially with oils.

On the 8th July, 1857, he wrote to his son, "I am, thank God, in very good health, and painting to enjoy myself."

Again, on the 13th August, 1857, he writes thus:—

"The weather has been so rainy and stormy that I have given up the idea of going to Wales. I hope you will come here, and perhaps we may go and make a few sketches.

"DAVID COX."

About this time a gentleman, who was a friend of David Cox, relates that he went one morning to call on him soon after breakfast. He was seated in his little smoking-room, of which the window looked into the garden. After the first greeting, Cox said, "I know I can trust you, so I will confide a secret to you about something in which I am so much interested. You see that rose-bush by the wall; a wren has built her nest in it, and there are five little ones lately hatched. I can watch her and her mate feeding them from where I sit, and I would not have them disturbed for all the world. I was afraid my cat, who often runs along the wall, might find them, so puss has been shut up in a room for several days. Poor puss! I am sorry she should be confined, and it gives Mrs. Fowler a good deal of trouble, you know, to carry up her food."

Shortly after this the friend called again, and the first words Cox exclaimed were, "Hurrah! hurrah! they are all gone, all safe. I watched the mother teaching her little brood to fly so patiently; and the nest is now empty. I would much sooner have lost twenty pounds," he rejoined, "than that one of the little ones should have been hurt!"

The tenderness of heart illustrated by the above anecdote was one of his characteristics through life.

He continued to paint in oils during the autumn, and on the 29th September, 1857, he wrote to his son, "I have finished four oil-paintings, which you will be quite pleased with. They are as much as I could paint. I have been quite happy to have my oil-pictures. Hurrah! hurrah!" He also continued to work through the following winter at water-colours, and in the spring of 1858 he again sent thirteen drawings to the Water Colour Exhibition. The principal works contributed by him this year were—"Snowdon," the "Vale of Clwyd, near St. Asaph," "Snowdon from Capel Curig," "Skirts of a Common," "Port Gyfing," "Penmaen Bach," "Kenilworth," and "Bettws-y-Coed Church." That there was no perceptible falling off in the quality of the works sent may be inferred from the following letter, written to Cox by a friend on whose judgment he relied:—

"April 8th, 1858.

"To DAVID COX, ESQ.

"DEAR COX,—I have been to Foord's. You have sent up a magnificent lot of pictures, better than you have sent

CHAP. XVII. — 1855—1859.

for several years. The largest of all is the grandest in colour; the most pleasing, and equal to it in all its perfections, is the 'Kenilworth.' The cleverest is the sea-coast, with the bathing-machine in the foreground. The Bettws-y-Coed is very good—more force, but not so much elegance, as in my oil-picture of the same subject. The sheep picture, too, is very good. The others are beautiful in different ways, and I congratulate you on having sent up such a very capital lot this year. There will be a sensation produced by your drawings this year, I am sure. There is one, with the bright light on the fields in the middle distance, that I thought delightful, and quite a new effect to me. But my oil-picture beats everything.

"Your affectionate."

Cox remained at Greenfield House all this year, but he was still able to paint, and also to take short walks and to go into Birmingham, as the following extract from a letter to his son shows:—

"Harborne, September 2nd, 1858.

"I have been to Birmingham, and saw the Birmingham Exhibition. It is a very good one. I am very well, and I wish I could walk well, so as to go to some greater distance."

Again he wrote to his son on the 23rd December, 1858:—

"MY DEAR DAVID,—In two days we shall have Christmas, and I pray you and my dear children every comfort and health for many days to come. I am in health, and I thank our God that Ann and Mercie are well and comfortable. I cannot see to work, paint, or at drawings."

This last remark referred as much to the dark short days as to the state of his health. The winter tried Cox very much; his sight and memory were to some extent beginning to fail him, and for some time past he had suffered from an infirmity, not very unusual with old people, of using wrong words in mistake, although knowing all the time the word he really wished to use. His son went down to see him as usual for New Year's Day, and found him far from well. He had caught a severe cold, and was very weak and depressed. By the 20th of January Cox had taken entirely to his bed, and for more than a week the symptoms increased in severity—great difficulty of breathing, and utter prostration—so that his medical attendants, Dr. Bell Fletcher and Mr. Bindley, considered that he was in great danger.

On the 24th of January, 1859, D. Cox, junior, wrote to his daughters:—"My dear father continues in a hopeless state, only taking notice occasionally to propose some kindness for me. I can hardly make him understand the simplest words, and he seems to be made restless by talking to him."

Happily by the 30th of January he began to rally, the symptoms improved, and he was able each day after this to take more nourishment. By the middle of February he had so far recovered that he was able to go into another room for several hours each day, and his son was able to return home. With the return of spring he continued gradually to gain in strength. He came down-stairs, and occasionally received the visits of his intimate friends, who delighted to send him any little delicacies which they hoped would tempt his appetite. Cox was also able again to dispatch seven drawings to the Water Colour Exhibition. This contribution—the last he ever sent—consisted of the following works:—"The Stepping Stones, Bettws," the "Mountain Tarn," "Darley Churchyard," "Rocks near Bettws-y-Coed," "Penmaen Mawr," "Kenilworth Castle," and "Twilight." Each of these was beautiful and grand in its way, proving, too, that in spite of ill-health and increasing years there was no failing in the artist's deep feeling for nature, nor in his powers of expression.

CHAP. XVII. 1855—1859.

I have already, in my chapter on water-colours, described the pathos and gloom of that very poetical drawing, the "Darley Churchyard," with the moon just rising, and the old gravedigger still at his work; and of the "Mountain Tarn," with its resistless, roaring torrent. I cannot do better than quote the following words from Mr. Ruskin's notes on the Exhibitions of 1859:—

"In the rooms of the Old Water Colour Society, the first thing to be looked at, after Hunt's, is David Cox's magnificent waterfall at the upper end of the room—unsurpassable in its own broad way, and giving in the foam examples of execution as broad as Salvator's, and infinitely more subtle and lovely."

Although unable this spring to do much in the way of painting, Cox was pleased to turn over his portfolios, and arrange work for the future that he still hoped to be able to carry out; but he unfortunately caught cold again in April, and each attack left him weaker. In a May number of *Punch*, (1859), page 192, the following interesting and touching notice of Cox occurred. I think it will be considered well worthy of insertion.

"PUNCH AMONG THE PAINTERS.—DEAR OLD DAVID,—and next to nature who can Mr. Punch have better than David Cox?—I feel as if you and I were shaking hands for a long, long parting. Is it the wavy mist of tears in my eyes, or the dimness of years in yours, that blears those Welsh mountains and wild western moorlands, the last, I fear, that your glorious old hand—true to the heart as ever, but now trembling—will create for the pleasure of all that have ever looked nature lovingly in the face? Alas! and is time drawing the veil between you and the looming hills and gusty skies? In brain and heart you see them still—bright and fresh as ever—perhaps brighter and fresher. But the eye will grow glazed, and the stiffening finger will flag, for all the wind's bidding, and the inward beauty and glory will pass faintly and more faintly into shape and colour, till what used to be noble, free, and generous transcripts of earth, and sea, and sky, are now hazy and indistinct landscapes of dreamland! CHAP. XVII. 1855—1859.

"All who have ever loved nature must love David Cox. How!—not love the man who for fifty years has done liege suit and service to the solemn purple of far-off hills, the sudden gleam of golden cornfields, the stately march or wild glee of summer clouds, the tossing of meadow grass on the uplands, or the flush of heather-bells along the moor!

"Well, let those who love him take their leave of him; for there hang his last works in the room of the Old Water Colour Society, touching in their mellow indistinctness, but honestly beautiful to the end. He leaves many good men behind, but no equal.

"There was, moreover, an intense sense of the solemnity, beauty, and variety of Nature, which made every drawing of his fresh and gladdening, familiar as his hand was to all of us, and much as he affected the same spots and subjects year after year. North Wales had his heart. He had absorbed its colouring and contours into himself.

"In one of Mr. Punch's country excursions—and where may not Mr. Punch set up, that is, set down, his pavilion, and sound his *roo-too it?*—he came after a successful pitch at Llanrwst to the bridge at Bettws-y-Coed (you will please supply the vowels), and looking round him exclaimed to himself, 'I know this country!' He *did* know it in David Cox's drawings, for it was to this very spot, as Mr. Punch found out in a confidential chat with the artists at the Oak that night, the faithful old man had resorted year after year, loving the place like a mistress, both hill, and field, and river, till they laid their hearts bare to him, and told all they had to tell—every year something new and always worth telling, and whispered to none, but to old David.

"So go, my dear young friends, reverently and tenderly,

CHAP. XVII. 1855—1859.

and give your farewell and God-speed to old David Cox, for he will draw no more. He will divide the shattered weather-stained, wind-rent old mantle among many, for whom the rags and tatters will make whole suits, wherein they will array themselves very proudly, and make no small figure in many exhibition rooms."

I have omitted to mention that, at the end of 1858, several friends and admirers of David Cox, residing in the neighbourhood of London, proposed that an exhibition solely of the works of that artist should take place. Clarkson Stanfield, R.A., Frederick Tayler, F. W. Topham, Tom Taylor, and Edwin Field, were of the number of those who interested themselves in this matter; they obtained the promise of assistance from some friends in Birmingham, and Mr. George Stanfield consented to act as secretary. It was shortly arranged that this exhibition should be held in the large room of the Conversazione Society at Hampstead. A large number of artists and amateurs assembled on the day of opening, and Mr. Edwin Field gave an address. Mr. W. S. Ellis, Mr. Norman Wilkinson, Mr. Tom Taylor, Mr. David Cox, junior, and others in London, sent many contributions. Mr. Mayou, and some others, sent drawings from the country, and likewise Mr. Hollingsworth, of Birmingham, contributed a great many drawings and sketches. He also induced David Cox himself to lend some. The collection was very interesting, and although not entirely successful, in the sense that it was not a thoroughly representative one of the artist's work, it afforded exquisite pleasure to a large number of his brother artists as well as to amateurs.

This probably led to the formation of a committee at the commencement of 1859, having for its object a more important Exhibition of the Works of David Cox, to be held in London, in the spring of that year. The use of the

German Gallery, New Bond Street, was secured, and at the end of April it was opened to the public. The collection consisted of one hundred and sixty-nine works, some in oil and some in water-colours. Messrs. John Allnutt, H. H. Betts, H. Bradley, G. Briscoe, W. S. Ellis, Robert Grundy, Edwin Gwyther, E. W. Field, John Henderson, John Hollingsworth, John Heugh, G. Layton, S. Mayou, J. G. Reeves, Tom Taylor, and Norman Wilkinson, were the chief contributors, besides some works lent by David Cox and by his son.

The following account of this Exhibition is from the *Art-Journal* of the 1st May, 1859:—

"There is no more severe trial to which the pictures of any artist can be subjected than by collecting them together, and when thus combined, by viewing them as a whole, or comparing them with each other. The critic is then in a position to observe and test the progress or retrogression of the artist, to compare him with himself, to scan his merits or defects, and to ascertain whether he has been conscious of either, and if so, whether he has laboured to correct the one and maintain the other; in short, the art-life of the man is placed before the spectator, and laid open to his judgment in indelible characters, which are the seal of his reputation; how few are those who can undergo the ordeal without apprehension of the result!

"To such a trial, however, has the veteran landscape-painter, David Cox, been submitted by his friends and admirers: an Exhibition of about one hundred and seventy of his works having recently been opened, and a rich treat the Exhibition is to all who can appreciate thorough English scenery represented in a style of art as original as it is true. We have sometimes heard people say they cannot understand Cox. We could only offer to such our pity—pity that they had not eyes for Art or Nature, that they could not see his glorious sunshine, the motions of his clouds as they 'float

CHAP. XVII. 1855—1859.

through the azure air,'—pity that they could not inhale the sweet breath of his hayfields and purple heaths, nor see the rushing of his summer showers, nor repose with him under the shadows of his thick umbrageous elms and his graceful ash-trees. Not understand Cox! why there is hardly a peasant in the land who goes to his daily toil by the hedgerows, or in the fields, who could not comprehend and thoroughly *feel* the truth and beauty of his landscapes, who would not acknowledge that what he shows them is just that which every villager sees above and around him each summer of his life. . . . From the first Cox seems to have founded a style of his own, and rarely if ever to have departed from the principles he laid down for his guidance. One of the few early pictures now exhibited, 'Meadows on the River Lugg, Herefordshire,' from the collection of an early patron, Mr. Allnutt, reminds us, in colour and handling, of the late George Barrett; but this is the only work in which can be traced resemblance to any other artist, living or dead.

"From the same collection is also another picture of his earlier time, and one which has been regarded among the best of his productions, 'George IV. embarking for Scotland at Greenwich,' a kind of subject very rare from the hand of this artist. It is an elaborate composition, gorgeous in colour and picturesquely treated."

After specially noticing many of the works, the article referring to the picture of "The Bull," remarks—"This is a highly poetical composition, one may almost hear the roaring of the affrighted animal, and the splashing of the heavy rain as it pours in torrents down upon the meadows, and the seething mists rise up as from a boiling cauldron." "To those who love and reverence such pictures (as we have described) the Exhibition now open in Bond Street cannot fail to prove a rich treat, and will convince any sceptic, if he has eyes, that David Cox must always stand in the first rank of British landscape-painters."

Great merit was due to the committee, I think, in having brought together this collection, which contained works of nearly every period in Cox's long career, from the earliest to the latest, and many of them were representative ones of the highest excellence. In the Appendix, No. III., is an additional notice of this Exhibition, which appeared in a London paper.

The improvement which had taken place in Cox's health at the end of February did not last long; early in April, one of his grand-daughters wrote:—

"I found grandpapa very poorly, his breathing at times is very distressing; I don't see that he is weaker, but he evidently thinks himself worse."

And again on the 24th April:—

"Though the weather is most trying, I trust dear grandpapa is not worse, indeed I think J. and I have done him some good. He has rallied since we came down, and though low at times, I see his appetite is good; he seems to enjoy what he eats, and has had three good nights."

From this attack he again gradually rallied, and on the 24th May Mrs. Fowler sent the following report:—

"I am thankful to say he (the master) is quite as well, or, I think, better; he has very good nights, and Mr. Bindley said yesterday his pulse was rather stronger. He was so well on Sunday that he was talking to Mr. Hall of trying to paint, but he has not begun yet."

Again, on the 26th May, Mrs. Fowler wrote:—

"Your dear grandpapa is pretty well for him; he has been out in the garden the last two days for a short time. He walks very much better than he did when he was out in

CHAP. XVII. 1855—1859.

April; he talks of having a ride soon, and he talks of writing to your papa. He sends his love to you all."

The improvement recorded in the preceding letters was, however, only like the flicker of the expiring lamp. At the beginning of June he again caught cold; until then he had been able to come down-stairs, and he was generally cheerful, but feeling a presentiment of what was impending, one evening when about to leave his parlour, he looked round the walls, which were covered with works of art, and, in a low, mournful tone of voice, exclaimed, "Good-bye, pictures! good-bye, I shall not see you any more!" This, indeed, turned out too true, for he never entered that room again.

On the evening of Monday, the 6th of June, Mr. Bindley, observing a change for the worse in his patient's symptoms, telegraphed to his son to come down at once. Mr. D. Cox, junior, travelled down at night, and arrived at Greenfield House at half-past six in the morning of the 7th, and soon afterwards he wrote thus to his daughters:—

"Your dear grandpapa is very weak and his breathing is difficult; he seems to have been failing for the last two or three days, and Mr. Bindley sent the message. I pray that I may have a better account to-morrow. My coming down as I did has been a great relief, and my dear father had been very nervously wishing it for a day or two past. Grandpapa has asked most affectionately after you all."

A few hours after the preceding letter was written by his son, this good man passed away. His peaceful end is thus described in a second letter, from which I am enabled to give the following extract:—

"Harborne, June 7th, 1859.

"MY DEAR CHILDREN,—My heart is full while I write a few lines, so contrary to the eager hope I expressed in my note only a few hours ago.

"At half-past ten o'clock, only a few minutes after sending my note to you by Mr. Hollingsworth, I quitted my father to give him, as I thought, a little opportunity for a nap, but, hearing his cough, I was going up-stairs to advise him to try something for it, when I knew from Mercy's alarm some change was taking place. He passed away with 'God bless you,' and not a sign more," &c., &c.

"DAVID COX, JUNIOR."

Although he had been in failing health for some time, he was not considered in any particular danger, until he again caught cold, which brought on an attack of bronchitis, and this, Mr. Bindley informs me, was the immediate cause of his death.

At last, at the advanced age of seventy-six, David Cox had finished his work. Of him it may be truly said, that his work only ceased with his life. Work which had brought delight and consolation to thousands, his mission as a true artist, had been well fulfilled. He had shown how beautiful and noble is the scenery of England and Wales, how lovable is country life at all seasons of the year and in all its phases; but, above all, how much there is in nature to elevate and refine the heart of man.

XVIII.

CONCLUSION.

CHAP. XVIII.

THE funeral took place in Harborne churchyard on Tuesday, the 14th June, 1859. There, under a spreading chestnut-tree, the remains of David Cox were laid to rest in the same grave in which his dear wife had been buried fourteen years before.

Many of his old friends attended, and the Society of Painters in Water Colours was represented by its president, who came down on purpose from London. The most touching part of the ceremony consisted in the deep interest shown by a great number of poor and aged persons, inhabitants of the village, who either followed the coffin of their dear benefactor and friend, or who stood round about in groups in the churchyard. An artist who was present has told me that he never before witnessed such evident signs of genuine grief among the poor as on that occasion, and that scarcely an eye was dry. There is no doubt that the expression made use of by a working man employed in one of the Birmingham printing offices, who lived in Harborne, thoroughly represented the feelings of his own class about David Cox, when, in reply to a question, he said, "Oh, sir, he is not only respected at Harborne, he is beloved by all the poor there."

An interesting picture of the funeral of David Cox was painted by his old pupil, Mr. C. T. Burt; it now hangs in the public gallery of the Midland Institute, having been lent by its owner, Mr. J. Hollingsworth. The sorrowful procession is seen in the distance passing up the avenue of trees towards the church, and in the foreground many old men, women, and children are standing about, and others are following in the wake of the mourners.

Soon after his death many sympathizing and appreciative notices appeared in the local and other newspapers. It would occupy too much space to quote these in full, but I have selected the following short extracts from some of the papers, which will show what the general feeling was at the time.

The *Birmingham Daily Post* wrote, June 8th, 1859:—

"Yesterday morning old David Cox, the contemporary of Turner and Girtin, and one of that small band of artists who have made the English school of water-colour painters the finest in the world, passed from amongst us, cheered by the presence of his son, possessing the love and veneration of hosts of friends, and occupying a foremost place in the grand galaxy of art of which England now boasts."

The *Midland Counties Herald*, June 9th, 1859, contained an article as follows:—

"The English school of landscape painting has lost one of its most distinguished ornaments, and Birmingham one of the sons of whom she had just reason to be proud, in the person of Mr. David Cox, who expired at a ripe old age on Tuesday last at his residence, Harborne. Although his health had been feeble for some years, the end was sudden and somewhat unexpected among his intimate friends, by whom, on account of his estimable personal qualities, his loss will be severely felt, while in the outer world of art its announcement will be received with sincere regret. In professional stature David Cox was indeed a giant among his fellows, and his ever-welcome productions will be sadly missed from the walls of exhibition rooms which they have long adorned."

I extract the following from the obituary in the *Art-Journal* of the 1st July, 1859:—

"A few weeks only have elapsed since we directed the

CHAP. XVIII. attention of our readers to the collection of pictures by David Cox exhibited in the metropolis, and now we have to record the death of the veteran painter, one whose equal, as an uncompromising and truthful delineator of English rural landscape, we never expect to see. It almost seems as if the collection in question had been gathered together to form a chaplet of flowers of his own rearing to be placed on his grave. Our personal knowledge of the artist and the recollection of his simple and unassuming character, would have restrained us from saying while he lived what we can say now that praise 'falls listless on unhearing ears.' Though by no means insensible to any commendation bestowed on his works, we never met with a man who received it with more diffidence or on whom it made a less self-complacent impression. He possessed, in its way, a genius as original as that of Turner. There are those who cannot or will not understand either. We sorrow for them as we do for the physically blind to whom the glories of nature and art are irremediably closed."

Cox's will was signed on the 2nd August, 1858, in the presence of two of his friends, the Rev. Edward Roberts, curate of Harborne, and Peter Deakin, artist, of that place. His only son David and Mr. W. S. Ellis were appointed trustees and executors. To the latter he bequeathed his large drawing of "Cader Idris," and to William Roberts and Charles Birch a drawing, each of the value of £20, to be selected by his trustees. He bequeathed substantial legacies to each of his four grand-daughters, and the sum of £500 to his faithful housekeeper Ann Fowler; his son being left residuary legatee of all his estate and effects. The executors proved this will in August under £12,000.

A sale (by Cheshire and Gibbon, the auctioneers) of such effects and pictures as were not selected to be kept by the family, took place a month or two after the decease of David

Cox; but his son retained *all* his father's own works—paintings, drawings, and sketches—and these have never as yet been offered for sale. CHAP. XVIII.

Many letters of condolence were naturally written to Mr. David Cox, junior, and his family, but of these I shall give only one; it is written by Samuel Palmer, one of the oldest members of the Water Colour Society, and I think it will be read with interest as indicative of the feelings of his brother artists.

"6, Douro Place, Victoria Road, Kensington, July, 1859.

"MY DEAR SIR,—But for severe illness I should sooner have expressed my very sincere condolements with you on your great loss. Sincere it certainly is; for, although it was not my privilege to have spent in your dear father's society more than an occasional half hour, yet that was sufficient to attach any one to such a man, in whom intellectual and moral were equally developed. Much as we all admired his works, in common with the nation at large, we might also see in him all that was kind and good, and at once honour the artist and venerate the Christian.

"Thus our profession, in losing one of its brightest ornaments, sustained a still heavier loss in his example, who showed the ardent students that devotion to art was not incompatible with devotion to God. . . .

"With every sentiment of regard and esteem, believe me,

"My dear sir, yours most truly,

"SAMUEL PALMER.

"TO DAVID COX, ESQUIRE."

The reference in the preceding letter to the devotional side of Cox's character suggests a dream which Cox once had of being brought face to face with Christ, who did not speak, but looked on him and smiled. The great beauty of the Saviour's countenance much impressed him, and he tried, but in vain, to paint it.

CHAP. XVIII. It was in the Royal Academy, in 1849, that, looking at a sacred subject with a lady, a remark of hers brought up the recollection of this dream to Cox, which he then related to her. "How I wish," she says, in a letter, "it were possible to give his simple, unconscious manner of telling it—so full of reverence and deep feeling!"

In the month following that in which David Cox died a movement, emanating from the Birmingham Society of Artists, for providing some monument, or permanent tribute to his memory, led to the formation of a committee.

On the 25th July, 1859, a meeting took place, Dr. Bell Fletcher in the chair, when the character of the memorial came on for consideration, and it was resolved that a bust in marble should be entrusted to Mr. Peter Hollis, the well-known Birmingham sculptor. At a subsequent meeting of the committee, after consultation with the subscribers, it was determined that the best situation in which to place the bust when completed would be the Public Art Gallery in Birmingham. There this bust, completed several years since, has been placed on a pedestal, and may now be seen by all comers at any time in the day. It is not so good a likeness as the portrait by Sir J. W. Gordon, but it is noble in expression, and represents Cox in deep thought, as if he were musing over the subject of one of his grand pictures. As a work of art it is carefully thought out in every part, and it is well executed. Within the last few months a subscription has been organized by Mr. Thrupp, to place a handsome memorial window of stained glass in Harborne Church, to the memory of David Cox. I understand it will probably be placed there before the end of 1873.

A short time before his death, Mr. Edwin W. Field, replying to a letter on the subject of the foundation of a trust for promoting the fine arts in Birmingham, wrote thus:—

"If the founder will not give his name to the fund, then call it 'The David Cox Fine Arts Fund,' and so honour one of the very truest, purest, and greatest artists England has produced, and a Birmingham man. *Deo Laudamus!*"

The idea was an excellent one, and although I believe it has not yet been carried out, there could hardly be a more appropriate or graceful tribute to the memory of Cox. I hope it may not be entirely lost sight of by the rising generation of art-lovers and patriotic men. Cox threw his whole heart and life into his works, and they are indeed a noble legacy for any man to have bequeathed to posterity. The whole nation may be said to have benefited by them either directly or indirectly, and they are surely deserving of more than a passing notice and recognition. Such as I have described, the man and the artist was David Cox. That he was an artist of extraordinary genius is now admitted by many who once slighted or ridiculed his works, and I expect, therefore, as time rolls on, that his fame will reach even to a higher place than it has yet attained. A supplementary chapter, on the genius and character of Cox, will complete my work, and with this I shall take leave of my readers.

XIX.

SUPPLEMENTARY.—ON THE GENIUS AND CHARACTER OF DAVID COX.

"Nature never did betray the heart that loved her."—W. WORDSWORTH.

CHAP. XIX.

HAVING arrived at the close of the narrative of the incidents and art-work which are comprised in the life of this great landscape-painter, I propose to offer a few concluding remarks on the most salient points of the genius and character of David Cox. I have endeavoured to show that the precious and noble gift of genius which had been bestowed on Cox was never allowed to lie fallow during a long life. Never sparing himself, and never induced for one moment to turn aside into other pursuits, art-work was to him "his being's end and aim;" ease and the allurements of "pleasure" were without attractions to him. Work, always work, was to David Cox true happiness; thus, with each succeeding year, his drawings became more broad, more pure in colour, and more entirely penetrated with a deep sympathy for, and an intimate knowledge of, Nature. I shall premise a few remarks on the chief characteristics of the landscapes of Cox by observing that in one respect I think they excel almost all others—that of *educating* the eye and the mind of the beholder in the beauties of English scenery, and showing how much poetry may exist in the merest field or lane, which I attribute to their great truth, simplicity, and originality. He strove throughout life "to hold as 'twere the mirrour up to nature;" to be able to gaze on Nature as she appeared to him, in other words, to see through his eyes, is a real benefit which I hold has been conferred on us by this artist, and which we should be ungrateful not to acknowledge. Until rather recently the belief prevailed in some quarters that he was only a water-colour painter; I have shown, however, how important and numerous were his works in oil, and how continually they are still rising in public estimation. In the same way doubt has been expressed as to his accuracy and correctness in drawing. Without doubt the imperfection of his eyesight during the two last years of his life offered some difficulties as to correct outline; but his knowledge of perspective was excellent, and his rapidity, power, and success, during the greater part of his life, in delineating important public buildings, difficult street architecture, and interiors, has rarely been surpassed. Cox had an unsuspicious nature, very gentle, and yet very sensitive; he had, moreover, a loving and child-like heart, which was full of charity and warm affection for his friends, and, indeed, for most created things. He loved the hills and streams, the woods, the meadows, with their wild flowers and "soft, countless, and peaceful spears," even the roadside weeds; nothing was too lowly or familiar to find a place in his breast. To children he was especially kind, as has been abundantly shown, and also how grateful he was for any kindness; how willing at all times to help the poor, and to give advice or assistance to brother artists who sometimes had recourse to him. As with all men of true genius, Cox felt that no person and no object in nature was too humble or too lowly to be deserving of his respect and regard; just as he also felt that, in matters relating to Art, nothing was really trifling or unimportant.

Disliking the whirl and bustle of great cities, display and luxury were alien to his nature. Essentially simple in his tastes and English in his feelings, he was of an independent though forgiving spirit; but when roused, he was well able to assert his own dignity. In the thorough transparency, simplicity, and guilelessness of Cox's character, is explained his wonderful sympathy with nature. If his character had been different, he never could have painted pictures so little alloyed with the dross of humanity.

He was, moreover, of an ardent and impulsive temperament, yet unassuming in his demeanour to all, with a keen yet quiet sense of humour, and withal social in his feelings. Perhaps too distrustful of his own powers, like some other great men, and rather erring on the side of modesty. Yet there are many indications that he was not altogether unaware of the great merits of his work. In his deep feeling, insight, and reverence for nature, he was a true poet, and rarely if ever equalled. His mind took in rapidly a complete and perfect impression of the natural objects presented to it, to which he gave utterance in the readiest, the most direct, and, indeed, the only way he could. His mode of expression was that to which he was impelled in order to express the broad and varied truths which moved him. His hand and thoughts worked most harmoniously together; the sweep of his large brush appeared guided and inspired by the working of his mind, and in the maturity of his powers he became truly a giant in art, and rendered at once, without apparent effort, and yet accurately, not only the forms, but the movements of the scenes before him, and thus produced those broad pictures of nature, so unsurpassed in truth, so rarely equalled in power, and so embued with the deepest love for the simplest by-paths of rural life, as well as for the wildest and grandest scenes of our island. The wider the range and the grander the subject of Cox's pictures, the simpler became the arrangement and the more imposing the masses; whilst rural and pastoral scenes of a more homely character were arranged on less severe principles.

In truth to nature, the works of Cox should be ranked especially high. Truthful they are if anything—truth not worked out with careful and laborious stippling, but conveyed as if by inspiration, in a rapid, almost loose manner, yet thorough and comprehensive, full of pathos, feeling, and sympathy with nature in all her moods and aspects. It is remarkable how wide this sympathy was, both with gay and joyous scenes, as well as with those that are solemn, grave, and severe. Thus Cox has rendered with equal truth pictures of the bustle and throng of market-places, of wide reaches of sandy shores melting away in the silvery light of early morning, or seas and skies bathed in the soft yellow glow of sunset, peaceful brooks fringed with broad-leaved water-plants, hay and harvest fields full of breezy daylight and the cheerful movement of pastoral life, and harmless rural frolic; or, on the other hand, angry torrents pent between crags and the débris of rocks, dark mountains wreathed with mists, and dreary moorlands swept by pitiless storms. Humanity, too, in its saddest and dreariest moments has not been overlooked—the humble funeral of the aged sons of the soil, or, sadder still, that of the young, where promise has been left unfulfilled; the aged sexton still at his mournful work by the light of the rising moon. No matter what the subject, it only required that the chord of sympathy should be touched, and his feelings stirred, and straightway those sympathies and feelings were re-echoed in his works.

Cox's work carries you in spirit into the very scene itself. You share in the joy or sorrow of the moment; you feel the summer's breeze on your cheek, smell the perfume of the new-made hay, see the birds soaring in the sky, the clouds driven by the wind, and hear the roaring of the wintry blast, and the wild roar of many waters—

"The divine voice of the water and the wind."

Although Cox was one of the hardest and most unwearied of workers, feeling, as Turner did, that thorough knowledge of form and mastery in drawing must be the only foundation

CHAP. XIX. of all true art, and that it could only be reached by a great amount of laborious chalk and pencil sketching, and pen and ink etching (practised by him greatly in his earlier days), yet it cannot be doubted that he had great powers of imagination. This imaginative power enabled him to seize instinctively all that was poetical in any scene, and, discarding the trivial and common-place, he produced rapidly with his brush, out of the simplest materials, a poem full of natural truth, but withal containing the most subtle knowledge and judgment.

Repose, also, is one of the qualities in which his works abound—a feeling of peaceful rest and permanence. His broad meadows, hills, and rocks lie around as if they had so remained for untold ages; his mountains, clothed with forests, have a massive appearance, the effect of which is often heightened into mystery by the clouds with which he loved to surround them. Cox sought for gloom and mystery as an expression of the infinite. This is especially evident in many of his later works—the solemn feeling increasing more especially after the death of his wife, which, although loose in handling, sometimes termed "blotty," are among the finest and most impressive he ever produced. He knew well the value of the streak of light close to the horizon, seen beneath a dark and lowering sky, when the departing day is deepening into night, or when the first flush of dawn is seen struggling through the rising mists, and illumining the mountain tops, the valleys being still shrouded in obscurity and gloom.

Cox's wonderful experience, knowledge of nature, and power of memory, enabled him to combine what was essential to the feeling and expression of the work in hand, and to reject all that was out of harmony with it. He knew what he wanted, and when once he had thought his subject thoroughly out he did it at once, without swerving to the right or left, in the most direct and apparently easy manner. His drawings are remarkable, too, for the very happy incidents introduced always in the right place, helping the composition, giving the point required, and tending to illustrate the season of the year, time of day, and action appropriate to each locality. His figures are generally of picturesque men and women, thick-set and often aged, yet full of life and action, or else of children in the full enjoyment of play and fun. CHAP. XIX.

The drawings of Cox are equally noticeable for their depth yet purity of colour and their atmospheric effects. The appearance of atmosphere, light, and space, in some of them is very remarkable. You feel that you can almost walk along his roads and wander round his forest trees. Many of his skies have a grand stormy character, and a lowering tumultuous aspect, rarely equalled. As already remarked, Cox's manner of work was impulsive. He appears to have held his brush in a peculiarly loose way, giving sideway strokes, and thus producing that effect of wind and movement so apparent in many of his works. This manner, although so truthful, may not be equally liked and understood by all; but I think there can be no doubt that to those who are the most conversant with natural scenery, and who are the most humble of votaries of Nature, the works of Cox convey a sense of reality and out-of-door life beyond those of any other artist. He cared more for the *feeling* and *effect* than for the actual subject of his sketch. He had great power of generalising what was too much cut up, and sacrificing what was immaterial. He had the habit, sometimes, when impressed with a rapid passage of light, movement of clouds, or other effect, of turning round with his *back* to the scene, and making a rapid memorandum, with chalk and colours, of the *effect* as it existed in his *mind*, as he said that the *impression* was more fresh, powerful, and vivid thus than if he had continued to gaze on the scene, which would have become weakened by looking. Some of my readers may, perhaps, be inclined to think that, by dwelling continually on the great beauty and

CHAP. XIX. truth of Cox's works, I have been led into the error of exalting them above their fair place in the commonwealth of Art. To such I would reply first, by asking them to go to his representative works described (how imperfectly I shall be the first to own) in these pages; and then, by referring them to the opinions recorded on the works and genius of David Cox by some of our most eminent art-critics, John Ruskin, Francis Turner Palgrave, Tom Taylor, and others.

Cox has exercised, I believe, rather an important influence on the landscape art of England. His example has tended to raise it out of that prettiness, gay colouring, and overcrowding of subject into one picture, which are unfortunately still the bane of so many works in our annual exhibitions. No one understood better, or obeyed more constantly the law of *sacrifice;* that law which is a stumbling-block to so many young artists, but without the observance of which good art is almost impossible.

Cox has also contrasted a broad, truthful, and simple rendering of Nature, to that exaggerated straining after effect and contrast, sometimes approved of for decoration or stage scenery, but which, in almost all circumstances and positions, is out of harmony with a refined and cultivated taste. Art ought never to be degraded to please and satisfy the bad taste of the public; it is, moreover, I believe, even from a monetary point of view, unnecessary; for the public in England, as well as on the Continent, are learning to discriminate between good and false art.

Cox's character, honest, unaffected, and truthful, shines out clearly in most of his works; he threw his whole soul into his work, and for that reason, I believe, it touches and moves you so deeply. Perhaps the fact that he relied less on the rules of art than Turner, Müller, and some other great landscape-painters, but was more entirely a worshipper of Nature, more humbly and exclusively, may account for some of his most eminent and unique qualities.

It has been remarked that men of original genius are impelled to do their work in this world for the benefit of mankind, irrespective of any idea of temporary gains; and thus that Milton worked daily at his "Paradise Lost," knowing full well that he should receive but £5 for that immortal work. The same remark applies, to some extent, to David Cox, who painted pictures of the highest excellence and truth, whilst expecting to receive for them, as I have shown, little more than the cost of the materials, and giving many of them away as presents to his friends. The thoughts and feelings enshrined in all noble work have a tendency to make the world better, brighter, and happier. That this applies to painting as well as to literature, need scarcely be insisted on. It is the only true and worthy aim of Art; and who shall estimate in gold the intrinsic value of such productions? The true artistic gift is one of joyfulness, and a fountain of freshness to all weary travellers along the stony paths and dusty highways of life.

Landscape art, pre-eminently, is allied to the poetry of Nature, and the more the artist, as well as the poet, has felt his innermost feelings stirred, and his deepest sympathies awakened by natural objects and events, the more power has he of touching the same chord in the hearts of others by his work. This is the true explanation of the supremacy of Robert Burns as a lyrical poet. The simplest incident in Nature awoke feelings in his breast with which all mankind are kin, but which he above all others knew how to express with perfect truth and touching simplicity. It has been well said that the crucial proof of a true poet lies in the power of his human sympathy; and there can be little doubt that the successful representation of the deeper poetry of Nature by an artist (in which Cox excelled) depends on the intenseness and truthfulness of his insight into Nature, and on the sympathy which exists between her and his own feelings. That Nature laid bare her heart and told her secrets to Old

CHAP. XIX. David, as to no other living man, is, I believe the simple truth, and *the reason* why his grand works are more touching than those of any other artist.

As the genius of Turner has been likened to the immortal Shakespeare, as displayed in the wonderful mental range of his drawings and paintings, and the sublimity of their conceptions, so that of David Cox may bė said to bear a striking resemblance to Wordsworth and to Burns, in the intense love for Nature, truthfulness, and pathos, which are the chief and noblest characteristics of his works.

Turner and Cox both lived to the age of seventy-six, but Turner attained to the zenith of his fame and power at a much earlier period of his life than David Cox did. This may be partly accounted for, perhaps, by the fact that in the earlier years of Cox's career so much of his time was taken up in the occupation of giving lessons.

Born in a humble position, and without influential friends, David Cox had to fight his own way upwards amidst great difficulties—difficulties that would have discouraged, if not entirely overwhelmed, a less ardent and courageous spirit. His early struggles, and eventual success, should be a great encouragement to young artists. Without any regular course of instruction in art, he turned, as we have seen, in his youthful days to Nature, as to his best teacher, and at her shrine he was an unwearied and constant worshipper, until he had considerably passed man's allotted space of threescore years and ten; and there the old and venerable man remained faithful until the last dark shadows closed around him. To enumerate the spots chosen as subjects by Cox during his long career would comprise, as I have shown, more than half England and Wales; but Bettws was the scene he loved above all others in his latter years. Thither his thoughts turned in his last illness, when he was sometimes heard to exclaim, "Dear old Bettws! how I wish I could see you again!"

That there is a solid and a truthful foundation for the high place in public estimation now attained by the works of David Cox, and that neither fashion nor caprice have assisted therein, is fully admitted, I believe, by most persons who take an interest in Art. It is a fact deserving of notice, that at all recent sales of importance, where the works of Cox have been offered side by side with those of other deceased British artists of reputation, such as Etty, Maclise, Sir Charles Eastlake, and D. Roberts, the latter have been occasionally sold at about the original price, or not much beyond, whilst the works of Cox, especially those in oil, have gone for two or three times as much as they were previously purchased at, and in some cases for far more even than that. The cause of this is, I think, easily discovered in their unconventional and broad truth—the truth of Nature as it appeared to an artist of original genius. It will be long, I fear, before we see his like again. If there had been anything conventional and meretricious in Cox's pictures they would scarcely have passed so unscathed through the adverse criticisms with which they were at one time assailed, but, like pure gold, the more it is subjected to friction and acids, the brighter and more resplendent it becomes.

"Honour to whom honour is due" was a favourite motto with Cox, but of all mottoes, the one most applicable to him is "Excelsior," for he was unceasingly striving upwards.

The life-long development of his genius may be well compared to a seedling of the forest, of lowly aspect and humble growth at first, and long forced to struggle with adverse circumstances; but which, by dint of ever sending forth fresh buds and branches, has risen higher and higher, increasing in beauty and strength each year, until in its fullest maturity it attains to that serene height above its fellows, where the light of heaven illumines its topmost boughs, and the evening sun sheds a ray of glory on its venerable head.

APPENDIX I.

DRAWINGS BY DAVID COX EXHIBITED AT THE SOCIETY OF PAINTERS IN WATER COLOURS, LONDON, FROM 1813 TO 1859.

1813.—Gravesend, Fishing Boat. Haystack, Sketch from Nature. Eton College. View on the Banks of the Thames, near Chertsey. Lane near Dulwich. Hastings, Fishing Boats returning on the approach of a Storm. Westminster Abbey, from Battersea Fields. Llanberris Lake. A Heath Scene. Cornfield, near Dulwich. Edinburgh Castle. A Barley Field. Stacking Hay. A Lee Shore, Coast of Sussex. Cottage near Windsor, Sketch from Nature. The Wrekin, Shropshire. Westminster Bridge, from Lambeth.

1814.—Cottage near Windsor. Oak Trees. Sketch from Nature. Twilight. Westminster Abbey, from Lambeth. Windsor Castle, from St. Leonard's Hill. Midday. Llanberris Lake, North Wales. View on the Thames below Gravesend. Millbank, Thames Side. Morning. Snowdon, North Wales. Dulwich Mill, Surrey.

1815.—Cox did not exhibit this year.

1816.—Sketch on the Banks of the Thames. Windmill in Staffordshire. Hastings, Boats. Cottages near Hereford. Chepstow Castle, River Wye. The Sands at Low Water, Hastings. Fish Market, Hastings.

1817.—Cox did not exhibit this year.

1818.—View on Sydenham Common. View in the Vale of Festiniog, North Wales. View on the River Lugg, near Hereford. Heath Scene. Gloucester from the Ross Road. Scene on the Beach, Hastings. Early Morning. A Stackyard. Three Figures, Cottage Child, Hastings Fisherman, Beggar. Ploughing, a Sketch. Cottage in Kent. Landscape, Morning.

1819.—Landscape Sketch. Dindor Hill and Rotteros Woods, River Wye, near Hereford. Windmill, a Sketch. Fish Market on the Beach at Hastings. View looking down the Valley from Dolgelly to Barmouth, North Wales. Hayfield. Part of Hereford, a sketch made on the spot. Cader Idris, from the Machynlleth Road, looking towards Tal-y-Llyn, North Wales. Distant View of Goodrich Castle, on the Wye. Stacking Hay, a Sketch.

1820.—Coast Scene, Evening. View in North Wales. Coast Scene. Haymakers. Coast Scene, near Hastings. Ploughing Scene in Herefordshire, with Stoke Park and the Malvern Hills in the distance. Cottage in Herefordshire. View in the Pass of Llanberris, North Wales. View of the City of Bath, from Beacon Hill. Sketch from Nature. Scene on the Sands at Hastings. Hayfield. Sketch from Nature, Lugg Meadows, near Hereford. View on the Coast, near Barmouth, North Wales. Ross Market House, Herefordshire, a Sketch. Llanberris Lake and Snowdon Mountains. Boy Angling, View on the River Lugg, Herefordshire.

1821.—Water Mill at Festiniog, North Wales. Cæsar's Tower and part of Leicester's Buildings, Kenilworth Castle. Comb Martin, North Devon. View on the Beach, near the Old Pier, Hastings.

1822.—View near the Village of Pipe, Herefordshire. Repairing a Vessel on the Thames, off Rotherhithe. Morning Scene on the Thames, near Gravesend. Evening Scene on the Thames. Scene on the Thames, near Northfleet. Scene on the Thames, near Gravesend. Domestic Ducks. Town and Castle of Hay, on the River Wye, Brecknockshire. View in the Pass of Llanberris, North Wales. Hayfield, Gloucestershire. Distant View of Harlech Castle, North Wales, Morning. Scene on the Beach, Hastings, Sussex.

1823.—LOAN COLLECTION. (Many of the pictures exhibited this year were on Loan). Cottage on a Heath (proprietor, the Earl of Essex). Scene in Herefordshire (proprietor, J. Allnutt, Esq.). View near Dolgelly (proprietor, J. Allnutt, Esq.). Angling (proprietor, Sir J. Swinburne, Bart.). Afternoon (proprietor, J. Allnutt, Esq.).

1823.—A Heath Scene. Rocky Scene with Figures. Hastings, Fishing Boats. North Shore, Liverpool. Hawkers crossing the Sands near Barmouth, North Wales. Dockyard, Building a Sloop. Gravel-pit Scene on the Thames below Greenwich. Scene on the Thames near Rotherhithe. On the Medway. The Pool of London. Vessels on the Thames. Embarkation of His Majesty George IV. from Greenwich, August 10th, 1823. Boats on the Thames, Gravesend in the distance. Boats on the Thames, Evening, Greenwich in the distance. Village of Bullingham, Herefordshire. Lane Scene near Hereford. Fishing Boat on the Thames.

1824.—A Hay Cart. Early Morning, on the Thames, near Battersea. Cader Idris, from the Barmouth Road. Fishing Boat on the Thames. Boys and Sheep, scene below Gravesend. Vessels coming up the Thames. Shepherds collecting their Flocks, Evening, from scenery in Herefordshire. Interior of Tintern Abbey. Gravesend Fishing Boats. Passengers landing at the Stairs, Gravesend. Vessels on the Thames, by the Custom House. Westminster Abbey, from Lambeth Palace. Rocks on the River Wye. Part of Goodrich Castle, Herefordshire. Windmill on a Heath. Great Malvern

APP. I. Church, a Sketch. Sands at Low Water, Hastings. Distant View of Harlech Castle. Greenwich, from Sydenham Hill. Vessels at Rotherhithe. Lymouth Pier, North Devon. Lambeth Palace, from Millbank, a Sketch. Hayfield, View near Hereford.

1825.—Boats on the Thames, near Battersea (purchaser, Mr. Wall). Distant View of Greenwich (sold). Haunted Vale, North Wales, Morning (sold). Vessels coming up the Thames (purchaser, Mr. Knyvett). View on the Wye (sold). Carthage, Æneas, and Achates. Aberystwith Castle, Evening. Coast Scene near Barmouth (sold). Evening (purchaser, J. Pye, Esq.). Goodrich Castle. Cader Idris, from Kymmer Abbey, North Wales (purchaser, Lord Northwich). Cornfield, Herefordshire (sold). A Sketch. A Heath Scene. Near Rome. On the Medway, Kent. Lane near Hereford. Hayfield. Hay on the River Wye. Evening. Billingsgate, from the Custom House Stairs, Low Water. View on the Wye. A Sketch. Chester. Boats on the Thames, near Battersea. Hayfield, from Nature. Battersea Bridge. Clifton, near Bristol. Gravesend Boats. On the Thames. Morning Landscape, with Sheep. Warwick Castle. Hereford, a Sketch from Nature.

1826.—View on the Thames. A Sketch. Vale Crucis Abbey, Derbyshire. Hayfield. Coast Scene, with Fishermen. Pirate's Isle,

> "A sail! a sail! a promised prize to hope!
> Her nation—flag—how speaks the telescope?"
> LORD BYRON'S *Corsair.*

Moelwyn, near Tan-y-bwlch, Merionethshire. Evening. Distant View of Cardigan Bay, from near Harlech. Boats on the Thames, Greenwich in the distance. Snowdon, from near Beddgelert. Westminster Bridge. Kenilworth, Evening. The Inn at Tal-y-Llyn, North Wales. View between Hay and Bwlth, Brecknockshire. London, from Herne Bay. Lymouth Pier, North Devon. Snowdon. Lane Scene. Westminster, from Lambeth. Cottage Scene. Hayfield, Harlech in the distance.

1827.—Dover, from the Sea. Debarkation, Composition. Hayfield. Fishermen, Hastings. Part of Kenilworth Castle. Canal, Birmingham. Festiniog, North Wales. On the Coast, near Towyn, North Wales. Great Malvern, from the Worcester Road. East Cliffs, Hastings. London, from Nunhead Hill. View new Dolgelly, North Wales. Shrimp Catchers going out. Fishermen on the Coast, Hastings. Cornfield. Scotch Drivers. Shrimp Catchers (for a lady's album).

1828.—Hayfield. View from Kinmer Abbey, North Wales. London, from Greenwich Park. The Grave. Cader Idris, Evening, the Storm clearing off. Ullswater, Morning. Welsh Drovers. A Windmill. Lymouth Pier, North Devon. The Dying Brigand, Evening. A Heath Scene. On the Beach at Hastings. Dolgelly, North Wales. The Aran Mountain, from the Beddgelert Road. Chelsea Reach. Bolton Abbey, Yorkshire. Hastings, Boats returning in approach of Storm. The Moelwyn, North Wales, Misty

Morning. On the Coast, near Towyn, North Wales. Scotch Drovers. Cader Idris, from the Barmouth Road. Snowdon, Twilight. Boats on a River, Twilight. On the Banks of the Thames, Battersea. South Side of Cader Idris, North Wales. The Aran Mountains, North Wales.

1829.—On the Thames, below Gravesend. Fruit and Flower Market at Brussels. Road Scene, with figures. From Little Malvern, Worcester in the distance. Pastoral Landscape. Entrance to Calais Harbour. Landscape. Shepherds. Rocks near Beddgelert. Vessels off Gravesend. Dutch Hay Boats. Heath Scene, Afternoon. Gravel Pit. Calais Pier. Returning from Market. Interior of Maentwrog Church, North Wales. Sand Carriers, Calais. On the Coast, Boulogne. Dutch Boats on the Scheldt. Tintern Abbey. Fish Market, Boulogne. Millbank, Thames side. On the Sands at Hastings. Hayfield. Vessels on the Thames below Greenwich. Wandsworth Common. Boats on the Thames off Greenwich. Westminster, from Vauxhall. Gipsies. Convict Ship. Beach at Hastings. Coast Scene. Gleaners, Afternoon. Coast Scene. Dover.

1830.—Cottages on a Common. Bolton Abbey. Cader Idris, Morning. The Severn and the Wye, from Wyndcliff. Village of Mansell, near Hereford. Boats on the Thames. Chelsea Hospital. Shrimpers. Calais. Shepherds. Sand-banks, Calais. East Cliff, Hastings. On the Coast, Boulogne. In the Garden of the Tuileries. Shakespeare's Cliff. Part of the Tuileries, at Paris. Pedmore Church, Worcestershire. Gleaners. On the Coast of Picardy. Coast Scene. Cader Idris, from the Barmouth Road. Evening. On the Thames. Drovers. Gleaners Returning, Afternoon. Goodrich Castle. Vauxhall Bridge. Ferry House. Coast, Hastings. On the Lake, Tal-y-Llyn. North Wales. Cornfield.

1831.—View on the Wye, near Chepstow. Pont Neuf, from the Quai de l'Ecole, Paris. Fort Rouge, Calais. Dieppe Pier. A Heath Scene. Harlech Castle, Twilight. The Arrival. Whitehall. Calais Pier. Bridge in Warwickshire. Cottage, near Hereford. Scene in Yorkshire. Chamber of Deputies, Paris. Wyndcliff, in the Wye. Goodrich Castle, in the Wye. Sketch from Nature. Battersea Fields. Cader Idris, North Wales. On the River Ure, North Wales. On the Wharf, near Bolton Abbey, Yorkshire.

1832.—Bolton Castle, Wensleydale, Yorkshire. Antwerp, Morning. Entrance to the Inner Court, Dudley Castle. A Hayfield. An Interior. Peat Moor, North Wales. The Great Hall, Haddon. Heath Scene. Cornfield. A Rocky Glen. Part of Windsor Castle. Stacking Hay. June. Lane, in Herefordshire. Westminster, from Vauxhall Bridge. Harlech Castle. Entrance to Haddon Hall. Ploughing. Windermere during the Regalia,—

> "But never yet, by night or day,
> In dew of spring, or summer ray,
> Did the sweet valley shine so gay
> As now it shines."—*Lalla Rookh.*

APP. I.

Langdale Pikes, Westmoreland. Westminster Abbey, from Lambeth. A Rocky Coast, after a Storm. Near Dolgelly, North Wales. Bedroom in Haddon. Pier at Dieppe. Shrimpers on the Coast, Calais. Bolton Abbey. Calais Boats off Fort Rouge. Coast, Boulogne. Recess in the Drawing-Room, Haddon. Rowsley Bridge, Derbyshire. Near Harlech, Morning. Snowdon. North Wales. The Garden, Haddon. On the Coast, near Barmouth.

1833.—Landscape, Showery Day. Calais Pier. Causeway, Boulogne. A Brig entering Dieppe Harbour. The Music Lesson. Landscape. On the French Coast. The Proposal. On the Sands, Calais. Coast, near Boulogne. Harlech Castle. Rocky Landscape. Dieppe Pier. An Old House at Amiens. Garden Scene. Ploughing. Bridge near Maentwrog, North Wales. From Richmond Hill. Boats on the Thames. Hayfield. Dieppe, Morning. Pont-y-Cysylty. Vale of Llangollen. A Landscape. Returning from Ploughing. Funeral of a Nun. Fort Rouge, Calais, Morning. Staircase at Haddon Hall. Boats on the Scheldt. On the Sands, Boulogne. Melham Cove, Yorkshire. Bolton Abbey, Yorkshire. Boats on the Thames. A Road Scene. Shakespeare's Cliff. Lane Scene, Herefordshire. Entrance to Calais Harbour.

1834.—Bridge over the Derwent, near Chatsworth Park, Derbyshire. On the French Coast. Lane Scene, Staffordshire. Rocky Landscape, with Figures. Bolton Abbey. Distant View of Bolsover, Derbyshire. On the Castle Walls, Harlech, North Wales. Snowdon. Landscape, Showery Day. Part of Kymmer Abbey, North Wales. A Villa. Barge on the Thames. On the Coast, near Boulogne. Near Cerniogc, North Wales. Lane Scene, Herefordshire. Penmaenmawr. Heath Scene. Road Scene, with Figures. Heath Scene. The Lady of the Manor. Lac de Gaure, Hautes Pyrenees, from Sketch made on the spot by Mr. J. H. Bland, scene of Mr. and Mrs. W. H. Pattison's Sad Loss. Woody Landscape. A Terrace, with Figures.

1835.—Ulverstone Sands. South Downs, Sussex. Waterfall of Pont-y-Pair, North Wales. Waiting for the Ferry Boat. Showery Day, Bolton, Yorkshire. Hope Green, Cheshire, a sketch from Nature. Returning from Ploughing. Heath Scene, with Figures. Lane Scene, Herefordshire. Lancaster, Morning. Richmond Hill. On the Thames, near Gravesend. A Fresh Breeze. Norwood, Surrey. On the River Llugwy, North Wales. Old London Bridge. Market People crossing the Ulverstone Sands. Holyhead Road, near Nant Frangon. Bolsover Castle.

1836.—Pass of Killiecrankie. Stirling Castle, Evening. Ellerside Peat Moss, Lancashire. Lane Scene. Lancaster Sands. Market People returning from Ulverstone. Haddon Hall. Bridge, near Capel Curig, North Wales. Windmill, near Kenilworth, Warwickshire. Harlech Castle, North Wales. Cottages, near Lancaster. Landscape, with Fern Cutters. Market People crossing the Lancaster Sands. Chatsworth Park, Derbyshire. Bolton Castle,

Yorkshire. Twilight. Harlech Castle, from Tan-y-Bwlch. Heath Scene. Boats on the Scheldt. Bridge near Coniston Lake, Westmoreland. Windmill, Morning. Waterfall on the Llugwy, North Wales. Landscape. Near Loch Awe, North Britain. On the French Coast, Evening. Lancaster Sands, Morning. Road Scene, with Figures. On the Road from Tremadoc to Beddgelert, North Wales. Cottages near Bettws-y-Coed, North Wales. Criccieth Castle, North Wales. Evening. Showery Day. Aston Hall, Warwickshire. Barden Castle, from Bolton Park, Yorkshire. Snowdon and Moel Siabod Mountains, from Pentre-Voelas, North Wales. On the Road from Sheffield to Baslow, Derbyshire.

1837.—Cottage on Gill's Heath, Warwickshire. A Mountain Road. Infantry on the March. Market People crossing Lancaster Sands. Water Mill, near Dolbenmaen. Lane Scene. Landscape, Cattle and Drivers. Pont-y-Cefn, near Capel Curig, North Wales. Cottage in Surrey. Vale Crucis Abbey, near Llangollen. Calais Pier. Lancaster Sands, Evening. Windsor Castle. Entrance to Calais Harbour. Cassybte Aquaduct. Haddon Hall, Derbyshire. Showery Day. Windermere Lake. Public House, side of Ulverstone Sands. Road near Ulverstone. Kenilworth Castle. Ploughing. Cornfield, Midday. Evening, Gleaners Returning.

1838.—Returning from Hawking. Haddon Hall. Ulverstone Sands. The Louvre and Tuileries, from Pont Neuf. Bolton Abbey, Yorkshire. Windmill, near Kenilworth Castle. Boat on the Thames. On the Coast near Aberdovey. Rocky Scene. Infantry on the March. Road Scene, with Gipsies. On the Thames, near Gravesend. River Scene, North Wales. The Pier at Ulverstone. Terrace in the Garden at Powis Castle. Near Bolton Park, Yorkshire. Gipsies. Garden Scene, Powis Castle. Dover Pier. Ploughing. Landscape near Woodstock. Lancaster Sands, Morning. Harlech Castle. Castleton, Derbyshire. Powis Castle, the Seat of the Right Hon. Lord Clive. Noon, Boys Angling. Going to Market. Penmaenmawr, North Wales. Going out Hawking. Barden Tower. On the Wharfe, Yorkshire. Drover. A Mountain Road. Stirling Castle. Cavalry on the March.

1839.—Market People crossing Lancaster Sands. A Farm in Staffordshire. Boys Angling. Barden, from Bolton Park. The Town Walls, Conway. Going to Market. Bolsover Castle, Derbyshire. Cavalry on the March. Going to Hayfield. View near Windsor. Rocky Scene, with Brigands. Cader Idris, North Wales. A Lane Scene. A Hayfield, Evening. A Sawpit. A Summer Day. On the Thames, Morning. On the Holyhead Road, near Penmaenmawr, North Wales. Bala Lake, North Wales. A Hay Cart. Inverary Castle. Battersea Fields. A Mountain Road. A Marine Village, Morning. A Castle in the Olden Time.

1840.—From the Tremadoc Road, looking towards the Pass of Pont Aberglaslyn, North Wales. A Brook. A Forest. Boats on the Thames. A Bay Window in the Portrait Gallery, Hardwick. The Portrait Gallery,

APP. I.

Hardwick Hall, Derbyshire. Throne in the Portrait Gallery, Hardwick Hall. A Farm Yard. Mill on the Trent. Water Mill in Staffordshire. Mountain Road. Rocky Coast. Harlech Castle, North Wales. Coast Scene. Pier at Liverpool. A Wood Scene. Bolsover Castle, Derbyshire. Hardwick Park. Bolsover Castle in the Distance.

1841.—Noon. Market People crossing the Lancaster Sands. Road through a Wood, Tan-y-Bwlch, North Wales. On the River Llugwy, North Wales. Landscape, composition, Brigands Reposing. Lancaster Sands, from Hest Bank. A Heath Scene. Vale Crucis Abbey, North Wales. A Brook Scene. Windsor Castle, from Sandpit Gate.

1842.—Brook Scene. Lancaster. The Old Holyhead Road, near Penmachno. Twilight. Distant View of Kenilworth Castle. Cornfield, Kenilworth Castle. Bolsover Castle. Powis Castle. Farm Yard, at Beckenham, Kent. Lane at Harborne, Staffordshire. Bolton Abbey. Gipsies. Going to Plough. Heath Scene. Powis Castle. Gate Tower, Kenilworth Castle. Fern Gatherers. Breiddyn Hills, from Powis Park.

1843.—Sands at Rhyl, North Wales. Penmaenmawr, North Wales. Cader Idris, North Wales. Bolsover Castle, Derbyshire. Stubble Field, with Gleaners. River Wrion, North Wales. On the Wharf, near Bolton Abbey. Sherwood Forest. Wharton Hall, Yorkshire. Chatsworth. Lancaster Sands, Morning. Harlech Castle, North Wales. Kenilworth Castle. A River Scene. Vale of Conway, from near Llanbedr.

1844.—Summons to the Noonday Meal, North Wales. Scene in Bolton Park, Yorkshire. A Mill near Bromsgrove. Bala Lake, North Wales. Lower End of the Llyn Dinas, North Wales. Merivale, seat of W. S. Dugdale, Esq., M.P. A Mill on the Trent. Mountain Road near Harlech. River Scene, Derbyshire. Powis Park. On the River Llugwy, near Capel Curig, North Wales.

1845.—Distant View of Kenilworth Castle. Gipsies, Early Morning. Market People crossing the Lancaster Sands. Distant View of Brough Castle. Knaresborough Castle. Cloudy Day. Garden Terrace, Haddon. River Wye, near Chepstow. Mill near Conway, North Wales. Hampton Court. Dryslwyn Castle, Vale of Towy, South Wales. Morning. Evening. Cottages in Cheshire. Midday. Going to Plough.

1846.—Hardwick Hall, Derbyshire. Outskirts of a Forest. Vale of Dolwyddelan, North Wales. Mill at Bettws-y-Coed, North Wales. The Watering Trough. Knaresborough Castle, Yorkshire. Cottages near Bettws-y-Coed, North Wales. Near Atherstone, Yorkshire. Harlech Castle, North Wales. Cornfield near Rhyl, North Wales. A Weedy Bank. Cottages at Rowley, Staffordshire.

1847.—River Llugwy, from Pont-y-Kefyn, near Capel Curig. Windsor Park. George's Dock, Liverpool. Mill near Llangadoc, South Wales. Bolton Abbey. Caer-Cennen Castle, South Wales. Vale of Dolwyddelan, North Wales. Cottages at Bettws-y-Coed. Mill in Staffordshire. Near Atherstone, Warwickshire. Moorland, near Kirby Stephen. Welsh Scenery. Vale of Clwyd.

1848.—Lower End of the Vale of Clwyd, North Wales. Going to the Hayfield. A Green Lane, Staffordshire. The Skylark. Windy Day. River Trent. Peace and War. Sherwood Forest. Haymaking, Festiniog, North Wales. Showery Bay. A Gravel Pit. Mountain Stream, Trefrew, North Wales. Village of Rowsley, Derbyshire. Holyhead Road, near Pentre Voelas, North Wales.

1849.—Barden Tower, Yorkshire. The Night Train. The Missing Flock. Cross Roads. Beeston Castle. Shepherds collecting their Flocks. Lane in Surrey. Going to the Cornfield. Cottages at Rowley, Staffordshire. Near Altrincham, Cheshire. River Leder, from Pont-y-Pant. The River Machno, North Wales. Bettws-y-Coed, North Wales. Rainy Day. From the Mountain above Bettws-y-Coed.

1850.—Summer. A Rocky Glen. Changing the Pastures. Beaver Grove, Bettws-y-Coed. Blackberry Gatherers. Cottages near Bettws-y-Coed. The Water Tower, Kenilworth Castle. The Vale of Conway. A Welsh Funeral Bettws-y-Coed, North Wales. River Machno, near Pandy Mill, North Wales. Rocks near Bettws-y-Coed. Flint Castle. A Farm at Bettws-y-Coed, North Wales. Near Pandy Mills, North Wales.

1851.—Rocky Scene near Capel Curig, North Wales. Going to the Hayfield. A Gipsy Encampment. Morning. Shearing Sheep, Vale of Dolwyddelan. Cornfield, Bettws-y-Coed, North Wales. Cutting Green Rye. Langharm Castle, North Wales. Beaver Grove, Bettws-y-Coed. Moel Siabod, near Capel Curig, North Wales. Sketch near Llanrwst, North Wales.

1852.—Cottages at Harborne, Staffordshire. Part of Conway Castle. On the River Conway, near Bettws-y-Coed. Bettws-y-Coed Church, North Wales. Besom Makers gathering Heath on Carrington Moss, Cheshire. On the Llugwy, near Bettws-y-Coed. Penmaen Beach, on the Coast between Conway and Bangor. A Peat Bog above Bettws-y-Coed. Lane near Llanrwst, North Wales. Gipsies crossing a Heath. Mountain Path above Bettws-y-Coed. Lane near Sale, Cheshire. On the Coast near Rhyl, North Wales.

1853.—Rainbow. Barden Castle. Near Bettws-y-Coed, North Wales. Mountain Rill. The Summit of a Mountain. The Challenge. The Old Road from Capel Curig to Bangor. North-east Point of Great Orm's Head. Windy Day. Coast of Rhyl, North Wales. Lane near Bettws-y-Coed, North Wales. Bathers.

APP. I.

1854.—Near Capel Curig. Keep the Left Road. Snowdon, from near Capel Curig. Peat Gatherers. Cutting his Stick. Ludford Bridge. Crossing the Downs.

1855.—Skirt of a Wood. Flint Castle. Snowdon, from Capel Curig. Hayfield. The Coming Gale. Besom Makers carrying Heath. Gipsy Encampment. Going to Market. Heath Scene. The Old London Stage. Asking the Way. Church at Bettws-y-Coed. Near Ludlow.

1856.—Driving the Flock. Peat Gatherers, North Wales. Near the Coast. Hayfield. On the Moors, near Bettws-y-Coed. Sultry Evening. Twilight. Wind and Rain. North Wales. Horses Drinking. Dover.

1857.—Near Capel Curig. On the Llugwy, Bettws-y-Coed. Gordal Scar. Carnarvon Castle. Shrimpers, Hastings. Warwick Castle. Near Ludlow. Forest Scene. Near Capel Curig. On the River Conway, near Bettws-y-Coed. Near Capel Curig. Near Capel Curig. Bolton Abbey, Yorkshire, Evening. Near Rhwy, North Wales.

1858.—Snowdon, from Capel Curig. Snowdon, near St. Asaph. Kenilworth. Skirts of a Common. Pont-Gyfyng. Penmaen Beach. Going to Market. Near Capel Curig. Coast at Rhyl. Bettws-y-Coed. Rhyl, on the Sands. Changing the Pasture.

1859.—The Stepping-stones, Bettws. The Mountain Tarn.

> "Resistless, roaring, dreadful, down it comes
> From the rude mountain and the mossy wild,
> Tumbling through rocks abrupt."
>
> THOMSON.

Darley Churchyard. Rocks near Bettws-y-Coed. Penmaenmawr. Kenilworth Castle. Twilight.

APPENDIX II.

AN ACCOUNT OF EIGHT OF THE MOST IMPORTANT COLLECTIONS OF WATER-COLOUR DRAWINGS AND SEPIAS BY DAVID COX OFFERED FOR SALE FROM 1856 TO 1872.

MR. CHARLES BIRCH'S Collection, February 27th, 1856. Water-Colour Drawings.—A Land Storm, 13 inches by 9 inches, 10½ guineas. A Road Scene, from the Bernal Collection, 11 inches by 9 inches, 9½ guineas. Richmond Hill, from the Bernal Collection, 11 inches by 7 inches, 16 guineas. Heath Scene, Windmill and Figures, from the Bernal Collection, 10 inches by 7 inches, 8 guineas. Ruins and Mountainous Distance, from the Bernal Collection, 10 inches by 8 inches, 9 guineas. Going to Market, with Passing Storm, from the Bernal Collection, 11 inches by 8 inches, 9 guineas. Figures with Cattle at a Watering Place, from the Bernal Collection, 14 inches by 10 inches, 22½ guineas. Tintern Abbey, 10 inches by 7 inches, 8½ guineas. Group of Cattle on the Edge of a Lake, 14 inches by 10 inches, 12 guineas. Travellers Passing a Ford, 11 inches by 7 inches, dated 1850, 9½ guineas. Cavern Scene, 8 inches by 5 inches, 5 guineas. Coast Scene, 10 inches by 7 inches, 9½ guineas. The Hop Gatherers, 19 inches by 11 inches, 27 guineas.

Mr. Charles Birch's Collection, February 27th, 1857. Water Colour Drawings.—Scarborough Castle, 10½ inches by 7½ inches. The Downs, 10 inches by 7 inches. A Village Scene, 10¼ inches by 7¼ inches. The Belated Traveller, 10½ inches by 7 inches. Wind and Rain, 10¾ inches by 7 inches. Scotch Drovers, 10 inches by 7 inches. A Coast Scene, 9¼ inches by 6¼ inches. Calais Jetty, 9 inches by 6 inches. Rhaiadr Bridge, Radnorshire, 9¾ inches by 6¾ inches. Bolsover Castle, effect of Storm, 16 inches by 11 inches.

Mr. Norman Wilkinson's Collection, June 14th, 1861. In Folios.—Beaver Bridge, Conway. Pont-y-Pair, River Llugwy. Rhyl. The Coast at Rhyl. On the Llugwy. Rowsley, Derbyshire. Bolton Abbey. Study for the Large Picture. Flint Castle. The Coast at Rhyl. The Strid, on the Wharfe. A Cornfield. Harvest Time. North Shore, Liverpool. At Rhyl. On the Wharfe, near Old Park. Pont-y-Gyffin. A Sketch at Bettws. Emigrants' Office, Liverpool. Ulverstone Sands. On the Road to Llyn,

APP. II. Crafnant. Waterfalls, Bettws-y-Coed. Near Rowsley. Staircase, Barden Tower. Pont-y-Pant. Bridge at Bettws-y-Coed. Near the Inn at Bolton Abbey. Salmon Trap on the Lledr. Interior of a Cottage, near Penmachno Mill, with figures. Bolton Abbey. St. George's Dock, Liverpool. Part of Bolton Abbey. The Coast at Rhyl. Cottage, North Wales. Mill at Bettws-y-Coed. On the Wharfe. On the River Llugwy. Penrhyn Castle. Barden Tower. Lancaster Sands. Melham, Yorkshire. Rowsley, Derbyshire. Near the Conway Falls. Salmon Trap, Bettws-y-Coed. In the Vale of the Lledr. Road over the Mountain, Bettws-y-Coed. Bettws Church. Mill near Bromsgrove. The Hall, Bolton Abbey. On the River Llugwy. The River Lledr, Dolwyddelan Valley. Framed Drawings.—In the Village of Bettws-y-Coed. Valley of the Lledr. A View of Bolton Abbey. Ford over the Lledr. Park Side. On the Llugwy, Bettws-y-Coed. Snowdon, from near Capel Curig. Mill near Bettws-y-Coed. Interior of a Kitchen. Fly Fishing, River Llugwy. From the Inn, Bolton Bridge. Near Llyn, Crafnant. On the Llugwy, Bettws-y-Coed. Pandy Mill, Penmachno. Pont-y-Pant, River Lledr. On the River Lledr. Barden Tower, from a distance. Interior of a Stable. View near Windsor. A Stormy Evening. Near Barden Tower. At Moel Siabod. First Peep of Bolton Abbey. Farm at Bettws-y-Coed. Barden Tower, from the Meadow. A View on the Llugwy. Men at a Well. A Scene in North Wales. Heath Scene and Waggon. Horse Fair at Birmingham. The Vale of Dolwyddelan. Near Bettws-ý-Coed. Bettws-y-Coed Bridge. On the Holyhead Road, near Capel Curig. In the Village of Trefrew. View in the Vale of Dolwyddelan. The Swallow Falls. Bettws-y-Coed Church. Barden Tower. On Barden Fells. Near Llyn Cranfant. Asking the Way. A Mountain Scene, North Wales. Bettws-y-Coed Village. A Girl Milking Cows, North Wales. On the Road to Llanrwst. Cottages and Cattle. Harborne. Pont-y-Pair, River Llugwy. Heath Scene. Mill near Bettws-y-Coed. View near Barden, Yorkshire. On the River Machno. Rock in Dolwyddelan Valley. Bolton Abbey, Evening. Sheep on the Way. Barden Tower, from the Bridge. A Welsh Cottage, with figures. Bettws Church. Stepping Stones over the Conway. Cottage near the Bridge of Bettws. Bolton Abbey. East End of Bettws Church, River Conway. The Vale of Dolwyddelan, North Wales (the large work exhibited in the gallery of the Water Colour Society).

MR. WILLIAM ROBERTS'S COLLECTION, May 21st, 1867. Drawings in Sepia.—After a Shower. Returning from Market, £10 10*s*. From Otley Bridge, £12 12*s*. Otley Bridge, £18 18*s*. Ilkley, £5 5*s*. Near Ilkley, £11 11*s*. Bolton Bridge and Abbey, £16 16*s*. Bolton, from the Tower Window, £7 7*s*. Bolton Abbey, north side, £12 12*s*. Bolton Abbey, south side, £15 15*s*. On the River Wharfe, near the Strid, £25 4*s*. Barden Tower, £13 13*s*. On the Road to Barden Tower, £19 19*s*. Barden Tower, £14 14*s*. Conway Castle, £3 3*s*. Water Colour Drawings.—A Lane Scene, with figures, a sketch, £5 5*s*. On the Wharfe, near Bolton Abbey, £8 8*s*. From Bolton Abbey, £6 16*s*. 6*d*. Near Bala, North Wales, £10 10*s*. A Sleeping Boy (not sold). A Scene at Windsor, £10 10*s*.

Traveller Asleep, Commercial Room, Lancaster (not sold). A Sketch near Kenilworth Castle, £12 12*s.* 6*d.* Cavalry, £19 19*s.* The Italian Garden, Powis Castle, £7 17*s.* 6*d.* Aberystwith, £37 16*s.* An Interior, £15 15*s.* On the River Wharfe, £36 5*s.* Harlech Castle, £28 17*s.* 6*d.* Ruins of an Abbey, Evening, £21. Battle of the Bridge (recollections of a drawing by Cattermole), £33 12*s.* A Scene on the Wye, £36 15*s.* A Landscape, with figures, £32 11*s.* A Landscape, Kenilworth, £28 7*s.* Kenilworth Castle, £34 13*s.* Hill Top, with Cattle, bright sunny effect, £28 7*s.* Landscape, with Cart Shed, £32 11*s.* A Cottage in Surrey, £31 13*s.* Blackpool, £4 10*s.* Blackpool, £12 12*s.* The Dying Knight, after Cattermole, £22 1*s.* A Mountain Landscape, Solitude, £31 10*s.* Peat Gatherers returning from the Moors, £89 5*s.* Crossing Lancaster Sands, £53 12*s.* Bolton Abbey, £27 6*s.* On the Wharfe, near the Strid, bequeathed to Mr. Roberts by David Cox, £77 16*s.*

MR. PETER ALLEN'S COLLECTION, March 6th, 1869.—The sale included forty water-colour drawings and five sepias. The following were the most important drawings:—Bolton Abbey, dated 1844, 125 guineas. A River Scene, with cows, dock-leaves in the foreground. Windermere Lake. Windsor Castle, from the Allnutt Collection, exhibited at Leeds, the view taken from Virginia Water, 240 guineas. Landscape, with a man travelling, showery weather. Haymakers, Vale of Carmarthen, 105 guineas. Windsor Castle, early morning, guard exercising, exhibited at Leeds, 210 guineas. The Hayfield, exhibited at Leeds, 95 guineas. Peat Gatherers, upright, from the Cox Exhibition, 200 guineas. Windsor, from the River. Barden Tower, with cattle on a road. A grand View in Wales, with a man and horse crossing a stream, exhibited at Leeds, 24 inches by 34 inches, 355 guineas. The Welsh Funeral, 24 inches by 34 inches, an original study for the drawing exhibited at Leeds, 110 guineas. Landscape, with windmill, and horses on road, 140 guineas. Flock of Sheep near a Pool of Water, early morning, 17 inches by 28 inches, exhibited at Leeds, 166 guineas. Woody Landscape, with figures at a stile, exhibited at Leeds 1851, 150 guineas. Going to the Harvest Field, 1845, 200 guineas. Broom Gatherers, 1854 (at Sir J. Heron's), 200 guineas. An open Landscape, with a pool of water, and swine in the foreground, 1840, 236 guineas. Wind, Rain, and Storm, dated 1845, exhibited at Leeds, 400 guineas. The Weald of Kent, exhibited at the Art-Treasures Exhibition at Manchester (No. 480), 345 guineas.

MR. THOMAS BROWN'S COLLECTION, June 5th, 1859.—Water-colour drawings. View off the Dutch Coast, with fishing-boats in a squall. View in Wales, with a woman driving geese, evening. The Gardens of the Tuileries, 1830. Part of Kenilworth Castle, with figures driving sheep. A Calm off Greenwich, with Boats, 1818. A Harvest Field, with gleaners. A Rabbit Warren. Changing the Pasture. Welsh Drovers, with a flock of sheep. A Landscape, with a lock and fisherman. A Sea Piece, with fishing-boats in a brisk gale. A View in Wales, with a milkman and cows. Conway, 1835, an important drawing. The Pass of Llanberris, with a coach and

App. II.

figures, an important drawing. Old Houses at Lambeth, old cottages. Hay-making. A French Street-scene. A Landscape, with a Welshwoman on a grey pony, and two other figures. Hay Barges in a Calm. A Meadow, with a windmill, morning. Windsor Castle. Rouen. A Pastoral Scene, peasants returning, 1826. A Landscape, with mounted figures, Aston Hall in the distance. A Welsh Landscape, with a man on a grey horse in conversation with two women. A Flock of Southdown Sheep near a Windmill. A Rocky Pass, with troops on the march. A Harvest Field, with sportsmen and dogs, Bolsover Castle in the distance.

Mr. Edwin Bullock's Collection, May 21st, 1870.—Twelve sepia drawings, including Rowsley Mill, Dudley Castle, Metchley Abbey, The Peacock, Rowsley, Macstoke Priory, &c. Water-colour drawings:—A Ruined Castle, £8. A River Scene, with figures, and a dog on a bridge, £30. The Entrance to a Château, with figures and horses, dated 1829, £29. Barden Tower, Yorkshire, £88. Near Sale, from Manchester. A Mounted Peasant driving a Cow, and other figures, £76. Interior of Bettws-y-Coed Church, £10. A Landscape, with a cottage, and ducks in a pool, £35. Bolton Abbey, £130. The Ferry at Oxford, £30. Malvern Abbey, £105. A Mountainous Landscape, with a cottage in the foreground, £50. Montmartre, dated 1829, £18. A Valley, with two cows near a river, £54. Crossing the Downs, 1854, £105. A Rocky Landscape, with a waggon and horses, £74. Four Miles from Sale, two peasants, with a cart and horses, £95. Hayfield, with a rainbow, figures, and horse, £37. The Waterfall at Bettws-y-Coed, £22. A Heath Scene, with figures, £28. A Welsh River Scene, with a woman carrying a pail on her head, £85. A Landscape, with a peasant boy driving cattle up a hill, £40. A Welsh River Scene, with an angler, a mounted peasant driving cattle in the distance, £65. A Landscape, with figures, after J. Cristall, £20. A Landscape, with two peasants, with a dog and sheep, £36. Windsor Castle, from the Forest, with cows, £50. A Rocky River Scene, with two figures and a cottage, £26. View of a Castle, £24. A Landscape, with a castle and cows, £30. View of an Abbey, with figures, £17. Interior of a Kitchen, £14. A Landscape, with peasants driving Cattle, 1823, £52. A Rocky Scene, with a horseman, £25. Hastings Beach, 1813, £25. Mill at Bettws, £100. Vale of Dolwyddelan, North Wales, £60. Peat Gatherers, North Wales, 1854, £90. Cutting his Stick, 1854, £135. A River Scene, with cows, £50. A Welsh Road Scene, with cattle and ducks, presented by the artist to Mr. Bond, 1846, £230. Cross Roads, 1847, £370. Keep the Left Road, 1854, £200. A Forest Scene, with three figures, with a white horse, £170. Royal Oak and Bettws-y-Coed Church, £95. The River Ure, Yorkshire, with peasants and horses, £52. A Landscape, with a boy and child about to cross a rustic bridge, and three other figures on a road, £295. Stoke-Say, near Ludlow, a woman and child on a road in the foreground, £130. Bolsover Castle, a man with a pony on a road, £340. Penmaenmawr, figures with a donkey descending the roads, 1853, £140. Boys Bathing alarmed by a Bull, £330. Ludford Bridge, West Ludlow, £76. A Mountain Scene, with a shepherd with a pony and sheep. Interior of the picture gallery at Hardwick Hall, upright, £75. The Companion Gallery at Hardwick Hall, £75. The Picture Gallery at Hardwick Hall, £300.

Mr. Gillott's Collection, May 4th, 1872.—Water-colour drawings. A Mountainous Lake Scene, 6⅞ inches by 10 inches, £28 7s. Showery Weather, 6½ inches by 9 inches, £12 1s. On the Thames, with hay barges and boats, 6½ inches by 9¾ inches, £57 15s. A Valley in Wales, with horsemen and cattle, 5⅛ inches by 7⅝ inches, £21. A Quiet Pool, 7¼ inches by 10½ inches, £58 16s. A Welsh Valley, with drovers and cattle, 10¾ inches, by 14⅝ inches, £86 2s. Milking Time, 10⅜ inches by 14¼ inches, £99 15s. Coast Scene, with figures and boats, 4⅞ inches by 6⅞ inches, £34 13s. The New Inn, Lynmouth, 6 inches by 8½, £19 19s. Old Cottages, 6⅜ inches by 9½ inches, £22 1s. An Overshot Mill in Wales, with figures, 8⅝ inches by 13⅛ inches, £85 1s. Gresmere Church, 7⅛ inches by 5½ inches, £19 19s. Tintern Abbey, 6½ inches by 9 inches, 1836, £30 9s. Lancaster Sands, with a farmer on horseback and fishermen, 1827, 8⅛ inches by 11⅜ inches, £120 15s. Val Crucis Abbey, 6½ inches, by 10⅜ inches, £26 5s. Mountainous Landscape, a sketch, £24 3s. Greenwich Hospital, 11¼ inches by 14⅞ inches, £92 8s. A Garden Terrace in North Wales, 7¾ inches by 10½ inches, £46 6s. A Rocky River Scene, with angler, 10½ inches by 14¼ inches, £189. Fort Rouge, Calais, 7¾ inches by 11¾ inches, £52 10s. Ploughing, 7¼ inches by 10¼ inches, £168. Lake Scene, with flock of sheep and figures, 1838, 1⅛ inches by 12⅛ inches, £278 5s. A Farm, with cows and ducks near a pool, 10½ inches by 14½ inches, £451 10s.

Mr. J. Tattersall's Collection, July 6th, 1872.—Of seventy fine drawings and sketches, the following were the most important: Sketches and Drawings in colours, Lots 22, 23, 25, 26, and 32, Hay, Brecknockshire; ditto, with Viaduct; Port Madoc; View on the Essex Shore of the Thames, and a ferry boat with sheep, all in sepia, 135 guineas (Agnew). Lots 39, 42, 56, 69, and 70, A Welsh Landscape, effect of Grain; Liverpool; Flounder Boat on the Thames; Peat Gatherers and Ulverstone Sands; Coming Storm —drawings in colours—160 guineas (Greenwood). Drawings in water-colours, Lots 81, 83, and 84, Harborne Lane; Watering of Horses; and Ploughing, a view in Surrey, 140 guineas (Tooth). Lots 86 and 87, A Hayfield; and Cader Idris from Kymmer Abbey, North Wales, 110 guineas (White). Lots 88, 89, Two Views on the Thames, Greenwich in the distance. Lots 90, 91, Views on the Coast near Barmouth, North Wales, and a Cornfield; View of the Black Mountain, North Wales, 145 guineas (Agnew). Lot 92, Greenwich Hospital, with boats and figures, 105 guineas (Greenwood). Lots 93, 94, A Coast Scene, with fishermen and boats; and View on the Coast near Towyn, North Wales, 100 guineas (White). Lots 95, 97, 98, East Cliff, Hastings—Moonlight; The Approach to Dunkirk; and Dry Sand Banks, Barmouth, North Wales, 108 guineas (Tooth). Lots 100, 102, View on the Wye below Tintern Abbey; Tintern Abbey—Evening; and Distant View of Harlech

APP. II.

Castle, North Wales, 130 guineas (M'Lean). Lots 103, 104, Milking Time; and Looking up the Vale of Llanwrog, 108 guineas (Noseda).

Recapitulation.

Mr. Charles Birch's Collection, February 27th, 1856; ditto, February 27th, 1857.
Mr. Norman Wilkinson's ditto, June 14th, 1861.
Mr. William Roberts's ditto, May 21st, 1867.
Mr. Peter Allen's ditto, March 6th, 1869.
Mr. Thomas Brown's ditto, June 5th, 1869.
Mr. Edwin Bullock's ditto, May 21st, 1870.
Mr. Gillott's ditto, May 4th, 1872.
Mr. J. Tattersall's ditto, July 6th, 1872.

APPENDIX III.

CRITIQUE ON THE COLLECTION OF WATER-COLOUR DRAWINGS AND PAINTINGS BY DAVID COX, EXHIBITED IN THE GERMAN GALLERY, BOND STREET, LONDON, APRIL, 1859.—*From the Standard.*

WE feel it necessary to express our fears that future exhibitions will not sustain the fame of the present one, unless they are made retrospective; because David Cox occupies the highest place among the living artists of the day as a sound and honest exponent of the English school. We mean that he is the repository of the traditions and principles of the English school as practised in the time of Reynolds, and recorded in his most valuable discourses to the students of the Royal Academy. It is, therefore, that we feel grateful to the committee for the opportunity they have given us of appreciating David Cox at his just value—of directing public attention to his great merits while he is still among us, and for enabling us, while so much uncertainty exists in the public mind as to what constitutes legitimate art, to vindicate its principles in the truly valuable and highly interesting collection now submitted to public inspection at the German Gallery.

David Cox is truly English in the choice of his subjects; the mode of treating them, and his execution for the most part is as original as his mind is genuine. He has, therefore, rendered an invaluable service to native art by adhering unshaken to its healthy practice amidst the fashionable vagaries of modern criticism. His sturdy love for early traditions enables him to vary his style of treatment without abandoning the fundamental laws of his art. In every subject there is so perfect a unity of intention, that, if it be fairly studied, the mind of the spectator is never distracted by tricks and trifling to entrap the admiration of the unlearned, nor is the connoisseur ever reminded of any other painter. The masses of verdure, rocks, and trees partake equally of the same touch, tone, and feeling. The real charms of outdoor nature are the motives which Cox labours to render manifest, and when he has adopted one of them as a starting-point, every accessory and each object is made subservient to that purpose. If it be his will to inspire the spectator with a sense of elegant repose, the general tone is delicate, the forms are pure, and the execution finished. Examples of this kind may be seen chiefly on the screen near the door. If it be his wish to display his powers on a larger scale and in a higher range of art, the masses are more simple, and become rather apparent as the leading features of the composition, while the forms of objects generally assume characteristics of approaching geometrical precision. Two examples of this arrangement will be alluded to lower down. If it be his intention to drench the country with rain, it pours down with a black intensity that makes the poor bull (110) bellow again with a sense of loneliness, desolation, and misery. If it be necessary to give an additional interest to an otherwise commonplace subject, he sends a strong wind across the scene, the herbage on the banks is separated by it into distinct portions, branches are bent, and leaves blown in clusters of foliage from their natural position; the boy's kite pitches madly overhead to break loose from its bondage; the gulls wheel wildly in the air; the old woman with the basket struggles almost in vain along the slippery road, which, with the grass recently watered by the passing shower, sparkles and glitters with intermittent beams of light as the clouds scud rapidly across the sun. And so real—artistically real—are all these phases of the atmosphere as they are recorded on the paper, that no stretch of the imagination is required to believe that the event occurred; nor is the slightest suspicion raised in the mind of the spectator that the artist was not present when it actually took place. These general remarks on the collection will be more directly verified by selecting such works as will illustrate them, besides others having different merits, which we have not space to enlarge upon.

Among the drawings of the more delicate kind, in which the effort of the artist has been to produce on the mind of the spectator a sensation of refined enjoyment, even when viewing scenes of rural occupation, we noticed the following:—The "Waggon and Horses," in which the line of the clouds arranges with that formed by the waggon and team of horses. In the "Heath Scene and Windmill" the sky contrasts with the dark form of the foreground. The same simple style of arrangement exists in the "View of Windsor Castle," and produces a most charming effect by the retiring curve of the foreground ending with the white turrets of the castle, illumined by a brilliant sun, and rendered conspicuous, although so distant, by a mass of light clouds placed immediately over the castle to attract the eye and increase the size of the buildings, as the principal point of interest. "Landscape" (76) is another example in which field occupation is pleasingly treated. "Hay Carting" is remarkably elegant, and will serve to show, when compared with "The Hayfield," with what variety the artist can treat subjects so similar. The latter has a more clear atmosphere, is cool in colour, and the whole scene is bathed in air and light. The tints of the distance and sky accord with those in the middle distance, conveying a sensation of repose, which is not disturbed by too much angular drawing in the heaps of hay. The figures, although small, are truly lifelike in their attitude, while the whole view is thrown into an aerial and a vaporous effect by contrast with the positive colours of their dresses, the force of which is sustained by those of the team of horses, the whole forming the strong line of the composition. The same feeling for classical elegance and refined serenity will be observed in the drawing entitled "Landscape" (80). In the composition of this there is not one object introduced which is not conducive to quietude, so that the eye may contemplate the smooth lake, under a tranquil sky, with graceful trees in the foreground, and the round tops of which gently contrast with the delicate forms of the distant mountains. "Meadows, Hereford," must be considered as taking a higher position in art. It is more important in size than most of the above, and is undoubtedly composed on principles of a more severe character. The unity and subdued light pervading the whole scene is more imaginary in its general aspect, evidently selected by the artist to produce more than the ordinary feeling of dreamy thought. The leading lines are extremely simple and few, arranged parallel to each other, and the stems of the trees contrasting with them at right angles assist in giving prominence to their simplicity. So anxious has the artist been to sustain his principal *motive* (to employ a musical term) in respect of his leading lines, that the flock of sheep introduced in the foreground to give life, movement, and interest to the subject are so closely kept together in their progress across the scene, that they do not disturb the straightness of the principal line in the foreground. "Near Carnarvon" is not so severe in character; but the "Meadows on the River Lugg, Herefordshire," is the largest water-colour drawing in the collection, and has been a very fine one, of the highly scientific class; but the colours have entirely changed by time, and little but the arrangement as regards lines and masses remains to record the merits of the artist. A flock of sheep, introduced in the same manner as the above, will serve to show his adherence to well-founded principles. They form a prominent feature, parallel with the base line of the mountains in the distance. The whole subject, although very fine as a composition, and belonging to the same style of art as "Meadows, Hereford," differs from it materially by being more full in subject, and was, no doubt, originally more rich and powerful in general treatment.

"Rhyl" presents at the first glance a fine effect of light and air; the clouds fly across the scene in rapid motion, the waves rush in quick succession towards the sands, the gulls are screaming and whirling in the air, and the ladies' dresses on the long line of the shore flutter in accordance with the movement which pervades the subject, and complete the intention of the painter in the representation of fashionable visitors to a popular watering-place, inhaling the sea air till they can taste the salt on their lips, and struggling against the sea-breeze, scarcely able to keep on their feet while enjoying the brilliant gleams of sun—free from London fog and smoke—darting down upon them from between the flying clouds. The picture is in oil-colours, and has a rather unfinished appearance; but the general effect of a seaside situation is most delightfully and truly represented. "Showery Weather" is another stormy effect. The men and the sheep going slowly into the gloom of the middle distance assist the sentiment of the composition, by seeming to resign themselves to their destiny. "Mischief" is a more rustic and lively scene, and the light is partial and brilliant. This drawing takes its title from a boy, who is driving some geese to the water, across which, on a rude bridge,

App. III. is an old woman threatening him with her upraised stick. The most tremendous storm of rain in the collection is represented in the drawing, to which we have already alluded, entitled "The Bull." The rain really descends in torrents, while the solitary animal seems to be bellowing hopelessly towards a distance, which is as cheerless in aspect as his own situation is miserable. The value of the light colour on his horns will be readily appreciated by an artistic eye as a set-off to the density of the background. In this way of treating stormy scenes, Cox differs from Gainsborough, whose disposition was so amiable, in a pictorial sense, according to M. Theophilus Silvestre, that if he painted a coming hurricane, it was evidently not so close at hand but man and cattle would have ample time to seek a place of shelter; but Cox, being of a more energetic character, and possessing a more sturdy nature in the thorough rendering of his single-minded intention, spares neither man nor animal, clouds nor trees; his masculine and relentless pencil rends the clouds into pieces, the branches are driven across stems that bend to the gale, and living things, whether man or beast, are as mercilessly dealt with as the brook forced over its banks, or the rushes by its sides when torn up by their roots, and blown away to wither on dry land. It is this singleness of purpose in all that he draws which makes his works so pleasing to the eye, invests them with so remarkable a character of variety, and with so much instruction for the researches of the young artist, and the improvement of the public.

Besides those drawings, which may be noticed as the stormy and classical, there are many examples in others of the same learning, but it is devoted to the production of simply powerful and striking effects. The roughness with which several of these is executed is very likely to induce persons not overskilled in art to think that they are the result of carelessness and want of thought; but that would be an error, for they are carefully studied, and full of meaning, which will be appreciated if the spectator will stand at a proper distance, and allow the scene to realise itself in his mind. The intention of the painter will then become gradually apparent, and that which at first appeared a slovenly sketch or a sloppy drawing, will assume all the unity of a finished picture. It is a remarkable fact that the roughest of drawings by Cox, when seen in an exhibition with works by other painters, will, at a proper distance, assume an appearance of more complete finish than any of those by which they are surrounded, with all their details minutely elaborated, and the objects most clearly and brightly coloured. "The Oak Tree" requires this precaution before the effect of wind will be perceived. The same degree of patience must be devoted to the examination of a "Woodbank Scene," which is dark and powerful. The little piece of pathway on the left, appearing at first a confusion of tints, will become perfectly true and real if time enough be spent upon it. "Children Blackberrying" has a fine mass of rocks in the distance, and is besides a splendid brilliant piece of daylight. "Peat Gatherers" is a drawing of remarkable power, in which the artist's intention is most completely carried out. The figures are trudging through a heavy shower over the marshy ground, and, with the exception of the dingy but positive colour of their dresses, the whole scene is an epitome of rain, slush, and bog—not a very agreeable subject, it is true, unless the undoubted merit displayed in it overrides, which it ought, all other considerations. The same mental energy is manifested, in a more solemn and dignified manner, in the view of "Barden Castle," where the only bright objects are the white clouds, which draw attention to the castle by their round forms contrasting with the angles of the turrets, rendering them sufficiently prominent, and giving value to the mass of secluded woodland scenery below. The gradations are admirably preserved in the dark tints, and the undulations of the ground are as carefully indicated; while the sheep, being only partially seen, and forming an irregular line across the middle distance, adding to the massiveness of the castle, although animated objects, really increase the sentiment of solitude and the magnitude of the whole composition. "Beeston Castle, Cheshire," is another example of the masterly manner in which Cox treats such subjects. "The Vale of Clywd" has a fine general character, and is painted in oil. The sheep, the labourers, and the man on horseback, all going into the gloom of the middle distance, bounded by a group of picturesque trees, produce an excellent effect. "A Heath," also in oil, is warm in colour, and differs in tone and treatment from any other work in the room, but is equally meritorious. "Going to Market," although roughly executed, is very charming, and the bank, with its portion of bare earth, is expressed with admirable truth. "Dover Castle" forms a relief to the darker subjects, for it is all light, motion, and air. Some pilots in the foreground, looking out to sea, are very slightly sketched, but full of expression in their attitudes. We return again to wild scenery in the view of "Penman Bach," which is a drawing so very freely pencilled, that it will require some attention to comprehend; but, after a while, a wave or two just peering out from the gloom in the distance will, with a little reflection, suggest a very perfect idea of the sea and its motion. A view, "Near Stoke-Say, Salop," may be classed among the drawings of a vigorous character, and is, like many others in this collection, remarkable for the freshness of its general effect. On the table in the middle of the room is a work, entitled "Streatham Common," which, we must admit, is dashed in with so much boldness, that it scarcely reveals, after a long examination, and at the proper distance too, any of those lurking beauties of nature so generally found under the same circumstances among those numerous productions to which we have directed attention.

As the genius of David Cox delights chiefly in English atmosphere, and the verdure of its landscape, he rarely seems to attempt securing effects expressed in glowing tints, nor does he indulge in any conventional displays of gorgeous colours. There is, however, a "View on the Sands," in which persons are going to market, under an appearance of the sun forcing its way through a fog; but among so many drawings of a decided character and striking effects, it seems rather feeble in its general management. "The Chat Moss Broom Gatherers" may be ranked as chiefly devoted to showing the force that can be obtained by the contrast of strong tints, the painter having been tempted, no doubt, by the rich lines of the growing broom; but, although the colour is caused to predominate as the leading feature of the scene, gleams of light are

APP. III. very skilfully introduced, and the figures, which, if we remember rightly, are larger in this drawing than in any other, attract no inconsiderable share of attention.

The last landscape we shall notice is one which, in point of feeling and conception, ranks higher in art than any we have seen from the same hand, and is entitled the "Mountain Top." The largest portion of the design consists of abroadly-defined mass of rock, leaving a small opening for the sky, where, against the bright spot of light, a dark blue cloud with its serrated edge cuts angrily across with most threatening aspect. Low down in the foreground, on a rocky fragment, the form of an eagle comes mystically off from amidst the deepest part ot the gloom. The sense of wild solitude and solemn quiet is increased by a sheep running through the dismal glen close under the rock upon which the watchful eagle sits. The sentiment of this desolate and romantic scene is heightened by the breadth of mournful darkness enveloping the side of the mountain, the contention indicated in the elements above, and the coming struggle for life below. This composition is, in our judgment, the most epic work that this artist ever produced.

However highly we have estimated the landscapes by David Cox, we are not disposed to pass over in silence the mode in which he indicates, we cannot say draws, his figures. His intention is expressed with so much certainty and truth, and his figures act with so much ease and spirit, that it is questionable whether he would not have succeeded equally well if he had devoted his energies to that branch of art. In addition to those we have mentioned above, we would direct attention to the labourers in the hayfield drawings, and the attitudes of the pilots in the small drawing entitled "Dover Castle;" but we would more particularly claim admiration for a very small subject, No. 167, "The Proposal." It is an interior, in which there are two figures, a young and gallant cavalier, and a maiden of high degree. The latter is seated with her back to an ancient bay window, the lover stands by her side bending gracefully over her while making the proposal, which she receives with a gesture expressive partly of pleasure, and of not a little coquetry. With scarcely any outline, in the ordinary acceptance of the term, the superior rank and the elegant forms of these two persons are very decidedly marked. The oaken wainscoting of the room, the crimson of the large arm-chair, and the rest of the furniture, are all tinted with extreme delicacy and truth. The sentiment of the whole scene is suggestive of retirement; the empty arm-chair intimates that the lover has taken a quick advantage of a temporary absence to make his proposal; and the mild light entering at the bay window, spreading its soft rays about the room, seems to imply a silence broken only by the confiding whispers of the cautious lovers. This is so charming a composition, that, while we do not believe we have a landscape painter equal to David Cox, we feel equally disposed to challenge the painters of "interiors and figures" to produce a subject so full of delicate feeling and refined art as may be found in the little gem now hanging in a corner of the German Gallery.

We are aware that David Cox, like Turner, Constable, and others who have displayed original genius in a peculiar manner, has but a limited number of admirers; but we feel that in noticing this collection so fully, we are doing but simple justice to the merits of the artist, and giving all the support we can to the admirable plan commenced by the Committee; and, as their sole object is to make British Art known to the world, for any profits arising from the exhibitions are to be given to "The Artists' Benevolent Fund," we wish them a success that may amply reward their endeavours in this excellent undertaking.

THE END.